Kimberly Dean

On The Prowl

Ellora's Cave
Romantica Publishing

An Ellora's Cave Romantica Publication

www.ellorascave.com

On the Prowl

ISBN # 1419952277
ALL RIGHTS RESERVED.
On the Prowl Copyright© 2005 Kimberly Dean
Edited by: Mary Moran
Cover art by: Syneca

Electronic book Publication: January, 2005
Trade paperback Publication: July, 2005

With the exception of quotes used in reviews, this book may not be reproduced or used in whole or in part by any means existing without written permission from the publisher, Ellora's Cave Publishing, Inc.® 1056 Home Avenue, Akron OH 44310-3502.

This book is a work of fiction and any resemblance to persons, living or dead, or places, events or locales is purely coincidental. The characters are productions of the authors' imagination and used fictitiously.

What the critics are saying…

…"This was a witty and sensually written story that kept me spellbound to the end." ~ *Sheryl Reviewer for Karen Find Out About New Books Reviewer for Coffee Time RomanceInterviewer for Coffee Time Romance*

…"*On the Prowl* is a hilarious and a vastly entertaining look at a good girl seduced by the exhilaration of thievery. I think I've found a new all-time favorite line - "Get your revenge. Womanhandle me". It was a rare pleasure to join Talia on her journey to learning herself. Wonderful job, Ms. Dean!" ~ *Michelle Fallen Angels Review*

Warning:

The following material contains graphic sexual content meant for mature readers. *On the Prowl* has been rated *E-rotic* by a minimum of three independent reviewers.

Ellora's Cave Publishing offers three levels of Romantica™ reading entertainment: S (S-ensuous), E (E-rotic), and X (X-treme).

S-*ensuous* love scenes are explicit and leave nothing to the imagination.

E-*rotic* love scenes are explicit, leave nothing to the imagination, and are high in volume per the overall word count. In addition, some E-rated titles might contain fantasy material that some readers find objectionable, such as bondage, submission, same sex encounters, forced seductions, etc. E-rated titles are the most graphic titles we carry; it is common, for instance, for an author to use words such as "fucking", "cock", "pussy", etc., within their work of literature.

X-*treme* titles differ from E-rated titles only in plot premise and storyline execution. Unlike E-rated titles, stories designated with the letter X tend to contain controversial subject matter not for the faint of heart.

Also by Kimberly Dean:

Fever

On the Prowl

Prologue

A thick layer of clouds drifted across the sky, blotting out the cool light of a full moon. Darkness fell onto the land, swallowing shadows as it went. The house that sat in the middle of the clearing was asleep.

It had been that way for over an hour.

A soft breeze trickled through the trees. The sound of rustling leaves was nearly imperceptible to those who wouldn't notice. To those who did, it was a signal. The lithe figure lurking in the shadows finally moved.

Damp grass muffled the figure's footsteps but it traveled quickly. Its motions were agile and confident, yet poised for any change that would signal danger. For countless heartbeats, the dark shape stood frozen in the shadows against the house. When no alarm was sounded, it went to work.

A rope swished upward through the air until a hook lodged itself around the railing of the second floor balcony. A quick tug ensured the hook was secure but caution made the figure pause once more. Once the plan was set into action, there would be no turning back.

At last, it was time.

The phantom attached the rope to a harness around its waist and began climbing. Soon, it reached the balcony and dropped into an alert crouch.

The house slept on.

A hand reached into a bag belted around a thigh and a set of tools emerged. Deft fingers worked magic on the weak lock of the sliding glass door and there was a soft click.

The intruder wasn't one to take chances. A small can of silicon was pulled from that same bag and sprayed into the door track. When the door was at last rolled open, it was silent as the wind.

The figure moved into the sleeping house and quietly rolled the door shut. The pathway through the rooms and hallways had been mapped out and studied in detail. It took twelve seconds to reach the head of the staircase. Three more allowed the figure to slide down the polished wooden railing and land noiselessly on the rug at the base of the stairs.

The target was ten steps away.

Light feet padded softly across the short distance and gloved fingers wrapped around the piece that sat so unprotected on the hallway table. The bronzed object quickly went into a pouch.

Coughing from an upstairs bedroom broke through the silence like a jackhammer.

The dark shape spun into the shadows and held itself motionless. One heartbeat turned into two — and then three. The coughing stopped as suddenly as it had begun and the house drifted back into peaceful tranquility.

It was time to go.

Retracing the path into the house was not the plan. Instead, the phantom moved quickly to the back door. The high-end deadbolt lock was effective against anybody trying to get in, but worthless against somebody trying to get out. It took forty seconds to leave the premises and retrieve the rope.

Rustling leaves greeted the figure as it slipped back into the darkness. Safe in the company of the trees, the thief finally opened the pouch.

They'd called it a "trinket". The fools didn't know what they'd had sitting right under their noses. The moon peeked through the cloud cover once again and the bronzed cat with the piercing eyes winked up at its new owner.

She winked back.

Chapter One

"Talia!"

The sound of her name broke into Talia Sizemore's daydream. Party sounds permeated her consciousness and she became aware of people laughing and talking around her. The quiet, elusive world she'd been fantasizing about shattered and she found herself in Brent Harrington's home. Blinking, she turned to face the man who'd just called her name.

"Uncle Roger." She smiled with relief. It was comforting to see a friend in this sea of vipers. "I'm glad you came."

"You were miles away," the older man said with concern.

"I'm sorry," Talia said, a touch embarrassed. She really needed to stop reading all those *Lady Midnight* comics down at the shop. "I drifted off there for a second or two."

"A second or two? You've been standing by yourself in the corner for nearly ten minutes."

Had it really been that long? She glanced disinterestedly at the partygoers around them. It was funny how the brain protected itself. Her daydreams had taken her far away but that world had somehow seemed so much more real. These people? They were all so...so *plastic*. Their smiles, their hair, their perfectly polished shoes... "Can you blame me?" she said tiredly. "If I had a choice, I wouldn't even be here tonight."

Roger smoothed the silver hair at his temple as his gaze shifted nervously to those standing nearby. God forbid that somebody should hear them talking disparagingly about the social event of the season. "I have to admit I'm surprised to see you here," he said. "I didn't think you'd attend an Arts Council function after what happened."

Talia's spine stiffened and she stood a little straighter. "I'm still a member of the Board. I'm not going to let them run me off that easily."

He looked at her worriedly. "I hope you're not planning on making a scene."

His eyebrows lifted when he saw the determined look on her face.

"Think about it, dear," he said quickly. "I realize that the Council's vote had to have been a big blow to you but you don't want to embarrass yourself in front of New Covington's elite."

New Covington's elite. Talia's temper flared. Wasn't that just typical? It always came down to appearances and social standing in this town. And money—the older, the better. "No, Uncle Roger, I'm not going to make a scene. I have more class than that."

"Of course you do. Of course. I didn't mean to imply otherwise." He relaxed and his eyes softened. "I just know how much that after-school arts program meant to you. You must have been crushed when the Arts Council voted to stop supporting it."

Talia pressed a hand to her stomach. She wished he would change the subject. "Crushed" didn't even come close to describing how she'd felt after the surprise attack. The hurt and betrayal were still taking a physical toll.

She couldn't help but take the Board's vote personally. After all, the inner-city after-school arts program had been her father's creation. The Sizemore Foundation had established it and nourished it through its infancy. She couldn't believe that now, just as it was starting to thrive, Brent Harrington and his minions had decided to pull the Arts Council's funding. Without that financial support, the program would wither and die. The Sizemore Foundation could administer the program but it couldn't support it on its own. "I just feel like I'm letting everyone down," she admitted. "The kids, the teachers…"

"Your father?"

On the Prowl

She flinched. Her father had left the foundation in her care when he'd passed away. He'd be so disappointed in her if he knew what had happened.

"Talia, dear. Ted was my best friend. He loved you to pieces. You could never let him down." Roger rubbed her shoulder comfortingly, but gestured when he saw the Board president. "Would it help if I talked to Brent?"

"No," she said quickly. Almost too quickly. She tried to rein her temper in. She couldn't take out her frustration on Roger. He was just trying to be kind. He didn't realize how upsetting this was for her. "I'm sorry, Uncle Roger. I don't mean to be testy. I just don't want you to get in the middle of it."

"Your father would have wanted me to get in the middle of it."

Daddy. Talia felt a dull pain near her heart. She missed him so much. He'd have known how to deal with this. He'd always known exactly what to say or do in any situation. She wasn't nearly as adept—and look at what had happened because of it. "I know you want to help but this is really something I need to do myself. I'll…I'll talk to Brent."

"Are you sure?"

No, she wasn't sure. She glanced Brent's way. As always, he looked tall, dark and sinful. Not to mention conceited, bull-headed, single-minded… Her fingers tightened until the blue beads on her purse threatened to pop off. Simply talking to him wasn't going to make him change his mind. He'd laugh in her face if she went to him and begged.

Then again, that might be exactly what he wanted—for her to subjugate herself in front of him. Get down on her knees and kiss his feet.

Or probably something a little higher.

The ringing of a champagne glass broke into her sickening thoughts. Turning, Talia faced their host and his fashion doll wife, Shelli. Her stomach rolled with revulsion.

She hated the idea of so much as even looking at the man but she had to try again for the kids. They deserved that much from her.

"I'm sure," she said dejectedly. "I'll try one more time to talk some sense into him."

Shelli's plastic smile glittered down on her guests and Talia squinted to shield her eyes from the glare. Shelli, Shelli, Shelli. Such a pretty package with nothing worthwhile inside. Brent bent down to kiss his wife's foundation-laden cheek and she actually giggled. Talia glared at her in annoyance. It was because of women like that that the blonde jokes would continue *ad nauseam*. If Shelli had half a clue about hubby dearest, she'd be packing some arsenic in that face powder.

Smiling like a king at his faithful party guests, Brent approached the microphone at the center of the stage that had been erected in the corner of the room. "Welcome, fellow art lovers," he said with a dramatic flair.

A sudden migraine shot through Talia's brain. How in God's name was she going to talk to that snake without screaming?

"I'd like to welcome everyone to our home—especially all you beautiful ladies."

The crowd laughed at the suggestive wiggle of his eyebrows but she saw nothing funny about it. Brent Harrington III. "The Turd" was more like it.

"The Council for the Arts is kicking off its fall campaign and, as president, I'm challenging all of you to make this season the best New Covington has ever seen!" He paused for the applause that rang throughout the room. "We've got some exciting performances scheduled and the Board is working on a few surprises for next spring. Our goal is to lift New Covington's art scene to the next level because, in the words of past Board president and my beloved grandmother, Sophia Harrington, 'culture enriches us all'."

Apparently, the kids in inner-city school system didn't count. Talia tucked her purse under her arm, swiped a glass of champagne off a passing waiter's tray and took a healthy gulp.

The situation had her at wit's end. She really didn't know what else she could do but try to convince Brent one last time that the program was important. To some of those kids, it was their only way out.

Why couldn't he see that?

"You don't look well, dear," Roger said as he laid a comforting hand on the small of her back. He moved protectively closer.

Talia looked lovingly at her stalwart defender. With Adam in Boston, Roger Thorton was the closest thing she had to family left here in New Covington. After everything that had happened, she had to admit she was feeling a bit alone in the world. His support bolstered her. He didn't need to take her side in this ugly affair but knowing he was there for her made her feel better.

"I'm all right," she said. She gently smoothed the lapel of his tuxedo. When she saw the concerned look on his face, she tried to smile. "Really."

"Roger. *Roger!*"

Out of the corner of her eye, Talia saw Lydia Thorton swooping in. Automatically, she stepped back. As always, Roger's wife had a glass of alcohol in her grip, pinky finger stylishly lifted.

Talia braced herself. It was hard to believe that Roger had been worried about *her* making a scene. She looked at him with empathy as Lydia stormed through the crowd like a bull in a china shop. The woman's wide hips bumped a waiter, nearly causing him to drop his platter of miniature quiche appetizers.

"For heaven's sake, you clumsy ox! Let me pass."

Talia's fingers tightened around the stem of her champagne glass. She should be used to Lydia's crass behavior by now but she still couldn't figure out how such a kind man could get involved with such a harpy. Roger looked discomfited as his wife bore down on them with nostrils flaring and gold sequins flashing.

"I should have known I'd find you with something in a tight skirt," Lydia said in a stage whisper that everyone within ten feet heard.

Roger fingered his collar as if it had suddenly gotten too tight.

"Lydia," Talia said coolly.

The woman lifted an artfully plucked eyebrow. "Well if it isn't poor little Talia Sizemore. Darling, I'm surprised to see you here. I thought the Council's vote would have sent you scurrying to a corner somewhere. I mean, *really*!" She let out a boisterous laugh and made a sweeping gesture that sloshed nearly half her drink onto the floor. "How embarrassing for you!"

Almost of its own volition, Talia's hand jerked. It was only the sound of her name echoing around the room that stopped her from throwing her drink in the offensive woman's face.

"Talia Sizemore?" Brent said loudly into the microphone. "Where is she, gentlemen? Believe me, you can't miss her in that blue dress."

The words finally registered and Talia looked to the stage. The other members of the Board were already there, apparently being recognized for all their "good work". She threw a glare at Lydia. It was hard to decide which was worse, taking verbal body shots from this woman or standing side by side with the people who had killed her program. With a shaky hand, she passed her half-empty drink to Roger.

She'd promised herself before she'd come here that she would hold the higher ground. Her pride was about all she had left. That, and the Sizemore name.

She held her head high as she walked across the room to the small stage, but whoops and wolf-whistles flummoxed her. Leave it to Brent to make her dress a topic of discussion. He met her at the top of the steps. It repulsed her but it would be impolite to ignore his assistance. She took his hand and busied herself with navigating the steps in her long skirt. When she looked up, though, he wasn't looking at her legs.

His dark gaze had clapped onto her breasts.

Shelli stood behind him, clapping like a giddy schoolgirl, but the Turd was unfazed. He openly admired her curves as he led her across the stage.

Talia mentally berated herself. She should have known better. The skinny straps of the dress hadn't allowed for a bra. Instead of going without, she should have found another outfit. With his stare on her, she could feel every sway and jiggle of her unbound flesh. The silk against her nipples suddenly seemed too rough and, inevitably, they popped to attention.

She came to a standstill by Edward Jones and flinched when Brent leaned toward her. The compulsory kiss he planted on her cheek was innocent enough but the brush of his fingers against her tightened nipple wasn't.

"That's better," he whispered into her ear.

Her face heated as he walked back to center stage. As indiscreetly as she could, she looked down at her chest. Her nipples had puckered under his touch and now stood upright like two sturdy tent poles. She felt Edward Jones' hot gaze sweep over her body and she fought not to cover herself and bring even more unwanted attention.

"Board members, if you'll take a seat, I'll introduce the entertainment part of our program."

Talia groaned inwardly, but sat down on the folding chair. She threw Edward a nasty look but he just smiled and kept ogling her. A string quartet started playing and she closed her eyes. Could they have chosen a longer piece?

"Nice nipple action, Tally."

Her eyes flew open when she heard the soft words. Brent sat down beside her and goosebumps rose on the back of her neck. As furtively as she could, she slid away from him. She didn't get far. Any further away and she'd be in Edward's lap.

Not that he'd mind. His eyes were practically bugging out of his head.

"So perky. It's a good look for you." Brent leaned in to whisper into her ear. "Reminds me of when we were teenagers, although you've filled out nicely since then."

Her breath hitched.

Damn him!

He knew exactly what to say to embarrass her the most. She stared straight ahead and fought not to react. It was what he wanted, she knew, and she refused to give him even that much. She just had to make it through the song. Then she could stand up and walk away. Preferably right out the front door.

"Oh, come on, Tally. Don't play coy. You remember the night I'm talking about."

She shifted uncomfortably in her chair, angry with herself for letting him get to her, but unable to stop it. Of course, she remembered that night. How could she forget?

"We were at Mimi Devonshire's party," he pressed. "I took your bra and paraded you around in front of the football team wearing only your tight, white T-shirt."

Talia finally gave in to the need to cover herself. As surreptitiously as she could, she crossed her arms over her chest. "Stop it," she whispered.

"Why?" he said, tugging playfully at her elbow. "You like having people look at you—at least you did then."

Her nipples tightened painfully and she couldn't hold back the memories any longer. She'd been fifteen at the time and he'd been a well-experienced seventeen. She could still remember how her knees had gone weak when he'd smiled at her. She hadn't been able to believe that the football quarterback had been interested in her! When he'd cocked his head, she'd willingly crossed the room. She could still remember how warm his fingers had felt when he'd caught her hand. She'd followed like a trusting lamb when he'd pulled her into the bathroom.

Oh, she'd been so naïve.

It had all been a game to him—a bet with his preppy friends. Well, he'd gotten her bra from her, all right. That hadn't been enough, though. Not for quarterback stud Harrington. He'd teased and fondled her until she'd looked like a slutty magazine centerfold.

"Don't try to hide them," he whispered, pulling her from that nightmare back into the one of the present. "Let me see those pretty titties of yours."

Talia turned her face away. She'd like to act affronted but she couldn't. What had happened in the Devonshire bathroom so many years ago had been a sexual awakening for her. Although she'd been humiliated by the outcome, she had taken pleasure in his touch. Debasing as it was, her body still reacted to him. To this day, he could arouse her with a look.

And he knew it.

So every board meeting, social encounter and business lunch, he'd look his fill and she'd walk away with hard nipples and a wet pussy. At least she'd kept that secret hidden from him. She had no doubt he'd use it to his advantage if he ever found out. The Turd had certainly earned the nickname.

The violin hit a long, high note and Talia closed her eyes in distress. It was taking everything she had not to squirm on the hard metal chair. His blatantly suggestive looks and words were having their usual effect on her body.

Taking a deep breath, she forced herself to remember why she was here. The after-school program. She needed to concentrate on that.

"Brent," she said quietly, turning back to face him. His gaze didn't stray from her breasts. It was degrading but she let her arms drop to her sides to give him an unrestricted view. At least that way she knew she had his attention. "I'd like to get you alone for a few minutes, if I could. Do you think we could find somewhere private to talk?"

His gaze finally lifted to meet hers and the air between them crackled. "Need some one-on-one time, baby?"

Not in this lifetime.

"Please," she forced herself to say. Applause broke out from the crowd as the quartet finished and she felt relieved. The sooner she got off this stage, the better.

"This should be interesting," he said. He gave her a wink. "Let me close this thing up and we'll find someplace quiet."

She cringed. Being alone with him was never a good idea but, then again, she hadn't had a chance to talk to him face-to-face. He'd brought up the vote on the funding when it hadn't even been on the agenda and she hadn't had much of an opportunity to make him see her side of things. Maybe speaking to him privately would help.

She sighed. And maybe the moon was made of cheese.

It was a pipe dream and she knew it. Still, she needed to make one last plea for the kids' sake.

She watched as Brent strode cockily up to the microphone. He wouldn't try anything with so many people around. Especially this crowd. He needed to keep these people's respect if he was going to keep his status in the community.

"That ends our program for tonight," he said in a velvet voice that carried throughout the room. "But please stay and enjoy the food and champagne. We've earned this night of celebration!"

Glasses tinkled and cheers of "Hear, hear" sounded. The board members began to disperse from the stage and Talia rose from her chair. Brent headed back toward her but stopped to talk to his wife. Shelli laughed at whatever he said and gave Talia a wave. Her hair bounced as she turned back to play hostess to her guests.

"This way," Brent said. He took her arm as the quartet started playing again. Couples began dancing but he deftly negotiated their way through the crowd.

Talia followed as he led her up the stairs to his home office. She knew she only had one chance at this. She needed to find the best way to approach him. Everything she'd tried before had been from the Arts Council's perspective. Maybe it was time to try a different tack. "Brent, do you know my associate, Sadie?"

"The sexy black woman who works at your antique shop?" he asked, looking over his shoulder. "I've drooled over her once or twice."

Talia's lips thinned but she refused to take the bait. "Her son, Lincoln, was arrested last week."

"Arrested?" Brent finally stopped his quick steps and turned to look at her. "For what?"

"Vandalism. He and some of his friends were caught spraying graffiti on his school's walls."

Brent shrugged and began moving again. "Sounds like he deserved to have the cuffs slapped on him."

"You don't understand," she said, hurrying along to keep up with him. "Linc's a very talented artist. He just doesn't have an outlet for his creativity now that the after-school program has been canceled."

"Aha! I knew you'd eventually come back around to square one." Brent opened the door to his office and let her pass through in front of him. "You were outvoted, Tally. Why can't you just let it go?"

"Let it go?" She whirled about on her heel. She'd vowed to keep her composure but that didn't mean she had to be a doormat. "That program was my father's brainchild. It's helped countless kids—several of whom have gone on to attend college on art scholarships."

"Once again, funded by whom?"

Frustration roiled in her chest. "If you'll just stop to think about all the implications, I'm sure you'll see what a pernicious decision the Board made."

"*Pernicious?* Oh, now you've gone and made me feel bad."

It took everything inside her not to slap the smirk off his face. How dare he make a joke out of this! "What do I have to do to make you change your mind?" she asked, her jaw tight.

The wicked grin that lit his face made her suddenly uneasy.

"The question shouldn't be 'what', but 'whom'." The lock on the door clicked ominously behind him. "And the answer would be 'me'."

The move he made was blindingly fast. Before Talia could realize her error in judgment, he'd caught her about the waist, spun her around and pushed her up against the door.

"Brent! What do you think—"

His hard lips cut off her words. Shock reverberated through her system and her fight-or-flight instinct kicked in. She dropped her purse and her hands came up to his chest. She pushed hard but he retaliated by sticking his tongue deeper into her mouth.

It stopped her cold.

He hadn't kissed her when he'd caught her in that clench so many years ago. She was suddenly glad he hadn't. She would have ended up losing more than just her bra.

His tongue swirled around hers and her knees wobbled. "Brent," she gasped as she tore her mouth away. "Get off me."

He leaned his big body more heavily against hers and nuzzled her ear. "Don't give me that crap, baby. You want me on you. You want me *in* you. You always have."

"I have not. Brent!"

His groping hands had caught the spaghetti straps at her shoulders and were pulling them downward. He didn't bother with the zipper at the back of her dress and the straps cut into her arms. Talia started to struggle again but she was caught between a hard door and an even harder man. She could feel his stiff cock bumping against her stomach as he wrestled to get her under control.

"Let's see what you've got hiding under here," he said with a callous smile. His hands caught the neckline of her dress and began rolling the bodice over her breasts. Without the zipper loosened, the fit was tight. With every tug on the material, another inch of her chest plumped out into view.

Talia tried to push him away but the straps bound her arms to her sides. Her stylish little party dress had just turned into a sexual bondage outfit. Things were suddenly getting scary. She didn't want to submit—not to him. "I'll scream," she said harshly.

"That's the idea," he said.

Her pussy clenched. Oh, God!

Suddenly, her nerves sizzled with a strange combination of fear and excitement. She couldn't let this happen—and for so many different reasons. She tried to roll away but, in that moment, he worked the silk material over her curves and her breasts sprang free. She froze at the look that entered his eyes. He'd seen her before. He'd touched her. Only this time, he wasn't going to stop after a little heavy petting.

His hard hands came up to cup her breasts and the feeling was electric. She closed her eyes as her nipples jutted into his palms. Traitorous pleasure swirled through her body.

"I never expected you to whore yourself for your little charity," he said, "but I'm an obliging sort of guy."

His hair swung forward onto his forehead as he bent down toward her. "Try your damnedest to convince me, baby. I should warn you, though. I'm feeling particularly pernicious tonight."

Talia squirmed against the door, fighting herself as much as him. "Damn you, Brent," she said, breathing hard. "Let me go!"

"Why?" he said, laughing softly. He pinched her nipples hard. "You wouldn't have come here with your titties bouncing all over the place if you weren't begging for a fuck."

The pain was sharp. Talia rolled her head against the unyielding door but he didn't ease the pressure on her tender flesh. Her distress and her pleasure mounted. He was going to make her do this.

"Please," she begged when his mouth skimmed down her neck. Her nipples felt like they were in vices. "It hurts."

"Admit it," he growled. "You've been annoyed with me for the last ten years because I didn't follow through."

His leg slipped between hers and pressed hard against her mound. Talia was in such a state of miserable arousal, she could hardly stand it. He had her nipples pinched nearly flat. "You debased me," she said, her voice catching. "You intentionally embarrassed me."

"You liked it. You liked having my hands and my mouth on you. You liked having all my friends look at you."

"No."

"Yes."

She whimpered. Her breasts were on fire but, like it or not, her hips were starting to rock against his muscled thigh.

He nipped at her neck. "You felt sexy then. Do you feel sexy now, Tally?"

Oh, God, she hated this man. She'd die before she admitted that to him. "I didn't come here for this."

"No? Well that's too bad, because it's what you're going to get."

One of his punishing hands mercifully left her breast. Talia gasped as circulation was restored to her tender nipple, but he leaned down and latched onto the red peak with his mouth. She jerked reflexively when his intent suckling brought a rush of blood to the delicate bud. Her neck arched against the door and she let out a piercing cry. The sensation was too fierce. Too heightened.

"That's more like it," he said as he hauled up the hem of her dress and began pawing at her panties. The protection they provided was laughable. He yanked them down and jammed his hand between her legs. Two thick fingers poked roughly at her opening.

The fit was tight but she was so wet, they slid in easily.

The surprise was enough to make him stop the plundering of her breasts long enough to look in her face. He worked his fingers higher into her and Talia was mortified. Closing her eyes, she rolled her head away from him.

He refused to let her draw back. "Look at me."

His fingers began pumping determinedly in and out of her and it was all she could do not to roll her hips in rhythm.

"Look at me!"

His thumb suddenly tweaked her clitoris and her eyes flew open.

"I get hard every time you walk into a room," he said in a voice like sandpaper. "Do you get wet?"

It was her deepest secret but she couldn't hide it from him anymore—not with his fingers dripping with her juices. "Yes," she whispered miserably.

"Did you want me to bang you in that bathroom when you were fifteen?"

"No!"

"The truth, damn it."

"Mmm," she whimpered. He was close to her G-spot. "Yes."

"Is that why you've been so prissy around me all these years?"

"I'm prissy because you're a jerk," she said, finding one last thread of her fighting spirit.

He laughed. "You don't know what you want, do you, sexy Tally?"

He pulled his fingers out of her so abruptly she groaned.

"Don't worry, babe. Big Brent will show you."

He pushed her panties down her legs. They draped across her ankles like a last defense surrendered. Talia tried to shove him away but she couldn't get any leverage with her arms restricted. All she could do was watch as he undid the zipper of his three-hundred-dollar slacks and pulled out his cock.

It was big and red — nearly purple, he was so hard. Her eyes rounded but she knew there was no escape.

She had to tell herself again that she wanted one.

He gave her no time to think before he was on her again. His hot mouth zeroed in on her breast. His tongue pressed her nipple tight against the roof of his mouth and she gritted her teeth at the bolts of electricity that shot straight to her core.

His fingers bit into the back of her thigh. With an abrupt tug, he lifted her leg up and to the side. With no preliminaries, he thrust into her.

"Ah!" she cried. His cock was longer and thicker than his fingers. And hotter. It felt like he was shoving a fat, red-hot poker up into her.

Brent grunted. He lifted her higher against the door until only the tiptoes of her left foot touched the ground.

Talia couldn't catch her breath. She felt dominated being trapped and spread so wide.

She couldn't move. Couldn't escape.

He nipped hard at her breast and thrust deeper.

"Ohhh!"

She could feel her pussy stretching under the invasion of his hard, determined cock. As exhilarating as it felt, accommodating him was an effort. Reflexively, her fingernails dug into the wooden door behind her. The discomfort was acute. He was having to be forceful but, of that, she was secretly glad. She wasn't welcoming him. She'd never have let him do this if he hadn't made her.

"Worth the wait, baby?" he growled into her ear when he was finally seated.

"Screw you," she panted.

"Since you ask so nicely," he said, nipping her earlobe. "I will."

He began to move and she nearly came unglued. In her constrained position, though, she could hardly budge. His mouth went to her other breast and, reluctantly, she threaded her fingers through his hair and held him against her.

She quickly learned that he wasn't one for shallow thrusts. He liked to work deep. He'd only pull out a few inches before ramming back into her. Her butt bounced against the door with every thrust he made and the knocking sound became faster and louder.

"Oh... Oh... Ohhh!" Talia moaned. Sensations spiraled through her. Pleasure. Loathing. Satisfaction. Compulsion. Her fingernails raked down his back. She hated him but she'd hungered for this forever.

Sweat ran down Brent's temples onto her naked breast. He grunted like a pig as he sucked on her tit and fucked her more and more fiercely.

"Christ," he snapped as he came up for air. He pressed her leg higher against her chest, opening her wider. He shifted his stance and his hips swung in a wide arc.

When he slammed home the next time, Talia's air caught in her lungs. He was banging directly against her clit. It took only a few rough thrusts before she went off like a house of firecrackers. She let out a sharp cry and his rhythm quickened as the orgasm rocked her. His cock swelled inside her and soon the unbearably tight friction had him shooting his load.

For long minutes afterwards, Talia had to depend on Brent's strength to keep her upright. Every ounce of energy had been wrung from her body. When he finally pulled out of her and let her leg drop, she couldn't let go of his waist. It was the only thing keeping her upright.

"I knew you'd be a Grade A fuck," he said, breathing roughly against her neck.

She kept her eyes closed and fought to find her center. She didn't know why his crudeness shook her. She certainly hadn't expected love talk out of him. Their whole relationship had been based on dirty, unwanted, sexual undercurrents.

"Don't you feel better?" he asked.

He let go of her and she sagged against the hard wooden door.

"Better?" she repeated in disbelief. She felt vile. Her breasts were red from his mouth and her dress was still wrapped around her waist. She felt cheap and sordid with her pussy naked and throbbing.

He patted the wet triangle of hair before turning toward his desk. "It must have been hard for you to fight your basic instincts. You've wanted to spread those long legs for Big Brent for a long time."

"I didn't... You made me..." Outrage made it nearly impossible to speak. "I came here to beg you to change your mind about the after-school program!"

He looked over his shoulder at her and his teeth glowed in the moonlight like a wolf's. "And you begged well. That after-school program is expensive, though. I'll need more convincing. Next time—"

Her head whipped back so fast, it banged against the door behind her. "There isn't going to be a next time!"

"Careful, Tally." He pulled tissues out of a box on his desk and cleaned off his limp dick. "Remember how badly you want the Arts Council's support before you say that."

"That's...that's blackmail."

He grinned again as he zipped up. "And just whom are you going to complain to?"

The fight drained out of her. She watched wide-eyed as he advanced on her again with the tissue box in hand. The bastard. She couldn't complain to anyone. She couldn't tell a soul what she'd let him do to her. He'd left her powerless. Distraught, she lurched away from the door but he caught her and pressed her back.

He pulled out a handful of tissues and reached between her legs.

"No!" she said, pushing at his forearm.

"You know, it's funny how your mouth and your body seem to disagree so much." He tossed a wet tissue onto the floor and reached for another one.

She gasped as the soft material brushed across her clit and gathered moisture from her wet tangles. "You are such a lowlife."

"And you love that about me," he whispered. His hot breaths blew onto her face as he leaned close. He emphasized his point by pressing a tissue-covered finger right up into her and swirling it around.

"Ahh," she cried.

"But I'm not an unreasonable man," he said, nipping her earlobe. "You pleaded your case well. I suppose a donation to your little charity is warranted."

He tossed the box of tissues aside and reached for his wallet. "Will this do?"

She was left utterly speechless as she watched him pull out a wad of bills and roll them up. Watching her with that wolfish smile on his face, he reached between her legs again. Horror suddenly gripped her. She groped for his hand but he pushed the money up into her damp channel and left it there.

"Use this in whatever way you see fit," he said with a smirk.

Talia couldn't have moved if the house had been on fire. She was staggered by what he'd just done. He gave her breast one last squeeze, set her aside and left her alone in the room.

Inside her head, all Talia could hear was screaming. After what could have been five seconds or five minutes, she finally reached between her legs. The wad of money clung to her but she dragged it out of its wet hiding place. Unrolling the bills, she looked at Brent Harrington III's "donation".

She was mortified.

He'd just paid her $120 for a fuck.

Chapter Two

He'd used her like a whore.

Bitterness rose inside Talia until a metallic taste filled her mouth. The money in her hand became hot to the touch. She dropped it on the floor before it could brand her. She'd had to deal with New Covington's twisted society strata ever since her family had moved to this town but she'd never felt so cheap. Brent hadn't thought twice about screwing her and paying her for her services.

Worse yet, she'd let him do it.

Her hand lashed out and hit the light switch. If she'd thought that things would look better under the harsh lights, she was wrong. Red marks dotted her breasts. Further down, her pussy was pink and swollen. Her dress was bunched around her waist and her panties were on the floor two feet away.

She looked like a tramp. She'd acted like a tramp.

And he'd made damn sure she felt like one.

Her hands shook with fury as she untangled herself from her silk bindings. She pulled her dress back into place but no amount of smoothing or stretching could erase the wrinkles. People were bound to notice.

Panic started to grab hold. They'd notice and they would talk. Once again, she was going to be dragged through the town rumor mill.

"Stop it!" she chastised herself. "Just stop and think."

She looked at her surroundings, not really knowing what she was searching for. A large oak desk was the focal point of the room. Dark leather furniture, a collection of antique riding equipment and a packed bookcase gave the room a masculine feel. Too masculine. Too much like Brent.

She had to get out of here.

Her gaze focused on the sliding glass door behind the desk. It led to a balcony and her mind was drawn back to her daydream. She considered it for a full minute before she decided it was too dangerous. There was no way around it. She was going to have to face the Edward Joneses and the Shelli Harringtons downstairs in order to escape.

A door in the far corner looked as if it led to a bathroom. She bent over to pick up her things and grimaced when her body protested. Her legs were unsteady as she wandered across the room. Her steps paused, though, when she saw the antique riding whip hanging on the wall in a shadow box. Fire burned in her belly as she took in the strong lines of the leather.

It was tempting.

She spun away before she could do something rash. She was a Sizemore. She refused to do anything to darken the family name—even if Brent deserved it.

Opening the bathroom door, she hesitantly looked at herself in the mirror. Her reflection made her wince. Her hair was falling out of its French twist and there was a hazy sultriness shining in her eyes. She looked as if she'd just had a great roll in the sack. Worst of all, there was stickiness between her legs that proved that she had.

Her chin dropped to her chest. She'd been screwed.

And in so many ways.

Brent had proven his political power over her in the Arts Council meeting. A quick rut against his office door had shown his physical and sexual power. He'd shown her in no uncertain terms that he could do whatever he wanted to her, whenever he wanted.

Her shoulders shook.

"This isn't over," she whispered.

On the Prowl

She had her pride. It didn't matter what he did; he'd never get that from her. She lifted her chin and straightened her shoulders. She did what she could to make herself respectable but nothing soothed her tattered ego. By the time she'd reapplied her lipstick and wiped the cum off her thighs, she was raging mad.

When she marched out of the bathroom, her steps were quick and sure. She kept her eyes strictly off the antiques display and headed to the door. She felt one last betraying flutter between her legs as she looked at it. Something brushed against her foot and she glanced down.

It was the money.

"I earned this," she said angrily. She swept the damp twenty-dollar bills off the floor and stuffed them into her purse. "I'm damn well going to keep it."

She shut the office door with a bang and strode toward the head of the staircase. Her confidence wavered, though, as she looked down at the crowd of people. Suddenly, she was fifteen all over again. This was exactly how she'd felt when she'd walked out of the Devonshire's bathroom looking like a wet T-shirt contestant.

"Damn you, Brent," she said through clenched teeth.

Holding her head high, she marched down the stairs.

"There you are, dear. I wondered where you'd gotten to."

Talia felt her flushed cheeks heat to the scorching point. Dear God, she didn't want to talk to Roger Thorton now. Her gaze darted around the room as she looked for an escape. He stepped in front of her, effectively blocking her path.

Humiliation made her cringe. Could he tell? Could he see that she'd just had sex? Could he smell it?

"Uncle Roger, I think you were right," she said, thinking quickly. She didn't even have to fake the tremor in her voice. "I feel as if I'm coming down with something. Perhaps I should go home."

"But of course, dear," he said. "You shouldn't push yourself like this."

She almost jumped out of her skin when he reached out and caught her chin.

"Do you want me to take you to a doctor? Your eyes are hazy and you've got a sheen of sweat at your temples."

"I just need some rest. Really." She turned her head to get away from his disturbing touch. Out of the corner of her eye, she saw Brent. She quickly gave him her back and focused on Roger. She needed to get out of here. *Now.* "Could you find my coat?"

"Stay right here." He stopped a passing waiter and grabbed a glass of water. "Drink this. It might make you feel better."

Her fingers gripped the glass hard as she took a long drink. The water felt good against her parched throat. She rolled the cool glass against her hot forehead and tried to calm down. So many powerful feelings were coursing through her veins. Embarrassment, shame and anger were warring for the top spot. When Brent moved into her line of view again and lifted a glass of champagne in salute, anger won out.

"Here you go, dear," Roger said as he returned.

Talia spun around and nearly threw her empty glass at a waiter. Her hands clenched into fists as she punched her arms through the sleeves of her coat. Her knuckles bumped against something hard and she felt it wobble. Instinctively, she grabbed for it.

It was the small, animalier bronze on the hallway table. A cat.

The rest of the world faded away as she looked at it. Her heart started pounding in her chest and a feeling of triumph threatened to cut off her air supply.

She was worth a hell of a lot more than $120.

She thrust the sculpture into her pocket and headed for the door.

Roger quickened his stride to keep up with her. "Are you sure you'll be okay?" he asked. "Do you need me to drive you home?"

"Oh, for God's sake, Roger. Would you stop following that sad sack around?" Lydia Thorton's inebriated voice cut through the din of the crowd. "The party's just starting to hop."

Talia kept her back to the woman. She couldn't deal with Lydia on the best of days. She certainly couldn't deal with her now.

"Thank you, Uncle Roger," she said as she nodded to the doorman. "I can get home on my own."

"Are you sure? I hope you'll be feeling better by Tuesday. Don't forget we're having that dinner party."

"I'll be there," she called over her shoulder.

She nearly ran out the front door of the Harrington mansion. Her footsteps were quick as she left the hell that was the Harringtons, the Thortons and the Arts Council. She quickly sent the parking valet for her car.

Her breaths were still shaky but she closed her eyes and inhaled the crisp night air as she waited. Her fingers tightened around the bronze cat in her pocket. It weighed heavily in her hand and the pressure in her chest eased.

"Now who's been screwed, Turd?"

* * * * *

Talia was in the shop early the next morning. She hadn't slept well. Her body was sore in places that hadn't been sore for a long time and her emotions were still touchy. It had taken a hot bath and nearly half a bottle of wine to calm her nerves after she'd gotten home last night.

At least she felt that she'd come out on top in the end. Sometime today, Brent was going to realize what had happened. Hitting him in the pocketbook had been pure inspiration. It was the place he would feel it the most. Soon, he was going to be regretting his actions.

She put the pretty cat on display. She'd been surprised to find it was a Mène but that made things even sweeter. The cat's eyes seemed to glitter in the morning sunlight. It would surely sell quickly and she'd already decided that the proceeds would go into the foundation. After all, Brent had said he was happy to make a donation. He just hadn't realized how big a donation it was going to be.

The bell over the front door to Coolectibles rang and she turned away from the new display. Sadie stepped into the shop and wiped her feet on the welcome mat. She cocked her head when she saw that they were already open for business. "You're up early."

Talia shrugged. "I couldn't sleep."

"Of course, you couldn't sleep. Who could after all the excitement last night?" Sadie tugged off her jacket and hurried over. "Tell me everything."

Talia stopped in the act of wiping dust off an old phonograph. Excitement? Last night? How in God's name had her assistant found out what had happened?

Her stomach turned. Brent. He'd already spread word of their tryst through the New Covington grapevine. She felt bile rise up in her throat. The rumor mill must be working overtime.

"Oh, come on, Talia. Did you see anything? The newscast was pretty vague."

The news? *The news?* Her common sense took over. There was no way that a story about her and Brent doing the deed would have been on the nightly news. She turned and looked at her friend. "What did they say?" she asked carefully.

Sadie rolled her eyes with impatience. "Just the basics. Robbery, Harrington mansion, party... You know. Tell me what really happened."

Robbery? Talia's head snapped up. Brent was calling it a robbery?

That bastard! He was trying to get back at her. Of all the—

Her stomach lurched as everything clicked into place. Reaching up, she slapped a hand over her mouth.

Of course, he'd reported it as a robbery—because that was what it had been. He didn't know that she'd taken the little cat. He didn't know why it had been stolen.

Dear God, she was a thief.

"Talia? What's wrong?" Sadie reached out and caught her by the arm. Gently, she led her to a chair. "Sit down before you pass out."

"Oh, no," Talia said as wooziness overtook her. *What had she done?*

"I keep telling you that you should take better care of yourself." Sadie crouched down in front of her and felt her forehead. "You don't feel as if you've got a fever."

Talia shrugged off the touch. No fever? Her skin prickled as if it was on fire. Every single nerve ending was flaring, signaling danger. She closed her eyes to try to block it out. That just intensified the thrum of her pulse in her ears. The pounding seemed to taunt "guil-ty, guil-ty" over and over again. "What was I thinking?"

Sadie rocked back on her heels. "You just need some sleep. Why don't you go back upstairs to your apartment? A nap might help."

A nap wouldn't cure what ailed her. She'd broken the law. She'd been justifiably upset but that didn't account for burglary. Brent had taken advantage of her—yes. But she'd been somewhat willing. What he'd done hadn't been a crime. Her revenge, though, could go down as a felony!

"What did they say on the news?" she asked.

"That's not important. Let's take care of you. I'll get you some tea."

Talia ran a hand through her hair. What was she going to do? Did anyone know what had really happened? Roger apparently hadn't seen but what about Lydia? Had she been too drunk? Had anyone else been around?

Sadie came back with a piping hot mug. "How long have you felt like this?"

"Last night," Talia said, her brain starting to kick into gear. If she stayed calm and thought this through, she could repair things. It was all just a big, horrible misunderstanding. Surely, everyone would understand once she explained.

But how was she going to explain? She couldn't tell the police what had happened in Brent's office! She couldn't tell Sadie, her best friend.

"I came home early from the party," she said, thinking fast. "I didn't even know there had been a burglary. Do the police have any suspects?"

"Not so far. The reporter said that they're looking through the list of party guests, the catering staff, the waiters, the parking attendants... It's going to take them a while."

Good. She had some time. She needed time to figure out how to straighten out this mess.

Maybe she should just return the cat to Brent and Shelli.

Yeah, right. And what was she supposed to say? "I'm sorry, it must have fallen into my pocket on my way out the door?" He'd laugh in her face. If anything could be more humiliating than last night, that might be it.

Talia looked over Sadie's shoulder and her eyes widened when she saw the telltale piece shining in the sunlight. "Could you find me some aspirin?" she asked quickly. "I can't believe how suddenly this has hit me."

"Of course," Sadie said, already turning. "You just sit still."

She couldn't stay still. She had to get rid of the evidence. She waited until her assistant was out of the room before she hurried to the display. Her hands shook as she grabbed the bronze. Where should she hide it?

Her eyes dropped to her briefcase. Hurriedly, she packed the cat inside, making sure it was well-protected in a roll of cloth. She was already putting on her jacket when Sadie came back with the aspirin.

"Where do you think you're going, missy? You park that butt back down in that chair."

Talia forced a smile. "That tone might work with Linc but I've got work to do."

She downed the two aspirin with one swig of tea. "Watch the shop?"

"Watch the shop? Where are you going? Talia!"

"I'm feeling better, I swear," she called. She ignored her assistant's protests as she darted out the back door. The briefcase weighed heavily in her hand. She couldn't sell the thing in her shop. She wanted it out of her hands.

Without thinking, she drove halfway across town to a colleague's gallery. She really didn't know what she was going to do once she got there but Arthur was a friend. More importantly, he detested the Harringtons. She could confide in him, tell him the truth. He'd help her; she knew he would.

As she walked in the shop, though, she saw that Arthur was busy helping a customer. Her nerves were frayed but she meandered about casually, pretending to look at the pieces he had on show.

Nerves made her stomach roll. How, exactly, was she supposed to go about this? She'd never tried to get rid of a stolen piece before. She didn't even know where to start.

"Talia," Arthur said when he saw her. "What a surprise. Come join us. Have you heard the big news?"

She made her way across the room uneasily. "What big news?"

"The Harringtons were robbed last night. This is Detective Riley Kinkade. He's working the case."

Talia's systems began shutting down one right after the other. First, her air caught in her lungs. Then her heart lurched to a stop. Her muscles went lax and she nearly dropped the briefcase. "Robbed?" she said in a quiet voice.

Kinkade. Detective. Case. Her eyes slowly turned on the man who'd been standing so quietly to the side. Her gaze caught him at shoulder level. Nearly frozen with trepidation, she forced herself to look up into his face. Dark brown eyes looked at her contemplatively.

"Talia Sizemore?"

"Yes," she whispered.

"You're next on my list."

List? She was on the list already? Reflex made her take a step back.

She never knew what happened next. She either caught a heel on the Oriental rug at her feet or her knees gave out. Whichever, she went flying backwards.

"Whoa!"

The detective had the reflexes of a tiger. Moving swiftly, he caught her about the waist. Her free hand latched onto his shoulder and, for the briefest of seconds, time stood still.

His dark gaze locked with her amber one and Talia felt him looking right into her soul.

He knew, she thought frantically. *He could see.*

Their bodies were sealed together from chest to knee, and she fought back her panic. There was no escaping now. His muscles felt like hot steel under her touch. His stomach molded against hers and a rock-hard thigh had slipped between her legs. As she clung to him helplessly, she felt another part of his body stiffen against her hip.

Her eyes widened and he let out a soft curse.

"Are you okay?" he asked, slowly bringing her upright.

No, she wasn't okay! Danger signs flashed inside her head. She was *not* okay.

"Ma'am?" he said again.

"I'm fine. Just clumsy." She tried to take a step back, but winced at the sharp pain in her ankle.

His hands at her waist stopped her. "Let me take a look."

Before she could clear her thoughts, he crouched down in front of her. His hand slid down her calf toward her ankle and a wild exhilaration ricocheted through her. Looking down, all she saw was the top of his head. A reckless part of her wanted to thread her fingers through his thick, brown hair and hold tight.

"I'm sorry, Talia. I should move that rug," Arthur said. "I keep tripping over it myself."

Her head snapped to the side. She'd forgotten there was anybody else in the room! "It wasn't the rug. It was my fault. Don't worry. I'm fi—"

Her words broke off sharply when the detective slid her shoe off her foot. The action felt as seductive as if he'd just slipped off her panties. She was thrown by her reaction but that didn't lessen it in the least. Her knees went weak again and she reached out to brace herself against the man's shoulders.

His gaze slid up her body slowly and she suddenly realized how short her skirt was. If he leaned only a few inches forward, his face would be in her crotch.

"How's that feel?" he asked.

"What?" she said in a haze.

"Your ankle," he said with the hint of a smile on his lips. "Does this hurt?"

He pressed against the soft tissue on her inner foot. The touch should have been impersonal but zaps of electricity shot right up her leg to her core. Talia felt her pussy twinge. "No, no pain," she said unevenly.

"How about that?" His fingers deftly touched her anklebone.

She pressed her lips together. She tried to pull her foot away but he glanced at her and she stopped. She couldn't afford to raise his suspicions.

Watching her closely, he slid his thumb to the bottom of her foot and pressed firmly against her arch. Oh, God! Her fingers tightened reflexively on his shoulders as arousal hit her hard. He might have missed the small sign but there was no way he could miss the curling of her toes.

"Everything looks good down here," he said, clearing his throat.

He slid the shoe back on her foot and slowly stood up. She thought she heard him say "real good" under his breath but she couldn't be sure. She'd already taken two steps back.

The man was dangerous.

"What were you saying about a list, Detective?" she asked hastily. Daddy had always taught her that the best defense was a good offense. At least in business. She hoped it was the same for crime.

He watched the wild gesture she made with interest and she forced her hand to drop limply at her side. His eyes glittered. "You were on the guest list for the Harrington's party. I'm talking to everyone who attended."

"Oh." She wasn't a suspect. Relief ran through her but she knew better than to let her guard down. Carefully, she tucked a stray hair behind her ear. His observant gaze took in the move and she felt unsettled again. The man had the instincts of a hunter. "I attended the party but I didn't notice anything unusual. Then again, I left early."

"Why was that?"

"I wasn't feeling well." It was the truth. She'd felt sick when she'd left the Harrington mansion and she felt even worse now. The dark circles she knew were under her eyes bore that out. She was particularly conscious of them with him staring at her so hard.

"Sorry to hear that," he said softly. "Since you haven't heard, the Harringtons noticed early this morning that an art piece they had on display at the party is missing."

"Really?" she said with just the right amount of shock. "Can I ask which one?"

"A bronzed cat. Something called an animali-er." He reached into his jacket pocket and pulled out a picture.

"It's pronounced animali-ae," she said politely. She forced her expression to remain calm as she looked at the photograph. The cat's eyes glared at her accusingly and her grip on her briefcase suddenly became sweaty. "I remember that. It's a very nice piece."

"The detective here was just asking if anybody had brought it into my shop today," Arthur said. "Anything like that come into yours?"

Talia felt faint. Thank God she hadn't gotten here fifteen minutes earlier. She adjusted her hold on the suddenly slippery handle. What if she'd shown the cat to Arthur before Kinkade had gotten here? She'd probably be in handcuffs right now. "No," she said feebly. "I would remember something like that."

"Why don't you set this down?" the detective said. From out of the blue, he reached for her briefcase. "You look like you're still a little shaky."

"No! That's okay. Really."

She tried to pull back but he was quick.

"Good God, woman," he said when he took on its weight. "What are you carrying in there?"

She smiled weakly as he set the briefcase on the counter. She didn't have to fake it anymore. She was beginning to feel truly nauseous. "Rocks. Anyway, that's what my associate always tells me."

One of his eyebrows lifted.

"Shelli must be very upset," she said, trying to change the subject. His scrutiny was just too intense. She wiped her damp palms on her skirt and his gaze finally dropped from her face to her legs.

That wasn't any better. A familiar tingle began low in Talia's abdomen. The power of the attraction she had for this man scared her. She felt like a moth being inexorably drawn to the flame.

"I'd say that Mrs. Harrington is more offended than upset," the detective said distractedly. He was still staring at her legs. "She hates that her party was spoiled."

"Yes, well, Shelli is a consummate hostess. I'm sure that the entire experience has been quite distressing to her." Talia couldn't take it anymore. The man had her nerves stretched to the breaking point. Her body was reacting on all cylinders and she had to put this ridiculous mating dance to a stop. He was a detective and, like it or not, she was his target.

"I'm sorry I couldn't be of more help, Detective, but I really need to get back to my shop." Trying to be casual, she reached for her briefcase. She gave it a firm tug and was relieved to feel the strain on her arm. "Good-bye, Arthur."

"Did you want something, Talia?" he asked. "You don't usually drop by in the middle of the day."

For a moment, her mind went blank. "I was in the area and I thought I'd just drop by to say hello."

"Oh, I wish you could stay a bit longer. A beautiful English tea set just came in. You'd love it."

"Maybe some other time."

"When exactly would be a good time, Ms. Sizemore?" the detective asked.

She looked at him sharply.

"I'm sure I'll have more questions for you."

It was funny how he could say so much more with his eyes.

Talia felt a tickle in her belly. It was attraction and fear all mixed up together. How in God's name had she gotten herself into this mess? "I'm sure it would be a waste of your time."

"You never know," he said softly.

Her insides began to quiver. She couldn't hold onto this façade much longer. "Then feel free to drop by my shop."

"I will."

Fear finally won out. She nodded mutely and spun on her heel. She walked quickly to the door but she could feel his stare on the middle of her back the entire way. It took everything inside her to keep herself from running to her car. She'd just met the consequences of her actions.

His name was Kinkade.

* * * * *

Riley watched the tall blonde leave. Good Lord, she even moved like sin. Trying to appear casual, he strained to watch those long legs of hers until they disappeared from sight. Fantasies about those legs were already making his head hurt.

Touching her had been the wrong thing to do but he hadn't been able to help himself. Considering what he'd wanted to do, massaging her ankle had been downright tame.

Only it hadn't felt tame.

"Damn," he muttered under his breath. He adjusted his jacket to hide the bulge behind the zipper of his pants. This wasn't looking good. He was a cop, for God's sake, and for all he knew, she could be a suspect.

She didn't seem to be the type, though. The dame was classy and she certainly didn't need the money. Still, she'd been wired. Her nervous energy had made the air around her crackle.

"What do you know about her?" he asked the gallery owner.

"She's single," Arthur said helpfully.

Riley grimaced and rubbed the back of his neck. So his casual behavior hadn't been so casual after all. "What's her relationship with the Harringtons?"

"They run in the same social circle. Talia sits on the Arts Council Board with Brent."

"Do they get along?"

Arthur finally picked up on the direction of the conversation. "Really, Detective. You can't suspect her. I've known Talia Sizemore for years. Why, she would no more steal than go running naked through the streets."

Now that was a vision. Riley shifted uncomfortably. "I've got to learn all I can if I'm going to track down that cat."

"Well, Talia didn't take it. She's a good woman. She runs a nice, friendly shop called Coolectibles over on Cavalier Drive. Why, she even has a foundation that helps bring the arts to disadvantaged kids. She's not a thief."

"Sounds more like a paragon of virtue."

"She is."

She wasn't. Riley had known it the moment he'd touched her. She wasn't virtuous at all. She was a red-blooded, sensual woman. He'd felt it in the way her body had melted against his. When he'd been crouching in front of her, he could have sworn her hips had swayed toward him. If the gallery owner hadn't been standing five feet away, he just might have taken her up on the invitation and gone rooting around under that short skirt.

His cock twitched at the intimate memory and he became irritated with himself. He needed to watch it. He had a job to do and getting tangled up with somebody involved in the case could be disastrous.

"She seemed nervous," he commented. She'd been wound tight as a top from the moment he'd laid eyes on her. Her palms had been sweaty and her breaths had been shallow. Come to think of it, his breaths hadn't been very steady, either.

"She seemed aroused to me, Detective."

Riley shot a surprised look at the seemingly demure Arthur but this time he couldn't hide his smile. "You think?"

"I think."

He nodded slowly. The idea appealed to him, although there wasn't a hell of a lot he could do about it. "Well, that's good, because I have a feeling that the lady and I will be seeing a lot of each other."

Turning, he looked toward the door where Talia Sizemore had just exited.

Getting to know her better intrigued him. There were things he wanted to know, like how those legs of hers felt up under that short skirt. Would her breasts fit into his hands as perfectly as he suspected they would? Did she like it better from the front or behind? Most of all, though, he wanted to know what was going on behind those sharp amber eyes, because Talia Sizemore, paragon of the art world, was hiding something.

He'd bet his entire month's paycheck on it.

Chapter Three

Talia drove without direction. Her fingers gripped the steering wheel so hard they turned white. The detective had known. He'd seen that she was lying.

What was she supposed to do now? Where was she supposed to go?

"How did this happen?" she asked incredulously. She'd never meant for things to go this far. She hadn't been thinking when she'd lashed back at Brent. Her emotions had overridden everything else. Looking back, it all seemed like some sort of chaotic dream.

But it hadn't been a dream. The police were involved now. That made everything just a little too real. And Kinkade had definitely been real. Just remembering him picking up her briefcase made her hands begin to shake so badly, she had to pull over to the side of the road.

"Settle down," she told herself determinedly. She leaned her forehead against the steering wheel and made herself take deep breaths. "You can't help yourself if you fall apart."

But falling apart was tempting. She knew that she hadn't fooled him. His sharp eyes hadn't missed a tremor of her hands. His ears had heard every catch of her breath.

She needed to get rid of the Harringtons' piece *ASAP!*

Lifting her head, she finally took in her surroundings. Unknowingly, she'd driven out of the city and headed to the shores. She was at the lighthouse. Fumbling with the door handle, she got out of her car. The sharp autumn wind smacked her in the face but the air cleared her thoughts and sharpened her concentration.

On the Prowl

The cat had to go; that was a given. She couldn't let it be found in her possession.

Wrapping her arms around her waist, she walked over to the lookout. Below, the ocean waves crashed against the cliff walls. The sight brought to mind an immediate solution.

Cautiously, she looked around. Only a few other visitors mingled about. Her gaze focused on her car and, in her mind, she could see the animalier's eyes sparkling at her. The smirk on the cat's face made her stomach clench.

It just wasn't fair. The Harringtons would collect on their insurance but what about her? She'd taken that stupid cat for a reason. *A damn good reason.*

"And what about the arts program?" she said aloud. The wind caught her words and carried them out to sea.

Her idea of selling the cat and using the profits for the foundation still had merit. No matter what Brent and the other members of the Arts Council thought, that after-school program served an important purpose. For some of those inner-city latchkey kids, the program was the only safe haven they had.

And then there were her sensibilities! That bronzed cat was beautifully crafted. It was an original Mène—not one of the extensive reproductions. The French sculptor's playful animals were highly desirable collectors' items. She couldn't destroy it. It went against everything inside of her.

"What am I going to do?" she whispered.

A chill ran down her spine and she wrapped her arms more tightly about her waist. Just how did one get rid of a stolen piece of art?

She tilted her head back toward the sky and groaned. She couldn't believe she was even thinking like this. She was a respectable art dealer. She was an appraiser, for heaven's sake. She sat on the Council for the Arts. If there was one subject she knew, it was ethics.

"Ethics," she said slowly. "Professor Winston!"

Her heart rate picked up as inspiration hit. The professor specialized in functional art history but he'd also taught her favorite class, Art Fraud and Ethics, at New Covington College. He knew everything there was to know about forgeries and scams. Wouldn't it make sense that he'd also know the inner workings of the black market?

She slowly drummed her fingers on the guardrail. "Maybe," she said.

Her mind began to turn. She could use her shop as a cover. She could say that somebody had tried to sell her a stolen piece. Her curiosity about the dealings of the arts underworld would be understandable. She just needed to play it better than she had with the detective.

Kinkade.

She trembled and turned sharply from the ocean view. Approaching Professor Winston was a risk she had to take.

* * * * *

New Covington College's campus was beautiful in the fall. Leaves fell from trees as Talia strode toward Jefferson Hall where she'd been told Professor Winston was teaching a class. She should have known she'd find him giving a lecture. The professor was a favorite among students. He had an amazing ability to take what could be dull subjects and bring them to life. Back in her day, his lectures on sexuality in art history were often standing room only — not to mention his lab classes on the techniques of art fraud. They were overbooked every semester.

Unfortunately, the professor's unusual teaching techniques often generated flack from conservative parents and alumni. He didn't let that dissuade him, though. He just continued with what he thought was best for his students' education. That, more than anything, gave her the courage to face him now. She was fighting for her students, too.

She found the room and watched through the window. The professor hadn't changed. His trademark wire-rimmed glasses were perched on the end of his nose and his bowtie looked starched and pressed. His animation was clear even from a distance. Watching his ebony hands gesture lavishly brought back memories but she waited anxiously for the class period to end. When it did, she stood aside as students poured out into the hallway. "Professor," she called as she stepped into the empty lecture hall.

Winston looked up from his papers. "Talia Sizemore," he said with a broad smile. "This is a pleasure."

She crossed the room and shook the professor's hand warmly. "It's nice to see you. It's been too long."

"That it has. Why, it seems like only yesterday that you were sitting right up there in the fourth row."

She glanced toward the desks. "Your memory is better than mine."

"I always remember my best students." Winston adjusted his glasses on his nose. "So what brings you here today?"

"Actually, I need your guidance." She looked around cautiously to make sure that none of the students had lingered. "Something happened at my shop yesterday and I need to discuss it with someone."

"Ah, yes. Coolectibles, isn't it? I keep meaning to drop by. I've heard it's quite wonderful."

The unexpected compliment made Talia momentarily forget her problems. The professor wasn't one to hand out gratuitous praise. It made her feel good that he had kept up with her work.

"So what happened?" he asked. "Did an interesting piece come in?"

The moment disappeared and her stress returned. This wasn't a social visit.

"You could say that," she said carefully. "Professor, what do you do when somebody tries to sell you a piece you think might have been...well, *stolen*?"

Winston straightened. "Stolen?"

She shrugged.

"Did you call the police?"

"Um, no."

His eyes narrowed behind the thick lenses. "Why not?"

She felt the color drain from her face.. This was going to be more difficult than she'd thought. "Could we find someplace else to talk?" she asked quietly.

One of the professor's eyebrows lifted above the metal rim of his glasses. He stared at her for so long, she almost lost her nerve. Finally, he gathered his lecture materials. "Let's go to my office."

The hallway was still busy with students but Talia followed Winston as he weaved his way through the crowd. Anxiety threatened to overwhelm her but she fought it back. The professor was the only person she could think of who might be able to help her. He opened his office door for her and she entered the small room. She heard the door click shut behind him.

"What is this about, Ms. Sizemore?"

The professor sat behind his desk and placed his papers in a drawer. His concentration was on her, though, and she fought to keep her composure. *Keep it together*, she ordered herself. "I hope we can maintain confidentiality about this discussion," she began.

He fingered his bowtie. "Of course."

Tentatively, she perched on a chair in front of his desk. She set her heavy briefcase on the floor close at her side. "As I said, I had an unusual item come into my shop yesterday. It started me thinking... I... Well, I was wondering if you could tell me how the black market works."

"The black market?" he said sharply. "Why would you come to me about that?"

Her heel began tapping nervously on the floor. This was not going the way she'd envisioned. "I remembered your classes on art forgery and I just..."

"You just what?" Winston shifted in his chair and looked at the door. "Who sent you here?"

"Sent me? Nobody sent me."

"I haven't seen you in years and now you show up asking all kinds of questions about the black market. Why?"

"Why?" Her eyes rounded. "Oh, no, Dr. Winston. I'm not accusing you of anything. I just need your advice."

The professor looked at the door as if he expected someone to come crashing through at any moment. "I think it would be best if you left."

"Left?" Her fingers curled around the arms of her chair. Her hasty plan was tumbling down around her like a deck of cards. "But I don't know who else to talk to."

"I'm sure you'll find somebody. The FBI, perhaps. They always have an interest in arts trafficking."

Panic swamped Talia as Winston stood suddenly and circled the desk. When he opened the door and gestured for her to leave, she came right out of her chair. "I can't go to the police," she blurted. "Professor, you've got to help me."

Her desperation must have been clear, because he finally looked into her eyes.

"I'm in trouble," she whispered.

He hesitated.

"Please."

Slowly the door closed. Winston's face was hard. "I want a full explanation. *Now*."

"It's...complicated."

"Isn't it always?" He stood, one hand on the doorknob, assessing her. The tension in the room thickened unbearably.

Talia wrung her hands. "I made a mistake—a big one. I don't know to fix it."

"And you think I do?"

"Maybe. Please, Professor." She was so scared, she thought she might be sick. "I swear I won't bring you into it. I just need someone I can trust."

Winston looked torn. His body was stiff and lines of strain crossed his forehead. Talia feared her nerves would snap as she waited for him to respond.

"If you truly want my help," he finally said, "you'll have to assure me you're on the level."

She lifted her hands, palms upward. She was willing to do whatever he needed to prove herself.

"Please remove your jacket."

Her head snapped back. "My jacket?" she asked in confusion.

"I need to make sure you're not wearing a wire."

She looked at him, dumbfounded. "You've got to be kidding me."

"I assure you, I do not 'kid'."

He turned back to the door and her nerves took off right along with her pulse. "No! I need to talk. There's no wire. I swear."

She reached up to undo her jacket. She slipped it off her shoulders and laid it on the chair. The professor stared at her hard. At last, he moved. He crossed the room but, for some reason, she still felt offended when he picked up the garment and began patting it, looking for electronic devices that might be sewn into the seams.

"Professor..."

"Please hold still."

She nearly came out of her shoes when he turned abruptly and caught her by the waist. He patted her down efficiently even as she recoiled and shied away from his touch.

"Now, wait just one minute!"

A shiver went down her spine when he lifted her hair to look for an earpiece.

"I need to check your bra," he said matter-of-factly.

She inhaled sharply when his hands settled over her breasts. *"Professor Winston!"*

"Monitoring devices have become incredibly high-tech, Ms. Sizemore," he said as his hands squeezed and prodded. "I've seen styles that use the underwire for antennae."

She didn't care. She hadn't given him permission to touch her! Although...

Her stomach clenched as the professor continued his impersonal fondling. He was truly more interested in her bra than in her flesh; she could tell by the way his fingers prodded at the underwire of the cups. That didn't stop her nipples from perking up. When she looked into Winston's dark eyes, though, she didn't see sexual sparks.

She saw suspicion.

It made her hold still until he completed his examination. Even so, she wasn't ready when he suddenly turned her breasts loose and dropped to a crouch. "What are you doing?" she gasped.

Her nipples were rubbing hard against the cups of her bra and she'd already surmised that her skirt was too short. The detective had made that perfectly clear.

"I'll be quick," he promised.

She stood in mute stupefaction as her respected mentor moved forward and put his hands on her again. His firm touch started at her waist, feeling for any suspicious bumps. It swept down her hips and she let out a huff when he clasped her buttocks firmly.

"Excuse me," he said politely.

Talia couldn't contain her surprised screech when his hands swept up under her skirt and did a thorough examination of her panties. One hand pressed firmly between her legs and she twisted away. Unaffected, Winston turned his attention to her shoes. When he was through, he stood and moved to her briefcase.

"Open it," he demanded.

"No!" she said, self-preservation finally taking hold. He didn't trust her; how could she trust him? Especially with the way he'd just crossed the line of their relationship. She lunged for her briefcase.

He was too quick for her. The briefcase was off the floor and on his desk before she could take it from him. He popped open the locks and she let out a soft cry. She'd come here for his help but this wasn't what she'd planned. She tried once more to grab the piece before he could see but the cloth slipped and the playful cat's eyes gleamed at them both.

Winston went still.

After a moment, he adjusted his glasses on his broad nose. Talia waited painfully for him to make some comment. Any comment.

He didn't.

Instead, he put the cat aside and ran his fingers around the edges of the briefcase's interior. Satisfied at last, he circled around his desk and calmly sat. He steepled his fingers together and looked at her. "That's the stolen Harrington piece," he said flatly. "I saw the story on the news."

She couldn't deny it. The cat sat there smiling up at her, building her guilt to an aching crescendo.

"Why bring it to me instead of taking it to the police?" he asked in a low, razor-sharp voice.

The police. She remembered Kinkade's dark, piercing eyes and she reached out to steady herself on the back of the chair. "I need to get rid of it."

He let the comment sink in. "How did it come to be in your possession?"

Her heart began hammering against her rib cage. Could she trust him? She had to. "I took it."

The only response the professor displayed was a slight widening of the eyes. "I see."

Talia stumbled over words as she tried to explain. "It was a misunderstanding. Brent... Well, he angered me, and I grabbed it out of spite. I wasn't thinking."

Winston's lips curled up slightly. "You were thinking enough to grab a very nice piece."

He picked up the cat and pulled it closer. Talia slowly sank back into the chair. Her knees wouldn't support her anymore.

"Very nice," he muttered. He turned the piece upside down and lifted his glasses off the bridge of his nose until he could see best through the lenses. "And it's an original."

"French," she muttered.

"Excellent craftsmanship."

She shifted in her chair. "The lines are flawless."

He nodded and continued his inspection. Talia rubbed her damp palms on her short skirt and waited with bated breath. Finally, he set the cat down with a gentle touch. Once again, he steepled his hands together and pursed his lips.

"We might be able to reach an agreement," he said softly.

Agreement? Agreement for what?

"My take is normally fifty percent."

She sat motionless for a solid minute until her brain finally clicked into gear.

Professor Winston was a fence!

Shock took her breath away. In a million years, she never would have believed that studious, bow-tied Dr. Winston actually dealt in the underbelly of the arts world. The idea that one of the most respected teachers at New Covington College could be involved in something so immoral was staggering.

Yet at the same time, so opportune.

Her train of thought came back on track. "Fifty percent is outrageous."

"I'd be taking all the risk."

"I'm taking it now. I had the Mène in my briefcase this morning when a persistent detective questioned me about it."

The professor dropped his hands to the desk as he judged her. "I could drop to forty percent."

The conversation had finally ventured onto her turf. Talia settled more comfortably into the chair. She bargained for items every day. If there was anyone who knew how to haggle over price, it was she. "I won't be taking any of the proceeds myself. The money will go into the Sizemore Foundation to help reestablish the after-school program for inner-city schools."

The professor's chin came up. "The one that Harrington and his pretentious Arts Council killed?"

"Precisely."

He looked at her contemplatively. "I'm beginning to understand how this all came about."

For the first time ever, Talia saw the cunning the professor hid behind the nebbish glasses and the prim bowtie. She watched as his gaze went from her to the cat—and back to her again. He took a slow breath and rubbed his chin as if in deep thought. The silence started to echo as she waited for his counteroffer.

"The money would be going to a good cause," he finally said. "My niece has taken part in the after-school arts program."

Talia blinked. "Really? I wasn't aware of that. What's her name?"

"Beatrice."

It wasn't a common name, especially for a child. "Beatrice Small?" she asked.

"Yes." He looked taken aback. "You know her?"

"Of course, but I didn't realize she was your niece!" Talia quickly picked up her purse and began digging inside. At last, she found her car keys. They jingled as she passed them to the professor. "She's exceptional with bead work. She made that keychain for me."

The professor went very still. When he reached for the keychain, his touch was as careful as if he was handling a hundred-year-old painting. His expression turned solemn.

"Twenty-five percent," he offered. "That's as low as I can go."

Talia took a deep breath. It was illegal and immoral but selling the cat on the black market would take it off her hands. That was the most important thing. If she could thwart the detective's suspicions before they could take root, it was worth it. "It's a deal."

Reaching across the desk, she shook Winston's hand.

"You'll be fairly compensated," he promised. He surprised her by throwing her an uncharacteristic wink. "I'll make sure I get a good price for your little pussy."

Chapter Four

Talia didn't remember the drive home. She was still stunned by everything that had happened. Brent. The cat. *Professor Winston.*

She couldn't believe the things she'd done. She shook her head. At least it was over. Misaligned planets, an unlucky horoscope, a bad tarot card reading... It didn't matter what the cause behind her aberrant behavior had been. She'd learned her lesson.

She wasn't cut out for a life of crime.

Letting out a long breath, she turned into the alley behind Coolectibles and parked in her designated spot. Her shaky legs made even the short walk to the back door seem long but the jingle of the bell comforted her. It signified home. Normalcy. She was more than ready for the world to right itself.

Sadie glanced into the back room at the sound and excused herself from the customer she was helping. "Where did you go?" she asked as she marched into the storage area. "Why did you run off like that?"

"I'm sorry," Talia said. "I didn't mean to worry you."

She adjusted her grip on her briefcase. It seemed a thousand pounds lighter but she couldn't unload her heavy conscience on her assistant. This story was going with her to the grave. More importantly, she couldn't implicate her friend—not even after the fact.

"What was I supposed to think?" Sadie said with a huff. "First you almost fainted. Then you ran out the door like your hair was on fire."

"I know. I just remembered...uh...an appointment that I'd forgotten."

"An appointment? Couldn't it have been rescheduled? You still look peaked."

For a moment, Talia drew a blank. She'd had so many other things on her mind, she hadn't taken the time to come up with an excuse. "The foundation," she said, quickly improvising. "I had a meeting with a potential donor."

"Oh." Sadie crossed her arms over her chest. "That is important. Did it go well?"

"You could say so." Talia's cheeks heated. It depended on how a person looked at things. On the one hand, she'd inadvertently found a way to bring more funding into the after-school program. On the other hand, her solution was a felony. "I think some money will be coming in soon."

"That's good news," Sadie said. "Real good. The kids need it."

She glanced over her shoulder to keep an eye on her customer. "Listen, I'm sorry I couldn't stop talking about the Harrington robbery this morning. I swear that sometimes my mouth isn't connected to my brain. I know you went to that party to try to convince that shifty snake to reestablish the funding. He gave you a hard time, didn't he?"

Talia forced her expression to remain calm. He'd given her something hard but they didn't need to get into that. "You told me not to go. I should have listened."

"That cheap bastard. He deserved to get robbed."

Guilt racked Talia. He might have deserved it but she couldn't have her assistant stumbling over the truth.

"I don't know what we're going to do," she said. "Without the Council for the Arts' funding, we have to find another steady source of income to keep the program alive."

Sadie rubbed her arm. "Oh, hon, don't worry. We'll come up with something."

"But what? Daddy would have known what to do but I don't even know where to start." Talia hung her jacket on the coat rack and her shoulders slumped. After all she'd been through, it was incredible to realize she was right back where she'd started. Wearily, she lifted a hand to her aching forehead.

"I knew it. You're still not feeling well." For all the sternness in Sadie's tone, her motherly tendencies surged to the forefront. She wrapped her arm about Talia's shoulders and gently turned her toward the back staircase. "Don't you worry about the money. I'll think of something. You just go upstairs and take care of yourself."

Talia caught her friend's hand and squeezed tight. "I'm so sorry I wasn't more prepared for Brent and the Board. If I had been, maybe Linc wouldn't be in trouble now."

Sadie's eyes flashed. "Linc's situation is not your fault. He's old enough to know better than to go running around with spray paint. As for the Board, who needs those snobs? We're better off without them."

"We're not better off without their money."

"Shush. We'll work on it tomorrow when both our brains are clear." Sadie shooed her up the steps. "Right now, you need to go crawl under some covers. I've got a Pennsylvania Dutch table to sell."

Talia glanced over her shoulder at the impatient customer and gave up the fight. She smiled weakly at her capable associate and started up the stairs. It took almost more energy than she had to spare. Her legs felt like lead as she dragged them up the steps one by one. Even her fingers were clumsy as she tried to find the right key for her apartment. Once inside, she dropped her briefcase onto a kitchen chair and made her way to the bathroom. Clothes hit the floor as she went.

The warm water of the shower was a soothing balm to her tired, aching muscles. The knot in her stomach loosened as the liquid sluiced down her form and she let her head drop back.

The water caressed her skin like a lover's touch. It snaked over curves and into secret crevices, lighting hypersensitive nerve endings. Her breasts felt full and tender. Further down, her pussy still ached deep inside. It brought back vivid memories of Brent.

She let out a soft whimper. The man had been nothing but trouble for her ever since they were teenagers. Why, *why*, couldn't she shake this unhealthy attraction she had for him? Look at what it had done to her.

Look at what it had made her do. Abruptly, she turned off the water.

Her father would have been appalled. He'd never had a problem with fund-raising. But stealing? Using a fence? Trading in the black market? She swallowed hard. He'd be so ashamed of her.

"It won't happen again," she said as she scrubbed herself dry. Leaving her hair wet, she walked naked to her bedroom. She pulled on a tank top and shorts before falling onto the bed. "I don't care what Brent said. Never again. I'll increase our marketing efforts. Maybe an email campaign or some new brochures would help."

As soon as her head touched the pillow, the ideas started to fade. The past day had been hell on her and most of her problems had been due to that damn bronze cat with the knowing eyes. Now that it was gone, her body was shutting down.

She could relax. Nobody ever needed to know about her slip of judgment. She was safe.

* * * * *

It was late afternoon by the time Riley finally made it to Coolectibles. Talia's assistant pointed him up the stairs to her apartment with a smile on her face but he got the feeling Ms. Sizemore wasn't going to be so cordial. He didn't know exactly why but she'd been skittish as a wild colt around him this morning. Their exchange had certainly been memorable.

Between the sight of her shapely legs and the feel of her satiny skin, he hadn't been able to get thoughts of her out of his head all day.

But what had made her so edgy? The instant attraction between them or something else?

He knew one thing for certain; he wanted to find out the answer to that question.

He climbed the stairs two at a time and knocked on the door. It had been a long day but he could feel his energy returning. Those long legs of hers would certainly wake him up.

He was a little surprised when she didn't answer. Her assistant had said she was home. He knocked again more soundly.

Still nothing. He was about to go back downstairs when he heard movement.

"This had better be important, Sadie," Talia mumbled when she opened the door.

Riley's air seeped out of his lungs.

Damn!

He'd caught her in bed.

She was rubbing her eyes in an attempt to wake up. Her hair curled wildly across her shoulders but one thing more than anything riveted his attention. She was practically naked.

Helplessly, his gaze dropped. She was wearing a tiny tank top and shorts that, for all practical purposes, weren't even there. Her nipples poked against the thin fabric and her tight belly was exposed. It was the long expanse of her legs, though, that nearly brought him to his knees.

"Kinkade!" she gasped.

He finally looked into her amber eyes. They widened expressively and she exploded into action. He jerked back as the door was slammed in his face and narrowly avoided a broken nose.

"Hey!" he yelled.

"What do you want?" she said loudly as the lock clicked into place.

"I told you I'd be dropping by to ask you more questions."

"Now's not a good time."

Riley planted his hands on his hips. She wasn't going to get rid of him that easily. He'd just seen heaven. She couldn't rip it away from him so mercilessly. "Listen, lady. I've had a hell of a day and you're the last stop on my list. Don't tell me it's not a good time."

"Can't we talk tomorrow?"

"Sure," he said through clenched teeth, "If you want to come down to the station."

The suggestion was met with silence.

"Oh, all right. Just give me a minute."

That's what he'd thought. There was the sound of more rustling before the lock clicked again. This time when she opened the door, she was discretely covered in a full-length robe.

"Come in, Detective," she said politely.

His gaze swept down her body. The satin clung to her curves and was nearly as sexy as the little number she wore underneath it.

He hesitated. "Do you have company?" he asked as he glanced over her shoulder.

Her eyebrows lowered in confusion until she saw the trail of clothes leading to her bedroom. "Oh!" she said with embarrassment. She hurriedly kicked her skirt so it covered a lacy pair of panties. "No. I was just taking a nap."

A nap. Now why the hell had she gone and painted that picture in his head?

With a heavy sigh, Riley pushed himself away from the doorframe and entered her apartment. Sometimes this cop-with-a-duty thing sucked.

She stepped back nervously.

"Are you feeling any better?" he asked.

She tightened the belt of the robe around her waist. "A little. I was trying to sleep off this headache."

"And your ankle?"

His gaze dropped down to her bare feet but even that seemed too intimate for her. She covered one foot with the other. He'd have bet ten bucks that, if her slippers had been nearby, she'd have put those on, too.

"You really didn't need to go out of your way to see me, Detective," she said as she raked a hand through her tussled hair. "I'm sure I have nothing to add to your investigation."

Nothing to add? She was the best thing about this investigation. He'd left her as his last stop so he'd have something to look forward to.

"You're not out of my way," he said. "Besides, I have some new information I want to discuss with you."

She looked at him sharply. The energy he'd felt radiating from her at Arthur's shop started pulsing again.

"Do you want some coffee?" she asked, turning away before he could see more. "I don't know about you but I could use some."

He watched the sway of her hips as she walked away from him. Damn, but she was something.

The case, Kinkade. The case.

Riley centered his thoughts. It didn't matter if her hair was mussed and her nipples were perky. He was here to work. He'd wanted to see her apartment. Now that she'd let him in, he'd better take a look around.

He let his gaze sweep the room and couldn't help but let out a soft whistle. Her apartment was dripping with expensive things. It had an understated quality that only made it all the more pricey.

"Nice place," he called.

He followed the trail of clothes on the floor. The lace bra draped over the coffee table probably cost more than he had in his wallet. Of course, that didn't mean he couldn't appreciate it. If he'd known what she was wearing under that sexy suit this morning, he would have had a hard time keeping his hands on just her ankle.

"Do you want sugar?" she called from the kitchen.

God, did he.

"Black's fine."

The sound of her rummaging through a cupboard caught his attention and he meandered into the kitchen. She had her back to him and his gaze swept over her nicely curved ass. The view stopped him cold.

Shit! Everything about the woman turned him on—her body, her perfume, her classiness, her complexity... Once he eliminated her from his suspect list, he was going to have to do something about the ache in his crotch. With the way his cock was twitching, he'd better get her off that list pronto.

"Have you been working on the case all day?" she asked.

She opened a cupboard, but reached for the can of coffee so quickly, it fell off the shelf. Old football reflexes had Riley jumping forward to catch it. The quick move caught her between his body and the counter.

The intimate contact put him on edge. He hadn't meant to pin her but, for the life of him, he couldn't make himself pull away. She was soft and warm, and suddenly very quiet. She'd been trying to ignore him, but awareness now simmered in the air. Awareness that she was a beautiful woman, and he was a red-blooded man.

"Careful," he said close to her ear. She'd gone so still, he could see the pulse at her temple fluttering.

"Thank you," she whispered. "I'm not usually so clumsy."

She took the coffee from his hands but her breath caught noisily when the twisting motion pressed her soft butt more firmly against his excited crotch. Riley stifled a groan. Damn, but she felt good. He could stand here rubbing his stiff cock against her all day. With the way she'd gone all rigid, though, he knew that probably wasn't such a good idea. Gritting his teeth, he stepped back a few inches.

Her hands trembled as she took the lid off the can. When more of the coffee grounds landed on the counter than in the filter, he took over. "I don't think you need any caffeine," he said. Circling his arms about her, he took the measuring scoop from her hands. "Do you have any tea?"

"Second shelf," she said, hardly above a whisper.

The proximity of their bodies finally got to her and she pulled away. He stopped her with a hand at her waist. "Don't go far. We still need to talk."

He felt a shiver run through her.

"I take it that you haven't found the Mène yet."

Riley paused. If she got any tenser, rigor mortis was going to set in. Why was she so jitterish around him? Some people got nervous talking to cops but this was above and beyond. Had he done something? Slowly, he let his hand drop. Or was there something more to it? "I've learned a lot from the people who were at the party. I was hoping you could clear up some things for me."

She looked him dead in the eye. "What do you want to know?"

His instincts went on alert. He could feel that stillness about her again. He held her gaze and the air started to sizzle.

Something was up with her—and he wasn't thinking about just his cock.

"Let's start with Harrington," he said casually. Trying to put her at ease, he turned to search through the cupboard. "What's the deal with you two?"

She was a foot away but he could feel the jolt that ran through her body.

"What do you mean?" she said quickly.

Interesting. He'd hit on a sore subject.

"I've been doing my homework," he said as he picked up the kettle from the stove and held it under the faucet to fill it with water. He wasn't really a tea sort of guy but he'd learned that, in order to get past people's guards, you had to cozy up to them. Standing with her practically naked in her kitchen was a good place to start. "I talked with a guy named Edward Jones. He said something was going on between you and Harrington at the party."

He didn't mention everything else Jones had said. The man had given a very detailed description of how Talia had looked in her dress. Riley had wanted to punch the son of a bitch but he couldn't help but glance down at the front of her robe and make comparisons.

"Brent and I have known each other since we were teenagers," she said in a strained voice. "It's no secret that we don't always agree on things."

"Such as?" he asked.

"I don't see what this has to do with anything."

He lifted an eyebrow.

Frustrated, she ran a hand through her hair. "Funding issues," she finally admitted. "We both sit on the Council for the Arts Board. We don't agree on its priorities."

"He's the Board president, isn't he?"

"Unfortunately, yes."

Riley couldn't help it. It was one of the first unveiled reactions he'd gotten from her and the infinite meaning in her tone made him smile. "I can't say I liked the prick much either."

Her lips twitched. After a moment, her body relaxed. She looked softer, sweeter. His dick swelled and he set the pot on the stove before he could drop it.

God, he wanted her.

"So is that what the two of you discussed last night?" he asked, desperately trying to keep his focus. "Priorities? His wife said you went to his office for a private chat."

The almost-smile disappeared from Talia's face and her cheeks flushed. Riley caught every nuance of her reaction and it intrigued him even more. He wasn't satisfied at all with the muted "yes" that left her lips.

"Want to give me more details?" he asked.

"No."

"Talia."

"We talked about Board business," she said. "It didn't go well."

He took a step closer. He was onto something. He could sense it. "From all accounts, you pretty much ran out of the house afterwards."

"My head was pounding," she said as she pushed herself away from the counter. She scooted past him and walked to the other side of the room. "I told you that I didn't feel well. After talking with Brent, I wasn't in a party mood anymore so I left. Is that a crime?"

"No," he said slowly. What the hell had happened in that room? She looked like she was about to come out of her skin. "I'm just wondering why you're acting so defensive."

"I...I'm not used to being questioned by the police. It's disconcerting."

Energy arced between them and Riley intentionally let the voltage crank up a notch. There was more to it than that. She was holding out on him. Gradually, he walked toward her. "Why do I make you so nervous?"

Her pupils flared. "You don't make me nervous."

"Liar."

He caught her chin between his thumb and forefinger. "I can see your pulse pounding at the base of your throat."

Her eyes went wide and her breaths shortened. Watching her closely, he slid his fingers down her neck. Her skin was warm and soft under his fingertips. He touched the fluttering artery and his arousal took on the sharpness of a knife's edge. "Your heart is rushing like a freight train."

She could feel it, too, this connection between them. How could she not? It was almost primal. He could feel it pulsating. Breathing. *Growing.* Compelled, he leaned toward her.

For a moment, she let him. Then, suddenly, she swallowed hard and stepped back. "I really should see if Sadie needs any help," she said shakily.

Riley dropped his hand and let it fall limp at his side. He could only watch as she made her escape. Desperately, he tried to get himself under control.

Shit! His cock was as hard as his head.

What the hell had he been thinking?

"Talia, wait," he called when he heard her at the apartment door. Forcing himself to act casual, he leaned against the kitchen archway. "Sadie's not here."

Her eyebrows drew together in confusion.

"She's gone home," he said. "I was supposed to tell you that she'd locked up."

"Locked up? What time..." She sought out the clock on the wall and bit her lip when she saw how late it was.

He ran a hand through his hair. He needed to get his act together. He'd come dangerously close to stepping over the line back there and now he had her on her guard. "Listen," he said. "I'm tired. You're tired. Can we just call a truce and get through this?"

She didn't move away from the door.

He glanced back at the pot of water on the stove. "What do you say to that cup of tea?"

The cautiousness in her eyes told him how bad of a tactical error he'd made. He needed to soothe things over with her quickly if he ever hoped to establish a rapport with her.

"You'll ask your questions and go?" she asked.

"I promise."

She still didn't look as if she trusted him but what option did she have? He'd follow through on his promise to make her come down to the station.

"All right," she said begrudgingly. "But you can't stay long. I slept the day away. I need to get caught up on my work."

"Fine. I understand."

Stiffly, she started toward the kitchen. With each step, the flap of her robe flew open and Riley was graced with the sight of long, smooth legs. He felt his control slip a notch. "Sit down," he said. "I'll get things. I saw the mugs in the cupboard."

Turning abruptly, he headed for the stove. Almost prophetically, the kettle began to whistle. He snarled at it. He didn't need it to tell him that impartiality was going to be a bitch on this case.

His grip on the pot was tight as he poured water into two cups and added the tea bags. They'd reached a tenuous truce and he needed to play by her rules. Even though everything about her made him think of sex, he needed to tone things down. At least for the time being. Once he ruled her out as a suspect, he could turn the heat back up.

Way up.

"That's a nice shop you have downstairs," he said as he carried the cups to the kitchen table. She hadn't taken a seat, but hovered nearby. He needed to get her to relax and her shop was the only safe ground he could think of. "It's different than all the others I've been in today. More approachable, you know?"

She looked at him suspiciously. "Thank you."

He wasn't trying to play mind games. He did like her place. It just wasn't what he wanted to talk about now. Small talk seemed to be working, though, so he went with it. "It's nice how you've got two rooms—one with the expensive stuff and one with things the rest of us lowlifes can afford. I was surprised to see all the kids."

"Our comic books are big sellers." The lines on her forehead smoothed. After a long moment, she reached for her tea. "I wanted a place where everyone could get interested in collecting."

"You like kids?"

She ventured a small smile as she lifted the mug to her lips. "I love them. I get more enjoyment out of selling a candy dispenser than a look-but-don't-touch lamp. Unfortunately, the lamps are what keep me in business."

She gave him a considering look. Finally, she sat down at the table. Riley followed her lead. Her briefcase was in the chair before him so he reached down to move it. The lightness of the leather case surprised him and he shot a look at her. In that split second, her body went taut and a closed expression settled over her face.

His instincts screamed. "You seem to have lost your rocks."

"Better than my marbles." She nibbled on her lower lip when he didn't laugh. "I cleaned it out after you commented on it."

Riley stared at her hard. He didn't like the direction his thoughts were taking. He didn't like it at all.

Her gaze broke away and she suddenly became overly interested in the pattern on the ceramic cup. She traced it carefully with her thumbnail.

"What do you know about the robbery at the Harringtons, Talia?" he asked, point-blank.

She didn't even flinch. "Nothing. Haven't any of the other party guests been able to help you?"

He glanced down at the briefcase. "The trail seems to have gone cold."

"Nobody saw anything?"

He sat down in the chair and intentionally leaned forward, crowding her again, but this time for an entirely different reason. He couldn't ignore the messages his gut was sending to his brain. "People saw a lot of things."

"Do you have any suspects?"

Oh, she was a gutsy one.

"I'm looking at somebody." Purposefully, he let his gaze rake down her body. With a distraction like that, who would notice her pilfering a small fortune?

She took a drink of tea with a strained air of nonchalance. "Why haven't you made an arrest?"

"I'm still trying to figure out the motive," he said softly.

She knew something. He could feel it in his bones. But if she was involved, it didn't make sense. Any way he looked at it, she didn't come off as being stupid and she seemed too classy for something so petty.

"Isn't it obvious? Somebody must have needed the money," she said as she carefully set her mug down.

He had a feeling it was more complicated than that. "It's not always that simple. People have many reasons for the things they do."

"Like what?"

"The thrill."

"I don't understand."

She looked at him so innocently, he wanted to grab her and shake the truth out of her. Then he wanted to carry her into the room at the end of the trail of clothes and ravage her until neither of them could walk.

"Think about it," he said, his voice rough. He moved his chair a few inches closer to turn up the heat. "The danger. The excitement. To some people it's a powerful aphrodisiac."

She scooted to the far side of her seat. "You can't be serious."

"But I am. Some people steal just to get their rocks off."

That, finally, unnerved her. "Don't be crude, Kinkade. I don't appreciate it."

"Can't you picture yourself getting horny over doing something naughty?"

Her cheeks turned red. "I can't imagine why you're saying these things to me."

"Oh, sweetheart," he said silkily. "I think you can."

Her chair skidded against the floor as it was abruptly pushed back. "Are you accusing me of this crime?"

Riley calmly took a sip of tea but all his concentration was on the gorgeous blonde standing over him. "No," he said smoothly. "I'm just making an observation."

"What, exactly, are you insinuating?"

He finally pushed himself away from the table and stood. At full height, he was a good six inches taller than she was. She tipped her chin up to look him in the face.

"I'm not insinuating anything. I'm saying outright that I can see through that veneer you show the rest of the world." He settled his hands on his hips and leaned into her personal space. "All they can see is the gloss, the icy perfection. You're high-class; I'll give you that, Sizemore. Inside, though, there's heat dying to get out."

"I don't see what—"

"You don't fool me, honey," he said, cutting her off. "You might manage to tamp down the fire when you're with other people but I can feel it. I know there's more going on beneath the surface."

"You...you don't know anything about me," she sputtered.

"No? Maybe you're right. But guess what? I'm willing to learn." He stared boldly at the spot where her robe gaped open to reveal rounded breasts. "And I'm going to be on you night and day until I find out *everything*."

Chapter Five

The messenger came three days later with a plain, unmarked manila envelope.

Talia sat staring at the money she'd found inside. It was so much—and so soon. Her heart thudded as she thumbed through the bills. She'd counted it a dozen times but her disbelief wouldn't go away. The professor had gotten better than a good price for the Mène.

But how had he done it? The robbery was still making front-page news. Hungry reporters were still broadcasting follow-ups. She couldn't believe that someone had purchased such an infamous item or that the professor had taken such risks to sell it.

No wonder he usually took such a large cut of the earnings.

Earnings? She dropped the money, suddenly unable to bear it. She hadn't earned this.

God, how could she live with herself? This money was dirty. She'd stolen to get it.

But she could put it to such good use.

Distressed, she ran her fingers through her hair. Guilt, fear and excitement kept jerking her from one extreme to the other. These ill-gotten gains were going to haunt her; she knew it.

She couldn't let that stop her, though. The money, no matter where it had come from, was going to buy a lot of crayons and construction paper.

And beads. It was the least she could do for Winston in return.

"That's it! I've got it!"

Talia's entire body jerked with surprise when Sadie yelled from the storage room. She heard her assistant coming her way and her heart jumped up into her throat. She couldn't let Sadie find her with this much money. She'd start to ask questions...questions that would need answers...answers that Talia didn't have! Hastily, she stuffed the money back into the envelope. Half of it didn't make it. She became flustered as she tried to scoop up the bills from her desk. She heard her assistant's quick footsteps as she shoved everything into her desk drawer and locked it. She spun around in her chair just as her office door opened.

"For God's sake, Sadie, what is it?" She'd been on pins and needles ever since the detective had visited her — or, she should say, harassed her. It didn't take much to startle her but her assistant's call had pierced the quiet of the shop like an air siren.

Sadie grabbed her by both arms. "I know what we can do! Come with me. It's perfect."

Talia let herself be pulled out of her chair but she stumbled over her own feet as she tried to keep up with her excited friend. "Perfect for what? What are you talking about?"

Sadie led her to the cluttered storeroom, but stopped so suddenly, Talia ran right into her.

"That," her assistant declared.

"What? Where?" Talia looked around the area but all she could see was the ugly Turkish rug they'd been trying to sell for over a year. She couldn't see that rug being perfect for anything.

"Yes, the rug!" Sadie rubbed her hands together like a mad scientist with a fiendish plot. "It's going to help us get the after-school arts program back on its feet."

Talia did a double take. "And how is it going to do that?" she asked cautiously.

Her assistant was showing all the telltale signs — the sparkle in the eyes, the gnawing of the lower lip, the cranking of the gears in her head... When Sadie got one of her grand ideas, it was usually best just to stand back and let her go.

"Don't you see? We'll sell it—and maybe that oak armoire with the big chip in the side. We'll donate the proceeds to the foundation and count it as a tax write-off for Coolectibles."

Talia shook her head and spoke very slowly. "Aren't you forgetting something? Nobody wants the rug or the armoire. That's why they're back here in the storeroom."

Sadie rolled her eyes. "Think outside the box, square peg. We won't sell them here. We'll sell them at a charity auction. *A charity auction!* I can't believe it took me so long to think of that. We'll donate pieces and ask others to contribute, too. I'm sure Arthur and some of our other competitors have something they're dying to get rid of."

"An auction?" Talia cocked her head. Sadie's grand ideas didn't always pan out but this one was intriguing.

"We'll invite everyone. We'll promote it as if it's the biggest social event of the season." Sadie suddenly turned and pointed a finger at her. "You're connected. You can invite all your hoity-toity friends. If we play it right, they'll be fighting to outdo each other."

Talia glanced at the rug again. "You know, that's not such a bad idea."

She'd been losing sleep over this funding issue. It seemed that the more she tried to come up with ideas, the more her brain went in circles. Visions of the detective or the animalier wouldn't stay out of her head. If her assistant had come up with a way to make the nightmares stop, she'd do whatever she could to help her.

Sadie spread her arms and turned in a slow circle as if she were channeling the inspiration. "We'll put ads in all the newspapers. It will be a black tie event. We're going for the big bucks here."

Talia walked over to the rug and ran her fingers through the fringe. She was starting to see the picture that Sadie had in her head. "We could rent out the community theater," she offered.

"Rent?" Her assistant planted a hand on her hip. "Honey, this is for charity. We ask them to co-host the event and put their name on the brochure as a benefactor."

Talia laughed. "You're much better at this than me."

"Then let me plan it."

She looked at her friend closely. "Are you serious? That's a lot of work."

"I'm dead serious. My son needs that arts program." Sadie self-consciously reached for her necklace and began playing with the pendant. She was a strong woman but her son's run-in with the law had affected her more deeply than she liked to show. "Besides, I'm having a devil of a time trying to find things to occupy his hands and his mind. Helping me organize this will count as community service time. Anyway, I hope the judge will see it that way."

Talia felt a familiar pang of guilt. "I'm so sorry about all that."

"Don't," Sadie said, pulling away. She straightened her shoulders and her chin came up. "It will be good work for him."

Talia finally had a bright idea of her own. "This could be an opportunity for all the kids who've used the after-school program. We should display their work—and maybe auction some of it off, too. It will show the people that their money is going to a good cause."

Sadie's eyes widened and Talia could almost see a lightbulb go on over her head. "You should bring up the idea at that dinner party you're going to tonight. If Roger Thorton lends some credibility to the event, others will fall all over each other to join in."

Ugh. The dinner party. Talia grimaced. She was so not looking forward to that. Still, she'd promised Roger that she'd go. At least now she had a reason. "You're right. I'll see if he has anything he'd like to donate. That's where we might have the biggest problem—getting nice pieces. Nobody's going to want to buy trash."

Sadie acted affronted. "This rug isn't trash. It's exquisitely made. The threads are of the highest quality and the workmanship is so detailed. It's just...just..."

"Butt ugly," they said in unison before bursting into laughter.

* * * * *

Talia's sense of humor was long gone by the time she drove to the dinner party later that evening. It was hard to believe that she'd once looked forward to visiting the Thortons. They lived out in the country along a winding, tree-lined road. Her father had always brought her along on his visits so she could play with Felicia, Roger's daughter. They'd swum in the pool, played tennis or rode horses as their fathers conducted business. Unfortunately, tonight she didn't anticipate having much fun.

The good old times were gone. She missed her father and Felicia lived far away in California. Thank God Roger was still here. He treated her like family and she loved him for that. It was Lydia she could do without.

As she drove up to the house, she saw something else she'd prefer to avoid. Brent's car was parked in the turnaround driveway.

"Damn." She hadn't known he and Shelli were going to be here.

Her thoughts went immediately to the envelope of money she'd locked in her safety deposit box at the bank. Could she really look the Harringtons in the face? The desire to turn around and leave was strong but Talia stiffened her resolve. She hadn't seen the couple since the night of the party but she couldn't hide from them forever. She might as well get it over with. Avoiding them might arouse suspicion—and she'd had enough of that.

She parked her car behind Edward Jones' sedan and was happy to see Roger waiting for her at the front door.

On the Prowl

"Talia," he said warmly as she walked up the steps to the house. "I'm so glad you could make it. I was worried you might still be under the weather."

"I'm feeling much better," she said with a smile on her face. She kissed his cheek and turned so he could take her wrap from her shoulders.

His eyes widened as he took in her dress. "Wow! Call me a dirty old man but you look fabulous!"

"You're not old," she said, laughing.

Secretly, she was pleased. She rarely obsessed over her appearance but, tonight, she'd taken special care. She looked good and she knew it. The red halter dress was classy, but eye-catching. The style complimented her figure and she felt sexy in it. She also felt powerful, a side benefit of having finally taken action, albeit illegal. That power was going to help her take a more established position as the Sizemore Foundation's president.

Roger's attention was still on her dress, so she made an obligatory spin. The skirt whirled around her legs and the long slit showed a liberal amount of skin. The older man's pupils narrowed and, suddenly, Talia was caught with a most inappropriate feeling.

"Roger, where are you?" came a voice from the next room.

Her happy, flirtatious mood abruptly ended. She braced herself as Lydia came into the entryway but her composure was severely tested when the woman was followed by her best friend, Ramona Gellar.

Great. The two of them. Together. It didn't bode well for the evening.

Both women already had glasses of Scotch. When she saw her latest guest, Lydia's face scrunched up. She acted as if she'd just caught a bad smell. "Oh hello, *Talia*."

The tone was textbook Lydia. Talia plastered a smile on her face. "Good evening, Lydia. Ramona."

"That's quite the number you're wearing," Ramona said as she patted her bouffant hairdo. "Or should I say almost wearing?"

Her raucous laughter echoed off the walls of the entryway and Talia's fingers bit into her clutch. She could feel people's attention being drawn from the next room. "Thank you," she said in a tight voice. "I appreciate being invited to dinner."

"Well, thank him. It was his idea." Lydia's Scotch swished in her glass as she gestured to her husband. "Really, Roger, would you get in here? I need you to speak to the chef."

Roger gave Talia a sympathetic smile and squeezed her hand. "Come. I'll escort you into the great room before I handle our latest disaster. An hour ago, we learned that there wasn't enough parsley to decorate all the plates. Oh, the horror."

Some of Talia's irritation evaporated in spite of herself. She didn't know how the man stayed in such good spirits but, if he could live with the witch, she could certainly stand one evening in her presence. Bolstering her resolve, she hooked her arm through his. There had to be at least one pleasant person here. She looked for familiar faces as they entered the room where most of the guests had gathered.

"Oh, there's Shelli standing all alone," Roger said. "I'm sure she has lots to talk about."

Talia stiffened and dug her heels into the carpet. Shelli was pleasant enough but she'd rather be insulted by the bitches in the kitchen. "I really don't think—"

It was too late. "Shelli, look who I found," he called.

Shelli Harrington turned and her curls bounced. Her blue eyes widened dramatically. "Talia!"

Talia took a small step back when the woman nearly pounced on her. For a split second, she was terrified that somehow the Harringtons had found out what she'd done.

"Did you hear what happened?"

The feeling fizzled when she realized that the blonde was just happy to have a new listener for her story. Talia looked beseechingly at Roger but he was already making a quick exit to the kitchen. In resignation, she turned back to Shelli.

"I heard," she said carefully. "I'm very sorry."

"Can you believe that my little kitty was stolen right out from under our noses?"

Talia glanced around, trying to find somebody to rescue her, but there was no one. She was trapped.

"And during our party," Shelli pouted. "I'm just so...so...*mad*."

"It was a very nice piece."

"It was my favorite. I tried to tell that to the detective but he didn't seem to care."

Talia's attention suddenly focused. "Detective? Do you mean Kinkade? Is he still working on the case?"

Shelli's pout deepened. "He says he is but I don't think he's working very hard."

Talia tried not to act too interested but it was nearly impossible. She hadn't seen the detective since he'd left her the other day. She'd tried to convince herself that was because he'd given up but she'd known better. The intelligence behind that man's intense eyes scared her. Thoughts of him haunted her day and night. Especially at night...

"Has he got any leads?"

"I don't know. If he was any good, he would have found it by now, don't you think?"

It was odd but Talia felt her spine stiffening. She didn't doubt Kinkade's competence in the least. "I'm sure he's using all his resources."

"Oh well, it doesn't matter. Brent bought me a new kitty." Shelli's spirits brightened considerably. "It's Egyptian. Did you know that they worshipped cats?"

"I'd heard that somewhere," Talia said, gritting her teeth. The woman's nonchalance was astounding. The school kids didn't have enough to buy finger paint but she could jump at whim from one priceless bauble to the next.

"Brent let me pick it out. Isn't he just the sweetest man you ever met?"

Sweet? Talia's jaw clenched so hard, her teeth nearly cracked. If that meant the same as "repugnant", then she agreed whole-heartedly.

"He really is. He's sweet and strong and faithful." Shelli paused and a wistful expression entered her puppy dog eyes. "I wish you could find somebody like him."

Talia had had enough. "Unfortunately, I'm still kissing frogs. I'm sorry but I really must find the ladies' room. If you'll excuse me…"

It wasn't the slickest of exits but, then again, the fashion doll probably didn't notice. Talia darted out of the room and down the hallway. It was mercifully empty.

Dear God, she thought as she sought the safety of the bathroom. If she'd known that the likes of Ramona Gellar and the Harringtons were going to be here, she never would have come. She'd only brought enough reserves to battle Lydia.

She scowled as she looked into the mirror. New Covington had never been known for its hospitality. Her father had made enough money for his family to be welcomed into the upper crust crowd; the money just hadn't aged enough for them to be welcomed graciously. She figured they had another two or three generations before that happened.

Sighing, she straightened her spine and tucked back a stray hair. She needed to concentrate on the auction. That was the real reason why she'd come. If she could get one or even two donations tonight, it would make the evening worthwhile.

Feeling determined, she opened the bathroom door and started down the hallway. She hadn't made it two steps before she sensed somebody's presence behind her. She gasped when, all of a sudden, she was caught and pulled backwards.

"Hey, Tally."

Warms hands slipped under her dress at the waist. She stiffened when they began to slide upward.

"Brent!" If she hadn't recognized the voice, she would have recognized the touch.

"Trying to avoid me?" he whispered.

"Let go of me!"

Her demand came too late. His searching hands had already made a discovery.

"Whoa!" he said dramatically. "What have we here?"

Talia was mortified. Absolutely mortified. She'd thought she'd learned her lesson after the other night. She hadn't wanted to go braless, so she'd found other means of support. She'd never dreamed that Brent would be here or that he'd find the pasties she'd specifically bought to go with the dress.

"Now this is interesting," he breathed into her ear.

His fingers traced the edges of the self-adhesive cups and her nerve endings tingled.

"Take your hands off of me," she hissed.

She couldn't believe his audacity. Did he assume he could get away with anything now that he'd had her? For goodness sake, his wife was in the next room.

She struggled to get away but she was no match for his strength. He pulled her bare back tight against his body. One leg slipped between hers and his hard cock prodded at her buttocks. She was infuriated by the answering twinge low in her belly.

"Are you sure?" he asked as his lips found the soft skin at the side of her neck. His hands pushed upward, plumping her breasts obscenely. "I think you like my hands on you."

"I don't." A shiver of disgust and excitement coursed down Talia's spine. She struggled but he just chuckled with amusement. She hated him. She downright hated him.

"You love it when I touch you. You've told me so."

She wasn't the violent type but she'd already had to deal with Lydia, Ramona and Shelli. The fuse on her temper was short. Clenching her fist, she swung her arm forward, intending to send an elbow straight back into Brent's solar plexus.

She wasn't given the opportunity, because he suddenly yanked on the material covering her right breast. The adhesive clung to her skin like a well-adhered bandage before ripping loose.

"Ahhh!" she cried as hot pinpricks of pain shot through her tender breast.

"Look at that," he whispered as he pulled the cup out from under her dress. He dangled it in front of her face.

"Brent!" she whispered desperately. "Please!"

Tears pricked at her eyes. Her breast felt as if it was ablaze but the sting of her humiliation was even worse. She'd known there would be consequences from the other night but she hadn't realized how heavy her penance would be. Was this how her life was going to be from now on? Brent had been bad before but now it was as if nothing was holding him back. Was she to be his plaything? A sex toy, ever at his beck and call?

He chuckled in her ear. "Since you ask so nicely..."

She went straight up on her tiptoes when her other breast was suddenly treated in the same harsh manner. The pasty clung to her sensitive skin and she bit her lip as he tugged and tugged. It finally turned loose and her belly clenched with excitement.

Brent nipped at her ear and wiggled the pasties in front of her face. He tossed them onto the floor and she looked at them anxiously. Anyone could find them there.

"That's better," he said.

She shuddered when his rough hands slipped under the material of her dress to cup her again.

"Such pretty titties," he crooned as his fingers captured her nipples. "I don't know why you keep trying to hide them from me."

The leg between hers pressed harder and Talia's body quickened. As much as she fought it, wetness was gathering in her pussy. His marauding hands plucked at her raw nipples and her resistance began to melt.

"Talia?"

The sound of her name had them both freezing.

"Brent? Dinner is served."

Talia batted at Brent's hands when she recognized Roger's voice. He reluctantly let her go and she moved as far away from him as she could get. She was unbearably self-conscious when their host came around the corner. Without the pasties, she felt naked. She almost died when Roger stepped on them.

"Are you two hungry?" he asked. "The rest of the guests are already seated."

He held out his arm and she quickly stepped forward to take it. She kicked the pasties under the hallway table as best she could and leaned on her adoptive uncle for support. The side of her breast brushed against his arm and she was discomfited when her nipple tightened reflexively.

Oh, dear God.

Heads turned as they entered the dining room. Lydia scowled and Talia's stomach dropped. She glanced down covertly to see how lewd she looked. Her red dress stood out like a beacon. Suddenly, the side slit seemed too high and the waist too snug. The halter style framed her overly perky tits and two matching bumps pressed at the material.

She quickly took her seat beside Edward Jones. Roger sat down at the head of the table next to her and she was horrified when his gaze dropped to her chest. He seemed embarrassed, but not enough to look away. The inadvertent attention made her want to just sink under the table and disappear.

To make matters worse, Brent sat down across the table from her. There was nothing she could do to stop his blatant stare. Her nipples seemed to stiffen at his command. Under the table, Roger's pant leg brushed against her bare calf and Talia's senses screamed. She'd never felt so finely tuned in her life. Even that slight touch had her system overreacting.

Good Lord, how was she going to make it through the evening?

Discussions broke out in small groups around the table and she found herself left with her two admirers. She had to count small favors, though. Even with them ogling her, it was better than sitting at the other end of the table with the shrew crew.

"So how are you keeping yourself busy these days, my dear?" Roger asked, finally tearing his gaze from her when the soup was served. "Are things going well at your shop?"

"We're having a good season," she said.

"And the foundation? How is that going?"

There it was—the opening she needed. She had to come away from this dinner party with something positive. Now was as good a time as any to broach the subject of the charity auction. "Actually, I wanted to talk to you about that."

"Of course," Roger said. He patted his napkin against his lips and leaned back in his chair. "How can I help?"

She was heartened by his response and sat a little straighter in her chair. She paused, though, when both men's attention was diverted to the jiggling of her breasts. With the way they were looking at her, she could practically feel them sharing her.

"Um, we're in the initial planning stages for a new fundraising event," she said, trying to push the thought from her head. "We've decided to put on an auction to raise money for the after-school arts program."

"Are you still on that?" Brent said.

"Yes," she said with a hard-edged smile. "The program was important to my father and it's important to me. I was wondering if either of you would be interested in donating an item to be auctioned off."

Brent winked at her. "You know I'll always be willing to donate to you, Tally."

She felt something suddenly press into her crotch. Looking down, she saw Brent's foot. Her pussy clenched at the memory of one particular donation and she was incensed. Reaching between her legs, she pushed hard at him until he removed his wiggling toes.

"We might have something around here that we could contribute," Roger said. His eyebrows lowered as he looked down the table. "What do you say, Lydia?"

Lydia continued chatting noisily with Shelli and Ramona.

Roger cleared his throat. "Lydia."

His wife threw him an exasperated look. "I was in the middle of a conversation, darling. What do you want?"

Roger ran a finger around the edge of his collar. "I'm sorry, dear. Talia asked me if we'd like to contribute something to an auction she's holding for her foundation."

Lydia rolled her eyes and settled her elbows on the table. "For God's sake, we've already given to so many causes. What does she mean by 'something'? More money, I assume?"

Talia felt heat creep up her chest and into her face. The woman was acting as if she wasn't even at the table. "Actually, we're not looking for monetary contributions," she said tightly.

"Well, thank goodness for small favors." Lydia threw back a king-sized gulp of her latest drink.

Talia struggled to keep her anger in check. "We're looking for art pieces. For instance, I'll probably donate a Turkish rug from my shop. It's for a good cause."

"And what cause is that, honey?" The question came from Ramona Gellar.

"The after-school arts program for inner-city kids. The Arts Council recently stopped its support." Talia threw a nasty look at Brent for good measure. "The program is languishing."

"I just don't understand that," Lydia said.

Talia was taken somewhat aback. She'd never known the woman to side with her.

"Why can't those people pull themselves up by their bootstraps? I mean, really. How many thousands of dollars have already been contributed to that black hole? That rinky-dink program should be self-supporting by now."

"Hear, hear," Ramona piped in. "Very astute of you, dear."

Fury caught Talia unprepared. Why, the snotty, rich bitches! Who did Lydia think she was? She hadn't earned a penny of the Thorton money. She'd been Roger's secretary when she'd lassoed him.

"Now, Lydia," Roger said cajolingly. "We've got more art around here than we know what to do with. Certainly we can find one piece. It's for charity."

"Certainly, we can not. I'm tired of all these so-called nonprofits taking money from my pocket."

Talia's half-finished meal threatened to come up.

Of all people, Brent came to her rescue. "Oh, what the hell," he said, "I'll find something. Come over to my place tomorrow and we'll discuss it."

The gesture would have been appreciated if it hadn't been accompanied by another provocative nudge of his foot. Talia knew the price she'd have to pay if he got her alone to "discuss" things. "Thank you, that's very generous of you," she said, sarcasm dripping from her voice.

She was so angry at Lydia, she could hardly think. If she'd been any closer, she would have been tempted to give a solid yank on the woman's frosted hair. Roger threw her a sad smile and shrugged.

"I'd like to—"

"Roger!" Lydia snapped.

"But I can't," he said, giving in. "Maybe another time."

"Over my dead body," his wife mumbled.

Something inside Talia snapped. *Wanna bet?*

She was so tired of being the woman's punching bag. It had been going on ever since she'd been a teenager. She'd done nothing to deserve it but she'd put up with it for years.

Tonight, Lydia had stepped over the line. The foundation's work was important but those children were priceless. She might not think they deserved a contribution but she was going to give one anyway.

A big one.

As soon as the decision was made, a soothing calmness overcame Talia. She was going to do it again—this time, willfully and knowingly.

She was going to steal.

And she was going to let herself enjoy it.

In her head, she knew it was wrong and immoral. In her heart, though, it felt right. Sometimes the end did justify the means.

"I understand, Roger," she said amiably. "I'm sure there are others like Brent who can help this time."

"You know I'll always take care of you, baby," Brent said seductively.

She felt his foot again but, this time, she was ready with her salad fork. She gave his intrusive toes a solid jab and his knee banged against the table. "We'd be delighted with anything you could contribute," she said, smiling brightly.

The rest of the meal passed as a blur. If anything snide was said, Talia didn't hear it. She was too busy planning. The adrenaline coursing through her body was nearly intoxicating. It couldn't be an impulsive snatch-and-grab this time. No, she was going to have to be more cunning than that.

Cunning and *careful*.

She couldn't undergo the scrutiny she'd suffered this week again. As handsome as Detective Kinkade was, she hoped she never saw him again.

The seven-course meal took forever. Even after her plan was fully mapped out, Talia had to suffer through discussions about the stock market, the Thorton's wine collection and Edward Jones' Civil War fascination. Lydia's verbal jabs and Brent's physical come-ons became tiring but she fended them off as well as she could. As soon as dessert was over, she excused herself from the table.

Roger was disappointed when she gathered her shawl but he seemed to understand. "I'm sorry about tonight," he said as he walked her down the front steps. "I'll look around the house and see if I can find something Lydia won't notice missing."

"So will I," Talia muttered under her breath as she slid into the driver's seat of her car. She rolled down the window. "Thank you for dinner, Uncle Roger. The meal was excellent."

"And you looked ravishing. Drive safely, dear."

"I will. Goodnight."

The moment she stepped on the gas, Talia felt her anticipation sharpen. She'd told herself she'd never get caught in this situation again but the fine line between right and wrong was blurring. Was it right for someone like Lydia Thorton to hoard money that others needed so desperately? Was it right for kids like Linc to go without?

She couldn't answer those questions anymore. All she knew was that she could do something about it. It was time to put her plan into action.

She pulled out onto the main road and, a quarter-mile down, took the turnoff to the Thorton stables. The road was dark but she took care to park in the shadows. Walking carefully in her high heels across the uneven ground, she let herself into the tack room.

The extra key to the house was still hidden in the same spot next to the bridles. The moment Talia felt the key in her hands, she felt a familiar power. It was strong and seductive.

"I wish it were over your dead body, Lydia, but this will have to do."

The night was dark as she began the long walk across the grounds to the house. Black clouds covered the crescent moon but she kept close to the tree line. Lights still lit the bottom floor of the house. A few more of the guests had left but she could see the Harringtons' car still parked in the drive.

She took a deep breath and let it out slowly.

Should she go now or wait until there were fewer people around? She didn't want to get caught but the guests provided a distraction. She could move around in the house more easily if the Thortons were busy entertaining.

Now, she decided.

She ran quickly to the back door. Her heart pounded as she slid the key into the lock. Bracing herself, she slipped inside.

Conversation from the front room hit her ears and, for a moment, she faltered. At the Harringtons' party, her actions had been instinctive. Here, they were deliberate. There was a difference. This was a lot more nerve-racking.

Why can't they pull themselves up by their bootstraps? Lydia's words rang in her head.

The risk was worth it.

Talia was up the stairs and on the second floor landing before she could catch her breath. The main bedroom was the first on her left. The door stood halfway open and she squeezed inside.

The room was so dark, she skidded to a stop. Adrenaline and fear made it hard to wait as her eyes adjusted.

"Ah!" she cried suddenly.

Something had brushed against her leg!

Meowwwww.

A soft body nuzzled against her again and she nearly fainted in relief. "Taffy," she whispered. Her body shook as the cat purred and stroked itself against her.

Talia ignored the Thorton's pet. She was listening hard to the people downstairs. Had anyone heard her?

She waited for an interminable moment but the chatter didn't break rhythm.

With a deep breath, she focused her thoughts. The cat wove its way around her legs but she didn't have time to give it the attention it craved. Instead, she clicked on a small table lamp. She hated to turn on a light but there was no moonlight to help her navigate. Hurriedly, her gaze swept the room.

There was a nice painting on the wall but it was large and cumbersome. *And a fake*, she realized when she looked more closely. A crystal vase stood on the bedside table. *Too cheap*, she quickly estimated. She finally saw the jewelry box. She reached for it but stopped herself.

She needed to think like a thief.

Reaching down, she caught her skirt. Using it, she opened the lid. A very nice bracelet immediately caught her eye. Still using her skirt to hide her fingerprints, she reached for it. She turned the bracelet over and looked at the markings on the back.

"Just right," she whispered.

It was time to leave. But first, she made sure to cover her tracks. She turned off the lamp and used her skirt to wipe it down. She couldn't remember if she'd touched the door handle but she rubbed it carefully. She was just about to go back down the stairs when she heard a sound.

Footsteps.

Somebody was in the laundry room.

And he or she was coming up the back staircase.

Talia's muscles clenched but then sprung into motion. She tried to move as quietly as she could but, in her ears, her plodding footsteps were as loud as a Clydesdale's. Gut instinct made her run down the hallway to Felicia's old room. Not caring about fingerprints, she gripped the door handle and pushed it open. She was just about to close it behind her when a little, buff-colored body darted into the room.

"Taffy, no!"

Her warning did no good. The cat just snuggled up against her legs and started purring loudly.

Talia tried to listen over the pounding in her ears. The hallway was carpeted but she could still hear heavy footsteps.

Whoever it was hadn't stopped at the master bedroom!

Oh, God. Dear God!

What was she going to do? She was trapped and she had Lydia's bracelet in her hand.

Instinct made her move again and she acted quickly. Still, she stood frozen with fear when the door to Felicia's room swung open and the light was suddenly switched on.

"Talia!" said a deep voice.

The glare of the light made dark spots jump in front of her eyes but she could quickly see that she'd made a mistake.

This room was no longer Felicia's. It was Roger's.

Chapter Six

"Talia!" he said in surprise.

She stood frozen in the center of the room. Oh, God. She'd been caught red-handed.

Roger stood in the doorway, obviously flummoxed. "What are you doing here, dear?"

Breaking and entering. Stealing.

She swallowed hard when her brain refused to come up with a lie. "I...I...oh, Uncle Roger," she said miserably.

The cat mewed and darted out the door. Talia wished she could do the same.

A sympathetic look crossed Roger's face. Reaching back, he closed the door. "There, there now," he said gently. "Don't upset yourself so."

"I'm sorry!" What had she been thinking? How had she justified doing this? Roger had never been anything but kind to her. She hadn't even thought of how she'd be hurting him. All she'd been able to think about was striking back at Lydia.

He crossed the room and pulled her into his arms. "I understand. She finally pushed you past your limits, didn't she?"

God, had she been that easy to read? Talia choked back a nervous laugh. And she'd thought she'd been so stealthy. She wrapped her arms about him and clung to the back of his jacket. "I couldn't help it," she admitted. "She's just so hurtful."

"I'm sorry about that, honey." He dropped a kiss against her forehead. "I know she's been especially hard on you all these years and it's partly my fault. You have to understand that she's just jealous."

He was the kindest man. Talia buried her face against his chest, incredulous over his generosity. He'd caught her in his house—in his bedroom—and he wasn't angry. Instead, he was sympathetic.

"She is not," she said, still stung over the treatment she'd received. She knew Roger was just being polite. His wife was *not* jealous. Why would Lydia be jealous of someone she considered no better than the scum on the bottom of her shoe?

"I know, I know," he said, rocking her like a child. "She hides it well but that's what it is. And really, I can't blame her."

The man was an absolute saint. He couldn't even bring himself to say a bad word about the ill-mannered bitch! Talia pushed back the thoughts. Her anger was what had gotten her into trouble in the first place. She let out a long sigh. "But why would she be jealous of me?"

"You're so guileless, dear girl." He pulled back so he could look at her. "She's envious because you're young, bright, beautiful—and important to me."

Talia had never looked at it that way. Still, it didn't make sense. Yes, she and Roger were close. That didn't mean that Lydia had the right to terrorize her every chance she got. "Our relationship has nothing to do with her," she said stubbornly.

"You and I know that. It's just hard for her to see."

Talia rolled her eyes. She hated it that he was making her see Lydia's point of view. Wearily, she laid her head on his shoulder. He'd always been such a rock for her. She needed his steady compassion now more than she had in a long time. The past week had been so hard on her. She hadn't been able to eat or sleep. It felt good to stand in his arms and let him protect her—even if it was from herself.

"I don't know what I was thinking coming here," she said. "She just made me so angry and upset. I know I shouldn't let her get to me but she does."

"Shhh," he murmured. He brushed his lips against hers. "We both know why you're here."

Talia went dead still.

He'd just kissed her. On the lips!

"I knew that one day she'd finally push you past your inhibitions." He stroked his hand downwards and gently cupped her bottom. "It was just a matter of time."

Talia was stunned.

This was her father's best friend!

He shouldn't be touching her like this.

"Relax, dear one," he said, hugging her. "Uncle Roger will make everything all right."

Talia felt like a deer caught in the headlights. She hadn't seen this coming. He couldn't want her *that way*. What could she say? What could she do?

She stood frozen as he reached up and caught the clip at the back of her head. Her hair fell loose across her shoulders and the soft ends brushed against her skin. The sensation made her shiver.

He gently raked his fingers through the blonde strands. "You're so pretty."

His gaze swept down her body almost reverently and she swallowed hard. The look of lust was clear in his eyes and she was thunderstruck. She'd seen that look before. Many times. She'd just been too young to identify it for what it was.

He ran his thumb softly across her lips. "I know this must be difficult for you but, if it makes you feel any better, I haven't slept with Lydia for years. As for your father, well, I respected him. That's why I waited so long. I wanted this to be your decision."

Her decision! She hadn't even realized an offer was on the table.

"Are you chilled, dear one?"

Suddenly, Talia realized she was shaking.

He smiled with understanding. "Come here."

Everything inside her went tense at the low words. They were so *sexual*. When he pulled her close, this time she felt an erection press against her belly.

An impressive erection.

Embarrassment flooded her. She shouldn't be thinking things like that. This was Uncle Roger, for God's sake!

"Relax," he whispered again. "I'll take care of things. You know how much I adore you."

The admission left Talia conflicted. She knew he was fond of her and she loved him — if not in that way. She couldn't bear the thought of hurting him.

When his head dipped, she couldn't deny him.

His lips pressed against hers delicately. The inappropriateness of it all made her uneasy but there was so much comfort in his touch. That comfort called to her. A safe haven was so tempting.

Slowly, he let her get used to the feel of him. He sipped at her lips as one hand gently cupped the back of her neck. *So much tenderness*, she thought, falling under the spell. When the fingertips of his other hand dipped under the material at her lower back, she felt warm arousal unwind in her belly. It was the same feeling she'd gotten when he'd first looked at her in her dress.

"So sweet," he murmured against her lips.

He turned his head and changed the angle of the kiss. As if it were the most natural thing in the world, she found herself opening her mouth for his tongue.

"Mmm," she sighed when it filled her mouth.

She could taste the whiskey and the chocolate he'd had for dessert. The intimacy made her head spin and she slid her arms around his neck for support. He was good with his mouth. Very good.

He kept the kiss slow and luxurious but the heat intensified. She heard a soft click somewhere close to her ear. Her eyes flew open when her halter top loosened.

She found Roger watching her closely. He was waiting for her permission, she realized.

Need suddenly pumped through her veins. She'd been so lost and anxious. Would it really be so bad to take consolation in his arms? They were consenting adults.

The material caressed her skin as it slid downwards and caught between their tightly pressed bodies. If she took even the smallest step back, she'd be half-naked.

The profanity of it all bewildered her. Roger Thorton was very special to her, yet the idea of sleeping with him appalled her as much as it fascinated her. If they crossed this line, there would be no turning back. She didn't want to turn what they had into something perverse.

But it didn't feel perverse. His touch was rife with reassurance and generosity. They really did care for each other. He'd obviously considered a physical relationship with her for a long time.

And what other reason did she have for being found alone in his bedroom so late at night?

Remorse made her eyelids drop. If anyone was trying to vilify their relationship, it was she. She'd come here to take what was his.

He sighed. Kindly, he began massaging the tight muscles at the nape of her neck. "Second thoughts, dear girl?"

He'd let her walk away right now if she said yes. He was that kind of man. Slowly, she looked up into his eyes. Emotion shimmered deep within them. She could feel his erection still pressing hard against her but, amazingly, his first inclination was to take care of her.

And she craved to let him, even more than he could know.

Slowly, she took that step backwards. Her dress slithered down her body and bared her to the waist.

His gaze zeroed in on her breasts like a laser beam. His breath came out with a whoosh and, for a moment, he stood unmoving. At last, his hands came up and cupped each rounded globe. "You are so beautiful."

His touch was startling. Talia looked down as his hands began working her flesh. He was more firm and demanding than she'd expected. His hands were callused from the work he did with the horses but the rough touch felt good. The sight of his hands on her did something to her. Her breath caught and her nipples pressed against his palms.

The forbidden nature of their actions was exciting.

"Let me know what feels good," he said as he leaned down and nuzzled her neck.

"This," she said with a groan. She wrapped her arms around his neck to keep him close. "*This* feels good."

He pulled back far enough to look at her. She flinched when he began drumming his thumbs across her nipples. "Do you remember the bikini that Felicia gave you for your eighteenth birthday?" he said with a secret smile.

"Mmm." His touch was insistent. "It was my favorite."

"Why?" he whispered.

She couldn't believe that this of all things would embarrass her. Shyly, she let her gaze drop. "It was so revealing. It made me feel all grown up and..."

"Yes?"

"Sexy," she whispered.

He took her breath away with a hard kiss.

"I picked that suit out," he said against her lips. "It was the skimpiest one I could find."

An unexpected thrill ran through her. He shouldn't be telling her this. The naughtiness of it all was burning her ears—and her pussy. She could feel the heat gathering between her legs.

"You were eighteen and I was nearing fifty," he said, looking straight into her eyes. "That didn't stop me from dreaming about stripping that little red string bikini off of you and fucking you right in front of everyone."

Talia gasped. He used the opportunity to duck his head and capture her nipple in his hot mouth.

Her back arched as shock tore through her. She closed her eyes tightly and groaned as reactions pumped through her. She hadn't been prepared for this—not for the sight of it or the feel. It was as if her nipple had just been caught in a hot, wet, suction pump that refused to let go.

"Ah, Roger!" she panted. The sensation was intense. She threaded her fingers through his silver hair and held on tight. She could hardly believe he'd lusted for her for so long but the pull of his mouth told her just how rampant his desire for her was.

He was a magician with his naughty tongue. Her breasts felt swollen to twice their size and her pussy was beginning to cry. He let out a grunt and turned to her other breast.

"I could just eat you up," he murmured before opening wide.

She arched back over his supporting arm and let out a sharp cry when his hand suddenly cupped her between the legs.

"God, I've waited too long," he said, his voice going rough. "Let's get you out of these clothes."

His hands smoothly undid the zipper at her lower back. The dress slipped over her hips and dropped into a pool at her feet. Talia was caught once again by the illicitness of what they were doing. She was standing exposed in front of her confidant, her father figure.

Before she could say anything, he gripped her by the waist and turned her. Their reflection was caught in a nearby mirror. She was startled by how sexy they looked together. The man she'd always referred to as Uncle Roger was standing behind her, fully dressed. She, on the other hand, was naked except for a tiny pair of panties and her high heels. She felt inexperienced and —

"Naughty," she whispered, unaware that the words had come from her lips.

"That's what makes it so good," he said as he nuzzled the side of her neck.

She watched as his hands came up to her breasts once more. The vision created an overwhelming sexual need in her and, suddenly, she wanted this more than anything. She wanted his hands on her. She wanted his mouth on her breasts. She pressed her knees together tightly to fight the hot fire in her pussy.

She wanted him.

"How do you like it?" he whispered into her ear. "From the front? From behind?"

She saw her face redden in the mirror.

He chuckled. "Don't be shy. I want it to be good for you."

It would be good; he wouldn't let it be any other way. Talia reached up and cupped the side of his face. He'd been waiting for her for a long time. "What's your fantasy?"

She was pleased when his cheeks flushed. "Do you mind if I... Would you let me tongue you?"

The request astounded her.

Her knees buckled but he tucked her against him and took her weight.

"Such a dear girl," he murmured. "Here, sit down on the bed. We'll take it slow."

Need was consuming her but Talia followed his orders. She watched as he began taking off his clothes. His hands were unsteady but he acted as if they had all the time in the world.

She couldn't believe this had been in front of her for so many years. Why hadn't she noticed sooner? It was so hot and powerful. And forbidden. Yet she felt surrounded by affection. How could she not have seen it?

Roger was soon naked in front of her and his cock pointed straight at her face. She took in a deep breath. He was in good shape for his age. His work with the horses had kept him lean and fit but, at the moment, all she could see was his magnificent cock.

May lightning come to strike her down, but she wanted it inside her.

"Oh, sweet girl," he said when he saw the look on her face. He slowly dropped to his knees in front of her. "Have mercy."

His arms wrapped around her waist and his head dropped into her lap.

They sat that way for a long time, with his head propped on her thigh and his hot breaths stirring the wet crotch of her panties. Talia knew he was giving her time but she didn't need it. Her panties were already wet and sticky. She tried to control her body but her hips twitched.

He lifted his head. "Are you ready? I don't want to rush you."

He licked his tongue across one of her pouting nipples and the effect was electric. The sensation shot straight to her core. Her hips pumped more aggressively and she had to bite her lower lip to keep from crying out.

"Please, Roger," she begged.

"I'm coming, little one. Just hold on. I'll take care of it."

He reached for her panties. "Lift," he said gently.

Talia did as she was told and she watched as he stripped her. She still couldn't believe this was happening. The vision was so bizarre. He pulled the wet silk garment down her thighs, past her calves and over her red shoes.

"You can leave those on," he said with a soft smile. "I like them."

Her excitement flared so hot, she thought she'd melt.

"Why don't you open your legs a little wider, so I can get at you better?" he suggested.

His hands settled on her knees and Talia's heart suddenly thudded in her chest. She needed this badly but she'd looked him straight in the face. This was Roger. *Uncle Roger.* Her thighs locked together. She couldn't spread her legs and show him her most private self. He increased the pressure, though, and she had to submit.

"Oh," he groaned. "You're so lovely."

His look was like fire. Talia's fingers clenched the comforter beneath her.

"Are you soft?" he asked.

She watched with frozen anticipation as he reached for her. He stuck out his middle finger and began probing her. The touch was like a firebrand.

"Easy," he said, as if he was comforting one of his mares. "Settle down, little one. It won't hurt."

His disquieting touch settled on her again. She groaned when his finger slid into her and pressed deep.

"God, you're as tight as a fist."

Talia felt out of control. She'd never been consumed by such wildness before. Her pussy finally had something to clamp down onto and she began to ride it.

"Wait," he said. "This will help."

He leaned forward and put his mouth on her. Her back arched like a bow. Looking down, all she could see was the top of his familiar gray head. The sight set her loose.

"Oh, God!" she cried. "Yes."

His mouth was hot as he suckled her and his wiggling finger set off tiny explosions. His tongue was wicked. It was thick, strong and raspy. He licked, suckled and probed until her body was one big, throbbing mass.

Talia couldn't think. She could hardly breathe. She felt his finger pull out of her and his hands settle on her thighs. He spread her legs wider and his mouth became more intimate. When his tongue pressed into her channel, she lost all control.

Her hands came down on his head to hold him and her hips began pumping obsessively. His mouth was voracious. She writhed underneath him and her cries turned into whimpers.

"Come, little one," he said, his voice muffled against her wet flesh. "Let me feel you come."

His nose brushed against her clit and a lightning bolt shot through her system. She fell back on the bed but he wouldn't let her go. His mouth continued working on her as the orgasm consumed her. Bright color flashed behind Talia's eyelids. At last, she collapsed against the mattress.

Roger crawled up over her with an intent look on his face. "So responsive," he said roughly. "If I'd known, I would have grabbed you when you were eighteen and run off with you. To hell with anybody who didn't like it."

He settled down over her and she felt his erection prodding at her. Her head was still spinning but she drew her knees to her chest, opening herself to him.

"I'm sorry, dear, but I can't wait," he said in a tight voice.

"Don't," she panted. "Please don't."

His hands slid under her bottom and he lifted her to him. With one smooth thrust, he slid into her.

"Oh, Roger," she moaned. She was astonished by the hard heat of him.

"That's my little one," he said.

He began thrusting slowly. Talia's body quickly rose to a response. He'd been so patient with her, making sure she took her pleasure first. She had to make this good for him. Her heart opened to him as she held him tightly. Taking care not to leave scratch marks, she raked her fingers down his back.

He jerked inside her. It told her how much he was holding back.

"Fuck me, Roger," she whispered into his ear. "Fuck me like you've always wanted."

His hips plunged and her back bowed. Oh, dear God. She'd never imagined...

His long cock was stroking deep and fast within her. She was so stimulated, she didn't know how long she'd last. She made herself hold back, waiting for him.

"You're so hot and wet. And tight," he said between thrusts. "My God, why are you still so tight?"

Talia rained kisses along his shoulder. Their connection felt so good. She never would have believed that she'd feel so natural with him like this. His fingers dipped deeper into the crevice of her bottom as he lifted her higher and she groaned.

"You like it," he said. "I can feel it. You're grabbing me."

She was. She couldn't deny it.

"Tell me how it feels."

"I... Oh, Roger," she gasped.

"Tell me," he coaxed.

"It's hot. And I feel... Oh, God... So full."

He kissed her wildly. "Such a dear young thing."

"Oh, please, Roger," she panted. "Harder. Please, harder."

He thrust almost savagely and the mattress bounced. Talia cried out in pleasure. At last, he wasn't holding back. He was giving her all he had.

"Get ready," he said. "I don't think I can last much longer."

She rolled her head to the side and saw their reflection in the mirror. She watched, mesmerized, as he rammed in and out of her. The picture they made together was as beautiful as it was obscene. His silver hair shined in the moonlight and her red high heels glowed against his back. It would be difficult to think of him as her uncle ever again.

"Roger," she cried. "Oh, Roger."

His hips were pumping and the sounds of their mating echoed around the room. It didn't take long for him to crest. Talia was right there with him. Her toes curled inside her shoes and her body tightened. Desperately, she pulled him down for a hot kiss. She moaned as his orgasm joined hers.

Afterwards, he lay upon her heavily, totally spent. She wrapped her arms around him and gently caressed his sweaty back. She felt so moved by what had just happened between them.

"I knew it would be like this," he whispered into her ear.

"I had no idea," she admitted.

"You must have been curious, though." He lifted his head so he could look at her. "Why else did you finally turn to me?"

The truth came crashing back.

Talia pushed away the feelings of guilt almost petulantly. She didn't want anything to spoil this. Tonight had been special. That was the way she always wanted to remember it. "You were right," she said quietly. "Lydia just pushed me too far."

"Don't let her get to you," he said. He rolled them onto their sides, taking care not to slip out of her. Leisurely, he gave her a full-mouthed kiss. "I'll give you a donation for the charity auction. She doesn't need to know."

Talia let her hand slide down to his tight butt. Once again, she was caught by what a sweet man he was. Too sweet and caring to be trapped in such a loveless marriage. "Why don't you divorce her?" she asked before she could stop herself.

He lifted one eyebrow dramatically. "She's cheaper to keep."

Talia let out a huff. "Why does it always come down to money?"

The look he gave her was gentle. "It's a harsh fact of life, dear. The world revolves around money. Those who don't have it, work to get it. Those who have it, fight to keep it."

And Lydia would fight to keep that bracelet. Talia knew it as well as she knew her own name.

The back of her neck tingled. It was dangerous for her to be here—and in more ways than one. She'd already stayed too long but she really hadn't had an opportunity to escape. She hadn't wanted one, either.

"I've got to go," she said reluctantly. "I don't want her to find me here."

"No, don't." His arm tightened around her. "Stay the night."

"I can't," she said. She tried to pull away but he caught her bottom and thrust deeper into her.

"Please," he said. He looked deep into her eyes. "For me?"

The look on his face was so pleading. He'd waited for this for so long and he'd shown her so much affection.

She couldn't say no.

"Just the night," she finally agreed. "You know that's all it can ever be."

"I'll take what I can get."

His hand skimmed up her body and cupped her breast. Talia gave herself over to the feelings coursing inside her. She needed this night as much as he did. Dangerous as it was, she'd take the solace he offered.

Come morning, though, she'd be gone.

Nobody could ever know what had happened between them.

Chapter Seven

"Help! My bracelet! It's gone!"

The alarm was sounded only a few hours later, catching Talia at a particularly bad time. She was astride Roger's cock and riding at a harsh pace. She froze with him deep inside her when the scream came barreling down the hall.

"Oh God, Lydia," Roger growled. "Not now."

Talia's body was on fire but a chill ran down her spine. The bracelet! How had Lydia noticed it was missing so quickly? Her fingers curled on Roger's chest. She'd been worried about getting caught but, if she were caught now, she'd be paying for more than just one sin.

Dread suddenly filled her, cooling her ardor. Why hadn't she left? She'd had the perfect opportunity half an hour ago but, instead of sneaking out, she'd chosen to wake Roger for one last go-around. Now she was trapped.

"Where is it?" The frantic voice echoed down the hallway. "Somebody's taken it!"

"Ignore her," Roger said. His hands settled on her hips and began guiding them up and down.

"I can't," Talia gasped. Suddenly, his cock inside her felt wrong.

"Try." With a smooth move, he rolled her onto her back and began thrusting hard. "I'll go see what the problem is as soon as we're finished."

Her hips automatically rose to meet his but the sound of the headboard bumping against the wall made her cringe. It was also making her cream. Her attention was split, heightening her sense of danger. Had he locked the door?

She couldn't remember.

Her neck arched against the pillow. Lydia was going to find her here!

And like this!

"Roger!"

A hard knock on the bedroom door made Talia buck. She tried to push Roger off of her but he just caught the back of her thighs and pressed her legs upward toward her chest. The position allowed him to plow even deeper into her.

She choked back a cry. He was getting off on this!

The doorknob rattled but refused to budge. "Damn it, you lazy fool," Lydia screeched. "Get out here and help me."

"Christ," Roger muttered. His cock stilled and he fought for air. He looked down at Talia with disappointment. With a groan, he dislodged his body from hers. "Remember where we were. This will just take a moment."

Talia's pussy cried out at the loss but she scrambled off the bed and crouched down to hide as he pulled on his pants. She'd been taking abuse from Lydia Thorton for most of her life but now she deserved it. She'd been caught fucking the woman's husband.

"What is it, Lydia?" Roger said as he opened the door. He stuck his head in the opening and blocked his wife from entering.

The crouched position made Talia's pussy throb. She pressed her lips together to keep from making a sound and risked a quick peek at the reflection of the two in the mirror.

For once Lydia didn't look tacky. She looked unkempt. Her hair was wild and, for the first time ever, her face was devoid of makeup.

"It's my bracelet, you idiot," the woman said. "Don't you have ears? I've been screaming my head off trying to get your attention."

Using the door as cover, Roger pulled on his robe and belted it. His hard cock formed a thick bulge beneath the tie ends. "What about your bracelet, dear? I was trying to sleep."

Sleep? Talia closed her eyes guiltily. They couldn't have been further from sleeping.

"It's been stolen." Lydia shoved her way inside and snapped her fingers in front of her husband's face. "Listen to me! It's just like what happened to the Harringtons."

"Now, dear." He gripped her shoulders firmly, pushing her back into the hallway and holding her away from him and the evidence of his hanky-panky. "Don't get carried away."

"*Carried away?*" Lydia batted at him and raked her hand through her hair. The overly-hairsprayed strands stuck nearly upright. "I've called the police. They're going to be here any minute."

Talia's blood froze in her veins. The police?

No.

She needed to get out of the house. *Now.*

"You've already called the police?" Roger threw a glance back into the bedroom and acted impatient. "I wish you hadn't done that. Don't you think you should have looked a little harder? Couldn't you have just misplaced it?"

"Misplaced it? Good heavens. I'm not a simpleton! You know very well that I take excellent care of my jewelry." Lydia's hands clenched into fists. "It was the antique silver one with the inlaid tigereyes—and it wasn't in my jewelry box where I left it!"

"All right, all right," he muttered. "Let's go look for it."

He closed the door behind him and Talia was off like a shot. She rounded the bed and found her dress still lying in a heap on the floor. Had Lydia seen it? She didn't have time to worry. She yanked the red fabric up over her hips and affixed the snap at the back of her neck. She yanked up the zipper at her lower back as she looked for her purse. She found it soon enough on the dresser where she'd put it.

A flash of color from the floor caught her eye and she saw her panties. Her mouth dropped agape. She could only hope that Lydia's mind had been on the missing bracelet. There was no other way she could have missed the telltale sign that her husband was cheating.

Talia frantically threw her panties in her in purse. Her shoes. Where were her shoes?

She found them but her attention was on the conversation down the hallway. Panic flew through her. They were in Lydia's bedroom, effectively blocking her escape route to the back door.

She spun around. She'd have to go out the front way.

Red lights flashed through the window.

Her hand went to her heart as she scurried over to look outside. It was too late! The police were here.

"Damn!" she whispered into the darkened room. "Damn, damn, damn."

She was trapped. She couldn't make it to the back door and she certainly couldn't go out the front.

Maybe sneaking out a side window was an option. The idea was quickly shot down when she peeked outside again. Three squad cars had gathered in front of the house, and policemen with flashlights were already taking a look around the premises.

There was no way out. She backed away from the window before she was spotted. There was nothing she could do but hide.

* * * * *

Detective Riley Kinkade arrived on the scene ten minutes after the first squad car. Before opening the door of his unmarked sedan, he took a long draw on his cup of coffee. Damn, but he hated the night shift. Fernandez better get back from vacation soon. The guy owed him big time. Look what he'd gotten for being a nice guy and covering for him—two high-profile robberies within a week.

A hysterical female clambered down the front steps of the house and he knew his time was up. Taking a deep breath, he got out of the car and walked toward her. The woman's silk robe flapped in the breeze and her hands fluttered in midair as if she were trying to take flight.

"My bracelet... Stolen! Just like Shelli's... Gone from my jewelry box..."

"Slow down, slow down," he said as her words tumbled over one another. She was upset, he could tell, but he hadn't been able to understand a word she'd said. "Let's start with your name."

"It's Lydia Thorton!" she said, offended for some reason. "I told that to the person on the phone."

She spun around, looking at the people in her yard. "Who's in charge here?"

"That would be me, Mrs. Thorton. I'm Detective Kinkade." He would have shaken her hand but her arms were still flailing about. He reached into his breast pocket for his notebook. This was going to be a long one; he could tell already. "So you're missing a bracelet?"

"Yes. Yes. How many times do I have to tell you people that?"

A sharp pain rippled through Riley's temple. Shrieking voices often did that to him. He didn't have much patience tonight but he called on the small reserve he had left. "When did you notice that it was missing?"

"Twenty minutes ago—approximately the time I *reported it*." She let out a harrumph. "I was getting ready for bed. I put away the earrings I'd worn for our dinner party tonight and I noticed right away that my tigereye bracelet was gone. It's an antique, you know."

The woman's initial enthusiasm was cooling in the autumn air. She'd wrapped her robe more tightly around herself and was rubbing her feet together as if they were losing feeling.

"Why don't we take this discussion inside where it's warmer?" he suggested.

"Yes, why don't we?" With a huff, she turned and stalked up her front steps. "As if I enjoy standing outdoors in my lingerie."

Riley sighed and caught a sympathetic look from one of the patrol guys. He shook his head. "Take a look around the house and the outskirts of the property."

He took a deep breath. "I'm going in."

He mounted the front steps and entered the house. He found Mrs. Thorton sitting on a sofa by the fireplace. An older man who looked familiar was handing her a drink. "Mr. Thorton? I'm Detective Kinkade."

"Call me Roger," the man said. He crossed the room and held out his hand. "I believe we spoke after the Harrington's robbery. I'm sorry you had to be called out here at such a late hour."

That's where he knew him from. Riley nodded and shook the man's hand. He'd talked to so many people over the past few days, the names and faces were starting to blend. At least the old guy didn't seem so bad. "It's my job. Can you tell me what you know?"

"Not much. I went to bed earlier than Lydia. I wasn't aware that anything was wrong until she started screaming." Roger rolled his eyes, showing how much he'd liked that.

Riley glanced up from his notebook. The guy didn't seem too concerned about this bracelet. "I take it that the jewelry is normally kept in the bedroom?"

Lydia nodded. "In the jewelry box I bought on our honeymoon."

He looked at the husband. "You didn't notice anything different about the room? Was anything out of place when you entered?"

At this, Roger Thorton looked discomfited.

"We have separate bedrooms," he said. He raised one eyebrow as if that was explanation enough.

It was.

Riley kept his face stoic as he noted down the fact. He glanced toward Lydia Thorton again. She'd quieted down for the time being and seemed intent on inhaling her drink. He looked at her raised pinky and suddenly things clicked. The drunk, gold-sequined lady! Damn, he hadn't recognized her without her makeup. These two had been at the Harrington shindig. He quietly filed the tidbit of information away.

"Could you show me the bedroom?" he asked. "Our forensics team will be here shortly but I should cordon off the area where the burglary took place."

"Oh, I don't know," Roger said, suddenly acting uneasy. "Maybe I should speak with our lawyer first."

"Heavens to Betsy. You go right ahead, Kinnear," Lydia said, nearly choking on a swig of brandy. "Do your little fingerprinting thingamabob."

"For God's sake, Lydia. It's *Kinkade*. How many drinks you have had tonight?"

Great. There they went. Riley tucked away his notepad. How could he have forgotten these two? He signaled for a patrolman to back him up. Permission from one was enough for him. "It's standard practice, Mr. Thorton. We'll try not to disturb anything."

"But… You only have permission to search her room," Roger called.

"It's at the end of the hall," Lydia said.

"Yes, ma'am."

Riley was already halfway up the front steps. Hell, this was just how he wanted to spend his night. He'd probably be cooped up here for hours with Mr. and Mrs. Happycouple. Why was it when people had money, they acted like it was all stuck up their ass?

He sighed. The biddy had been right about one thing, though. This was too much like the Harrington case for his liking. A swanky party. A missing trinket. Sounded like one of New Covington's socialites had come down with a case of sticky fingers.

At least he hoped that's all it was.

He'd just hit the second floor landing when he saw a flash of red at the other end of the hall. His muscles tensed and he reached for the gun at his hip. It wasn't necessary. The figure was already gone. "Runner!" He yelled to his backup. "Going down the back staircase."

The patrolman turned on his heel and quickly headed down the stairs to try to cut the person off. Riley ran down the hallway at a full sprint. He took the stairs at the other end two at a time. He had to admit whomever he was chasing was good. They were swift and silent—excellent traits for a burglar.

He leapt down the last four steps when he heard somebody fiddling with the lock on the back door. It was too dark to see. The moon was still hidden by the clouds and the lights from the living room didn't extend back this far. Letting his ears guide him, he moved swiftly across the room and shoved the perpetrator up against the door. It slammed shut and a soft cry wafted through the darkness.

"What the hell?" He'd caught a woman. If the voice hadn't told him, the soft expanse of bare skin under his hands would have.

The patrolman arrived from the opposite direction and turned on the lights. Riley blinked, but recognized the long-legged blonde immediately. He grabbed her by the shoulder and spun her around. "Talia Sizemore."

Her eyes were big as saucers as she looked at him. Riley swore. "What are you doing here?"

"Don't hurt her, Detective," came a worried voice from over his shoulder. "Ms. Sizemore has been my...my *guest* for the evening."

It was then that Riley saw Talia's rumpled clothes and her mussed hair. There was an unmistakable look of passion in her eyes and red dots colored her cheeks.

Fuck!

He felt as if he'd just been kicked in the gut. Suddenly, he didn't give a crap about the missing bracelet. This was worse. She'd been here screwing the old man. The old man! Jesus!

"Get in the living room," he barked.

"But..." she stammered.

He caught her by the arm and pulled her away from the door. She was warm to the touch. Too warm. His fingers bit into her skin when he pictured how she must have been exerting herself. "You're not going anywhere until we've had a little chat."

This put her in connection with both robberies. That was two robberies too many. He wanted an explanation.

For everything.

A sickly green color swam across her face. "Please, can't we talk here?"

It didn't take him long to catch on. "The wife doesn't know?"

"No," she said softly. Her eyelids dropped in embarrassment.

Riley had a strong inclination to punch something. Anything. The wall would do fine. "Jesus, Talia."

"Talia? Did you say *Talia*? Is that bitch still here?"

Riley gritted his teeth hard as a shrill voice rang into the room. This was just what he needed—a domestic disturbance thrown in for good measure. The paperwork tomorrow was going to be a real pain in the ass.

Lydia Thorton pushed her way into the tiny mudroom. When she saw Talia standing at the door, she went off like Mount Vesuvius. "You," she hissed. "You were the reason why Roger left the party so early."

She lurched forward and the patrolman caught her about the waist. She clawed at the air, trying to get at the younger woman. "I knew it! I've always known. How long? How long have you been doing my husband?"

"Mrs. Thorton," Riley said, using a straight arm to keep her away. "Calm down. We need to talk about this."

"Calm down? That little tramp has been flaunting her body in front of my husband since she was a teenager and you want me to calm down?"

She launched herself out of the patrolman's arms and Riley did what only seemed natural. He pushed Talia behind him and planted himself in front of her. Mrs. Thorton's claws came at him but he caught her by her wrists. Fury made her strong but he held her off until the patrolman could pull her away and into the other room.

"It wasn't like that," Roger Thorton said agitatedly. He pushed his hands through his silver hair as he looked from one woman to the other.

Riley wasn't really in the mood for excuses. "Go after your wife."

The old man left with his shoulders drooping and Riley took a moment to calm himself. He hadn't expected to walk in on a scene like this. It had him agitated and he could commiserate with Lydia more than he'd like to admit. His blood was pumping and the desire to rip into something was strong. He stilled, though, when he felt Talia clutching the back of his jacket like a safety raft. Her forehead rested against him as she took shuddering breaths.

His gut twisted. As much as he tried to fight it, the need to protect her was still strong. *Damn it, Kinkade. Don't do it!* He fought with himself for a moment longer but then finally turned. She gave up her hold on him reluctantly.

He looked at her downturned face. Her pink cheeks were now scarlet red. She'd been caught dead-to-rights and the humiliation had her close to tears. It went against every grain in his body but he couldn't stop himself from reaching for her. He ran a hand over her soft hair. It took two to put her in this position but she was the one taking the brunt of the backlash.

"Can I go now?" she asked. "Please?"

"No."

Her wobbling chin came up. He was prepared for the pleading look, though, and it bounced right off him.

"You can't leave," he said. "I've got a robbery to investigate."

Suddenly that pissed him off more than anything. He pulled back, removing his hand from her hair. He'd come here to do his job—not get all entangled in an adultery mess. Damn it, what was she doing screwing that old geezer? "Get your ass into the living room," he said flatly.

She flinched. "Lydia... She won't want me in there."

"Tough." Talia looked away but Riley caught her chin and made her look at him. "Listen, the quicker you get in there and answer my questions, the quicker you can leave. I promise she won't come after you. If she does, I'll charge her with assault."

The assurance didn't ease her nerves. Her white teeth worried her lower lip and he was again taken at how sensual she looked. Damn, but he hated seeing her fresh from another man's bed. If anybody should be scared right now, it was Roger Thorton.

"Come on," he said. He started to wrap his arm around her shoulders, but stopped himself as soon as he touched her. Her shoulders were bare. The feel of her skin was too much for him to handle right now. He jerked his hand away and pointed the way instead.

He led her into the living room and guided her to an overstuffed chair as far away from Lydia Thorton as he could get. The old biddy's glare cut across the room like a knife. He purposely ignored it. Emotions were ricocheting about the room but he needed answers regarding the theft. It was the reason he'd been called here.

He had to remember that.

"Mrs. Thorton, you said you hosted a dinner party tonight." He schooled his features and reached for his notes again. By the book. He had to do this by the book. "Who attended?"

She glowered at Talia. "The Harringtons, Edward Jones, Ramona Gellar and *this whore*."

The response was inflammatory. It made the muscles at the back of his neck clench but he promptly moved on to another question. His purpose was twofold. One, he had to keep control of the situation. Two, he wanted to get Talia out of this house as soon as he could. There was no need to draw out her degradation and he wanted to talk to her. One-on-one. The best way to do that was to work quickly and efficiently.

"When did your guests leave?" he asked. "In what order?"

Petulantly, Lydia answered.

"Do you have any pictures of the missing jewelry? Was anything else missing?"

As hard as he was concentrating, he still made sure to take good notes. His brain wasn't as centered as he'd normally like it. He ignored Talia as much as the questions didn't pertain to her but it was difficult. She seemed to have the attention of everybody in the room—including the patrolmen.

That red dress was like some sort of neon sign. Hell, if she moved wrong, her breasts were going to pop out. He knew that's what everyone was waiting for.

At least, he knew he was.

The lead of his pencil snapped and he cursed. He borrowed another one and continued. Finally, the only questions he had left were for her. He took a deep breath before diving in.

"You were invited to the dinner party?" he asked.

"Yes," she said.

"What time did you leave?"

"Around ten o'clock."

"When did you come back?"

"About a half hour later."

"Why?"

She paused. "To see Roger."

The answer burned a hole in Riley's gut. His voice was curt as he got more personal. "Was this a planned interlude?"

Again, she hesitated. "No, I surprised him."

Wonderful. He'd been having dreams about her surprising him but she was running around town, popping into this old fart's bedroom. The guy's teeth probably weren't even his own. "How did you get into the house without anybody noticing?" he asked, his voice suddenly gruff.

"I came in the back door."

"Wasn't it locked?"

"I had a key."

"She has a key?" Lydia shrieked. "To my house?"

"No," Talia said quickly. She stared down at her tightly clasped hands in her lap. "I grew up with Felicia Thorton. I know where the spare key is kept."

"So you surprised Mr. Thorton in his bedroom," Riley said, his head starting to pound. Damn it all to hell. "Did you stop by Mrs. Thorton's bedroom along the way?"

"No, and I don't appreciate the implication."

Apparently she wasn't offended enough to look him in the eye. His frustration with her escalated. He wanted to shake her up, make her notice him. "Did you see anybody else on the second floor?"

"No."

"Did you hear anything?"

"I don't remember anything unusual."

Probably too busy. Riley felt like he was going to be sick. Mr. Geriatric sticking it to a gorgeous babe like her was what he called "unusual".

He shook his head. He got the distinct impression she was lying but he didn't know why. She was embarrassed; everybody in the room knew that. Still, the shake in her voice and the timidity of her gaze could be due to something else entirely.

Like larceny.

He tucked his notebook back into his pocket. "Would you stand, Ms. Sizemore? I need to search you."

"That's not necessary," Roger Thorton said hurriedly. "She's got nothing on her."

If the guy had been standing anywhere close, Riley would have decked him. Instead, he fixed his best don't-mess-with-me glare on the bastard. "I'll do my job as I see fit, Mr. Thorton. Now, Ms. Sizemore, if you'd please."

She stood slowly, but said nothing.

"Lift your arms to the side," he ordered. The words were hard to say with the way his jaw was clenched. "Now just stand still."

He patted her down as quickly and impersonally as he could but there wasn't anything impersonal about it. He was laying his hands on her, but under the most constrained of situations. He'd have given just about anything to spend a few more seconds weighing her breasts or feeling the curve of her tight waist.

And those legs. God, those legs were going to be the death of him.

"Turn around."

To anyone watching, he behaved like the professional he was. Only he and she knew, though, the few extra seconds he spent cupping her bottom. It was just so damn perfect, he couldn't help himself. Turning her slightly so the room couldn't see, he finished the last part of the search. Slipping his hand between her legs, he cupped her mound.

She made a soft, surprised sound and he felt her dampness start seeping through the material. Son of a bitch! He pulled back as if burned. He hoped he was treating her to a small measure of the torment she was giving him.

"This is all your jewelry?" he asked as he grasped her hands.

She looked blindly over his shoulder, her face a fine shade of crimson. "Yes."

"That cheap crap certainly isn't mine," Lydia Thorton hissed.

"How much do you estimate your bracelet was worth, Mrs. Thorton?" Riley said, letting her words roll off his back. "Have you had it appraised?"

"It's worth $2,500 if it's worth a penny."

Riley just nodded. He'd grown accustomed to rich snobs' indifference to the value of money. He looked at Talia again and caught the lifting of her chin. Now, that was surprising. He wasn't sure but he could have sworn that she agreed with him.

But she was a Sizemore. From all accounts, she was set for life.

Remembering her briefcase, Riley became uneasy. "I need to see the contents of your purse."

She looked at him and, for a moment, he thought she'd refuse.

"Of course," she said. "I have nothing to hide."

She sat back down in her chair. With a defiant look, she reached for her purse and opened the clasp. The effect was ruined when they both saw the red panties inside. The desire to hit something came over Riley again and he turned away from the sight. Running a hand through his hair, he got hold of himself. When he turned back, he saw that she'd tucked the panties in the chair beside her hip.

"Don't you get any of your stinky cum on my furniture," Lydia griped. Her words were getting slurred as she drank more and more brandy.

"Place the items on the table," Riley ordered. If he ever made it through this, he was never switching for the night shift again.

Talia looked nauseous but she moved the panties onto the coffee table. They sat there like a bright red flag and Riley's cock twitched. She wasn't wearing anything under that dress. When he'd cupped her mound, that filmy red dress had been all that stood between her and his hand. The thought alone was enough to make him break out in a cold sweat.

"I'm going to have to get that table sanitized."

"Shut up, Lydia!" Roger Thorton finally snapped.

"Your purse," Riley encouraged Talia. "Can we see the rest of its contents?"

Her lips pressed into a straight line and he wasn't surprised when she upended everything onto the table. She sat back in her chair, her look defiant, but he could see the hint of tears in her eyes. Her humiliation was complete.

And it made him feel like a heel.

With a detective's eye, he looked through the pile of items on the table. He saw at once that the bracelet wasn't there but he spent his time cataloguing the rest of the contents. They gave him insight into Talia Sizemore, the woman. Call him a glutton for punishment, but he wanted to know as much as he could.

For the case and for himself.

Quickly, he sorted through her things. There was a pack of gum, a package of tissues, a hairbrush and a tube of lipstick. A beaded key chain with her name caught his eye. It seemed out of place for what he knew about her. Definitely not haute couture. He picked it up to look at it more closely.

"One of my kids made it," she said.

"Your kids?" he said, his head snapping up.

"My father's foundation supports an after-school arts program."

"Oh, yeah," Riley said, relaxing. "That's right."

She'd surprised him again. He remembered Arthur telling him about the foundation but he'd thought she'd be the standoffish kind, running the charity from arm's length. If the kids were making her things, though, that couldn't be the case. This silly little key chain made it a lot more personal.

He liked that and he felt his anger toward her soften.

He reached for her pocketbook and saw her flinch. Her fingers tightened on the arms of the chair. His instincts told him to pay attention but the bracelet wasn't in the pocketbook either. From the balance in her checking account, he could tell he was right about one thing. She didn't need the money.

"Are you quite through?" she asked in a deceptively quiet tone.

"Yeah. You can pack up your things."

He started to help but she snatched away her purse and her panties almost before he could move.

"I'll do it!"

"Fine." He pushed himself to his feet and stretched his legs. "I have a few more questions for the Thortons. Wait for me and I'll walk you to your car."

Her amber gaze swung up to him. "I'm free to go?"

"I've got no reason to hold you."

"Good."

Riley wandered over to the Thortons as she swept everything into her purse. Literally. She opened the bag, held it against the edge of the coffee table and used her forearm to push everything inside.

No rush there.

He'd just turned his focus on Roger Thorton when he saw movement out of the corner of his eye. He pivoted sharply. Talia had her wrap about her shoulders and was heading determinedly toward the front door. "Hold on," he called.

She glanced at him, but didn't break stride. "You said I could go."

"I said that I'd walk you to your car."

"I know where it is."

"It's dark out there."

"Doesn't bother me." As if that were the end of that, she walked out the door. A cat bolted out of the house to follow her.

"Good riddance, you slut!" Lydia yelled.

Riley was torn. He wasn't finished here but he couldn't let her go out there alone. Although slim, there was the possibility that the robber could still be in the area.

Yeah right, Kinkade. That's the reason.

"Excuse me," he told the Thortons. "I'll be back."

He heard Lydia bitching as he hit the door but he ignored her. He stopped on the stoop. "Where's the leggy blonde?" he asked the patrolman that was still out front.

He followed where the man pointed and eventually caught up with Talia as she walked across the open field. "Where the hell are you going?" he asked.

Her head jerked toward him. With one look at her face, he could tell she didn't want him anywhere near her. Well, that was tough. He'd warned her he'd be on her until he found out all her secrets.

It was her own damned fault this one had been such a doozy.

"To my car." She wrapped her arms around her waist and increased her speed. The cat bounded ahead, almost as if it knew where she was heading.

Riley didn't have a clue but he was ready to follow her anywhere.

He kept pace with her as they headed deeper into the meadow. Shadows loomed all around them. The moon peeked through the clouds and he saw his own breath in the cold air. He glanced at Talia. She had to be freezing in that filmy little number. Looking down, he saw that her feet were bare. She was carrying her shoes. Sighing, he shrugged out of his jacket. "Here, take this."

She glanced at it for a long moment. She was ready to refuse before a gust of cold wind changed her mind. "Thank you," she said quietly.

He held the jacket for her as she pushed her arms into the sleeves. "I take it that you parked far away from the house so Lydia wouldn't catch you."

"That was the idea."

He'd had about enough of her short, clipped answers. "Done this much?"

Her head wheeled toward him, her expression aghast. "No!"

His patience snapped. Reaching out, he caught her by the arm and spun her around. "What were you thinking, Talia? Jesus, the guy's old enough to be your father."

She blanched and pulled back from him. "I don't have to explain anything to you."

"Can the guy even get it up?"

"That's none of your business."

"No?" he snapped. "While you were banging him, a pricey piece of jewelry turned up missing. That makes it my business."

That was stretching it a bit but he'd spent enough time thinking about her over the past few days to feel like she was his business. His personal business.

"So find the bracelet and leave me out of it." She turned and began walking hurriedly. The cat weaved its way around her feet as she went.

"I can't." His strides matched hers as they walked under the dark sky. He could barely see where they were going. The moon had gone back behind the clouds. There was a chill in the air but he hardly felt it. His anger was getting hot enough to keep them both warm. "Every time something disappears, you seem to be around."

"Ever hear of coincidence, Detective?"

"I can't believe in coincidence." He raked his hand through his hair. "Just like I can't believe that you'd fuck that guy."

"Stop it."

"He's an old man. He's married. Christ, you could have any man you want and you pick him?"

The cat bounded away when he raised his voice. It ran toward a building that he assumed was the horse stable. The long walk finally made sense. That was probably where she'd picked up the key.

"There's my car." She pulled his jacket off her shoulders and thrust it at him. "Would you leave me alone now?"

Riley couldn't let it drop. "What did he do for you, Talia? What did you need from him?"

She finally turned on him. He could see her temper simmering in her amber eyes.

"What did I need from him?" she said in a throaty rasp. "Try understanding. Comfort. Yes, Detective. He might be older but he's a sweet, desirable man. That's more than I can say for a hot-tempered, bullheaded cop like you!"

That was it. Riley caught her and pushed her up against her car. He pressed his hips against her and his cock settled against the vee at the top of her legs. The hot contact stunned even him for a moment. Their bodies fit together with stunning accuracy. "Careful, baby. You don't want to make me prove anything."

Their breaths mingled in the cold air. His hands were at her waist and hers were on his shoulders. Their attention, though, was focused much lower. Riley's cock was so hard, it was near to bursting out of his pants. He knew her pussy was naked and vulnerable behind that red dress and the knowledge was driving him mad.

They stood there watching each other carefully for what could have been minutes.

"I could sue you for assault," she finally whispered.

"It wouldn't be assault, baby. We both know that."

She stood silent within the circle of his arms until a shiver ran through her body. "Please let me go, Kinkade. I'm tired and I've been humiliated. I just want to go home."

The despair in her voice finally got through. Riley pulled back slowly. She wasn't trembling because of him. She was cold. The night air was downright frigid and he'd pushed her up against a metal car. He looked down at the cat winding its way around their legs. Her bare feet had to feel like ice. "Damn, I'm sorry."

He ran his hands up and down her arms. She was having none of it. "Goodnight, Detective."

"Take my jacket. I can pick it up at your shop tomorrow."

"I can manage on my own."

"Talia."

"Don't you have work to do?"

Riley knew how to pick his battles and this wasn't one he could win. Not right now. Not after he'd made her put her wet panties on the table for the world to see. "Drive carefully," he said, taking another step back.

She didn't respond as she turned and unlocked her car door. He couldn't help but notice how her hands shook. She quickly slid into the driver's seat and reached for the heater controls.

He took the hint. Turning, he began the long walk back to the house. He knew better than to look back.

It was too bad he didn't. If he had, he might have seen Talia reach down for the cat. That, in and of itself, might not have been suspicious. Seeing her remove a very expensive collar from Taffy's neck, though, would have been downright incriminating.

Chapter Eight

Talia shivered as she drove away from the stables. Cold racked her from the inside out. Between the wind chill and Kinkade's icy demeanor, she was a wreck. A shudder ran through her and she reached down to turn the heater on high.

"What have I done?" she whispered over the whir of the fan.

She was mortified by the evening's events. She'd stolen. Again. And this time, she'd committed adultery to get away with it. She raked a shaky hand through her hair. If that hadn't been bad enough, she'd gotten caught in the worst possible way—by Roger's wife and the *police*!

There was going to be no keeping this quiet.

Guilt and dread mixed like a deadly cocktail in her stomach. *What* was making her do these things? She'd been out of control ever since Brent had manhandled her. He'd pushed her to the end of her rope and now she couldn't seem to subdue her instinctive reactions. Lydia had angered her tonight. Her gut response had been to strike back. She'd taken that bracelet without an ounce of guilt.

She glanced at her purse, knowing that the tigereye antique was tucked safely inside. She'd been anxious at coming so close to being caught, but guilt? She still couldn't find any.

As for Roger...

She did feel guilty about being with him, although the detective, not Lydia, had made her feel that way.

As cold as it was, she felt her face flush. "You had no right, Kinkade."

She didn't want to regret what she and Roger had done together. She didn't want anything to cast a bad light on their connection. Other people might not understand but the time they'd shared had been pure. He'd made her feel safe and protected. She didn't want to taint their liaison with an ugliness that shouldn't be there.

But the ugly words had already started to fly. Lydia's contempt, she could understand. The woman had apparently known about her husband's lusts for years. But Kinkade?

"Just who do you think you are?" she said, her fingers tightening on the steering wheel.

The detective's outrage had been a tangible thing. Her body remembered the press of his as he'd trapped her against her car and she became flustered all over again. He'd been angry with her. Livid, even—as if he'd caught her cheating on him. Some of the things he'd said to her...

"It was none of your business!"

She didn't know who she was angrier with—him or herself. He'd caught her in an embarrassing situation but, instead of being discreet, he'd put her on display as a common whore in front of everyone. Maybe her behavior had justified such treatment but the situation could have been handled better. The man certainly wasn't one for subtlety.

He'd let her know exactly how he felt about her stripping and spreading her legs for Roger Thorton.

At last, a rush of heat ran through her. "Roger," she said, shaking her head in disbelief.

She hoped he'd be able to avoid most of the fallout from this, although she knew Lydia would never allow him a moment's peace. The poor man. He couldn't help his feelings and he'd held them back for so long.

Talia sagged into the driver's seat. She'd never forget the look that had been in his eyes when he'd caught her in his bedroom. He'd looked at her as if she was a cherished gift and he'd treated her with just as much care. Even now, her pussy ached for his long, hard cock. He'd left her in such a precarious state, hungry and unsatisfied.

She shifted uncomfortably in the driver's seat. She hated the detective for belittling what they'd shared.

And she hated him even more for using her arousal to make her wonder how it would be with him.

"Damn you, Kinkade," she hissed.

His anger and aggression had only made the desire between them take on an even more excited edge. She'd seen the look in his eyes. She'd heard the unspoken words in his tone. And his touch... He'd nearly made her come in front of the entire living room when he'd groped her between the legs during that supposed pat-down.

She shuddered, close to orgasm just thinking about it.

He'd told her that stealing excited some people sexually.

He'd been right.

She was riding right on the razor's edge. She knew he'd been suspicious of her before but, tonight, everything had just been cranked up a notch. His suspicion. Her thrill.

Their attraction to each other.

Nothing was going to stop him now. He'd promised to stay on her until he knew everything. She'd just never understood how all-encompassing "everything" could be.

* * * * *

Talia went home long enough to shower and change clothes but she was too keyed up to stay put. She wanted the stolen bracelet off Coolectibles' property. With Kinkade on the case, she knew she had to get rid of it fast but her only option was to wait for the long nighttime hours to crawl by until she could go see Professor Winston.

She had another job for him.

A diner just off campus proved to be a good waiting spot. Her rolling stomach couldn't stand the notion of food but cup after cup of coffee helped her pass the time. With her hair in a ponytail, she blended in well with the harried students pulling all-nighters around her. Her stress fit in, too. It seemed to float in the air of the place as naturally as oxygen.

She just wished her greatest fear was a midterm exam. By the time the sun rose, caffeine had her nerves stretched to the breaking point. That, and the looming threat of Riley Kinkade. No doubt he'd put the word out. The police had to have been looking for the bracelet for hours now. She could feel the danger increasing with every second that passed. When the breakfast crowd started to pour in, she had to leave. She could wait just as well in the hallway outside the professor's office.

Adrenaline gushed through her veins as she walked across campus to Jefferson Hall. She opened the door to the building and found the hallway empty. Her boots thudded loudly against the floor and she glanced around nervously. No wonder the professor had been paranoid when she'd first visited him. She couldn't help but look over her shoulder with every turn she made.

At last, she saw his office. It was dark but her shoulders sagged in relief when she saw the light on in his laboratory. Thank God for small favors. He must have come in early to get some research done before classes began. She quickly covered the rest of the distance and knocked.

"Yes?" came a sharp voice. "Who is it?"

She could hear the professor's surprise even through the door. She couldn't imagine he got many visitors at this hour.

"It's Talia Sizemore," she called. "I need to speak with you."

There was a long pause before she heard a shuffling noise. After another moment, the professor opened the door. He didn't invite her in. Instead, his alert gaze swept the hallway. Finally, he looked at her. "Did you not receive the..." He cleared his throat and glanced around one more time. "*Donation*?"

"Uh, yes, I did." Talia hitched her purse higher on her shoulder and gave him a tight smile. "I wasn't expecting quite so much. Thank you. It will be very helpful."

Winston fingered his bowtie but stayed planted in the doorway. "Then is there a problem?"

She could sense his tension and it brought hers back with a punch. She couldn't help but shift her weight nervously under that acute stare. "I was hoping you'd consider making another...contribution."

The professor's dark eyes sharpened behind the lenses of his glasses. "Come inside."

Finally, he stepped back. Talia followed him into the lab. She'd always been curious about his research. He was known as one of the foremost experts on functional art history. She'd nearly opted to continue with graduate studies under him until her father had agreed to finance her antiques shop. Even then, it had been a tough decision to make.

Her steps slowed as the professor locked the door behind them. The lab space was cramped. Books and manuals took up one entire wall, while art pieces were scattered everywhere else. The lab had all the look of the absent-minded professor but she had no doubt he knew exactly where everything was. The energy emulating from the space was palpable.

"I'm sorry to disturb you," she said. "You're probably here early in hopes of getting something accomplished."

He brushed her apology aside. "What is this about, Miss Sizemore? You have *another* piece?"

Her hand covered her purse protectively. Trust was still a tenuous thing between them. "I've come upon something. I was hoping we could make the same arrangement we made last time."

One of the professor's eyebrows rose but he indicated that she take a seat on a lab stool. She sat down in front of an interesting antique that he'd obviously been studying when she'd interrupted him. He cleared off another seat for himself but, when he sat, Talia found him eyeing her speculatively.

The look didn't inspire confidence.

"Can you help me?" she asked.

"I don't know if I should," he said bluntly.

Her jaw slackened. She'd never dreamt he'd refuse her. Panic slipped under her skin, hard and fast. If he didn't help her, it had all been for nothing!

And Kinkade was coming for her!

He held up his hand when she started to protest. "What, exactly, is going on with you, Ms. Sizemore?"

"Going on? Well, I..." She'd been asking herself that same question all night long and she didn't have an answer. She fell back on the only plausible explanation she had. "The after-school program is in great need. I'm doing everything I can to keep it alive."

"And you find this your only recourse? Stealing? Working through the black market?" He shook his head. "You seem to have put yourself on a slippery downward slope."

Her grip tightened on her purse. In her head, she knew what he was saying was true. She just couldn't seem to help herself. "You don't understand. This wasn't supposed to happen. I *was* working on another fund-raising idea. Everything with it was supposed to be on the up-and-up."

She took a sharp breath. When had she had to start clarifying which of her activities was legal? She licked her suddenly dry lips. "My associate and I are planning a charity auction. I went out last night to ask for items to be put on the block. Unfortunately, the donors weren't as enthusiastic as I expected them to be. I had to get them to... *ahem*...contribute in *other* ways."

The professor picked up a well-worn pencil and began tapping it on top of the lab bench. "I must be candid with you. I find your behavior disturbing. The first time you came to me, I noticed your adrenalized state. Stealing that bronze cat energized you. From my experience, people who undergo that kind of a heightened rush often become addicted to it. Is that what's happening here?"

Talia blinked. He wasn't the first to make that observation. The detective had keyed in on it from the very beginning.

Kinkade! She had to get that dreaded man out of her head.

"I admit I find it exciting," she said carefully, "But I haven't intentionally set out to do these things."

"Yet."

With one word, he summed up all her uncertainties. A week ago, she would have put a definite end to this trail of conversation. Then again, a week ago, she never would have been having this conversation in the first place. A lot had changed in a short amount of time and even she didn't know what she was capable of now.

Winston folded his arms across his chest. "Frankly, I'm not comfortable working with... How can I put this delicately? An amateur."

Talia didn't know why she felt offended. "I assure you, Professor. I was very careful."

"Who was it this time?"

A bad taste filled her mouth. "Lydia Thorton."

"Ah."

"Please, Professor." She didn't like to beg but she would if she had to. "Would you at least take a look at it?"

He pushed his glasses up to the bridge of his nose. For all his contained quietness, she could sense the battle going on inside of him.

Finally, he let out a heavy sigh. "Your Robin Hood tendencies do strike a chord within me. Let me see what you've got."

"Oh, thank you." She'd waited hours for this. Her heart began pounding as she pulled the bracelet from her purse. She'd found a cushioned box on her quick visit home and she'd put the bracelet inside for protection. Like a student waiting for praise from her teacher, she slowly opened it so he could see inside.

"My, my," he said softly. He gently clasped the edge of the box. "Might I have a closer look?"

She let him take it and watched his face intently. He was so hard to read.

"Tiger-eyes mounted on interlocking silver squares," he commented. "Very nice. I should be able to get two thousand for this."

Her brow furrowed. "That's it? I know for a fact it was appraised at $2,500 and that must have been some time ago. If it were brought into my shop, I'd offer closer to three. I wouldn't have taken it if I didn't think I could get at least that much."

One side of his mouth lifted. "So you were paying attention in class."

A test. It had been a *test*. At once, Talia was miffed. She was going to have to watch this man like a hawk if their unusual partnership was to continue.

Her nerves jumped.

Continue?

"What's this?" Turning, Winston grabbed a pair of tweezers from his workbench. Ever so carefully, he used them to remove a short, cream-colored hair that had gotten caught in the clasp.

Talia drummed her fingers along the edge of the desk. She really hadn't wanted to get into this. "It's cat hair. I had to be creative to get the bracelet out of the house."

His sharp gaze drilled her. "Are you certain nobody noticed?"

"I'm sure." She felt heat flood her face. "Lydia and Roger were too busy fighting over me to notice their cat had a new collar."

"Fighting over you? I don't understand."

She refused to answer. "They didn't notice it and, if the police had, they wouldn't have let me go."

The professor stood so abruptly, his glasses slipped down his broad nose. "The police?"

Damn! Her lack of sleep was making her careless. Talia mentally chastised herself for the untimely slip of the tongue but it was too late to take it back. Nervously, she began playing with the antique on the workbench in front of her. "His name is Kinkade."

"If I remember correctly, you mentioned a detective the last time you were here."

"Same guy."

Winston's body stiffened and his ebony features hardened. "You said you were careful."

She frowned. "I was."

"This is totally unacceptable! I put myself at risk for a ridiculous payoff. I am not putting myself back into that kind of jeopardy, especially not with the police already sniffing around."

He pushed the bracelet back toward her. "Get this out of my sight and don't ever come back."

Talia held up her hands, refusing to accept it. "No, it's clean. I swear. The only thing I'm suspected of is—"

Oh, this was awkward. She didn't want to spread this gossip herself! Especially to someone as asexual as Professor Winston. He'd never understand.

She bit her lip in embarrassment. She had to tell him. It was either that or get thrown out of his office. Then where would she turn? "The only thing I'm suspected of doing is sleeping with Roger Thorton," she said, hardly above a whisper.

He retreated one step, physically taken aback. "You had relations with him?"

"It wasn't like that," she said miserably.

Winston's brow furrowed. "Lydia found you two."

It wasn't a question.

"And she called the cops?"

Talia couldn't meet his gaze anymore. She focused on the antique and toyed with it absently. "If you'd please, I'd rather not talk about this."

A chuckle erupted from the professor's throat. "You are a surprising creature, Ms. Sizemore."

Her head snapped up and she gaped at him in astonishment. That laugh wasn't asexual in the slightest.

A wide grin split his face as he picked up the bracelet again. He nodded as he used his thumb to polish the tigereyes. "I think we can come to terms on this."

His sharp about-face in attitude made her uneasy. Very uneasy.

"You are a most delightful, if unpredictable, supplier." Walking across the room, Winston began twirling the lock on a small wall safe. Glancing over his shoulder, he silently instructed her to turn away. "Knowing what I know about you now, it's all the more disappointing to me that you didn't continue with your graduate studies. You're very innovative."

Talia turned on her stool and looked at the assortment of antiques in front of her. The one she'd been playing with was unfamiliar, but intriguing. It was a wooden instrument with a crank and several moving parts. As old as it was, the gear teeth looked worn and smooth. She couldn't imagine its utility but the piece had been put to good use. "Grad school was tempting," she said, "but I wanted to get out into the real world."

She rolled her eyes over the implications of her decision. It would have been safer to stay in school. The real world was turning out to be much darker than she suspected.

"Graduate school might have been more educational than you realize."

She ran her finger questioningly along the wooden device on the lab bench. The protruding feature looked familiar but, for the life of her, she didn't know what it was. "Professor, what is this?" she finally had to ask.

At once, he looked discomfited. He paused for a long moment but, at last, looked her in the eye. "It's an orgasmic manipulator."

She looked at him uncomprehendingly. "I'm not familiar with—"

"It's a sex toy, Ms. Sizemore."

She snatched her hand back.

He sighed. "That kind of reaction is why I normally keep this line of my research quiet."

"But...but why would you be studying this?"

"It's functional art," he said simply, "And the sponsors were quite generous with their funding. In this day, one can't be choosy. You should know that better than anyone."

"Yes, but—"

"It's really quite interesting work." He cocked his head and looked at her inquisitively. "You took my courses on sensuality in the arts. Human sexuality is expressed in all art forms from songs to paintings to sculptures. Theater and movies have long portrayed the condition of human attraction."

Talia hurriedly wiped her palms on her jeans. Who knew where that thing had been? "But functional art is something that incorporates art but is used for a different purpose. It's furniture, pottery...peace pipes."

"And dildos," Winston said, matter-of-factly. He reached for the apparatus.

"You're an art aficionado; you should be able to appreciate this. Look at this piece carefully," he said, holding it up for her perusal. "You'll note the intricate carving and the smooth sanding that was done to create this piece. Some craftsman obviously put in a lot of time and effort."

It was like a car wreck; she couldn't tear her gaze away.

"This artifact is really ingenious," he said. "If you'll watch as I turn this crank, the phallic module moves in a lateral fashion, thus simulating the thrusting motion of a man's hips."

"Um, yes," Talia said, shifting on her stool. She could feel her nipples tightening and her pussy beginning to throb as she watched the workings of the wicked device. It wasn't that long ago that Roger had left her mid-intercourse, and Kinkade had pawed between her legs.

This wasn't helping at all.

"With this lever," the professor continued, "an added feature is engaged. This donut-shaped structure will traverse the length of the faux penis, giving additional stimulation to the walls of the woman's vagina."

How could he touch and describe that devilish thing with such clinical detachment? She couldn't take it. Awkwardly, she slipped off the stool and put a good distance between them. "I'm sorry, Professor, but I find it hard to believe that the college supports this. No respectable publisher would print this type of research."

Winston pushed himself upright, obviously offended. "Oh, but they do. Feel free to ask the provost. It isn't something we promote due to the sensitivities of the parents and the alumni but we are known worldwide as a leader in the field. Several respected companies in the sex market regard me as an authority. I'm also well-known in the medical community."

He gestured to the bookshelf and she looked closer at the titles. There was volume upon volume of books relating to the subject. Many had his name on them and several were co-written by a professor from the Nautington Institute with whom she was familiar.

"This is serious research?" she asked.

"Do you think I would risk procuring these collectors' items on the black market if it were something perverse?" the professor asked, affronted.

Talia was taken aback. *That* was why he worked as a fence?

The realization nearly knocked her over.

"Of course not," she said hastily. She just couldn't say anything right about this. Whatever tack she chose, she was bound to be embarrassed or learn more than she ever wanted to know.

Even worse, just looking at that devious machine was agitating her.

And making her too curious for her own good.

She nearly jumped out of her shoes when she heard a key in the lock on the door.

Winston merely glanced at his watch. "Relax. It's my graduate student, Jennifer. We tend to conduct our studies before the more conservative students and faculty arrive."

Grad student? Talia looked quickly at the sex toy in the professor's hands. Heat flooded her entire body. She didn't want to know. She did *not* want to know.

She reached for her purse. "I really must be going, Professor. I've already interrupted you enough and I have to get back to my shop before anyone becomes suspicious."

"Of course," he said. He set the piece down carefully.

Talia turned, but stopped dead in her tracks when the door opened and a beautiful young blonde walked in. A tall, beautiful, blonde wearing jeans and a ponytail.

"Oh! I'm sorry," the girl said. "I didn't realize you had a visitor, Professor."

Talia was speechless. It was like looking in a mirror from ten years ago.

"It's fine, Jennifer," Winston said. "This is Ms. Sizemore, a former student of mine."

An amused, but interested, sparkle entered the student's eyes. "Hello," she said as she stuck out her hand.

"Undergrad!" Talia blurted. She felt her face flush at her outburst. Hastily, she shook the girl's hand. "I received my bachelor's degree here. I...uh, never went to grad school."

Vivid images flew through her mind. If she'd continued with her education, would Winston have involved her in this line of research? Just how in depth did the research go? And what exactly was Jennifer's contribution?

Moisture pooled in the crotch of Talia's panties and she pressed her thighs together tightly.

"Ms. Sizemore runs a foundation that supports the arts for school children," the professor explained. "She was just telling me about a charity auction they'll be holding in the near future."

"Um, yes," Talia said, distinctly uncomfortable.

"That sounds interesting," Jennifer said as she took off her backpack.

Talia glanced away from the girl's lush body. "I'll provide the details once I have them, Professor Winston."

"Wonderful," he said, rubbing his hands together. "And I'll let you know about that donation I promised."

She nodded stiffly in understanding. She tried hard to shake off her unease. He really was putting himself on the line for her and he deserved more gratitude than she'd shown. Who was she to judge anyway? Had her actions been any better? "I know I've been a nuisance but I do appreciate all you've done for me."

"I'm doing it for the children."

She smiled. "That makes it all the better."

Talia nodded at Jennifer and headed for the door but every step she took made the ache in her lower belly intensify. She couldn't block out the heated visions that were rushing through her tired mind. She could see Roger kneeling in front of her spread legs, the professor demonstrating the sex toy, Kinkade searching her for the bracelet...

Kinkade doing anything!

Her fingers turned white when she gripped the door handle. What had gotten into her?

Why was she suddenly feeling so reckless?

Had the detective been right? Was she becoming addicted to the rush?

Whatever it was, this had to stop. This wasn't her. She was a dependable, sane person. She had to get herself under control before this wildness got her in trouble.

Or worse yet, got her caught.

Chapter Nine

It was still before hours when Talia arrived back at Coolectibles. The sun had risen and the newspaper was on her doorstep. A new day had begun but to her it was just the continuation of an already lengthy night. She looked longingly at her bed when she went upstairs to change into work clothes. A quick nap was tempting but she couldn't do that again. Once her head hit that pillow, she wouldn't wake for hours. She couldn't get into the habit of sleeping the day away. Sadie would get worried and others would get suspicious.

Or more suspicious than they already were.

She forced herself to eat a muffin but the comfort food didn't help her relax. The events of the night before had been too exhilarating. Tired as she was, she still had a buzz.

And that wasn't good.

All sorts of new inclinations were bubbling up inside her. Roger Thorton and Professor Winston had certainly stirred the brew. It all added up to trouble with a capital "T" and she knew what that meant.

Consequences with a capital "K".

She shivered as she remembered the detective's hard, angry body.

Where was he right now? What would his next move be? Was he still as outraged with her as he'd been last night?

She picked fretfully at a walnut in the banana bread. She hoped he hadn't grilled Roger too much. The thought of those two together...discussing her...analyzing her behavior... The muffin crumbled onto the table and she pushed it away.

Raking a hand through her hair, she tried to get herself to settle down. She had to stop this. Obsessing was not going to help. It would just make her a nervous wreck and elevate her to the top of everyone's suspect list. What she needed to do was lie low. Keep her head down.

She forced thoughts of the detective to the back of her brain. She knew he wouldn't stay there but the best way to handle him was to continue with her life as normally as possible.

And today, "normal" meant... She glanced at the calendar. Oh, hell and tarnation. Today, she was supposed to host a field trip visit from Mrs. Tuttle's third grade glass.

Twenty-three eight-year-olds were about to invade her shop.

She dropped her head as fatigue pressed on her like a two-ton weight. Twenty-three loud, rambunctious children. Lord help her.

She rubbed her temple. Maybe she could reschedule. She groaned. She couldn't back out; the visit had been on her calendar for a month. She'd promised to talk to the kids about history and antiques. Besides, she knew she didn't deserve a break. This could be her penance for her crime.

As normal as possible, she reminded herself.

Muscles aching, she pushed herself away from her breakfast to go make preparations.

Sadie still hadn't shown up when the class arrived, so Talia made do on her own. The youngsters' kinetic energy made her head spin but their interest in collecting was contagious. When she finally got them gathered in the showroom away from the pricier items, she heard all about their baseball cards, race car collections and dolls. In return, she showed them toys, kitchen gadgets from the 1900's and a collection of bottle caps. Each item had a story behind it and she had a rapt audience.

She felt a second wind come over her as she worked with them. That was the way it always was with kids; when they were interested in something, they became totally absorbed. That was why she loved them so much.

She'd just turned the class loose to explore when she heard the back door open. Turning, she saw her assistant. "There you are," she called. "I was starting to get worried."

Sadie hung her coat on the rack and hurried into the room. "I'm sorry. It took longer than I thought it would."

It. Talia looked at her assistant blankly until the lightbulb went on inside her head. At once, she felt guilty. She'd been so wrapped up in her own issues, she'd neglected her friend's problems. "Your meeting with the judge! I forgot."

Sadie looked around at the chaos. "That's understandable. I meant to be back before the rug rats arrived."

"They've been fine." Talia reached out and straightened her friend's collar. She hadn't needed to rush. Work should always come second to family. "What did he say?"

For the first time since her son had gotten into trouble, Sadie looked encouraged. "He thinks having Linc help with the charity auction is a good idea and he'll allow it to count as community service time. Little does my son know, but he's going to start working this afternoon as soon as he gets home from school."

Talia had insisted that Sadie begin leaving work early so Lincoln wouldn't have those late afternoon hours to get into any more trouble. Her assistant had been reluctant about the arrangement but she hadn't seen any other solution. Until Linc fulfilled the terms of his probation, he couldn't be left alone. It wasn't as if Sadie was sloughing off her duties. She was working on the auction's preparations at home. It was more than an even trade and well worth her full-time pay.

Sadie shoved her purse under the counter and patted her hair to make sure it was in place. "So, about the auction... Did you get buy-in from the la-di-da crowd? How did the dinner party go?"

The dinner party. Talia felt her face flush. She was going to have to tell her friend everything that had happened, but not here. Not now. "We'll talk later," she said.

"Why? What happened?"

She grimaced. What happened? It sounded like such a simple question. She hesitated before answering. She had no idea what was already floating through the rumor mill. "I would have assumed you'd heard by now."

"Heard what? I was too busy scrambling around this morning to hear anything."

A little boy came to the counter and Talia smiled at him weakly. "The Thortons had a burglary last night."

Sadie's nimble fingers paused on the register's keypad. "It happened again?"

"Can you believe it?" Talia turned away to find a sack for their young customer's marbles. She didn't like lying to her best friend and she knew it would show on her face.

"My goodness. Were you there?"

She nodded as Sadie handed the boy his change.

"What happened?"

"I'm not sure," she lied. She nervously hooked her hair behind her ear. "I believe that Lydia is missing a bracelet."

Sadie rolled her eyes. "I'm surprised that loon noticed anything was missing. She usually isn't that coherent. Besides, she has more jewelry than I'd know what to do with."

"Mm," Talia murmured. That had been the idea anyway. Lydia wasn't supposed to have noticed that one little bracelet was missing so soon. Her unusually quick wits had started this whole mess.

That was, if you didn't count the theft in the first place.

A shiver of shame ran down Talia's spine and she was grateful when she saw the schoolteacher waving at her. She caught Sadie by the shoulder. "We really need to talk after they're gone."

Her assistant's eyebrows lifted. "Okay," she said hesitantly.

Talia wove her way through the crowd and was appreciative when Mrs. Tuttle thanked her for her hospitality. All the same, it was a relief when the schoolteacher indicated that it was time for the class to leave. It had been an enjoyable but exhausting visit. Twenty-three children on no sleep? She suddenly had unending respect for those in the teaching profession.

The schoolteacher began rounding up her charges and Talia took the opportunity to sit down. Her adrenaline was starting to wane and it wasn't even lunchtime yet. How was she going to make it through the afternoon? She closed her eyes and reached for the kink in her neck.

She didn't get to relax for long. She'd barely begun to work on the knot when someone poked her in the shoulder. Opening her eyes, she found one of her most loyal patrons. "Bobby, I didn't know you were in this class."

The rough-and-tumble little boy smiled broadly, showing the gap where a front tooth had been. "I brought you something."

Talia ruffled his hair. The kid might be young but he had a bit of a shark in him. That made him one of her favorites. "What do you have today?" she asked.

"Something you'll like."

"Stop teasing! Show me."

With a grand gesture, he pulled a carefully packaged comic book from his backpack. "The Patroller Number 407—the last issue of Year One. It's the one where Lady Midnight first wears her blue catsuit."

Talia's eyes widened. Not bad. It wasn't that old—late '80s if she remembered correctly—but it was one in a short series that told how the modern-day Georgina Miles became Lady Midnight. Carefully, she wiped her palms on her skirt and reached for it.

Bobby laughed at the automatic gesture. "Your hands always get sweaty when I bring you Lady Midnight stuff."

"Really?" said a low voice from a few feet away. "I've been wondering what gets her wet."

Bobby looked up sharply and Talia froze. She found her gaze drifting up, up, up a very rumpled police detective. Oh, God! What was he doing here?

Bobby was the first to respond. "She likes Lady Midnight."

"Does she now?" Kinkade said slowly. "Isn't that interesting?"

Talia quickly pushed herself to her feet but the kink in her neck protested. She winced and reached for the pain. It was all she could do not to flinch when the detective caught her elbow to steady her.

"My palms are not sweaty; it's the proper technique for handling comic books. The oils on your hands can interact poorly with the ink," she said. She shrugged away from his hot touch. "Besides, I should be excited about this issue. Lady Midnight is a popular villain."

"Really popular," Bobby said, piping up. "I should get ten dollars at least."

Talia looked nervously from one male to the other. Great, she had a shark and a wolf preying on her. At least all the little one wanted was money.

She dreaded to think what the big one wanted.

"Ten?" she said, raising one eyebrow. *As normal as possible*, she reminded herself. *As normal as possible*. "I know you've done your homework. This issue is worth five, tops."

"Oh, come on. Give me eight. It's in fine condition. Very fine, even."

She tried not to show her impatience. She wasn't up for this today but, for the detective's benefit, she had to pretend. Carefully, she pulled the comic book from its protective sleeve and laid it flat in her palm. Ever so gently, she thumbed through the pages. "It's very good plus, maybe fine if I stretch it a bit. The corners are blunted and there's some creasing on the cover. I'll give you seven," she said firmly.

Haggling was usually a game between the two of them but she couldn't have any fun with the detective looking on. Her voice was too high and her movements were stiff. She wished she hadn't jinxed herself by wondering where he was. His unexpected appearance was making her distinctly uncomfortable.

"All right. Geesh." Bobby sighed in disgust. "Seven bucks."

"Deal," Talia said. She used the opportunity to escape behind the counter. "Hold on, I'll get your money."

The detective wasn't ready to let it go so easily. He turned to Bobby, surprising her. It was the first time since they'd met that he'd paid more attention to somebody else in the room than her.

"So, kid. What makes Lady Midnight so popular?" he asked.

"Patroller likes her."

"Likes her how?"

"Duh." Bobby rolled his eyes. "Like a girlfriend."

Kinkade crossed his arms over his chest, considering that new bit of information. "But The Patroller's a good guy. I thought Lady Midnight stole things."

"She does but she's not totally evil," the boy explained. "She doesn't hurt people and sometimes she helps Patroller."

"She helps Patroller," Kinkade said softly. "Wouldn't that be nice?"

Talia patently refused to acknowledge the detective's insinuations. She marked down the transaction in her record book and retrieved the money from the cash register for her young client. She loved the kid but it was time for him to go. "You better hurry, Bobby. I think the bus is about ready to leave."

"Thanks," he said as he stuffed the money into his pocket. He turned to hurry away, but stopped long enough to look over his shoulder at the detective. "You should read it sometime."

"I will, kid," Kinkade said. He stuck his hands deep in his pockets and watched the last of the kids get on the bus. Only once they were all aboard did he finally turn to face her.

Talia suddenly wanted the energetic crowd back. Without the kids as a buffer, she and the detective were too alone — even with Sadie still in the room. Her stomach tightened when he emphasized their intimacy by leaning toward her. He settled his elbows on the glass countertop and eyed her speculatively.

Suddenly, she found it hard to breathe. The room seemed to close in on her and she took a step back. He was too close for comfort. She didn't like having him here in her territory. She was supposed to be safe here. He watched her reaction closely. "Why don't you just wrap that up for me?"

"Wrap what up?"

"Lady Midnight."

The way he said it was unmistakable and it unnerved her even more. Was that the real reason for this visit? Was he here to wrap her up in handcuffs and cart her off? Had he found evidence against her?

"What are you doing here?" she blurted.

"Buying a comic book."

She gave him a long, hard look. A five o'clock shadow emphasized his ragged, tired look but she knew better than to let down her guard. His temper might be reined in but his frustration was still running wild. She could see it in his eyes.

He was here about last night.

He was here because of Roger.

Her fingers curled into fists. Why couldn't he just let it go? The man was as bad as a dog with a bone. The robbery, she could understand, but he had no business prying into her private affairs. She wanted him out of her shop and out of her life. "That will be ten dollars," she said impatiently.

"Ten? What the..." He suddenly stood upright and pointed at the door where Bobby had just left. "You just told him it was worth five."

"What can I say? Inflation is an evil thing."

His eyes narrowed. "I'll give you seven-fifty. That way you make a profit."

"Nine."

"*Nine?*" He raked a hand through his hair. "Ah, hell. Here's eight bucks."

He pulled his wallet out of his back pocket and plopped the money down on the counter. "I'm here to apologize, damn it."

Talia blinked. The words sounded so foreign coming off his lips. "Apologize?" she said at last.

"Yeah, I was out of line last night."

He was serious. She looked at him in disbelief and felt her defenses waver. He couldn't be nice to her. She couldn't fight him if he was nice to her. He reached up to rub the back of his neck in a gesture similar to her own and the tense ache in her belly slid dangerously lower.

"Can we talk alone?" he asked. He nodded toward Sadie who was watching them unabashedly.

Alone?

Talia looked over at her assistant. She wanted desperately to keep her around for moral support but this was one discussion she didn't want Sadie to overhear. She still hadn't told her friend the abridged version of what had happened last night and she certainly didn't want to confess her flirtation with Roger with the detective prodding her in the back.

She closed the cash register drawer. "Let's go in the other room."

He led the way and she followed him apprehensively. It didn't matter why he was here; the man just plain made her nervous. He was too big, too curious. Too...too male.

For all their intention to talk, once they entered the more private room, they both fell silent. Kinkade stuffed his hands into the pockets of his trench coat and Talia folded her arms across her chest. They eyed each other carefully.

He looked as rumpled as she felt. His brown hair was mussed, his raincoat was wrinkled and dark circles underlined his eyes. As unwise as she knew it would be, her fingertips itched to touch him.

She'd never seen him look so dark and sexy.

"Listen," he finally said. "Last night wasn't a good night for either of us. I don't usually work the night shift, so I was cranky to begin with. Then I had to deal with that über-bitch, Lydia Thorton. I figured I'd drawn the crap job of the night."

His dark gaze suddenly met hers dead-on. "But then I found you there. I wasn't ready for that."

Talia swallowed hard. He was doing it again. Remorse and shame weighed upon her heavily. "I wasn't expecting to see you either."

"No shit." He looked away and a muscle ticked in his jaw. "Once I found you on the premises, I had to treat you the way I did. I'm not apologizing for doing my job. I'm sorry about what happened at your car."

The honesty in his words surprised her. He meant it. As far as apologies went, it wasn't the sweetest she'd ever heard but she doubted Riley Kinkade apologized for much. "You had no right to talk to me like that," she said quietly.

"I know." His pockets bulged as his hands curled into fists. "It's just that the thought of you with that old guy hacks me off."

The proprietary tone made her toes curl. "Why? My love life isn't any of your business."

His look nailed her where she stood.

That look said everything she needed to know. He wanted her, case or no case. Her knees went weak. This man was dangerous to her in every possible way.

Because she wanted him back. Desperately.

She just couldn't let herself be susceptible to him. He was a cop, through and through. She couldn't let him get to her. If she did, he'd take her straight to jail.

"Fine. Whatever." She waved her hand in front of her face as if it didn't matter. "I accept your apology. Go home with a clear conscience."

Her nonchalance backfired.

"Damn it, woman!" he suddenly exploded. "You make me so crazy."

He came at her and her self-preservation instincts flared. If he touched her, she was a goner. Her resolve simply wasn't that strong. She bolted but he caught her by the arm before she could escape. Her heart pounded wildly in her chest. She was too tired and vulnerable for this. She struggled when he caught her chin but the look in his brown eyes made her resistance melt.

"I'm trying to say I'm sorry," he said gruffly. "Let me, damn it, or I won't be able to sleep at all."

His face just made her ache. He was so tired, he looked haggard. His eyes were bleak and dark whiskers covered his chin. Everything inside her screamed at her to invite him upstairs. She was tired, too. "Haven't you been home yet?"

"No, I had to go back to the station and start on the report."

The police report. Her stomach dropped. "Did you have to put me in there?"

"Yeah. Why do you think it was so hard to write?"

Her heart thudded once, then twice. He wanted to protect her. As much as he might try to deny it, she knew it to be true. She'd seen it when he'd protected her from Lydia. He'd stepped right in front of her and had used his body as a shield against the woman's wrath.

Talia's mouth went dry. He was vulnerable to her, too.

Suddenly, she realized how close he was standing. She could feel his body heat radiating toward her. The sensation was so appealing, she found herself drifting toward him to ward off the chill that still racked her body. He could warm her; she knew he could set her on fire.

The jingling of the doorbell made both of them jump. Somebody entered the shop and she jerked away from the detective. Her breaths were short and her pulse was fast. Closing her eyes, she reached for her sanity. Talk about good timing; she'd nearly let herself do something stupid. Composing herself, she turned to her customer, sure she'd find an eight-year old who'd forgotten something.

The person she found was no child.

"Brent." She felt as if somebody had just thrown a bucket of cold water on her. Of all the people in the world, he was the last person she needed to see right now. What was he doing here?

"Hey, Tally." He looked at the other man in the room and his attitude cooled. "Detective."

"Harrington." Kinkade's tone was like ice.

Talia felt her apprehension grow. And she'd thought the tension in the room had been unbearable when it had just been the two of them.

"Found my wife's cat yet?"

"We're working the case."

Brent's eyebrows rose dramatically. "You must be busy. I heard the Thortons were hit last night, too."

Talia felt Riley stiffen even though he was two feet away.

"There was an incident last night at the Thorton residence," he said. "We're looking into it."

"Looking into it," Brent said. He clicked his tongue as if that just wasn't enough. "The newspaper is saying that we've got a serial thief on our hands—the New Covington Cat Burglar.

Any idea on when you'll actually be tracking the perpetrator down or is that too much for me to ask?"

Talia winced. What did Brent think he was doing? She glanced at Kinkade. His jaw was set and his eyes had narrowed to slits.

"We're looking at similarities between the two cases but we haven't determined if there's a connection yet. Be assured, I'll let you know if we do."

Brent let out a comical laugh. He set down the box he carried and planted his hands on his hips. "You don't see any connections? I'm a simple civilian but even I can see the similarities."

He held up his fingers and started ticking them off. "One, in both cases a valuable antique was taken. Two, Roger Thorton and I travel in the same circles. Three... Well, hell, three could be Talia. She was at both our houses when the robberies occurred."

Talia's heart lodged in her throat. Oh, God! Had he figured it out? Had she been so careless that even he could see it?

"Me?" she said, struggling to find a way to defend herself. "What about...*you*? Or Shelli? Or Edward Jones, for that matter. You were all at both parties."

She'd taken a step forward but Kinkade smoothly moved in front of her. "I've already talked to your wife about what she witnessed at the Thorton party but you've been harder to catch. Where did you disappear to this morning, Harrington? Nobody seemed to know."

"I was up in the attic of my house." Brent rolled his eyes. "And to think I'm relying on you to find my Mène."

Instinctively, Talia reached out and caught Riley's arm. The tension in his muscles was tactile. He was exhausted and she could feel his patience crumbling. She knew how he felt. He looked down sharply at the feel of her hand on him but she ignored him. "What's in the box, Brent?"

"It's my donation."

She looked at him in confusion.

"For your foundation's little auction?" he said. He shook his head impatiently. "You said you'd come by today to pick it up but I got tired of waiting."

"Oh, that." She'd forgotten his promise to donate but there was no way in hell she would have dropped by his house to pick anything up. "You didn't need to bring it by. I could have sent somebody for it."

He smiled slickly. "Now what fun would that have been?"

Talia felt Riley's muscles pop under her grip. He took a step forward, but then cursed under his breath. "Hell, this is your business. I should—"

She panicked. He couldn't leave now!

She didn't want to be left alone with the Turd. She didn't want to be left alone with either of them but if she had to pick and choose...

Instinctively, she reached for the one she wanted to stay.

* * * * *

Riley stopped mid-sentence when he felt cool fingers wrap around his. At once, he was hit by two impressions. One, she shouldn't be able to get that close to him. He wore a gun. If she could catch his hand, she stood a good chance of grabbing his weapon if she wanted.

It was the second impression, though, that rocked him back on his heels. She didn't want to be alone with this creep. He didn't know why but, whatever the reason, it wasn't good. He'd been told that they didn't get along but this was something different. Something more.

His protective instincts surged and he wrapped his hand tightly around hers. Her fingers were so cold, he automatically pulled her closer.

"You should what?" Harrington asked.

I should kick your ass, Riley thought.

Going with his gut, he carefully hid his and Talia's clasped hands in the folds of his coat. "I should take a look in that box, too," he said.

The look on Harrington's face almost made him laugh. The guy definitely didn't like the fact that he was sticking around for Show and Tell. Talia, on the other hand, seemed to visually relax.

What in the hell?

"I'm interested to see what you've brought, Brent," she said, her tone distinctly *dis*interested.

"You can look at it later." Harrington's pretty boy face turned hard as he watched the two of them standing so close together. "I can see you're busy right now."

Riley stood up a little straighter at the silent challenge. "What's in the damn box?"

"Oh, enough already," Talia said, coming out of her shell. "I'll just look and see."

She tugged at her hand and Riley reluctantly let her go. Everything inside him told him to plant himself between her and Harrington but she walked to the box and began opening it. Pretty Boy moved forward to help and Riley clenched his fists together to stop from grabbing him by the nape of the neck.

"Oh, my," Talia said as she began lifting wooden figurines out from the protective popcorn padding. She threw a confused look at her donor, but then seemed to shrug. Like a pleased little girl on Christmas morning, she began lining the figures up on the counter. "Brent, these are beautiful. Are they African?"

She seemed to genuinely appreciate what Harrington had brought for her but Riley wasn't buying it. He knew the guy's type. Charity wasn't in his nature. There had to be something more to it. He looked at the carvings closely. There was something about them but he couldn't quite put his finger on it. The figurines ranged in size from little to big. They looked like a tribe of men with stubby bodies and bulb-shaped heads.

"They're fertility symbols," Harrington said.

Riley watched the guy like a hawk. He saw the grin that pulled at the cocky bastard's lips and he knew.

He knew and, before he could stop himself, he pictured Harrington using them. On Talia. He could see him bending her over the counter...hiking up her skirt...pulling down her panties...lubing her up...

Riley lost it.

He had the creep by the lapels before he could wipe that nasty smirk off his face. "What the fuck do you think you're doing?" he said, his voice like steel.

Harrington's hands came up as he was caught off guard. "Man, get off me! What's wrong with you?"

Riley jammed him up against the glass counter. He couldn't help the fury that seethed inside him. "Is this some sort of joke? Did you think it would be funny watching her auction off a box of butt plugs in front of a packed house?"

"Butt plugs?" Talia said with a gasp. A sickly green color flooded her face and she dropped the one she'd been examining like a hot potato.

Her innocent reaction made Riley all the hotter.

"What kind of a sick bastard are you?" he growled.

"Riley, don't," she cried.

He wasn't ready to ease up. He had Harrington off balance and he wanted to mess him up bad. Pretty Boy didn't look like he'd gone through many street brawls in his life but he sure did know how to play dirty.

Was this the kind of shit he liked to pull on her? No wonder she went pale every time his name was mentioned. The idea of her dealing with the son of a bitch alone...

Riley saw red.

"Listen," he snarled. "I don't know what the deal is between you two but, from now on, you stay away from her. If I catch you harassing her like this again, I'll take you down to the station so quick, you'll think your ass is on fire."

He shoved the man away and he stumbled before he regained his balance. His nose was the first thing that found its place. It went straight up in the air as he straightened his tie.

"If anyone is charged with anything, it will be you for police brutality," Harrington said huffily. "Are you forgetting who you work for, Detective? Aren't you supposed to be finding a stolen possession of mine?"

Riley nearly snapped before he felt Talia's fingers take hold of the back of his jacket. She was too close again but her touch had a message. Harrington's face needed rearranging but now wasn't the time or place to do it. Slowly, he unclenched his fists. "I work for the citizens of New Covington, Mr. Harrington. All of them."

"Brent, thank you for the...well, the 'collection'," Talia said calmly, desperately trying to keep the peace. She pulled hard on Riley, making him step back. "I doubt that I'll use them at the auction but I might have a buyer who'd be interested."

Harrington smoothed his jacket, trying to regain his polished look. He scoffed. "What the fuck do I care about your crappy little auction?"

Riley's blood pressure skyrocketed but the guy had already turned and walked out the door. "That son of a bitch!"

"That's what I like to call him."

He spun around, still itching for a fight. "What the hell was that? Why would he bring you something like that?"

He watched Talia closely, hoping he wasn't going to see any of her tells. He was beginning to pick up signals when she was lying but for once he didn't want to see any of them.

Her face was pale but she met his gaze. "He likes to do things that unsettle me. It's unfortunate but I've become used to it."

It was the truth but it pulled at Riley even harder. "What kind of things?"

Her lips thinned into a flat line and her gaze flickered away.

"Sexual things?" He erupted. "God damn it! Him, too?"

"Quiet!" she hissed. Her gaze flew to the doorway that opened into the adjoining room.

"Just how many men are you fucking, Talia?"

She turned on him with fire in her eyes. "I am *not* sleeping with him."

"But you want to." Riley felt sick at the certainty that filled his gut. "What is it with you and married men?"

He wanted to shake some sense into her. She was worth more than that. Why couldn't she see it?

Her jaw dropped open in shock but she advanced on him like a warrior princess. "That's not fair, Kinkade! It wasn't fair last night and it's not fair now. I don't want anything to do with that man. He disgusts me!"

Riley began to stalk around the room. He didn't like it. He didn't like how they'd looked at each other. He didn't like the body language. He didn't like the intimacy in the way Harrington harassed her and he especially didn't like the way she didn't fight back.

Every time he went at it with her, she was right there in his face. Toe-to-toe. He liked seeing her that way a whole lot better.

Fuck!

He dragged a hand through his hair. He was sick of the position this case had put him in. She was a witness and a potential suspect. He wasn't supposed to be getting involved in her personal life but, damn, he wanted to.

The woman needed a keeper.

"Who's this pervert buyer?" he asked, turning on her again. The anger burning in his chest refused to let loose. "Who do you know who collects old sex toys?"

She went white. "He's not a pervert! He...he collects African art."

Riley stopped pacing. Truth or lie? He didn't want to know.

Rolling his shoulders, he tried to let go of his tension. He was tired and it was beginning to make him dizzy. Taking a deep breath, he walked over and stood beside her. Bracing his hands on the counter, he looked at the set of grown-up toys. They stirred up all kinds of conflicting emotions.

Hell. He shouldn't do this.

But he had to.

He nodded toward the box. "If your 'African art' collector doesn't want them, I'll take them."

She looked at him in shock. "You'll what?"

"I'll take them." Unable to stop himself, he reached out and caught her by the chin. "There's no way on God's green earth that Harrington is going to get them back.

"I don't trust him with them. Or with you."

Chapter Ten

The following week was the worst of Talia's life.

She'd thought that Kinkade's reaction to finding her and Roger together had been bad. Little had she known that he'd just be the start of it. Rumors abounded throughout New Covington. Nasty, hurtful rumors. She heard murmurings at the beauty parlor, the post office and even a wedding she attended. Lydia was doing her best to drag her name through the mud.

And she was doing a good job of it.

Talia took a drink of wine and curled her feet up underneath her on the sofa. She sat in candlelight to ease the pounding in her head. She'd taken a long, hot shower but nothing was helping. She felt miserable.

Today had been especially bad. Lydia's minions had lined up to take their shots. It was as if they'd planned a strategic, orderly attack. Ramona Gellar had started things. She'd marched right into the shop this afternoon and started screaming at her. Talia had been so surprised, she hadn't been able to fight back. If Sadie hadn't been there, she didn't know what she would have done.

Good old Sadie. Talia felt tears press at her eyes. Her assistant hadn't approved of the latest development in her relationship with Roger but she wasn't one to judge. She was a good, stalwart friend with a swift right foot. She would have kicked Ramona out of Coolectibles if she'd needed to. Fortunately, it hadn't come to that.

Talia let out a choked laugh. Too bad Sadie hadn't been with her tonight. She could have used the backup.

The meeting of the Council on the Arts had been an utter disaster. Edward Jones had gotten into the fray this time. He'd practically made an announcement to the entire Board. Once Brent had gotten wind of the news, it had been all over.

She closed her eyes, feeling absolute remorse. She'd never felt more tortured in her life and there was nothing she could do about it. Everything they were saying was true. She'd brought this down on herself.

With a shaky breath, she leaned back against the cushions of the couch. She'd made herself fodder for the rumor mill. It didn't matter that she could tell everyone of Brent's philandering ways, Ramona's failed visit to an alcohol treatment center or Edward's penchant for wearing women's clothing. No matter how they behaved, she couldn't bring herself to sink to their level.

She contemplated the reflection of a candle's flame dancing against the wall. Life was so ironic. She was at an all-time low whereas her alter ego had become something of a cultural icon. The headlines were full of the New Covington Cat Burglar's daring deeds.

She'd already hidden money from the professor's sale of Lydia's bracelet in her safety deposit box with the take from the animalier heist. It was counterintuitive, really. Whereas "hot" property was usually difficult to sell on the black market, anything associated with the New Covington Cat Burglar was going like hotcakes. Winston said that he'd never seen anything like it.

Talia watched the wine swirl around in her glass. Life at the top wasn't without its problems, though. Mainly a big, six-foot-two problem, if she guessed right. Kinkade wasn't going away.

She'd caught him following her all week long.

He was hunting her like prey and he wanted her to know it. He was probably out there right now, biding his time. Waiting for her next move. Studying her...

The phone suddenly rang. She jerked in surprise and wine sloshed onto a throw pillow. Muttering under her breath, she set down the glass and reached for the receiver.

"Hello?" she said as she blotted the pillow with a tissue.

"Hey, sis."

"Adam!" Talia said, her head coming up. A delighted smile spread across her face. It was a relief to hear from her brother. It had been too long since they'd talked and she needed the distraction. "How was your trip?"

"It was good but you know Seattle. It rained the whole time I was there." He let out a laugh. "I suppose that helped me concentrate on work, though. I made some progress on the acquisition."

She felt a bittersweet twang somewhere around her heart. "Dad would be so proud of you. He always wanted to take the company bicoastal."

"Yeah, well, it was a good idea. I'm just following through on it. Before I'm done, we'll be global."

Adam wasn't one to be modest, but why should he be? Under his leadership, Sizemore Appliances had increased its profits by fifteen percent even though the market conditions weren't ideal.

"Are you going to be in Boston for a while?" she asked. "Maybe I could drive down and spend a weekend. I've been craving some clam chowder."

And some friendly company. The idea of getting away for a weekend was more than appealing. She needed time to think. She needed to get away from the pressure and the questioning looks in order to do that.

"That would be nice. It's time we got caught up with each other."

"I'd say. I haven't seen you for over a month."

"So what's going on with you?"

"With me?" Her life was in the slow lane compared to his.

Her brother cleared his throat uncomfortably and she went on the alert. Something was off. He never asked her questions like that.

"What is it, Adam?" she asked.

"I've just been hearing some things. Rumors, really. I'm sure they're not true."

She went still. Oh, God. Please not this. Things were bad enough. She leaned forward on the sofa. She had an unexpected ache in her stomach. "What rumors?"

"About you and Roger Thorton," he admitted.

Her stomach cramped and she felt sick. No. This couldn't be happening.

"Lydia called me," he said. "She was very upset."

Lydia. Fury began rolling through Talia's veins. She'd known the woman wouldn't just let it lie. She'd thought that she'd just stick to the New Covington rumor mill, but no. She'd gone for the jugular. "Lydia tracked you down in Boston to tell you that?"

"Yeah, and I'd just gotten in from that long flight. It was really hard to hear what she had to say but then I got to thinking. Well, Roger always did have a thing for you. You haven't had anybody in your life for a while and I thought that maybe…"

Talia was torn between anger and shock. She was livid with Lydia but Adam's comment about Roger unsettled her. "You saw it, too?"

"Saw what? Uncle Roger eyeing you?" He paused. "Then it's true?"

"No," she blurted. Dismay immediately consumed her. Now she was lying to her family? She raked a hand through her damp hair. "Yes. No… It wasn't like that."

"So you didn't sleep with him?"

Family or not, her sex life was private. Years ago when she'd had questions about her brother's relationship with Felicia Thorton she hadn't pried. Not once. "It's nobody's business," she said quietly.

Adam let out a low curse and she knew that her secret was out. One of her secrets, at least.

"Sis, I know that things between Lydia and Roger haven't been good for quite some time but you're playing a dangerous game."

He didn't know the half of it.

"Lydia has always been good to me," he continued. "I can't defend your actions to her."

"I realize that," Talia said. It had always been a point of contention between them. As smart a businessman as Adam was, he was naive when it came to the social scene. Lydia had seen that weakness and used it to her advantage. "Divide and conquer" had been her strategy. She'd made sure that Adam had never been around when she'd torn into his sister. She'd even gone so far as to pamper him like a beloved aunt. For all Adam's good points, he'd never been able to see what the woman was doing.

"As long as Roger treats you well, I'll stay out of it," he said, obviously trying to stay on impartial ground. "But next time, you need to prepare me better. You know I don't like getting caught in the middle."

Talia sighed. "I didn't put you in the middle. Lydia did."

And next on the list would probably be Felicia. And then Aunt Cordelia. She closed her eyes and rubbed her throbbing temple. Her headache had just become a migraine.

"Point taken." Adam's voice brightened. "All right, enough of that. Let's talk about something else. What's happening with the old foundation?"

Tension crept into Talia's shoulders. She loved the big sap but, as with all brothers, he knew how to get under her skin. "The old foundation." She put her heart and soul into their family's non-profit charity but he always acted like it was some sort of hobby.

She brushed her hurt feelings aside. With all that had happened, she knew she was just being touchy. At least he was showing interest. "We're having a fundraising event next month," she said. "You should come."

"A fundraiser? Wow, I remember when Dad used to drag us around to those things. I hated them."

"And I loved them."

"Yeah, well you didn't have to wear a tux. I swear, those things were out to choke me to death."

He let out a gagging sound and she laughed because she knew he wanted her to.

"Think you can brave strangulation just one more time?" she asked. "We're planning a charity auction. I promise it will be fun."

He groaned. "Do I have to?"

"It would be nice to have a strong Sizemore showing." And some much needed moral support.

"Are you that hard up for money? Can't I just send a check?"

She counted to ten. Adam was the last person she wanted to know about the seriousness of the foundation's fiscal problems. After all, it was her responsibility and she was the one who'd let things get into such bad shape. On the other hand, it frustrated her that he didn't keep better track of the foundation's status. She read all the annual reports for Sizemore Appliances. Their father had always put equal importance on both the family business and the charity. She sighed.

"A check would be fine. Brent Harrington cut off the Council for the Arts' support of the after-school program," she said. "I'm trying to find a way to fund it solely through the foundation."

Adam let out a long whistle. "I hadn't heard about that. Dad would be pissed. No wonder Lydia said I should check on you."

Talia went very still. *"Check on me?"*

"Well, you know… She's worried about you."

Oh, *really*. "Adam, what, exactly, did Lydia tell you?"

"Forget about it. I shouldn't have said anything and I don't want to get you all riled up again."

"Spill it."

He cleared his throat. "She just thought that you might be having some problems. You seemed to be pushing the foundation work pretty hard at her dinner party and then she caught you in bed with Roger. She thought that maybe...well, maybe you're missing Dad."

Talia choked as revulsion pushed its way into her throat. Of all the vile things to say! "That sick, underhanded, manipulative bitch!"

"Now, now. She didn't mean it that way. It's just that... God, I don't know how to say this. She and Ramona talked. They thought that maybe I should take the foundation work off your hands."

Talia sprang to her feet. "And why would you do that?"

"To ease the pressure on you."

"And?"

"With your state of mind, they don't think it's a good idea for you to be around kids."

Talia let out a strangled cry. "Adam!"

"Whoa. Hold on now. They said that, not me."

"But you're repeating it."

"And I shouldn't have. I'm sorry."

"That's it!" she snapped. "That's absolutely the last straw."

She'd been teetering on the edge of a big decision but it had just been taken out of her hands. There was no question now as to what she should do.

"Talia, what's going on with you? You're not acting like yourself."

"There's nothing going on with me," she said tightly. Nothing a little nighttime thievery wouldn't cure. "I'm just fed up with life in New Covington. Your buddy Lydia is making life hell for me. I can't believe you listened to her sick lies."

"I'm sorry," he repeated. "She's obviously just lashing back. I trust you with the foundation. You know I do."

"You'd better."

"Hey, about that visit. Why don't you come next weekend? It sounds like some time off would be good for you."

"Fine. I think I'm going to need to get out of town around then anyway."

"Wait! Now, you've got me worried."

"I'll see you soon, Adam. Welcome home. And don't worry about the foundation. I've got things well in hand."

Talia slammed down the receiver but her mind was already elsewhere. Oh, yes. She'd made her decision. Guilt was no longer a problem. Lydia Thorton and her cronies deserved whatever they got.

And a world of hurt was about to descend upon them.

"The New Covington Cat Burglar," she said, letting the words roll off her tongue. "It's got an awfully nice ring to it."

* * * * *

A month later, Talia stepped out of the shower and reached for a towel. Winter had New Covington firmly in its grip and the air in the bathroom was downright chilly. Briskly, she rubbed the terrycloth over her skin.

"That will teach you to work on a night with temperatures below freezing," she muttered to herself.

She was still learning the tricks of her new trade. Hiding in the bushes behind Edward Jones' house for two hours had been torturous. It had been necessary, though, because tonight had been the night. She'd been charting his activities for weeks. Every night, he'd let his dog out to do its business. The problem was, he didn't have a set time. On this, the night with no moon, she'd had to wait longer than ever to greet the friendly little poodle.

Over the weeks, she and Noodles had become friends, mainly due to the doggie treats she fed him. Tonight, she'd added a little something else to the mix—a leash. When Edward had opened the door to let Noodles back in, the pooch hadn't been waiting.

It had been such a simple, but effective, plan. She was finding that they worked the best. When Edward had wandered outside to look for his dog, she'd slipped into his house through the unlocked door. By the time he'd found Noodles chained to a bush, she'd been long gone with her loot.

"You're getting pretty good at this," she said to herself in the foggy mirror.

This was the third job she'd pulled since she'd made her decision and she was finding herself better suited to her new avocation than she ever would have expected. The planning stage was actually turning out to be fun. It exercised her mind and developed her creativity. Physically, she was more fit than she'd ever been in her life. She was taking rock-climbing classes and T'ai Chi. Her focus had never been clearer. The actual execution of her plans, though, was the climax. Almost literally. She got so excited when she was pulling a heist, she could hardly stand it.

The adrenaline. The danger. She was feeling the effects right now. Her face was flushed and her nipples were hard. And between her legs... She reached down to dry herself and groaned as the rough terrycloth created friction on her sensitive skin.

Her thoughts immediately rushed to Kinkade. It was hard for them not to.

The man was relentless.

He was everywhere. Every time she turned around, he was buying comic books at her store, talking to Sadie or questioning her about the latest robbery.

He knew.

Excitement sizzled through Talia and she squeezed her thighs against the ache.

He knew what she was doing; he just hadn't been able to prove it. Their cat-and-mouse relationship was escalating and she knew if she ever were to make the slightest mistake, he'd pounce.

A shiver of anticipation ran down her spine. She couldn't help but wonder what that would be like.

A sudden pounding on the downstairs door jerked her out of her steamy thoughts.

"What in the world?" She reached for her robe.

The doorbell started to buzz nonstop and she became alarmed. It was after midnight; something had to be wrong. She ripped open her apartment door and flew down to the stairs to the main showroom. Had there been an accident? Was it Adam? Sadie? Her footsteps slowed when she saw her visitors.

Police. Everywhere.

A jolt of fear hit her in the chest but her alarm eased. There were too many of them for it to be about someone else. They were here for her.

She took a steadying breath that faltered when she saw Kinkade at the head of the pack. So the time had come already. He was pushing things to the next level. Her control over her emotions wasn't what it should be but she reached for it now. She couldn't let him see any signs of weakness. She steeled herself and calmly walked to the door. A blast of cold air hit her when she opened it. "What do you want, Detective?"

"I've got a search warrant," he said roughly. "You finally made a mistake, baby."

He waved the piece of paper in front of her face and she gasped when he pushed his way into the store. A deluge of policemen followed, bringing snow and muck in with them. Soon Coolectibles was swarming with uniformed men.

"You can't just come in here like this!" She looked in dismay at the puddles already forming on the floor.

"The judge disagrees," Kinkade said as he shoved the warrant into her hand. Turning around, he addressed his men. "You two take this side. You three take the other. Hendricks, search her car. Keep your eyes peeled, everyone. We all know what we're looking for."

"This isn't right," Talia said sharply. She'd been prepared to tangle with him but she couldn't take on the whole department. She watched as the men fanned out and a scary thought occurred to her. What kind of authority had they been given? Were they at the bank, too? The stash of money was still in her safety deposit box, waiting for the auction so she could slip it in the foundation account unnoticed. She looked uncomprehendingly at the court order but was distracted when a silver umbrella stand teetered dangerously. "For God's sake, tell them to be careful."

"You're with me," Kinkade said as he grabbed her by the arm.

His grip was tight and uncompromising. It shook her out of her dream state. This was for real and it was serious. "No. Let go!"

He gave her a sharp look. "Don't mess with me tonight, sweetheart."

Her stomach dropped. His voice was dark and almost unrecognizable. She knew how it felt to be pushed to the edge of one's limits and he was at his.

She'd put him there.

"How did you get this order?" she demanded, instinctively going on the offensive. She couldn't let herself be intimidated. If he was going to bring her down, he was going to have to do it all by himself. She wasn't going to help.

"The Cat Burglar used a dog leash tonight—a new one."

She shook her head. "So? I don't have pets."

He smiled harshly. "And yet I've got a picture of you coming out of the mall last week with a Pet-n-Pet bag on your arm."

Damn!

"That's not proof," she sputtered. Her mind raced. "I was buying a gift."

"Yeah, right. Tell it to the judge."

He started pulling her to the staircase and she looked frenetically over her shoulder. The sight of so many people pawing through her inventory made her queasy. One didn't paw through collectibles! "What are you searching for?" she asked.

"I think you know the answer to that."

She stumbled on the stairs but his firm grip dragged her inexorably upward. She glanced at him again and her uneasiness intensified. His jaw was set and his eyes were flinty. The only time she'd seen him this angry was when he'd caught her with Roger.

God help her.

"I've had enough of this," he said in clipped tones as he pulled her into her apartment.

Her breath caught when he closed the door. He wasn't at the end of his rope. He'd lost his grip entirely. She stumbled away but he came after her and pushed her right up against the back of the couch. He loomed over her and, suddenly, oxygen seemed to be in short supply.

"This might be a little game to you but I'm tired of it," he said.

"I'm not playing any games." She managed to keep her tone calm but her nervous fingers dropped the search warrant and curled into the sofa for support. She wasn't lying. She'd never considered any of this a game.

"Stop with the crap, Talia. I know what you're doing."

"And I don't know what you're talking about." It was hard to stand up to him, especially with him looking so cold and uncompromising. Snow was melting in his hair and the wind had chapped his cheeks. He looked like a dangerous man with a short supply of patience.

His lips flattened. "Don't act dumb with me. I've been watching you for weeks."

Didn't she know it? The hair on the back of her neck rose. She could feel the charge in the air whenever he was around. It was like she'd developed her own internal alarm system that was set to detect only him. Right now, it was screaming.

"Watching me? You've been *stalking* me," she said boldly. "I should go to your judge and file a restraining order."

"I'm stalking you?" He raked a hand through his hair. "You're driving me fucking crazy but *I'm* harassing *you*."

"What would you call it? Every time I turn around, you're in my face."

"That's not the only place I'd like to be," he sneered, leaning even closer. "Enough with the lies and double-talk, Talia. You're caught. I've got you. Now, give me the truth. Why do you do it? Why do you steal? For once, just tell me flat out."

"You're out of your mind, Kinkade." His proximity was forcing her to arch back over the couch. The position unbalanced her even more than she already was and she reacted instinctively. She pushed hard against his shoulders but he didn't budge.

"I need to know and you owe me at least that much." He stepped closer until the tips of his wet shoes bumped against her bare toes. "Nothing about you makes sense. You don't fit any of the profiles. You're rich, so you don't need the money. You're kind to animals, you're polite to the elderly and Bobby, the comic book kid, thinks you're the bomb."

"I like kids," she said, her eyes flashing.

"Too bad you're such a bad role model."

Of anything he could have used as a weapon, that was the worst. Her temper flared. Before she could think better, her hand whipped up. He caught her wrist before she could make contact.

"Where is it?" he demanded.

"Where is what?" she snapped back.

He twisted her hand behind her back and drew her up tight against him. Their bodies sealed together from breast to thigh and Talia gasped at the suggestive contact. She tried to sidestep away but he took that last small step that scrunched her body between him and the couch. "You know what," he said, "The spyglass you took from Edward Jones' house tonight."

She fought to breathe. His thighs were rock hard against hers and his chest was wide. She began to feel claustrophobic as he blocked out everything else in the room. "I don't know anything about a spyglass," she said, struggling to keep control.

He let out a harsh laugh that rubbed his chest against her tight nipples. "Nah, you probably only know the year it was made, the battle it was used in and its value down to the precise penny. Jones said it was a valuable part of his Civil War collection."

Talia bit her lip as reactions rocked her system. Could he feel what he was doing to her? Was that why he was so close? To break her down?

Of course, it was.

"I'm sorry for Edward but I don't know what that has to do with me," she said, lifting her chin defiantly. Jones hadn't seen her. She hadn't left any traces behind. She knew it. She'd been very, very careful. They could test that leash all they wanted; they wouldn't find any prints.

Kinkade caught her by the chin and looked at her with those penetrating brown eyes. "It has everything to do with you. You're the New Covington Cat Burglar."

Her heart stopped.

When it kick-started a full minute later, it was in hyperdrive. "You *are* crazy."

"Am I?"

"Yes," she spat.

His hand slid silkily down to her throat. He watched her with hooded eyes as he measured her racing pulse. "If I am, I'm crazy like a fox."

Talia felt lightheaded. Make that a hungry fox. He'd been hunting her for weeks but, for the first time, she felt as if he might have her by the throat. Literally. She fought back the only way she could.

"That's right, Detective," she whispered hoarsely, "Leave a mark. It will only strengthen my case when I charge you and the NCPD with harassment and slander."

One side of his hard mouth curled upward. "It's not slander when it's the truth—and we both know it is.

"Just look at you, baby. You're the ideal candidate. You've got the brain for it and you know the art field inside and out." His voice dropped to an intimate tone. "Our little kitty cat only takes the best of the best."

Talia swallowed hard. His disconcerting touch was sending dangerous flares across her sensitive skin. "That proves nothing. I'm in the art business."

His thumb brushed the line of her jaw. "As much as I hate to admit it, Harrington was right about one thing—you run in the same crowd. You know all the victims."

She licked her lips. "That's purely coincidence."

"Yeah, right." His gaze swept over her and he reached out to touch her wet hair. "That's why you were a guest at two of the crime scenes."

"I told you. It's coinci—"

"Dence," he completed for her. "So you say. Rumor is that you've been asking people a lot of questions about their collections."

For a moment, she couldn't respond. Had she been more obvious than she'd thought? Had she given herself away? Wait a minute. "I've been asking for donations for a fundraiser for the after-school arts program. That's the reason I'm talking to people. Nothing more, nothing less."

He looked at her so hard, she got the feeling he was trying to look right into her very soul.

"Where is it?" he asked again. His voice had an element of steel to it that hadn't been there ten seconds ago. "Give me the damn spyglass."

She looked up at him bravely and refused to cave in. "I don't have it. I didn't take it."

His unwavering gaze dropped and she suddenly realized how little she was wearing. She hadn't had time to grab more than her robe when she'd heard the pounding on her door.

"I'm only going to give you one more chance," he said softly. "Where is it?"

"How many times do I have to—Kinkade!"

He'd warned her. In the flash of a split second, he'd reached out and caught the sash of her robe. With a quick tug, it came undone. She tried to cover herself but he was already pulling the material open, baring her.

"Tell me where it is," he demanded.

His eyes were hot on her naked flesh. Talia hardly heard the question as she struggled to pull the flaps of the robe together. Her breasts heaved as she pushed at him but he was like the Rock of Gibraltar. Hard and unmoving. She couldn't fight against his strength. She squirmed against the couch, unable to hide from his raking look.

"All right," he said on a note hardly louder than a whisper. "If you won't tell me, I'll have to look myself. Assume the position."

His hard hands settled on her waist, turned her around and bent her over so she was braced on the back of the couch. Her fingers sunk into the cushions as her mind raced. He wouldn't do this. He couldn't do this!

He flipped her robe up so it lay on her lower back and astonishment froze her. She wasn't wearing any panties. He could see everything!

Her entire body lurched when he suddenly shoved his cold hand between her legs.

"Kinkade!"

"This was your choice," he said. He held her still and began determinedly probing her pussy. "All you had to do was be honest with me."

"Don't!" she gasped. She was staggered by his aggressiveness. Her breath worked hard as she shifted, trying to get away from that shockingly intimate touch. "You can't."

"I can," he said gruffly. He pressed his leg between hers and widened her stance. "I've got a search warrant."

"Not for this, you don't!" His fingertips were probing all her crevices and valleys. Two fingers rimmed her opening and she cried aloud. No, this wasn't right! She couldn't let him do this. Those thick fingers suddenly penetrated her and her hips rolled. Oh, God! Unwanted pleasure raced through her. "I'll have you fired," she panted.

"I'd like to hear you tell the judge about this." He was breathing hard, too. His air rasped in and out of his lungs as he bent over her, holding her down with his weight. Talia shuddered. She'd pushed him too far and now there was no pulling him back. He was angry, betrayed and out of control. She'd known she'd have to face the consequences but she'd never dreamed they'd be like this.

"Have you got it hiding in a safe place?" he growled. "I always wondered if this was how you got away with the Thorton bracelet."

She tried to twist her hips away but those insidious fingers lodged deeper inside her. The pressure increased as they began stretching her, searching and seeking. The arousal she'd felt stepping out of the shower came back with a vengeance and, to her horror, her juices started flowing. She could feel the wetness dripping onto her thighs.

He groaned into her ear. "Tell me where you stashed it, baby."

She bit her lip to hold back a moan. "I can't," she said. "I didn't stash anything anywhere."

Her last word turned into a squeal when he used his other hand to flick her clit.

"Where?" he demanded.

"I won't talk to you like this. Get your fingers out of me!"

"Out of your pussy?"

"Yesssss."

"All right," he said with a rasp. "Maybe you've got it somewhere else."

His fingers left her abruptly but she went stock-still when she felt his touch move further upward between her legs. Her head whipped around and she looked at him helplessly. His face was like granite but a dark fire burned in his gaze.

"No," she whispered.

"Yes," he grunted.

His fingers trailed fire across her perineum and settled against the bud of her anus.

She frantically reached back and caught his arm but there was no escaping his scandalous touch. His free hand spread wide on her lower back, keeping her firmly in place. The pressure on her sphincter increased and she whimpered. Her body fought him momentarily before conceding to his strength.

Two fingers sunk knuckle-deep into her most private spot but it was too much. She let out a sharp cry and her fingernails bit into his forearm. He pulled one finger out but wiggled the other one deeper. Her mouth opened in a silent scream.

"Christ Almighty," Kinkade swore. He bent over her again, cocooning her body with his. "Where is it?" he growled into her ear.

Talia's eyes pressed tightly together. She couldn't think. She couldn't move. His free hand slid up her thigh and grasped her buttock hard. He kneed her legs open wider and spread her cheeks so he had better access. She felt his finger push harder against her resistance. He wanted her to submit.

Her legs gave out and she sagged onto the couch.

"Tell me the truth," he ordered. "Tell me everything."

"Stop," she begged.

"You don't want me to. Your pussy is dripping all over the floor."

She cried out. Her excitement was undeniable. Nobody had ever touched her there—and he wasn't just touching. He was *burrowing*. It felt absolutely wicked.

"Where is the spyglass, sweetness?" he asked. "It will be easier for you if you just tell me. You know I'm going to find it."

"Not there, you're not!"

"No, but I'm finding something else," he grunted as he inserted that second, insistent finger again.

Talia's neck arched. She felt positively overwhelmed. Any second now, she was going to break into a million pieces. "Oh, please."

His thumb slipped into her pussy and the double penetration sent her entire body shaking.

"Where...is...it?" he grunted.

His cock was grinding hard against her hip and she suddenly realized that he was in just as much torment as she was. "Riley," she moaned.

"That's it, baby. Give it to me."

"Ri-ley!"

A sharp tap made both their heads snap toward the door.

"Detective," a voice called. "We haven't found anything down here. Do you need help searching the apartment?"

"Fuck," Kinkade muttered.

"Ahhh," Talia cried. Not now!

"Hold on a second," he called.

She looked over her shoulder, fraught with incompletion. His smoldering gaze captured hers. It was full of lust and something else she couldn't quite interpret. She had to look away when he began pulling his fingers out of her. He moved so slowly, she could feel the friction along every millimeter of her internal flesh. She winced when she was finally left empty.

Kinkade recovered first. He quickly wiped his hand on his coat and reached for her. She was still too stunned to move. He peeled her off the couch and pulled the flaps of her robe together. She had to hold onto his shoulders for support as he tightened her belt.

He let out another soft curse and wiped the sweat off his brow as he moved to the door. Talia walked unsteadily around the couch and sat on it stiffly as he let his men into her apartment.

"Did you make any progress, sir?" Hendricks asked as he stepped inside.

Riley didn't answer. "Search every inch of this place with a fine-toothed comb."

Talia felt ready to shatter. She'd nearly given in to him.

And, unbelievably, she still wanted to.

She heard the men spread out but her internal radar kept Kinkade on-screen. He hadn't moved from the doorway and he was watching her like a hawk. She could feel it. She looked straight at her lap. At last, she heard his distinctive footsteps head to the kitchen. The sounds of water running and paper towels being torn soon followed. When he returned, he furtively wiped away the puddle of wetness she'd left on the floor.

Talia bit her lip. She was horribly embarrassed but that little display of intimacy was nearly her undoing.

She didn't dare look at him. With the way he'd left her, so close to the finish, she just couldn't. She was in too much distress. She'd thought it had been bad when Roger had left her on the edge of orgasm. That was nothing compared to this.

She wanted to roll her hips against the couch so badly, she could almost cry. Instead, she sat staring at her clenched fingers, waiting in agony for the men to finish their search.

It took hours—or so it seemed. Time had a way of standing still with Kinkade scrutinizing her every move and emotion.

At last, he had to walk away empty-handed.

His men came up with nothing.

Without a word, Talia ushered the policemen out of her apartment and away from her place of business. Kinkade stopped in the doorway as if to say something but she caught his arm and pushed him outside.

He wasn't one to be pushed. He caught her by the nape of the neck. She went still when he began gently massaging the tense muscles in her neck. Her heart thudded when she finally looked up into his eyes. They were dark and dangerous.

"I'll get you yet," he whispered.

Her muscles began to quake. "Good-bye, Kinkade."

"I thought we'd gotten to 'Riley'."

"Get out."

"Sweet dreams, baby."

She shut the door firmly behind him but a whimper escaped her as she locked it. He'd figured out what her weakness was. *Him.*

He'd be back to test that vulnerability again.

Gingerly, she turned and mounted the steps. Her pussy throbbed with every move she made and her anus felt disturbingly tender. By the time she made it to her bathroom, she was in agony.

The steam from the shower had disappeared long ago but she was heated from the inside out. Slowly, she bent over and opened a drawer.

"The one place a man would refuse to look," she said without humor as she pulled out a box of tampons. Digging deep, she found an Alvin Clark and Sons spyglass, *circa* 1860. She set it carefully on the vanity.

Hands shaking, she undid her robe and let it slide to the floor. Tentatively, she spread her legs. She stared at the spyglass and pictured Kinkade. Memories of how he'd touched her pulsed throughout her body. She let herself feel how his fingers had stroked her…how his breath had brushed her neck…how his palm had cupped her ass. Her pussy throbbed as it begged for penetration.

She gave it what it needed.

Closing her eyes, she pressed her fingers deep. They slid home and her groan echoed off the walls.

It just wasn't quite enough.

She took a deep breath.

"Riley," she groaned.

With one soft brush of her thumb against her clit, she finished what he'd started.

Chapter Eleven

A week later, Riley sat in a box seat of the New Covington Community Theater. A crowd of people mingled below, oblivious to his scrutiny. Hiding in plain sight was sometimes a good strategy. People rarely looked up but he could look down on them all he wanted. And he watched them closely, every single one of them. He was on guard for anything out of place, anything suspicious.

Something was brewing tonight. He could feel it. The hair on the back of his neck had been standing on end all day.

The Sizemore Foundation Charity Auction was *the* place to be on this unseasonably mild winter night. He knew how hard Sadie had worked on promoting the event and it looked as if her tireless efforts were paying off. The turnout was good. The upper crust was certainly all here.

The red carpet theme made the community theater look upscale and classy. People were wearing their Sunday best, although a few of the women looked as if they hadn't attended church for a while. The men were doing their best James Bond impersonations but some pulled it off better than others. Riley knew which group he fell into. He couldn't wait to get out of the monkey suit he'd rented.

A shiny silver head caught his attention in the first row and he felt the muscles in his shoulders tighten. Roger Thorton looked as if he'd been born in a tuxedo. The old fart looked comfortable and pleased as punch. Why shouldn't he? He was Lydia-less and probably thought he might get lucky again tonight.

Fat chance of that.

Riley forced himself to look away. He was here to work tonight, damn it. He needed to remember that. Everyone from the media to the mayor had come down on him and his captain for the "slowness" of the NCPD's response to the Cat Burglar robberies.

Slowness, hell. He'd been working his butt off for nearly two months.

He pulled at the tight collar of the tuxedo and forced himself to concentrate. Working fast wasn't going to solve anything. That was the way details got missed. The only way he was going to crack this case was the old-fashioned way—with hard work. If he had to suffer through old fools and dress like a penguin, so be it. He was more than ready for the payoff.

He let his gaze sweep the crowd one more time. Edward Jones and Ramona Gellar sat halfway back in the sea of seats. He'd come to the conclusion that those two were just hangers-on. No big threat there, although one of them had already been a victim.

The doors at the back of the theater swung open and his gaze shifted to catch the latest arrivals. Acid started burning in his stomach when he spotted Brent Harrington.

Now there was a threat.

"Son of a bitch," Riley muttered. His hands clenched into fists. He wished Talia hadn't stopped him from pounding the guy's face. Just one punch would have messed up that cocky smirk. Just one.

Heads turned as Harrington and his wife walked into the theater like the King and Queen of New Covington but Riley couldn't stand the sight. He glared down at the stage instead. He knew he was getting too personally involved in the case but he couldn't help it.

When it came to anything involving Talia Sizemore, he felt possessive. And why shouldn't he? Thoughts of her filled his working days and dreams of her consumed his nights.

The woman was rapidly becoming his obsession.

A wave of heat ran through him. Just look at what had happened the other night after the Edward Jones hit. If she ever reported what he'd done, his career was dead in the water. No search warrant gave him the right to paw at her pussy and stick his fingers up her ass.

But she'd liked it.

And that was the problem.

He shifted in his seat as the memories blistered his brain. She'd been hot, tight and unbelievably responsive. She'd enjoyed everything he'd done to her and he'd gotten off on it, too.

It made him hard just to think about it.

He ran a hand over his face and tried to clear his head. He had to get past this. This overpowering attraction between them was interfering with his work. He needed to put his personal feelings aside and do his duty. The fact that she turned his insides to mush was neither here nor there.

She was the key to breaking these cases wide open.

He knew that with every breath he took.

There were just too many "coincidences". She'd outsmarted him the other night but even smart people eventually made mistakes. Gut instinct told him it wouldn't be long until she slipped up.

That was why he was here tonight—to catch her when she fell.

The curtain behind him stirred and Riley glanced over his shoulder.

"Oh," a young boy said in surprise. "Sorry, mister."

Riley relaxed. The swarm of kids at the event had brought the stuffiness factor down a notch or two. "You looking for someone?" he asked.

"My mom was supposed to be sitting up here."

Sadie's kid. Riley looked at him with interest. He liked Talia's assistant. She'd always been friendly whenever he'd dropped by Coolectibles, which had been quite often over the past few weeks. Her son was a good-looking tweener—old enough to want to act cool, but young enough not to know how to hide his excitement about the auction. Like his mother, the boy nearly vibrated with energy.

Riley gestured to the seats below them. "Sadie traded seats with me. She's down there near the back of the theater. She said she wanted to be in the thick of things."

The kid glanced over the edge of the box seat. "That sounds like her."

"What's your name?" Riley asked.

"Linc." The boy pulled at the bow tie of his miniature tux as he sized him up. "Who are you?"

After skirting around New Covington's rich folk for so long, Riley appreciated the candor. He held out his hand. "I'm Riley Kinkade."

Linc looked at the offered hand uncertainly. "You're the cop that likes Talia?"

Riley paused but there was no getting around that question. Besides, if that's how Sadie looked at him, he could use it to his advantage. "Yeah, that's me."

He didn't like the kid's instinctive reaction. Linc looked ready to bolt. For the life of him, Riley didn't know why. Was it because the kid had a crush on her, too? Or was it because he was a cop? He hoped not. The force had been doing a lot of work within the school system to strengthen its relationship with New Covington's next generation. The goal was to earn kids' respect and encourage trust in the boys in blue—not scare them to death.

"Are you here to check up on me?" the boy suddenly blurted.

"Check up on you?" Riley asked in confusion.

"I've been doing the work, mister. I swear!" Linc began to breathe hard as he pointed unsteadily at the program balanced on Riley's thigh. "I designed that cover and I folded all of the programs. There were over five hundred of them."

"Hey, kid. Whoa! Settle down."

"I...I helped my mom decorate this place for tonight." Linc's breaths started to hitch. He grabbed the program and flipped through it. "Number 27. That's mine, too. I drew it and it's going to be auctioned off tonight."

Riley reached out and grabbed the boy by the arm before he fell down. He was nearly hyperventilating. "All right. Sit down, buddy."

He tugged Linc into the seat next to him and pushed him over until his head was between his knees. "Breathe."

"I'm...I'm...try-ing to do...what I'm s-supposed to do."

He patted the kid on the back. "Relax, kiddo. I'm not here to check up on you. I'm just here for the show."

"Re-Really?" Linc asked, risking a glance at him.

Riley palmed the back of his head and gently pushed him back down. "Come on, now. Inhale. Exhale."

He glanced at the cover of the program. Huh. He never would have guessed that an eleven-year-old had drawn it. It looked almost professional. He rubbed the kid's back and waited for him to calm down. After a moment or two, the boy took a deep, lung-filling breath. Riley felt the tense muscles under his hand relax.

After a moment, Linc glanced at him sheepishly. "You gonna push me back down if I try to sit up again?"

"Nah," Riley said with a chuckle. "We wouldn't want to wrinkle that fancy tux of yours."

Linc slowly sank back into the chair. "Sorry," he said. "I'm not usually that big of a wuss."

Riley let the statement go by without comment. The kid was embarrassed enough as it was. "Want to tell me about it?" he asked instead.

"About what?"

"Whatever trouble you're in."

Linc glanced at him sideways. "I thought you weren't here for that."

"I'm not."

The kid looked at him suspiciously but then shrugged as if he appreciated straightforwardness, too. "I got picked up for spraying graffiti. Working on this auction is part of my community service time."

Riley drummed his fingers on the back of the kid's seat. Things were becoming clearer. Little Linc had run astray of the law and he hadn't liked the nip in the butt he'd received in return. "Was it any good?" he asked.

"The time?"

"The graffiti." Riley held up the program. "Looks like you're not a half bad artist."

Linc shifted in his seat but one corner of his lips twitched and some of that excited energy returned. "It was pretty cool," he admitted. "I drew a big T-Rex. I'd never worked on that big of a canvas before."

"Canvas?"

"The wall of Covington Elementary next to the basketball courts."

"Ah." Riley supposed that if one wanted to draw a life-sized T-Rex, that was the place to do it. "Just couldn't resist?"

"Kind of." Linc shrugged. "I didn't have anything else to work on."

Riley paused. Now that was one he hadn't heard before. Graffiti artists were notorious for putting up their messages to mark their territory. Others did it maliciously to deface property. That wasn't what he heard going on here. He sat forward and braced his elbows on his knees. "What do you mean?"

"I used to go to the after-school art classes with Mr. Albright but they were canceled. I filled up my sketchbook at home and Mom wasn't around—"

"But the school wall was."

"Yeah."

Riley nodded. "You're just a man with restless hands."

Linc sat a little straighter in his chair. "That's right. That's what I am."

"So who's working your case?"

Their uneasy trust wavered as Linc shot him another look. "What do you need to know that for?"

"I thought I'd talk to the guy tomorrow when I go in to work. You know, put in a good word for you."

Linc's eyes widened. "You'd do that?"

Riley shrugged and looked around the theater. "Looks like you've been working pretty hard to me."

"I have."

"And are you going to keep working hard?"

Linc nodded fiercely.

"Are you going to paint graffiti again?"

The nod quickly switched directions. "Nuh-uh."

Riley nudged the kid with his shoulder. "You tell your mom to talk to me. She can give me the information I need."

Linc practically sprang out of his seat. "For real?"

"Why not?"

"I'll go tell her right now."

"But Linc..." Riley called as the kid sprinted for the staircase.

The boy spun around in his tracks.

"Next time you need something to draw on, use a napkin or something."

"Right." Linc smiled. "See you later, Kinkade. Watch for Number 27."

Riley settled back into his chair as he heard footsteps bounding down the stairs to the main floor. Poor kid. Idle time often spawned trouble but Sadie was doing a good job. Linc would turn out fine with his mother keeping track of his hide. There were other wayward little souls who weren't as fortunate.

The houselights dimmed and Riley's attention focused on the stage. It was about time this show got started. He'd been watching out for Talia ever since he'd arrived but she'd been frustratingly elusive. A flash of white in the wings caught his eye and, suddenly, his wait was over.

"Damn," he hissed when he got a good look at her.

He'd thought he'd been prepared for everything tonight but he hadn't been ready for *that*.

Applause filled the air as she walked to center stage but he couldn't move. She looked incredible. She was wearing a crisp, white, wrap-around top that made him think of Christmas. He knew what that snug material hid. One little tug on the bow at the side of her waist and a very nice present would be revealed. Two, in fact.

She came to a stop behind the podium at mid-stage but he couldn't take his eyes off of her. She turned slightly and a groan left his lips when he saw the way her leather skirt hugged her ass. The slit up the side came to nearly her hip. Long legs, firm breasts and a hidden treasure between her legs...

Did she lie awake at night looking for ways to torture him?

He rubbed his palms against the arms of his chair. He wanted to put his hands on her again like he'd never wanted anything in his life.

"Ladies and gentlemen," she said warmly. "Welcome to the Sizemore Foundation's First Charity Auction."

The smile she sent out to the crowd was so warm and inviting, it hurt. She'd never looked at him like that. Not even once. From the moment they'd met, everything between them had been strained.

"We're here tonight to show our support for something near and dear to my heart," she said. "My father created the

After-School Arts Program for Inner-City Schools nearly twelve years ago. I'm here to carry on his work."

Riley felt himself break out in a cold sweat. Would it really hurt that much to scratch this itch? Get it out of their systems? Ease the tension?

"The money raised tonight will be used to purchase much-needed supplies such as crayons, paints, ceramics..."

They both wanted to hit the sheets. If Hendricks hadn't knocked on her apartment door at precisely the wrong moment, he wouldn't even be asking himself these questions. He would have already nailed her.

"Art pencils, glue..."

Was he just prolonging the inevitable?

"Sketch pads and canvas paper..."

Because delayed satisfaction had never— His lustful thoughts skidded offtrack. Wait a minute. Had she just said *"canvas paper"*?

His attention focused.

"The funding will also be used to support teacher pay. Space rental. Heating bills. Electricity. But best of all, it will be used to put smiles on kids' faces."

Riley went still as a very dim lightbulb went on inside his head.

Oh, shit. Could it be?

"Will all the children who've participated in the after-school program please stand?"

Kids bounded out of their seats in every corner of the audience but his gaze sought out one very energetic little boy at the back of the room. One little boy who hadn't had any paper to draw on because his class had been canceled...

"These children are the reason why we're here tonight," Talia said, her voice catching. "They deserve to experience all the joys and wonders of art. Let's make sure they can."

"We love you, Miss Sizemore!" a group in the back yelled.

Riley became entranced when Talia's chin quivered.

"I love you, too," she said hoarsely. She quickly wiped away a tear that coursed down her cheek.

The crowd responded with the thunder of applause and he sagged back in his chair. The lightbulb in his head was now so bright, it was blinding. "I'll be damned."

He'd just figured out the "why".

"I hope everyone has fun tonight," she said, smiling bravely. "So sit back, grab your paddles and be prepared to do some serious bidding! Thank you!"

She waved to the crowd as she walked offstage and Riley watched until those long legs of hers disappeared behind the curtains. He was dumbfounded. Why hadn't he seen it before? It was so clear. He'd just been coming at things from entirely the wrong angle.

Ah, hell.

The altruism of it all made him ache.

What was he supposed to do now?

* * * * *

Talia's legs felt shaky as she climbed the stairs to the box seats. She'd never expected to draw such a large crowd. Sadie had passed her the message backstage that the event was a sellout—the first for the community theater in three years. Speaking in front of so many people had been daunting and her excitement was still warring with her nerves.

She hoped that she hadn't come off as too needy—or too greedy. She couldn't quite remember what she'd said. She just wanted things to go well tonight. The auctioneer's voice came over the sound system and her footsteps quickened. At least her part in the show was over. All she had to do now was sit down and let the fast-talking man take over.

She finally made it to the landing. Not wanting to disturb anyone, she quietly opened the curtain. The lights were dimmed but she was surprised when, instead of Sadie, she saw a man sitting in the seat next to hers. *Overflow,* she thought happily. "Excuse me," she whispered.

The man politely stood and turned. Talia smiled at him as she moved toward her seat but shock knocked the wind out of her when she recognized Detective Kinkade. For a moment, she was speechless. He looked so good in that tux, her mouth watered but, at the same time, disappointment and fury rushed through her.

"Riley," she said flatly. Why wouldn't he leave her alone for at least this? Couldn't he give up the constant harassment for just one night?

"Hello, Talia."

The tone of his voice threw her—as did the look on his face. For once, he wasn't angry or aggressive. Instead, he sounded tired and maybe a little bit concerned.

An unexpected feeling of empathy caught her but she pushed it away. That was tough. She was tired, too. She was tired of the way he'd steamrolled over her life and she wouldn't stand for it. Not tonight. Police detective or not, she'd have his head if he jeopardized this fundraiser. "What are you doing here?" she demanded.

"I heard so much about this foundation of yours, I thought I'd come check it out." He cocked his head. "I'm glad I did. It's helped me understand you better."

The look in his eyes was so piercing, she actually took a step back. Understand her? It looked as if he was trying to see right inside her mind.

She felt goose bumps pop up on her arms. His behavior was starting to disturb her.

"This event is very important," she said in a raw voice. "It's for the kids. So help me, if you do anything to spoil this, I'll have your badge."

"Easy, baby," he said, holding his hands up in front of him. "I have no intention of making a scene."

"Riley," she warned. She was upset with herself when tears pressed at her eyes.

"I'm not here to make trouble, Talia," he said. "Sit down."

He caught her by the elbow and heat ran up her arm and into her chest. She was embarrassed when she felt her nipples stiffen but, like him, she didn't want to garner any attention. She let him lead her to her seat but she sat down stiffly.

He sat down beside her and, in typical male fashion, spread his legs wide. His pant leg brushed against her ankle and a sizzle ran up her calf. She quickly crossed her legs the other way. She felt his hot gaze immediately clap onto the free display of thigh offered up by the slit in her skirt and arousal warmed her belly. Disgusted with herself, she planted her feet flat on the floor and pressed her knees together.

She didn't like this side of him. She could deal with the bull in the china shop but this quiet, contemplative side was scary. She didn't know what he was thinking. She didn't know what he was planning.

And she didn't know how she was going to react once he made his move. After the other night, she couldn't trust herself around him. Her body would betray her every time.

She accidentally bumped against his arm. She quickly scooted away but there wasn't far she could go. He had the shoulders of a linebacker.

"Relax," he sighed. "Watch your auction. We'll talk when it's over."

Talk? About what?

Arthur's tea set was on the block but, no matter how hard Talia concentrated, she couldn't ignore Kinkade. He had her nerves singing and he seemed uncomfortable, too. She'd never seen him so contemplative. He wasn't paying any more attention to the auction than she was.

"What is up with you tonight?" she finally asked.

He shook his head. "Let's not get into it now."

He expected her to suffer until he finally dropped the bomb? No way. "Tell me," she insisted.

He let out a low curse. "I've got a problem," he admitted. "A big one."

She didn't know why that concerned her but it did. "What is it?"

"You."

She fell silent. He was a problem for her, too.

He finally looked at her with heavy lidded eyes. "Remember the question I kept asking you the other night?"

She felt her cheeks flame under that steady, challenging stare. "You found what you were looking for?"

His gaze glittered darkly but he cleared his throat. "No, the other question."

She shrugged uneasily. She couldn't remember the other question but that didn't surprise her. "Where is it?" was still ringing in her ears.

Her pussy throbbed every time she heard it.

"I know why you steal," he said softly.

She came back to Earth with a thud.

"I finally figured it out, baby."

Talia felt the blood drain from her face. Suddenly lightheaded, she fought the weakness that swept through her. He couldn't know. This was just a new tactic. He was fishing. "Must we go through this again tonight?" she said tightly. "If you haven't noticed, I am busy."

Applause rang out as the auctioneer yelled "sold" and she determinedly looked at the stage, dismissing him. She nearly jumped out of her skin when he caught her chin and redirected her attention back to him.

"Do you realize how much you light up whenever you talk about kids?" he asked quietly.

She flinched when he brushed his thumb across her jawline. "I'm very proud of the work the Sizemore Foundation does," she said.

"You should be. You've helped a lot of people. Linc, for one."

A caution sign went up inside her.

An all-too-knowing light gleamed inside Riley's eyes but it wasn't mocking. It was the intimacy of a shared secret.

A secret he couldn't possibly know.

A feeling of dread overcame her.

"He told me how he'd gotten in trouble without the after-school program there."

Oh, God. Dear God. Talia took a deep breath to try to still the apprehension brewing inside her chest. "He's just a kid," she said, deliberately avoiding the topic. "He didn't realize what he was doing when he painted on that wall."

"There it is again," Riley said. He leaned closer. "Your eyes are flashing and your body's humming. I can feel it from here."

Her body wasn't humming. It was shaking from the top of her head to the tips of her toes. "Kinkade," she whispered.

She had to find a way to trip him up. He was venturing too close to the truth.

"Kids are your passion," he said, ignoring her warning. "That's what tipped me off."

He reached up and caught her by the nape of the neck. He began to massage the tense muscles he found there but Talia couldn't relax. She was so close to panic, she could feel it bubbling up in her throat.

"I couldn't figure out why you would need to steal," he said softly. "But it's not for you, is it? It's for them."

Her thoughts scattered in a million directions. He knew. She'd been so careful but he'd figured it out.

Applause rang out again but it sounded like gunfire in her ears.

Run! Her instincts screamed. *She had to run!*

Her muscles clenched and she was halfway out of her seat before she realized that would only confirm his suspicions. She locked her knees to force herself to stay put. Flight was not an option—but neither was sitting here doing nothing. Her mind raced out of control. She had to do something to sidetrack him. Anything to shake him loose. Her self-preservation instincts surged and she reached out blindly. She caught them both by surprise when her hand settled over his crotch.

"Shit!" Riley's hips bucked and his hands flew up in the air. "What are you doing?"

Talia's breath caught and, for a second, she couldn't answer. She stared wide-eyed at the sight of his firm bulge filling the curve of her palm. What *was* she doing? A tiger had just come at her and she'd decided to catch it by the cock? What in God's name did she think this would accomplish besides getting her into even more trouble?

Think! she screamed inside her head. Why would she—

"Do you know what I remember about the other night?" she said on impulse. She hesitated only the briefest of moments before rubbing him suggestively. He let out a soft curse and an amazing sense of power filled her. "I remember you nearly breaking down the door of my shop."

Emboldened, she trailed her thumb across the swell of one of his balls. His hand clamped down on her forearm and she nearly smiled.

Before she'd started her life of crime she never would have used sex as a weapon but her new hobby had freed her of many inhibitions. This wasn't the sanest of tactics but she could feel it working. She had the upper hand—literally. "I remember you and your men tracking snow into my showroom. I remember them pawing through my collection."

He started to push her away but she cupped his thickening erection and ground down hard. "I remember you manhandling me," she hissed.

Two could play at this blackmail game. If he was going to hold the truth over her head, she'd do the same to him. What he'd done to her the other night wasn't acceptable behavior for any lawman.

"What the hell? Is that what this is about?" he said as his eyes met hers. A sheen of sweat had broken out on his brow. "Are you still mad about that?"

"Mad? No! I'm not...*mad*!" she sputtered. Of all the egocentric things to say. "But your captain will be once he hears about it."

Riley looked at her for a long moment before a Cheshire cat grin spread across his face. "You are! You're upset that I stopped. You can't stand that I left you hanging."

Talia let out a soft cry. Was he dense? Or really that self-centered? "You violated me," she accused.

"You liked every second of it."

"I did not. You held me down and did things to me."

"And you enjoyed every nasty touch right up to the moment I stopped."

"No," she said, shaking her head.

"Bullshit."

She was flabbergasted. How could he sit there and smile at her when she was threatening him? She squeezed his cock tighter. "I'll tell him," she warned. "I swear I will."

Riley gritted his teeth as his hips rocked toward her punishing touch. "Why don't I just let you even the score instead?"

Talia looked at him blankly. "What?"

She pulled back sharply as he reached for his zipper. It slid down with a rasp and he looked at her in challenge.

She sat frozen in astonishment.

"Come on, baby," he said. "You don't want to back down now. After all, turnabout's fair play."

"Have you noticed the crowd of people here tonight?" she hissed.

"We're up high. They can't see us from the waist down," he said, smiling wickedly.

He quickly undid his pants and pulled out his cock. Talia's eyes went round. Good God, he was hung like a horse. She panicked. This hadn't been her intention. She started to push herself to her feet but he caught her hand and dragged it back down to him. Her heart leapt as her fingertips brushed against his heated skin.

He blew out a gust of air. "Well, come on, sweet Talia. Get your revenge. Womanhandle me."

Talia squeezed her legs together tightly. She'd pushed things too far. He was thick and hot under her fingers and her pussy itched for that long, steely cock.

Damn it, she was supposed to be the one in control. He was quickly turning the tables on her but she couldn't let him. One by one, she wrapped her fingers around him. He groaned and she bit her lip to keep from joining him. He actually pulsed in her hand. There was so much power in this, the heart of him, she couldn't help but dream about how he'd feel sliding up inside her.

She forced herself to look him in the eye. She couldn't let herself get carried away. She couldn't forget how dangerous he was to her. "I've heard your accusations before, Kinkade. They're getting tiresome."

"Still, they seem to have gotten you riled up." His hand circled her wrist and he showed her a pumping motion. "Like this, baby."

A soft sound left the back of her throat. Oh, God. She liked the feel of hot friction almost as much as he did. Together, they watched as her hand slid up and down the velvet rod, making it grow even redder. When she rubbed her thumb over the plump head, his grunt echoed over the crowd below them.

"Fifty dollars, bid by the gentleman in the box seat," the auctioneer said.

"Shit," Riley breathed.

Talia swallowed hard. She had to stay in command of the situation. Determinedly, she swirled her thumb again. She had to know one thing. "That's an interesting theory you have but do you have any evidence against me?"

His hips came right off the chair. "I'll get it."

If the situation hadn't been so dire, she might have felt relieved. As it stood, her concentration was on the huge cock she held in her grip. Her pussy was practically crying for it. "You won't. You couldn't find any the other night."

"I found something else, though. Didn't I, sweetheart?"

He moved quickly and she gasped in surprise when his hand dove under her skirt. She pressed her legs together but he used the opportunity to grind the heel of his hand against her pubic bone.

"Ah," she cried softly.

"Open for me, baby," he demanded.

Talia struggled to get away from that intrusive hand but he was too strong. His fingers prodded at the crease between her legs, tickling her. She looked frantically out at the crowd. Could anyone see what they were doing?

"Spread your legs, Talia."

Oh, God. His hand felt red-hot under her skirt—almost as hot as the cock in her hand. She looked down at him. He was near to bursting. She couldn't believe what they were doing to each other. Hesitantly, she spread her legs. He palmed her possessively and she felt herself start to spiral out of control.

"Riley," she panted as her head dropped back.

"God, you and leather," he grunted. "It's like a wet dream come true."

Both their hands began working feverishly. Talia jerked on his cock as his fingers played with her through the cotton panel of her panties.

"I want you so bad," he growled into her ear. "Talk to me, baby. Tell me the truth and I'll work my ass off to find a way to make this thing between us work."

A whimper left Talia's throat. She didn't want him to be nice to her. She couldn't fight him when he was like this.

His devious fingers finally found their way to her slick pussy. "I'll tell the D.A. to go easy on you," he coaxed. "Maybe you can get off with a fine and minimal time."

She closed her eyes tightly. She couldn't think when he did these things to her.

"Trust me, baby," he whispered. "Trust me to make everything okay."

She wanted to. Badly. She wasn't a criminal, not at heart. She'd just gotten herself into a fix and she couldn't find her way out. Not alone. She was confused and scared but his touch felt so protective. The urge to confide in him was strong.

But was that all part of his plan?

Her eyelids fluttered open and she looked at him warily.

Could she trust him? This was the same man who'd pursued her relentlessly. Just an hour ago, he'd wanted to put her in the slammer and throw away the key. Now he wanted to help her?

Apprehension shot down her spine.

It was a trick. He'd found her weakness and he was using it against her.

She felt pressure as his fingers started to penetrate her and she cringed away from his touch. He hesitated and looked at her sharply.

"No," she said.

He looked at her uncomprehendingly. "Why?"

Applause echoed off the walls and she looked to the stage. The auction had just finished and she took the cue. She sprang away from the detective and pushed his hand away from the slit in her skirt. He lunged for her but she sidestepped away from him on wobbly legs.

Riley cursed from his seat beside her but he was in no condition to stand—not in front of such a crowd. His erection was pointing straight up like a flagpole. His jaw was hard as he glared at her. "Damn it, Talia. Don't do this."

She felt her anger surge.

"Am I leaving you hanging, Detective?" she said sweetly. She looked pointedly down at his lap. "Hmm. Guess not."

With a flourish, she turned and swept aside the curtains. She heard another curse as he tried to cover himself and she used the precious seconds to escape. She hurried down the stairs, her heart pounding like a big bass drum.

"Curse that man!"

She'd underestimated how devious he could be and she was upset with herself for playing his mind games. No more. He knew too much. He knew about the foundation and he knew about her attraction to him. She had to stay as far away from him as she could get.

Deep down inside, though, there was a part of her that was happy she'd gotten close. At least now he knew how it felt to be left riding on the edge.

Chapter Twelve

Talia hit the lobby, intent on making a quick escape. Her plans were dashed as she became caught up in the tide of well-wishers exiting the theater.

"Great job, Talia."

"What a wonderful idea."

"Are you going to do this again next year?"

"Thank you," she murmured absently. "It's nice to see you."

Years of attending society functions had ingrained a certain sense of propriety. She couldn't just walk away from the very people who could keep her charity alive but she also knew how foolish it would be to stay where she was. Riley wasn't going to let this drop.

She glanced over her shoulder anxiously. He'd be on her tail as soon as he could zip up. If he caught her, he'd be on her tail literally.

Automatically, she started moving with the flow of people toward the coat check. She smiled, shook hands and said all the things she was expected to say. With each person she greeted, though, she worked her way toward the door. She was almost there when a hand caught her by the arm and spun her around.

"Don't you touch—Adam!" she said with surprise.

"Hey, sis. Sorry I got here late."

"You came," she said in astonishment.

He pulled her into a tight hug. She was thrilled to see him but, over his shoulder, she caught sight of Riley. He was cutting through the crowd like a blade and fear pricked at the back of her neck. His mood looked treacherous.

"Why didn't you tell me you were coming?" She pulled back from her brother's embrace and grabbed his hand. "Let's go somewhere we can talk."

Adam glanced around. "Shouldn't you stay here and say your good-byes? I can wait."

Talia grabbed her coat from the coat check girl and whipped it around her shoulders. She started backing toward the double doors, dragging her brother with her. "Sadie can handle it. Are you hungry? Let's go get a bite to eat."

"What's the rush?"

"Nothing. Claustrophobia. Please, Adam."

It was too late. Riley had caught up with them. He'd seen the hug and his gaze practically smoldered as he stared at their clenched hands. The lines of his face were hard as he glared at the new arrival. "Who the fuck are you?" he snarled.

Adam's head snapped to the side and his muscles went taut. "Adam Sizemore." He quickly sized up the unexpected aggressor. "And just who *the fuck* are you?"

"This is Detective Kinkade," Talia said, quickly stepping in to defuse the situation. Adam was tall but he wasn't a match for Riley's brawny physique—or the explosive knowledge the detective carried with him. "He was here for…uh, security. Riley, this is my brother."

At the word "security", Kinkade shot her a look that could have cut steel. Talia took an involuntary step toward her sibling.

She shouldn't have pushed things so far.

Cautiously, she looked at the detective's crotch. She felt her face flush. It was a wonder the material was holding.

"Security, huh?" Adam said, relaxing a bit. "I suppose that's a good idea with that Cat Burglar running around town."

Talia's heart nearly stopped. She looked at Kinkade with wide eyes.

He was going to have her for lunch.

He folded his arms over his chest, his gaze never wavering from her face. "Yeah, that's why your sister hired me for tonight. She wanted to make sure she was the only one handling the family jewels."

Talia looked at him in bewilderment even as her pussy throbbed. What was he doing? Her attention ping-ponged back and forth between the two men. Why hadn't he said anything? He'd had the perfect opening.

"That's my sis, Ms. Overprotective." Adam chuckled and threw her a wink. "Actually, that auction wasn't half-bad if you don't count the kiddie stuff. I didn't realize you were going to be auctioning off such valuable pieces."

As grateful as she was for her brother's presence, the backhanded compliment wasn't appreciated. "People were generous with their donations but the 'kiddie stuff' came from the heart," Talia snapped.

"I still wouldn't hang any of it on my walls." Adam reached out and pinched her cheeks playfully. "You must be excited with the way things turned out, though. You're all rosy."

Riley let out a grunt. "Tickled pink, actually."

Talia batted away her brother's hand as embarrassment swept through her. Damn Kinkade. He was toying with her!

"I've got to admit," Adam said, oblivious to the undercurrents, "Dad would be proud of you."

"What?" she said, her head spinning around. The unexpected compliment threw her and she looked at her brother in shock. "Really?" she said softly.

"Sure. You've kept his little foundation puttering along. Hell, pretty soon I'll have to be looking over my shoulder. Who knew you'd turn into such an astute businesswoman?"

Her happiness faded. "Puttering little foundation" or not, it wasn't her business acumen that was bringing the programs back on track.

"So what do you do, Adam?" Kinkade asked unexpectedly.

Her brother stood a little straighter and his head took on a familiar tilt. "I run the family business out of Boston. Maybe you've heard of it? Sizemore Appliances?"

"Heard of it?" One side of Riley's mouth curled upward. "One of your dishwashers is leaking over my kitchen floor as we speak."

A surprised snort rose up in Talia's throat. She covered it with a cough. Aggravating as he might be, Kinkade had just achieved something she'd never been able to do. He'd popped Adam's pompous balloon with one well-placed pinprick.

"Well, now, I don't like to hear that." Ever the consummate businessman, Adam reached into his pocket for a business card. Still, he looked as if he was suffering from severe heartburn as he passed it to the other man. "Call my secretary and we'll get a repairman out there pronto. No charge."

The smirk settled fully on Riley's face. "I'll do that."

Even a blind man could see the pissing match starting. Talia bit her lip when her brother pulled at his gold cufflinks. He always got fussy when he was annoyed.

She took a step forward.

"So, Detective. Are you working on that Cat Burglar case?"

She stopped dead in her tracks.

One of Adam's eyebrows lifted contemptuously. "I don't know if I'd have hired you for security, what with the way that guy is giving your department fits."

She cringed. No! Don't provoke him.

She waited in agony to see what Riley would do.

He hesitated for a long moment before finally letting his gaze rake down her figure. "That one's a slippery one, all right."

Self-consciousness made Talia want to sink through the floor. He knew her panties were wet; he'd made them that way!

Enough with this double-talk. Why was he keeping her secret?

Adam wrapped his arm around her stiff shoulders. "You guys better get your act in gear. I don't like the idea of my sister being a potential target."

"You don't need to worry about her," Riley said. His eyes held a dangerous glint. "I've got her covered."

Talia's mouth went dry.

It was time to leave.

She didn't know what kind of mind game the detective was playing but she wasn't up for it. Plastering a smile on her face, she turned to Adam. "What about that dinner?"

"Talia," Riley said tersely.

Adam sent him a glare. "Sounds good to me. Maybe the company will be better there."

The thought of food turned her stomach but she nodded. "Oscar's should still be serving."

"Don't you even think about leaving."

The warning came across soft and low. It made a shiver run down her spine and she paused. It was an order—one she should probably follow if she knew what was good for her.

Feeling impetuous, she slid her arm through her brother's. Safe, stodgy, by-the-rules Talia had disappeared weeks ago. "Thank you for your work tonight, Detective."

"We're not finished here."

She let her gaze drop to the bulge pressing at his zipper.

"Sorry," she said sweetly. "You'll have to finish the job yourself."

* * * * *

By the time Talia got home that night, she was in a state. Dinner with Adam hadn't improved her frame of mind. If anything, it had made her even more agitated.

"Why do I let him get to me?" she asked in frustration. She let herself into her apartment and slammed the door behind her. Her steps were quick as she threw her coat at the couch and tossed her purse onto the table. It slid across the surface and dropped helplessly to the floor.

She didn't care. She was already stomping into the kitchen. Opening the refrigerator, she found a bottle of wine. She drained it into a glass and took a long drink.

It didn't help. Her brother knew just what buttons to push.

Was he really that inconsiderate or was he just oblivious? Tonight was supposed to have been about her and the foundation. Would it have killed him to be more supportive?

She trudged back to the living room but left the lights off. She didn't want them on. More and more, the darkness was becoming her friend. If anything could soothe her nerves, it was the night. It was during this time that she felt the most confident.

She had to remember that. She was a confident and competent woman. Adam was just being…well, Adam. His little snipes about New Covington weren't directed at her. He'd grown up here, too. Just because he was a Boston bigwig now didn't mean that he was belittling her.

But if he said one more thing about her "little" shop, she was going to smack him.

"Or the foundation," she said, taking another sip of wine. "One more criticism about that, and I'll…I'll…I'll grab his Rembrandt."

The idea was tempting. Just going out on a hunt sounded enticing.

Sighing, she wandered over to the window. The winter sky was dark and clear. Stars glittered in the heavens, beckoning her to come out and play.

She leaned against the window frame. It wasn't just Adam that had her so upset. It seemed that everybody had been intent on aggravating her tonight. The Turd, Uncle Roger, Riley…

When she'd been in the lobby of the theater welcoming guests, Brent had had the audacity to feel her up in front of his wife. If that hadn't been bad enough, Roger seemed to think that he'd put a stamp of possession on her. He'd kissed her on the lips, for heaven's sake. She'd been hosting an important event and neither man had shown an ounce of respect for her. All they'd been intent on was getting a piece of ass.

"Kinkade nearly did," she muttered, disgusted with herself. Almost unconsciously, she pressed her thighs together. Who was she kidding? Detective Riley Kinkade had gotten her more hot and bothered than anybody.

"That aggressive, arrogant, bull-headed...Grade A, prime piece of beefcake."

Desire washed through her. God, he was hot. Was there a woman on the planet that could resist those dark eyes, that mussed hair, those bulging muscles, *that cock*?

Her eyes drifted shut as she remembered the things they'd done together up in that balcony. It had been like a flash fire—all heat, sighs and moans. Her pussy still ached with need and her fingers itched for the feel of him.

Lord help her, but she wanted him.

Him. Detective Riley Kinkade. The man who wanted to put her in prison.

Goose bumps popped up on her skin and she hugged herself. Could things get any more complicated? She was infatuated with the one man who could change her life forever—and not in a good way.

She let her forehead rest against the cool windowpane. How was she going to handle this? She'd thought she'd been so careful. How had he put it all together?

It didn't matter. The bottom line was that he knew what she was doing and why. All he lacked was solid, concrete proof.

And she'd seen fit to taunt him.

"Oh, Talia," she said. "What have you done?"

She downed the remaining wine and began pacing restlessly. She'd never been so aggressive with a man before. She just hadn't known what else to do. He'd been pressuring her about the foundation and she'd felt herself panicking.

So naturally, she'd reached out and started pumping his cock?

The memory of his hot, steely flesh made her palms tingle and she set down her wineglass before she could drop it. If she was still this worked up, she couldn't imagine how he felt.

Her gaze fell on the couch and she stopped short. Oh yes, she could.

"You are in such trouble," she whispered.

She wandered back to the window. Where was he right now? Was he suffering like she had? Or had he gone home to jack off?

"Ohhhhh." A vision of Riley standing in a cloud of steam in the shower made her knees go weak.

That, of course, would be the best thing that could have happened. If he hadn't taken care of his little—ahem, big—problem, it could still be fueling his anger.

The thought alone sent a jolt of uneasiness through her. Just how pissed was he? Enough to go back to work to investigate his theories? Enough to follow her to dinner with Adam?

"Or enough to be sitting in an unmarked police car outside my apartment!"

Her jaw dropped. She could see him. The moonlight reflecting off the snow was nearly as bright as sunlight. He was staking out her place.

She froze. Was he going to come up here and finish what they'd begun?

No. Disappointment surprised her. He'd changed out of his tuxedo into more comfortable clothes. From the looks of it, he'd settled in for the night.

"What is he doing here then?" What did he think he was going to accomplish? Why was he watching her?

The answer rang in her head.

"He thinks I'm going to go out tonight!" She shook her head. "But why? We raised good money for the foundation at the auction. Why would I—"

Her fingers wrapped around the curtain sash. "Oooo, you think you're so smart."

This wasn't about money. He knew that she'd been horny as a mink when she'd left the theater. If he couldn't assuage the heat burning low in her belly...

He knew what would.

Talia sprang back from the window. That smug bastard! He was practically daring her!

A wild recklessness gushed through her veins.

He wanted to throw down the gauntlet? Fine. She was more than willing to pick it up.

Determinedly, she walked to the bedroom. She'd been planning her next job but she hadn't expected to go tonight. Things were in place, though, and a surprise burglary might throw him off her trail. If she could just get away from the building without him noticing, it would be perfect. After all, how could she be the culprit when he was watching her every move from outside her window?

Her every move...

A cunning smile spread across her face. He wanted to watch? She'd give him an eyeful.

"You deserve this, Riley."

With a flick of the wrist, she turned on the lamp in her bedroom. Butterflies took flight in her stomach as she walked sensuously toward the window. Weeks ago, she never would have had the nerve to do this but this cat-and-mouse game was making her bold.

She positioned herself in full view of the man outside in the dark car. She knew the backlight put her silhouette in clear focus but she was careful not to get too close. He had to think she was getting ready for bed, not putting on a show.

"Easy," she whispered to herself. Her heart was thudding. She'd never stripped for a man before.

But she wanted to. She wanted to set Kinkade on his ear.

Reaching up, she removed the pins holding her hair in an elaborate updo. Blonde tendrils dropped softly onto her shoulders and she shook her head. It felt good. More relaxed.

She needed to relax if she was going to pull this off.

She reached for the bow at the side of her waist and the butterflies in her stomach started dancing. Her fingers were clumsy as they worked on the knot but, just when she was about to lose her nerve, the wrap-around top came undone.

She took a shaky breath. It was now or never.

She let the crisp white shirt slip off her shoulders.

She didn't have to see Riley to feel his attention sharpen. For a moment, she was paralyzed with her arms caught in the sleeves of the top. Excitement and apprehension rushed through her. What if she'd calculated wrong? What if he got out of his car and came to get her?

Her pussy tightened. What would be so wrong with that?

She finally relaxed into the role. "Bring it on, big boy."

She'd suffer through whatever consequences he wanted to dole out.

She draped the shirt across a chair. Feeling more confident, she reached back and undid the zipper on her skirt. The weight of the leather pulled it rapidly over her hips to the floor. She could almost hear Kinkade's groan. With a devilish smile, she stretched. The move lifted her breasts high in the cups of her bra.

Oh, yes. This felt good.

She let her arms drop and raised one foot behind her. She slipped off the high heel and gave the shoe a careless toss. The other one followed close behind. With a sigh, she let her toes curl into the carpet.

Was he enjoying this as much as she was?

Because she was getting turned on.

"Only for you, Riley. Only for you."

Thinking of him actually made things easier for her.

Teasing did have its advantages.

She slid her hands sexily up her stockings to her garter belt. With a practiced flick she undid the tabs. Feeling like a porno actress, she bent her leg and balanced her toes on top of the dresser. Ever so slowly, she rolled the silk down her thigh, over her knee and along her calf. It left her foot with a whisper. She switched legs and a new, more intense feeling settled low in her belly.

What was she going to do about this man?

Look at the extremes he was pushing her to. Look at how he was making her feel.

When it came to Kinkade, her feelings were complex. She knew what a purely physical reaction felt like; this wasn't it. She was sexually attracted to Brent Harrington. With Riley, there was something more. A whole lot more.

He'd gotten inside her head.

Danger signs flared and her hands shook as she reached for her garter belt. She let out a groan when the elastic slipped and snapped against her thighs. This little striptease was quickly getting out of control.

She straightened but suddenly realized how naked she was. All she was wearing were her bra and panties.

He's seen you in less.

The memory didn't help. She vividly remembered the feel of his hand between her legs...the penetration of his fingers...the stretch in her most private place... Arousal made her eyelids heavy.

She was too far gone to stop. Biting her lip, she reached for the front clasp of her bra. The cups dropped to the side and her breasts jiggled as they were released. Her nipples perked up, red and turgid, and heat suffused every centimeter of her exposed skin. She lifted her hair off the back of her neck but realized too late that the motion only emphasized the lift of her breasts. In profile, Riley could see every curve, valley and peak of her body.

"Oh, God," she moaned.

She shrugged out of the bra and let it fall to the floor. It left her wearing only the damp, uncomfortable bikini panties.

They needed to come off.

Not stopping to think, she hooked her thumbs inside the material and pushed it over her hips. Bent over as she was, she could see the wet curls at the juncture of her legs. Her breasts swayed and her arousal soared. She didn't even want to imagine the erotic picture she was casting against that window.

Muscles resisting, she forced herself to stand upright. Her nakedness reflected in the mirror and she had to look away.

She wanted to touch herself. She wanted it so badly she thought she might cry. Need screamed at her but she couldn't.

Not with him watching.

Not if the point of all this was to distract him so she could go out thieving.

She let out a moan of disappointment.

"Show's over," she whispered as she kicked her panties away.

Hands shaking, she yanked open the top drawer and pulled out a royal blue chemise. Her movements were stiff and jerky as she pulled it over her head. The satin slid down over her curves, making her whimper. The sensation was like a lick against her stiff nipples.

Bed. She was supposed to be giving the appearance she was going to bed. *To sleep.*

Turning, she made her way to the lamp. Her thighs stuck together with every step she took and shudders racked her body. Everything inside her told her to reach down and ease her tension but, if she made even the slightest motion in that direction, Riley would come crashing through her door.

Of that, she was certain.

She nearly knocked the lamp over in her haste to stop this voyeuristic game. The harsh light was doused and she stood at the table taking deep, calming breaths.

She'd gotten carried away. She needed to tamp this desire down, muffle it somehow. A laugh of disbelief escaped her. And just how was she supposed to do that? She'd been in a permanent state of heat ever since she'd met Riley Kinkade.

And a permanent state of anxiety.

She had to pull herself together. It was time to go to work.

She needed to pull this heist to get him off her scent.

Reaching deep into the bottom drawer of her dresser, she found the beginnings of her uniform. Her night waiting for Edward Jones in the cold had taught her a lesson. She needed to dress for both mobility and warmth. The catsuit provided both.

She held the lace and nylon confection up in the moonlight. It was provocative as hell, and most definitely not intended for the uses she put it to. It was meant for sex. She used it for crime.

Quickly, she began to get dressed.

"Work with me," she growled after several seconds of fighting with the constricting suit. The material clung to her from the tips of her toes to the tips of her fingers. With the state her body was in, the sense of bondage was only heightened.

She finally worked herself into the undergarment and layered a pair of dark pants and a black turtleneck over it. A down-filled jacket, gloves and boots completed the outfit. She strapped her bag of utensils to her thigh, pulled a stocking cap over her blonde hair and blended into the darkness.

Carefully, she checked outside her window one last time. Riley was still there. Hopefully, he was too distracted by his hard-on to notice that the New Covington Cat Burglar was about to go on the prowl.

"Catch me if you can," she said, her breath fogging the window.

She was playing with fire now. Riley Kinkade was not going to be a happy man.

But she was a happy woman. The detective might be aggravating but he'd been right about one thing. She did steal for pleasure...

The pleasure of making him squirm.

Chapter Thirteen

The next morning, Talia hummed a happy tune in her office as she poured herself a cup of coffee. The day was getting off to a wonderful start. Snow had fallen overnight and the scene outside looked just like a postcard. Tree branches bent under the weight of puffy white powder, while chimneys blew out clouds of smoke. She watched as her snow service boy shoveled her sidewalks and was glad that she was inside where it was warm and comfy.

Snow could be such a wonderful thing. Its crisp, white blanket made everything look prettier. It made her shop feel more inviting. Best of all, it covered any potentially incriminating footprints that might be found leading from her shop to Ramona Gellar's condo ten blocks away.

Talia smiled. Things had gone well last night.

The bell over the back door jingled and she automatically reached for another cup. Sadie blew through the door on an Arctic blast and slammed it behind her.

"Brrrr," she said, her teeth clattering. "It's like a freezer out there."

"The snow moved in fast," Talia called. She walked to the storage room and waited until her assistant had taken off her coat. She helped her with her scarf before handing her the coffee. "Last night, it seemed almost warm."

"That's Mother Nature for you. I'm just glad she held off until after the auction." Sadie wrapped her hands around the mug and savored the heat. A twinkle lit her eyes. "We did good, didn't we?"

A grin split Talia's face. "We did great!" She gave her friend a quick squeeze. "Thank you, thank you, thank you for all your hard work."

Sadie shrugged modestly. "It was worth it. Besides, it was a hoot watching all those muckety-mucks squabble over the same items they ridiculed here in the shop. Did you see how intense the bickering got over that garden gnome? Why, if I hadn't known better, I would have thought it was the *Venus de Milo*."

Garden gnome?

"Mm," Talia murmured. She took a quick sip of coffee. Maybe she'd missed a thing or two up there in the balcony.

She followed Sadie into the showroom. The snow boy was finishing up but it was doubtful that they'd have any customers for a while. On days like this, the world seemed to wake up a little slower. That was fine with her. It would give her and Sadie the opportunity to chat. They never seemed to have the time to do that anymore.

"I'm sorry I left you to do all the cleanup work," she said as she reached out to straighten a rack of comics. Her behavior last night had been uncharacteristic on many levels. "I should have stayed but things got so chaotic. I felt like I was being pulled in a million different directions."

"Ack, don't worry about it." Sadie tossed her purse under the counter and took a drink of hot coffee. "The parents helped me. We finished in a snap."

"Still, I owe you dinner."

"Italian?"

"Whatever you want."

Sadie threw her a wink before a more serious expression settled onto her face. She leaned forward onto the counter and propped her chin up in her hand. "I saw that Adam made it. How did that go?"

The trials and tribulations of the Sizemore clan weren't a secret. Talia had shared her frustrations about her brother, just as Sadie had talked about her problems raising a pre-teen. Sadie and Adam had even gone a few rounds themselves, with Adam playing the clueless antagonist, of course.

"Fine," Talia murmured. She immediately rolled her eyes. She'd lied to her friend enough. "Same as always, if you want the truth."

"Must have been better than usual. You look almost chipper this morning."

Talia brushed a hand over her cheek self-consciously. She was refreshed — but not because of her brother. She'd just finally gotten a good night's sleep.

It had been months since her body had allowed that to happen. In spite of the challenges, it seemed that pulling the job at Ramona's had been well worth the risk. She'd acquired a valuable piece, she'd confused Kinkade and she'd built her self-confidence back up to where it should be. She couldn't help but feel that she'd won this battle.

Of course, the color in her cheeks could be due to the way she'd masturbated herself into exhaustion after she'd gotten home. It had been impossible to resist the temptation knowing that Riley was right outside.

"I feel good," she admitted. "I'm glad the auction went well but it was a lot of work. I'm relieved that it's over."

"Me, too." Sadie got a dreamy look in her eyes. "I celebrated with a bubble bath complete with candles and leftover champagne. I didn't know what I was getting into when I volunteered to take over that thing."

Champagne. Talia's mouth tightened involuntarily. If she'd felt an ounce of remorse about burglarizing Ramona Gellar, it had vanished when she'd found two champagne glasses from the auction on the woman's kitchen counter.

The witch had had the nerve to steal from a charity! Of all the targets so far, this one felt the most justified — except for Brent, of course.

"Talia?"

"Hmm?" She shook her head as she came back to the present.

"You were a million miles away."

"Oh, sorry. Just thinking." She hooked her hair over her ear. A good night's sleep should help her keep her wits about her better. She couldn't drop her guard like that. "What about Linc? Did he have a good time?"

Sadie slapped her hand down on the counter. "Are you kidding me? With his drawing selling for twenty bucks and Kinkade promising to put in a good word with his case worker, he was over the moon."

Talia only heard one thing. "Kinkade?"

"He talked with Linc last night and really made an impression." A resolute look crossed Sadie's face. "I like that man. If you don't snatch him up quick, I might make a play for him myself."

Talia blinked in surprise. "What?"

"You heard me."

"But...but... There's nothing going on between Riley and me."

"So it's Ri-ley now, is it?" A self-satisfied smile settled onto Sadie's lips. She traced the lip of her coffee cup with her finger. "Nothing going on, my foot."

Talia's mouth worked helplessly. Where was this coming from? Riley had been hanging around the shop for months but Sadie had never commented on it before. She certainly hadn't expressed any interest in him to her assistant. She hadn't admitted her feelings to even herself until last night. "You've misinterpreted things."

"Sweetie, I didn't have to interpret anything. I know attraction when I feel it. That stud's like a magnet to your steel armor. I've learned to stay out of the way so I won't get caught up in the field."

A thought occurred to Talia and she set down her coffee with a *whump*. "You put him in that box seat on purpose."

"There wasn't anywhere else to seat him. We were already sold out when he bought his ticket."

"Sadie!"

"Okay, okay. Even magnets need to be flipped sometimes. I figured it wouldn't hurt to give things a little shove."

Talia let out a huff and spun away. She walked aimlessly as she tried to get her mind around her friend's ill-timed matchmaking. "Why would you do that? You've seen how the two of us argue."

Sadie shrugged. "Foreplay."

A jolt went through Talia's body. "Excuse me?"

"You're not arguing. You're juicing each other up. Honey, there's nothing wrong with that. He's a hunk. A *bona fide* hottie. A woman could go all moony-eyed over that strong jawline, those wide shoulders and those big hands. You know what they say about a man with big hands…"

Talia's stomach dropped. She knew better than anyone how apropos that saying was. Whipping around, she held up her hands to stop the embarrassing tirade. "Okay, you're right. There's chemistry between us but it's not the good kind. It's the kind that blows things up!"

"You're just not used to how he challenges you." Sadie planted her hands on her hips and shoved her head forward like a snapping turtle. "I think he's a perfectly nice man. The fact that he's easy on the eyes is an added bonus. He's certainly better for you than Roger Thorton."

A choked sound erupted from Talia's throat.

"That old fool," Sadie said tetchily. "It was absolutely disgraceful the way he shoved his tongue down your throat in front of all our patrons."

Talia covered her face with her hand. She'd passed the point of discomfort long ago. "Can we just drop this?"

"And the obvious display he made buying that Turkish rug. I swear."

Talia peeked through her fingers. Oh Lord, Lydia was going to love that. "Roger bought the rug?"

"Of course he did. You were there; you saw him." Glee suddenly lit Sadie's eyes. "Unless you were busy with the detective at the time."

Talia looked at the ceiling and counted to ten. What was this woman doing working at an antiques shop? She should be with the CIA.

She pivoted on her heel. "I'm going to get the paper."

"Oh my gosh! I was just kidding!" Sadie flew out from behind the counter. "Don't you run away from me. What happened up there?"

Talia's heels clipped steadily across the floor. "Nothing."

"You didn't know about the garden gnome either!"

"Sure I did."

Sadie grabbed her by the arm. "What color was its hat?"

"This is ridiculous." Talia pulled her arm free and opened the front door. The wind shot straight through her sweater and skirt, making her grit her teeth. She hurried over to where the paper sat on the sidewalk. Dumb paperboy. She'd asked him to put the thing in the mail slot a million times.

She ran back to the entrance but Sadie blocked the way.

Talia stood shivering outside her own shop. "I'm getting frostbite. Let me in."

"The hat," her assistant said, pointing at her head. *"What color?"*

Talia hunched her shoulders against the cold. She didn't have a clue. "Green?"

"Wrong! Purple!" Sadie pointed at her with the finger of death. "You were making out with the detective."

Not exactly.

She hurried into the shop and rubbed her hands up and down her arms. Trying to distract her assistant, she tossed the paper onto the counter. "There should be an article about the auction in here."

Sadie was on her heels like a bull terrier. "Is he a good kisser?"

The question stopped Talia as she flipped by the sports section. She didn't know.

How was it that with everything they'd done together, he'd never kissed her?

Damn. Now Sadie had put *that* thought into her head.

Her assistant let out a cackle. "From the expression on your face, he must be fantastic."

She wouldn't doubt it. He'd proven himself to be quite skilled at other things. She shook off the thought and began pawing through the newspaper. "Where's the society section?"

"Come on. Share. I haven't had a date in three— There!" Sadie said abruptly. She pushed aside a grocery store's advertisement so the New Covington Life section was on top. "What does it say?"

The bold headline made Talia go numb.

"Are we in there?"

"No," she finally said, her voice like ice. "*But Brent is.*"

Sadie let out a screech.

"Brent? As in Harrington? Why in the world would he be in there?" She nudged Talia aside so she could see. Swiftly, she skimmed the page. She let out another wail when she saw the column. "That no-good, two-timing fiend!"

Talia pressed a hand to her stomach. The anger inside her burned.

"*Art Council Supports School Programs?* Where did they get that? Why would they print this garbage? It's an outrage!"

Talia's gaze fixed on the black and white picture of Brent and Shelli in all their finery. Her teeth ground together as she read the caption. "Council for the Arts President Brent Harrington III and wife, Shelli, show their support at local fundraiser."

"The Art Council isn't supporting this," Sadie fumed. "They twisted the words around. The Council chose to rescind their funding. That's why we had to have this auction. Where's the phone book? I'm calling the editor and asking for a retraction."

"It won't do any good," Talia said, her fury mounting. "Whatever they write will be in tiny print that nobody will see."

"We've got to do something!"

She took one deep breath, then two. This was the second time Brent had pushed her temper past its limits. Last time she'd chosen to run away. This time, things were going to be a whole lot different.

He couldn't walk all over her anymore. She was a different person now. She was stronger, more confident and just a little bit ruthless.

Turning, she marched for the back door. "I'll take care of it."

"Where are you going? What are you going to do?"

"Watch the store."

Talia was halfway to her car before she even got her coat over her shoulders. How dare he? "Ooooh, you *turd*!" she growled as she slammed the door.

Her tires spun on the snow, sending muck flying. She was in too much of a fit to notice that Kinkade's car swung in behind her. It didn't matter. Her mind was clearly focused on another man who liked to cause problems for her.

Brent Harrington III had been a pain in her side forever. She was tired of being manipulated. The man was a master of spin. He could take the worst of situations and still come out smelling like a rose. This time, though, he'd gone too far. She wasn't going to let him get off easy. If he'd thought the loss of his animalier had hurt, he hadn't seen anything yet.

On impulse, she made a quick left turn that had three cars slamming on their brakes and honking their horns. She didn't notice the blue sedan that took the turn with her. In minutes, she was at Harrington Manufacturing. She parked in Shelli's open space and slammed the door behind her.

"Old money," she growled under her breath.

Of course the reporter had gone after Brent. The Harrington family and their hunting implements company had been around for seventy-five years. Guns were sexy, the company was solid and, most importantly, old. In New Covington, that was as good as aged wine. Second generation wealth from an appliance company didn't rank nearly as high. With the Harrington name in the tagline, the society reporter had earned herself a bonus.

Talia yanked open the front door to the building and stormed across the entryway.

"Ma'am. Excuse me, ma'am?"

She glanced back and saw a redhead in impossibly high heels trying to catch up with her. She punched the up button for the elevator anyway. "What?" she snapped.

"Do you have an appointment?"

"No."

The elevator arrived and Talia stepped inside. She hit the button for the top floor with enough force to make the jiggly redhead take a cautious step back.

"I can't let you enter if you don't have an appointment," Red said nervously.

"Tell Brent I'm on my way."

"But I don't know your name." The woman's voice faded as the metal doors closed.

"Don't worry," Talia said. Her eyes narrowed dangerously. "He's expecting me."

* * * * *

Brent was leaning back against his desk with his arms crossed over his chest when Talia stormed into his office. A smirk settled on his face. "Hi, Tally," he said softly. "I've been waiting for you."

Her fingertip hold on her temper slipped. She slammed the door behind her, nearly breaking the nose of another secretary who'd tried to get in her way. "You bastard."

"Not a bastard," he said with a chuckle. "I assure you, I'm a full-blooded Harrington."

"Same difference."

She started toward him but a newspaper on a nearby table had her pausing mid-stride. The society section glared up at her like a neon sign. In a flash, the paper was crumpled in her hand. Crossing the room, she threw it in his face. "Sadie is calling the editor right now, demanding a retraction."

"A retraction?" he said, cocking one eyebrow. He smoothed out the paper and held it up to the light coming in from the window. "I thought it was a good article. It's a damn fine picture, that's for sure."

She tore the paper from his hands. It ripped with a loud rasp. For emphasis, she tossed the remnants onto the floor. "It's full of lies. I can't believe you, Brent. Last night was important to a lot of people. Why does everything have to be about you?"

"There isn't one thing in that article that isn't true. I'm the Arts Council president. I supported the auction with a donation, my attendance and even a purchase." He reached out and touched a lock of her hair. "Where was my donation, by the way?"

Talia's face flared. How dare he bring those up? She swatted his hand away. "You spun that story to make yourself look good."

"Hey, you're in there, too."

"The Sizemore Foundation name doesn't even appear until the third paragraph."

"No press is bad press, baby."

"Don't you 'baby' me." She closed the remaining distance between them. The slick smile hadn't disappeared from his lips. She was sorely tempted to remove it for him. "You don't care about this program. You were the one who pushed the Council to drop it. Why can't you leave it alone?"

"What fun would that be?"

"This is fun for you?" she said in a raw voice.

He reached out suddenly and caught her about the waist. With a jerk, he pulled her firmly between his outspread legs. She unbalanced and fell against his muscled chest. "It's fun for both of us," he said as he buried his face in the crook of her neck. He licked her pounding pulse suggestively. "And you know it."

Talia's eyes widened. His cock nudged at the juncture of her legs, domineering and insistent. Her hands flailed for his shoulders. She pushed him hard but his fingers bit into her hips, making her rub her mound against him. "Damn it, Brent," she said through gritted teeth. "Coming at me through the arts program is low. I won't let you do it."

His teeth scraped against her tender throat and he pushed her coat off her shoulders. It dropped to the floor. "You'll let me do anything I want."

His voice was low but the message was loud and clear. He expected her to submit.

And it made her sick.

Remorse filled her. How had she allowed herself to be subjugated like this? Where was her pride? She hadn't realized until this very moment how far this thing between them had unraveled. Brent was always ogling her and stealing a quick touch. He'd been doing it for years. She was used to it.

She shouldn't be used to this!

She pulled back to look at him. His eyes were full of steely intention and his touch was just as determined. Awareness sizzled across her skin. With that frenzied coupling at his party, things had risen to another level. Now that he'd screwed her, he wasn't going to be satisfied with anything less.

"I am not yours to order about as you wish." Her lips flattened but she couldn't help the unsteadiness in her voice. "I'm not your sex toy."

His lips curled upright. "The hell you're not."

To prove his point he lowered his mouth to her breast and gave it a solid nip. Even cushioned by her soft sweater and bra, the pain was sharp and hot. Talia let out a surprised yip. "Ah! Brent! What do you think you're doing?"

"Playing." His teeth clamped down harder.

She let out a whimper and pulled at his hair. The stinging pain hurt but pleasure followed close on its heels. The two were a combustible mixture and she felt an unwanted twinge low in her belly. Heat radiated from her throbbing breast straight to her core.

"No," she said, more to herself than him. She wasn't giving in this time. She refused to let it happen again. Still, her grip on his hair loosened.

He took it as sign of concession. The vice on her nipple loosened and he nuzzled his cheek against her. "You're wearing a bra again. I thought I'd taught you not to do that."

Her pussy pulsed at the rebuke. Even as she fought him, she felt a delirious sexiness overcome her. "I don't take orders from you."

His attention shifted to her cleavage, left bare by the low cut of her lavender cashmere sweater. He pressed his face between the swells and inhaled deeply. "I didn't like it last night either. That dress would have been fantastic if your perky nipples had been on display. With that white top, they would have shown right through."

"Brent, let me go." Talia took a shaky breath, only to realize too late that it pressed her breasts more tightly against his face. Hands trembling, she smoothed back his hair, trying to calm him. Things were too volatile. If she didn't approach him rationally, he'd have her on her back with her ankles somewhere around her ears. "We need to talk."

"Talk, talk, talk," he mocked. "I want to suck your tits."

His grip suddenly moved to the hem of her sweater. He pulled it up over her curves, yanked the cup of her bra to the side and latched onto her left breast.

"No!" she said, this time meaning it. Energy coursed through her body and she began to fight.

She remembered how ruthlessly he'd pushed his fat cock into her. He'd pumped her like a jackhammer and she had been helpless against the onslaught. Her orgasm had been powerful but she hadn't wanted it.

She didn't want it now—no matter how much her pussy was itching for attention.

"Let me go. Damn you. Don't!"

His teeth punished her again, this time with the added rasp of his tongue.

"Get rid of this damn thing," he said as he tore at the front clasp of her bra.

Talia struggled harder but the bull had caught her scent. She wasn't going to get away. Her nerves shimmered when she felt the catch give and her breasts swing free. He caught her stiff nipple in the hot, wet confines of his mouth and began to suckle lustily.

"Mmm," she groaned. "No, I don't want this. I don't...want... I want... Nooooo."

"God, you're hot," Brent said, his mouth making slurping noises against her raw flesh. "Are you creamy?"

His hand shot up under her skirt. Talia tried to kick him but it was to no avail. His fist curled around her hot pussy. She cried out as unwanted arousal coursed through her. She'd worn nylons, but no panties. All that saved her soft flesh from his intrusive fingers was a thin cotton panel.

He rubbed her clit through the fabric. "Your mouth says 'no' but your cunt is dripping, Tally."

"I swear if you—"

"Oh, cut the crap and get on your knees," he growled. "I want your mouth."

She stood there, breathing hard. She'd come here to make a point but look at her. She was half-naked, clutching at his shoulders for support as she humped his hand.

She hadn't made the point; he had.

A little light inside of her flickered out and tears pressed at her eyes.

"I hate you," she whispered.

He flicked her nub and her back arched. "Hate me all you want," he chuckled, "but you love what I do to you."

She did and that's what killed her. She'd loved his touch even at the tender age of fifteen when he'd flaunted his control over her at the Devonshire party. She'd let him do whatever he'd wanted to her that night. She could have left but she'd stayed. She'd even danced, knowing that her breasts were making an entire room of horny teenage boys drool.

For years, she'd let Brent look. He'd stared at her breasts without an ounce of shame and she'd complied by throwing her shoulders back and giving him a better view. She hadn't worn bras to events she knew he'd be attending. Unconsciously or consciously, she'd played just as much a role in this sick seduction as he had.

"What's wrong with me?" she asked, not meaning to let the words slip out.

"There's nothing wrong with you, baby," he said, his voice for once amazingly gentle. His hands slid up her rib cage and cupped her breasts possessively. "I'm your master. I've always been your master."

Talia tried to look away, but couldn't. The sight of his big hands molding and shaping her was too erotic. He'd fondled and suckled her tender breasts to the point where they were a riot of nerve endings. Every time he squeezed his hands, she felt her pussy clench.

"We're connected," he said seriously. "We always have been. You can't deny it."

"No, I can't," she said, her voice aching at the admission. She licked her lips and tried to find a shred of self-respect. "That doesn't mean I have to like it."

His eyes narrowed. "Do you like it better with the cop?"

The question was so jarring, he might as well have reached out and slapped her. "What?" she said, her eyes flying open.

She didn't want the detective inside her head. Not now.

"Kinkade. The two of you have been connected at the hip—or maybe I should say groin?"

The sneer in his voice surprised her. He sounded almost jealous.

"There's nothing going on between—" She sputtered to a stop. She didn't have to talk about her personal life with him. "That's none of your business."

His forehead scrunched and, for the first time that she could remember, he looked angry. "Yes, it is."

Talia was taken aback. Things were quickly spiraling out of her comfort zone. "You don't own me!"

"You're mine," he growled. "You always have been. I'm not going to give you up to some blue-collared slab of meat."

The conversation made her uneasy. It was too twisted, too obscene. "Brent, you're married. Shelli is your wife. I can be with whomever I want."

"Not the detective, you can't. I won't allow it."

She looked at him, dumbfounded.

He pinched her nipples hard and she gasped. She tried to pull away but he used his hold on her to pull her close until her forehead rested against his. "You can fuck other men," he whispered, staring straight into her eyes. "I like the idea of you lubed and ready but you'll only do it with my permission."

The submissive part of her creamed.

"I don't want Kinkade wasting time looking for your pussy when he should be looking for mine. You remember it—bronze, about this big." He gestured with his hands against her breasts.

Her nipples burned as circulation was restored. Oh, she remembered his kitty, all right. She felt absolutely no guilt at what she'd done with it. "The detective has been working very hard to find your Mène. Believe me," she said in a hard voice.

"Seems to me he's been working you harder than the case."

Talia couldn't help it, her hips swiveled. Brent saw her unconscious reaction and he let out a swift curse.

"I don't want that son of a bitch laying his hands on you. Do you understand me? You're not to let him touch you." His hands fell heavily on her shoulders and pushed downwards. "On your knees. Suck me now, damn it."

Her knees buckled under the pressure. She dropped to the floor and her feet tangled in her coat. When she looked up, she found her face in Brent's crotch. The sight of tented fabric made her muscles stiffen. It reminded her all too much of Riley.

Suddenly, she realized why Brent was so touchy about the detective. He realized that Kinkade was the one man who could take her away from him.

Self-realization made Talia rock back on her heels.

She didn't want this.

For once, she truly meant it.

For years, she'd been telling Brent "no" and not really meaning it. She'd said it to make things hotter and to relieve herself of any blame. This time, though, she was being brutally honest with herself. She had to break herself of her Harrington habit.

There was another man she wanted more—even though she could never have him.

An oppressive weight suddenly lifted from her shoulders. She'd been tied up in a sick obsession for Brent Harrington for so long, she hadn't been able to think straight. She felt as if her head had just been cleared of a fog.

She shook her head, feeling almost sorry for the man who'd harassed her since they'd been kids. As a willing accomplice, she'd only helped him along. "I'm sorry, Brent."

His hard touch went still. "What?" he said, uncomprehendingly.

She looked up at him. "I'm sorry," she repeated. "I'm done doing this."

She braced herself against his thighs and felt them tense. Slowly, she pushed herself to her feet. With grace and dignity, she pulled her bra together and did the clasp.

He reached out to stop her. "What are you talking about?"

"I don't blame you, although I'm sure I will later." She brushed his hand aside and smoothed her sweater down to her waist. "I've been enabling you but, as of now, it's over."

"What are you talking about?" The look on his face was almost desperate. "What's over?"

"I won't degrade myself for you anymore," she said calmly. "You're right. There is something happening between Riley and me and you've got Shelli. We need to put all these perverse teenage games behind us."

He yanked her back to him, clutching her almost frantically. "It wasn't a game. I would have married you, Tally. Shit, if you just would have had the bloodline, we'd be together now."

It was sad but, in her heart, Talia knew it to be the truth. Prick that he was, if he'd asked her to marry him, she would have run full speed to the altar.

She wouldn't have been able to deny herself.

She cupped his face and felt his jaw tighten. "Take care of yourself, Brent."

She pulled back and their fingertips brushed as he caught her hand, but slowly let it go. He acted like a five-year-old who'd been told "no" for the first time. He looked uncertain, unhappy and on the verge of rebellion.

She turned her back on him. It would be best not to drag this out. She picked up her things and headed for the door.

"We aren't finished," he finally called, his voice hoarse. "I won't let us be."

"You don't have anything to say about it." She paused in the doorway and calmness washed over her. "Not anymore."

And never again.

Chapter Fourteen

Riley followed Talia down the alley behind Coolectibles. He'd given up all pretense of laying low. It was time they had this out. When she parked, he pulled into the spot beside her. He was out of his car and waiting for her before she even undid her seatbelt.

She sat for a long moment when she spied him, almost as if she didn't want to get out of the car. When she finally opened the driver's door, a wary look was on her face. "Detective," she said.

He was taken aback when she closed the door, turned and started to walk away. He could hardly believe it. He'd never suspected Talia Sizemore would turn tail and run. "Don't even think about it," he said, suddenly incensed.

Snow scrunched under her feet as she kept right on walking.

"Talia," he warned.

"Are you stalking me now?" she asked wearily.

He reached out and caught her arm. She was going to at least look at him, by God. With a tug, he turned her around. "What happened back there?"

She stiffened. "Where?"

"At Harrington's. You walked in there like you were on a warpath." He ducked down to get a better look at her. The way she was keeping her face averted was pissing him off.

"You followed me?"

"Yeah, that's what stalkers do. Detectives, too."

She fumbled with her purse. "Either way, it's none of your business."

"Try again."

She shrugged uneasily. "It was nothing. I just needed to talk with Brent."

"Must have been quite the conversation. You didn't even see me in the lobby when you walked out." He caught her chin and forced her to look at him. "Should I send the paramedics back there or—"

The look on her face nearly cut him off at the knees. Her face was pale, almost ashen. She had that utterly defeated look about her—the kind that people got when they fought back and realized it was of no use. Riley felt everything inside him harden.

"That fucking bastard," he said hoarsely.

She looked as if she could shatter into a million pieces. Possessiveness hit him like a two-ton hammer and he moved closer to her.

"What happened?" he asked. "What did he do?"

She took a cautious step back and held up her hand to ward him off. "Don't. Please. I can't deal with you right now."

"Sorry, baby," he said gently. "I'm not liking the way this conversation is going. You deal with me or I'll go get Harrington and we'll all deal with this down at the station."

She didn't like that idea at all. As a policeman, he was trained to see details and, boy, were they flying at him now. At the mention of Harrington's name, her lips thinned and her nostrils flared. It was the look in her eyes, though, that really stopped him. She looked wounded. He'd seen women act like this before and he didn't like the implications.

Self-consciously, she brushed her hair away from her face. "Can we not talk about him?"

The son of a bitch.

"He touched you," Riley said in a flat tone.

"I… He…"

"Don't try to deny it. I've seen the way he looks at you." Riley's stomach began to churn as his mind automatically went to the worst scenario. He didn't want to ask but he had to know. "Did he rape you?"

Her entire body rocked. "No!"

He wasn't ready to feel relief yet. If anything, the churning only got worse. "What exactly did he do?"

She swallowed hard and Riley felt his rage build. "Did he hurt you?"

"Not the way you think." She tugged at her purse again in agitation. "Please, just let it go. You wouldn't understand."

"Try me."

"You'll just think I'm being oversensitive."

"I doubt it. I've met the asshole."

It was the right thing to say. Her gaze jumped up to meet his and Riley tensed. She was judging him. He suddenly found himself wanting to be worthy of her trust.

"Did you see the morning paper?" she finally asked.

He shook his head. He'd been parked outside her apartment but he had a feeling she knew that.

"He took credit for the auction." She took a deep breath that hitched halfway through. "I don't know why I was surprised; it was classic Brent. He has the power to do things like that—change things that shouldn't be changed—just because he has the Harrington name. It was the last straw."

Riley wasn't quite sure he understood. She was jittery, though, and he definitely got that. Carefully, he reached out and rubbed her shoulder. "From what I hear the Sizemore name is no slouch."

He took it as a sign of encouragement when she didn't flinch away from his touch. Instead, she wrapped her arms about her waist in an unconscious hug. "Did you grow up in New Covington?"

He hesitated. She'd never asked him anything personal before. "No."

"Then you don't know what it's like. My family moved here when I was ten. People wouldn't accept us, though, because our money wasn't old enough. Brent Harrington and his friends have looked down their noses at me for my entire life. Today was just the capper. Sadie and I worked long and hard on that auction but the *Turd* stepped in and took that away from us, too."

Riley heard the hurt in her voice and it ticked him off more than he would have expected. The pain sounded deep and inbred. Harrington hadn't hurt her physically but he'd hurt her feelings—and not for the first time. It was a pattern that he didn't like.

At all.

"Talia, you can't let him get to you like this," he said soothingly. He slid his hand across her shoulder and cupped the back of her neck. The muscles there were stiff as a board. "People know who put that auction together and what it was for. The newspaper isn't going to change their minds."

"But anybody who wasn't there won't know."

"So you'll tell them."

She let out a frustrated sigh. "You're not helping."

He rubbed his thumb against a knot at the base of her skull. "Would it help if I went over there and kicked his ass?"

That earned him a soft smile. He liked the look of her smile. It made something squeeze inside his chest.

"It would be my pleasure," he admitted. "The guys down at the station actually have a pool going as to how long I'll be able to hold out."

She bit her lip and shot him a look of regret. "Has Brent been giving you trouble about…well, the case?"

They both knew full well who was giving him trouble about the case but neither wanted to bring up that subject. Riley sure as hell didn't. This was the closest she'd ever let him get. He was finally getting inside her head; he wasn't going to jeopardize that. "Harrington has done everything he can to mess with our investigation. He calls me daily to demand a progress report on that damn cat of his."

"Cat?" Her cheeks turned pink. She took a step back, breaking their contact.

He slowly dropped his hand. He knew she was more aware than anyone what had happened to that bronzed sculpture but he got the feeling that wasn't why she was embarrassed. "Did Harrington say something about the investigation?"

Her agitation returned. "Maybe."

Riley could feel his impatience growing. "What did he say?"

"It doesn't matter."

"It matters to me."

Her foot began to tap an abstract pattern in the snow. "He said... Oh, don't make me repeat it."

Like hell. He planted himself in front of her, totally messing up her design. "We're not going anywhere until you do."

"Damn it, Riley," she said miserably. Clearing her throat, she stared somewhere over his shoulder. "He thinks you're looking for my pussy harder than you're looking for his."

The sound of the word "pussy" on her lips nearly knocked Riley over. He stared at her helplessly and felt his cock jerk. "The guy's an idiot but he might be onto something there," he said hoarsely.

The cold, winter air snapped. Talia shifted her weight, obviously not immune to the sudden tension that filled the alleyway. "Could he cause trouble for you?"

It wasn't the response he expected and he looked at her in confusion. She sounded like she was actually concerned. For him.

It didn't help his aroused condition one bit.

"Like I give a rat's ass. Bring him on."

She stared at him in amazement.

He sighed. "Baby, in case you haven't noticed, I'm a tough son-of-a-bitch. He can't touch me. And you've got to realize you're not ten years old anymore. For all his puffed-up ego, Harrington can't hurt you or degrade you if you don't let him. You've got to break free of this hold he has over you."

The most indescribable look crossed her face. "I have. That's what just happened back at his office."

Riley felt a tingle at the back of his neck. The truth. Finally. "Good," he said softly. "It sounds like it was past time you set him straight."

She stared at him for so long, the tingle became pinpricks. He watched her just as intently. He wished to God he knew what she was thinking. Thoughts were whirring inside her head; he could see the gears turning.

Her puzzled gaze dropped to his mouth. "He's jealous of you," she whispered.

Riley's mind went blank. Harrington was *what*?

She blinked and seemed to snap out of it. Unusually flustered, she turned away. "I should get back inside to help Sadie."

He latched onto her arm. The tingle had worked its way into his chest. "Wait a minute. You can't say something like that and just walk away."

"Sadie likes you, you know," she babbled, not even listening to him. "She thinks you're a nice guy and that I should—"

"Talia." He grabbed her by the lapels and pulled her so close their noses nearly brushed. "Why should Harrington be jealous?"

The look in her eyes was hot and frantic.

A soft sound erupted from her throat. Before he could figure out what the hell was happening, she leaned into him and pressed her mouth against his.

The contact shocked him senseless.

Her lips felt cool but the kiss she planted on him was red-hot. It didn't take long for him to catch up. His grip on her tightened reflexively and, with a growl, he slanted his mouth across hers.

God, she was sweet.

Changing angles, he sent his tongue deep. She murmured softly and her arms came up around his neck. Even with the layers of winter clothing between them, her curves fit against him perfectly. Riley let out a grunt of pure pleasure. He slid one hand up to cup the back of her head and sent the other down to her ass. He pulled her tight against him as his hips ground against her. After an unsatisfying night, his cock was more than ready for some action.

An unsatisfying night.

Godammit!

He jerked his head back. Breathing hard, he peeled her off of him. So help him... "What is this? Another trick like you pulled at the theater?"

Her eyes were glazed with passion and her lips were swollen. She was caught up in the moment and it took a while for understanding to dawn. When it did, her face tightened in embarrassment. She remembered the auction—and she remembered missing most of it with her hand stuck in his fly. She pushed at his shoulders, suddenly wanting to get away from him.

He jerked her back. "Enough with the games."

The look on her face was far from mischievous. She looked like she might cry.

He went still.

She wasn't playing a game.

His cock hardened to the point of steel. She'd kissed him because she'd wanted to kiss him.

He crowded her right up against her car.

"Look at me," he demanded. "The truth, Talia. Did you like the feel of my cock in your hand last night?"

Her face flamed but she didn't say no.

He leaned closer, letting her take his weight. "Did you like it when I strip searched you after the Jones robbery?"

She closed her eyes but he could feel her body softening. It only made his all the more rigid.

"Did you like it when I pushed my fingers into your pussy?"

"Stop it."

"And up your ass?"

A whimper left her throat.

He wasn't about to ease up. "Did you strip for me last night?" he growled.

Her eyelids fluttered open in surprise. For a full minute, she stood frozen in his arms. When she finally spoke, her voice was hardly louder than a whisper. "Why are you doing this? I thought you were convinced I was the New Covington Cat Burglar."

"You *are* the New Covington Cat Burglar."

"But...but you're assigned to the case."

"Right now, I'm past the point of caring."

She bit her lower lip and Riley felt his fingertip hold on his control slip. "I want the truth. Are you just jerking me around or do you want me?"

She almost lied. He could tell. Her lips pressed together and her gaze skittered away. Determinedly, he ground his cock against the vee at the top of her legs. She let out a soft moan and sagged against him. "I want you," she whispered.

Three little words and his fate was sealed.

He kissed her then almost savagely. Their lips clung and his tongue plunged deep. Her taste made him groan.

Forget the job. Forget everyone else. This was all that mattered.

Rolling with her in his arms, he turned so he was the one settled back against the car and she was draped over him. She wasn't fighting him anymore. Her tongue rasped against his and she snuggled to get closer.

He was more than happy to help. Wedging his hands between their bodies, he started working on her coat. The minute it took to open it was too long. He thrust his hands inside. He had to touch her.

Her sweater was impossibly soft but he wanted skin. Hot, smooth, tender skin. He tugged up the material and laid his hand flat across her stomach.

She inhaled sharply.

He rubbed her in slow circles as he ate at her lips. She trembled against him and her hands threaded through his hair. She acted like a woman who needed to be held. A woman who needed long, slow lovemaking.

He didn't know if he could manage the slow part...

"Riley," she moaned. She wiggled closer and ran her hands across his thighs.

He nearly bucked her off. Damn, but he was ready to detonate.

He jammed his fingers under the waistband of her skirt. The fit was tight. His other hand tore at the zipper at her back and he managed to work it down halfway. She gasped and caught at the material before it fell to the snow at her feet.

He'd gotten what he'd wanted, though. Room to work. He slid his palm down her quivering belly and found cotton. Plain old cotton.

God, now! She'd made him wait too long. He needed to get inside her *now*.

He tore his mouth from hers and looked over her shoulder toward the back door to Coolectibles. The thought of Sadie inside stopped him. He'd never get her up to her apartment. He'd take her right on the goddamn staircase.

And with the way she was shaking under his touch, he didn't think she'd mind.

She caught his forearm and her fingernails dug into his skin. "Don't stop," she said raggedly. "Make love to me, Riley. *Please*. Show me there's still good left in this world."

"Shit," he cursed.

Where? The car? He hadn't done that since high school and he'd prefer more room. He looked around a little frantically before his gaze settled on the Coolectibles company van. "There," he said.

He backed her quickly toward the vehicle. "The keys," he said. "Find the keys."

Her hands shook as she tried to keep her skirt on and dig into her purse at the same time. He knew he didn't help matters as he kissed his way down to her neck but he couldn't help himself. At last, he heard the jingle of heaven.

He swiped the keys out of her shaking hands but his weren't much better. Finally, he managed to jab the key into the keyhole. He opened the back of the van but swore when he saw the pile of things Sadie had stored inside. No doubt supplies from the auction. Still, there was a little room right up against the door. He lifted Talia inside and sat her on her butt. "It'll work. Get on all fours."

The look she gave him was part shock, part excitement and part offense. "I will not!"

Classy dame. She'd never screwed in a love mobile before.

Well, she was about to be initiated.

"The hell you won't." Spreading her legs, he scrunched up her skirt and ground his erection directly against her mound. "If I don't get inside you soon, I'm going to jack off right inside my pants. Do you understand?"

Her head dropped back and her legs wrapped around his waist.

That meant "yes" to him.

Urgency pressed at Riley hard. Hands shaking, he pushed her coat off her shoulders. His gaze went straight to her stiff nipples. They were so hard, her bra couldn't hide them. He could see the firm peaks through the soft sweater she wore. He wrestled the coat all the way off her and threw it into the van, uncaring where it landed. "Doggy style," he grunted as he unwound her legs from his waist and turned her onto her knees.

He was already reaching for his zipper as he climbed in behind her. With one hand he slammed the door behind them. It made for a tight fit but he didn't care. He was looking for a tight fit.

He had himself out of his jeans before she even had her loose skirt worked up to her waist. With an impatient hand he pressed her forward so she was on all fours in front of him. The sight alone almost set him off.

"Christ," he groaned.

The panties he'd found were built into her nylons. It was a turn-on knowing that she wasn't wearing anything underneath. The cold air in the van quickly heated. Reaching out, he traced a run down the back of her thigh. "You've got a snag," he said quietly.

She shuddered violently at his soft touch and her hands slipped against the metal floor. "Riley," she begged. "Please."

So she didn't want it nice and polite. Neither did he.

He grabbed the waistband of her nylons and yanked them down and out of his way. Her white cheeks popped into view.

"Damn."

She had a great ass but it would have to wait until later. It was her pussy he wanted. He pulled the nylons down just far enough to where it was naked. Naked and vulnerable.

Hunger tore through him when he found her pink and swollen. Hell, he'd hardly touched her and she was already primed? What would she be like if he made an effort? The devil made him decide to see. She cried out when he stroked her. He did it again, purposefully spreading her lips and flicking her clit until she was shuddering in front of him.

The sight made his blood thunder. She was so responsive. Bending down over her, he pressed his lips against her ear.

"Did you know that I could see your blonde curls in the lamplight last night?" He threaded his fingers through the springy hair and gave a soft tug. He felt her pussy spasm and she nearly sobbed with need.

"Are you ready for me?" he said with a quick lick to her earlobe.

"Yes!"

There was no time for foreplay. Moisture was already dripping from the tip of his cock and she was running like a river.

He sat upright and hooked an arm under her waist.

"No more teasing, Talia. This time we're going all the way." He lined himself up with her opening. In one motion, he pulled her back toward him and thrust. "All...the...way."

Her back arched. "Aye! Oh... Oh, God!"

"Take it," he growled.

She was like a fist around him. Her nylons kept her from spreading her legs and it made his entry difficult. Her kneecaps pressed tight against the outside of his as he kneeled behind her. The result was the tightest, hottest fit he'd ever experienced. He penetrated hard and kept pushing until he was balls deep.

Her cry resonated in the close quarters and splotches of color flashed behind his closed eyelids. She wanted this; he could feel her pulsing around him. Uncontrolled, he began pumping into her.

"It's too much," she gasped.

"Relax. You can take it, baby." He slowed down, but guided her hips with the iron band he kept around her waist. Soon, she found the rhythm. "There you go," he crooned.

She let out a moan of pleasure.

He knew how she felt.

He slid his free hand over her bunched-up skirt and under her sweater. Her skin was like silk. He caressed her spine as she rocked back and forth. He didn't have to help her anymore. The sound of their harsh breaths filled the van and fogged the windows.

Need was consuming Riley. Reaching around her, he loosened the front clasp of her bra. It fell open and he wrapped both arms around her. Her swaying breast filled his hand and her nipple jabbed at his palm.

Short cries left her throat with each thrust he gave and soon the entire van was rocking with them. The suspension system creaked and a box slid forward, nearly falling on them.

"Ri...ley..." Talia panted. Her arms gave out and she dropped down onto her elbows.

The position, head down and ass up, sent him off. He rammed into her, spreading her tight pussy with his thick cock. He wanted to dominate her, make her his. If he could get her to submit to him, they had a chance.

He pounded into her like a madman and watched as her hands raked along the floor. She was helpless to his onslaught but she was a willing recipient. She took everything he had to give and pleasure permeated the chilled air. It didn't take long. The pinnacle came quickly and violently. She let out an eager cry and her pussy clamped down hard.

"Fuck!" Riley growled as he threw his head back.

The tendons in his neck stretched taut as the orgasm rocked him. His cock finally spurted its wad. Holding her tightly, he jerked two more times before collapsing forward onto her. Their ragged breaths blended and echoed off the walls of the van.

"Oh, my God," Talia said weakly. She sagged against the cold metal floor like a limp rag. Riley's weight pushed down on her heavily and she felt pinned. It didn't matter. She couldn't have moved if she'd wanted to. She was absolutely stunned. She couldn't believe what they'd just done. They'd gone at each other like two animals in heat.

She pushed aside something beside her head and realized it was one of the ribbons that had been used to decorate the theater. For heaven's sake, they'd just rutted in the back of her company van.

"Holy shit," Riley said, somewhere close to her ear.

He pulled her with him as he sat back on his haunches. She gasped as she felt his cock shift inside her. Even halfway limp, he felt huge inside her.

He muttered under his breath when he saw how her thighs had turned white where the nylons pulled. Still holding her about the waist, he reached down and rolled the constricting material down to her knees. The tenderness in his touch made her uneasy.

"Better?" he asked.

"Yes, thank you," she said inanely.

"No, thank you," he teased. "That was fucking amazing."

It was. She'd had good sex before, but nothing close to this. She'd never had such an earth-shattering orgasm. There were scratch marks from her fingernails on the floor of her van and she was sure her knees would be black and blue for weeks. Her pleasure had been absolutely mindless.

And incredibly stupid. She'd just screwed the man whose job it was to arrest her!

Her exhilaration cooled. What had she been thinking? How could she have made herself so vulnerable to him? She might as well have surrendered. "We shouldn't have done that," she said shakily.

"We're still doing it," he said as he nipped her ear. He swiveled his hips and embedded himself even more firmly inside her. "Or hadn't you noticed?"

Astride him as she was, it was impossible not to. He was hardening again already and she bit her lip to keep from moaning. Dangerous or not, she still wanted him, too.

His wandering hands found their way under her sweater. He spread his fingers wide to explore her. She shifted in unconscious enjoyment and the move was almost like a tiny little thrust onto his stiffening cock. He let out a grunt when he felt it, too.

The sound ricocheted inside her head. No. She couldn't let it happen again. If she did, she'd be a goner.

The muscles in her thighs tensed and she almost leveraged herself up and off of him. "We can't," she said desperately. "Let me go."

"What the— No!" He pulled her down firmly, impaling her on his stiff cock. "What's wrong? Settle down."

His jeans felt rough against the backs of her thighs and his cock felt hot and unyielding inside her. Talia wriggled in his lap but that only made the sensations intensify. She felt her body beginning to melt and she fought to steel her mind against him.

As tender as his touch might be, she couldn't let herself be fooled. She knew him. He was a good cop, one who wouldn't be able to look the other way. This wasn't going to change his mind about her.

If anything, it was changing her mind about him.

Anxiety raced through her when she realized how badly she wanted to confide in him. The deep-seated urge scared her and she clawed at his hands to try to free herself. "I'm not going to fall for this. I won't turn myself in to you. You've got no proof against me. You just want to gain my trust so you can throw me in prison."

"Throw you in prison?" he barked. "Damn it, woman."

She wasn't settling down, so he did what came naturally. He began fucking her.

"Why would I want to throw you in prison when I could have this?"

"Ah!" She tried to pull away but the feel of him shafting her was too good. "Drop the investigation," she begged.

"No."

Distress clogged her throat.

He pressed his mouth against her ear. "But I will do everything I can to make sure you get off easy."

His hands pinched at her nipples and her neck arched in pleasure. She fought the feelings surging through her. She wasn't ready to give in. "Why would you do that?"

"Why? In case you haven't noticed, I've got a thing for you." His breaths sounded loud in her ear. "Your ways are twisted but your intentions are pure. You've got a big heart, you're beautiful and you're cunning as hell. Somehow, the combination turns me on."

"But we couldn't ever be together," she said, her voice tight. "I know that. You're just trying to confuse me."

"We aren't having a problem being together right now."

He juddered into her almost roughly and her breath caught in her lungs. He didn't give her time to regain her poise. He started humping her hard and fast. The electricity started to zap again and she reached back to catch his hips.

"Ah! Riley!"

"Too deep?"

"No." In this way, she couldn't fight him. "Just like that."

She was feeling every inch of him but he wasn't satisfied. Reaching down between her legs, he sought out her clit. Her body bowed when he found it and her fingers raked across his butt cheeks.

"We'll find a way," he growled into her ear. "Trust me and I'll do everything I can to protect you."

Resistance drained out of her as she gave herself up to his capable hands.

Her body soon became slick with sweat and she could feel her juices slathering everything—his thighs, her bottom, his balls... His hands were everywhere. On her breasts. Raking up and down her thighs. Probing between her legs. She gritted her teeth when she felt the familiar zing start low in her belly.

Please, dear God, she thought. *Don't let him be lying.* She wanted to believe in him.

She bounced on his lap until the rush went through her. Her entire body arched and she called out his name.

"Trust me," he demanded one last time.

"Yes!" she cried as her body seized.

He held her tight as he fucked her through it. When his own orgasm hit, he thrust so hard, he lifted her right off her knees, impaling her as far as he could go.

When Talia finally found her air again, they were both leaning against the wall of the van and groping at each other for support. She reached out to brace herself and found the window fogged over.

His grip on her tightened.

"I'd never hurt you, baby," he said between breaths. "But things have got to change. You've gotten yourself into one hell of a mess. If somebody else cracks the case first, I won't be able help you."

"I know," she said softly. "I need you to understand. I—"

The ringing of a cell phone made them both flinch. Talia looked around but realized that her coat was on a box near the front seats and her purse was nowhere to be found. She'd probably dropped it outside.

"Shit. That's me."

"Don't answer," she said instinctively.

"I've got to. I'm on duty." He reached down into the pocket of his leather jacket and pulled out his cell phone. "Kinkade here."

Kinkade.

As in Detective.

The call was business. It broke the intimate little cocoon they'd made for themselves and Talia felt her bliss fading. She didn't want the real world in here. It brought back all her fears and doubts.

"Where?" he said, his attention focusing on the call. "Damn it. Okay, I'll be right there."

Her warning signals started bleating. *Ramona!* Oh, dear Lord. She'd forgotten about that.

Fear ripped through her. Riley would go off the deep end when he discovered that her striptease hadn't been for his enjoyment alone. She couldn't believe how close she'd come to admitting her guilt.

He hung up the phone and silence screamed throughout the back of the van.

"I'm sorry," he said, nuzzling her shoulder. "I have to respond to that call."

"Do you have to?" she asked, trying to forestall the inevitable. When he discovered what she'd done, they'd be adversaries again.

"I wish I didn't."

His hands settled onto her hips and gently guided her off of him. There was a distinct slurp as their bodies disconnected. Talia felt empty. She knew she was losing more than just that part of him. She concentrated on straightening her clothing rather than look at him.

"This is important," he said as he zipped up his jeans. "I wouldn't go otherwise."

"I know," she said as she zipped up her skirt and pulled it back down over her hips. Her throat felt tight. She just wanted to bawl. She'd screwed things up so badly. "Go ahead. Go do your cop business."

He leaned forward and rocked her composure with a hot, possessive kiss.

"I'll be back. Don't worry, baby. We'll talk and we'll find a way to work things out. Everything will be okay."

She nodded.

Deep inside, though, she knew it wouldn't.

Chapter Fifteen

Talia was stressing out as she drove to New Covington College. The call Riley had taken in the van had her scared. Flat-out, plain scared. It had been about the robbery at Ramona's place, she knew it. She had to find Professor Winston. She needed to get rid of the crystal paperweight she'd stolen *now*. Once Riley saw all the telltale signs at the condo, he'd be back for her. She had no misconceptions about what would happen then. He'd search her place. If he found the stolen property, he'd arrest her.

It didn't matter what had just happened.

Her foot jammed harder on the accelerator. *What had just happened?*

Good Lord, she hadn't been prepared for that. She hadn't been prepared for *him*. She'd known they were attracted to each other; she'd felt it from the moment they'd met. She just hadn't expected that their coming together would be so incredibly explosive.

And she'd thought that Brent Harrington had power over her.

"Don't," she snapped at herself.

Things between her and Riley were nothing like that. With him, she felt... different. Emotions and feelings got all jumbled up in the mix. Her body heated at the memory of his intimate touch and she squirmed in the driver's seat to ease the ache in her sex.

"Stop thinking about it!" she ordered.

Looking down at the speedometer, she forced herself to ease up on the gas. Getting caught for speeding was the last thing she needed. Things were already convoluted enough and she'd left herself no margin for error. She had to settle down and concentrate on getting herself out of this mess.

Analyzing what was going on between her and the detective would have to wait until later.

Slippery roads made the drive take longer than normal. The sidewalks weren't much better but the need for discretion made Talia park at the diner and walk the rest of the way. By the time she made it to Jefferson Hall, she was a nervous wreck. Why had she waited so long to pass off the take to Winston? She knew better than that. Her heels clipped a fast pace down the hallway and the briefcase weighed heavily at her arm.

What if Riley was already searching for her?

She bypassed the lecture hall and went straight to Winston's office. The light was on. She took a calming breath as she gripped the handle and swung open the door.

"Professor—" The words died on her lips as she found a slew of people inside. Heads snapped toward her and she took an unconscious step backwards. "I... I'm looking for Professor Winston."

"He's been detained."

The quiet but lethal voice from the back of the room sent a shiver down her spine. A woman with a fingerprint kit stepped to the side and she saw the man with the voice like ice. Her stomach plummeted. "Riley."

He was looking at her with fire in his eyes. In his hand, he held one of Brent's African pieces, which she'd sold to the professor.

Her entire body began to shake.

The gig was up. It was over. *They* were over.

And they'd hardly gotten started.

"Ms. Sizemore," he said in that same, scary tone. His gaze raked over her, but froze on the briefcase in her hand. The tension in the room became suffocating. "Do you have business with the professor?"

Talia's heart was pounding so loudly, she feared she might have a heart attack. She got the insane urge to hide the briefcase behind her back or toss it down the hallway. Self-preservation instincts warned her not to do anything foolish.

"I took classes from him," she said in the steadiest voice she could manage. "I often consult him when an unusual piece comes into my shop. Is there a problem?"

The look on Riley's face was tortured. "Yeah, there's a problem."

She fought the urge to run. "Then I'll come back at a more convenient time."

"Like hell you will."

The words exploded, making everyone in the room jump. Looks that had been trained on her suddenly swung toward him.

"Shit," he hissed. He raked a hand through his hair. His shoulders shifted up and down as he took deep breaths. The room went quiet as everyone waited but looks of uncertainty were exchanged.

Only Talia understood what was going on.

He was deciding her destiny.

And there was absolutely nothing she could do about it.

Suddenly, he turned and swept up the box of wooden carvings.

"Finish up here," he ordered his team. "I'm going to take Ms. Sizemore for questioning."

A whimper escaped Talia's throat. This wasn't how she wanted things to end. She watched Riley anxiously as he came at her. The lover who'd taken her so greedily was gone. In his place was a police detective filled with ice-cold determination. She held up her hand to fend him off. He caught her and turned her with a jerk. She had to practically run to keep up with him as he dragged her down the hallway.

"Riley," she said, her throat tight. "I can explain."

"Save it."

The anger radiating from him was blistering. It scared her even more. He'd been upset with her before, but never like this. He led her out of the building to his car. When he opened the passenger door, she meekly got inside. She knew better than to fight him.

"Put on your seatbelt," he snarled as he sat down in the driver's seat.

She quickly snapped herself into place. "Please listen to me."

He slammed his hand against the steering wheel. "Not another word! *Don't you get it?* Things have changed. An entire NCPD crime scene unit just put you at a third crime scene. I can't cover for you anymore."

"I'll tell you everything."

"Don't. I don't want to see any evidence or hear any confessions. The time for that has passed. Don't give me anything I might be forced to use against you."

The words buffeted her and she sank into the seat. Muck flew from under the tires as he threw the car into gear. The back end fishtailed as they pulled out of the parking lot and she instinctively reached for the dashboard. She risked a glance in his direction.

His profile was stony. Lines of stress crossed his forehead and red slashes marked his cheekbones. The lips that had kissed her so hungrily were now pressed nearly flat. He didn't look just angry.

He looked hurt.

Guilt suddenly assailed her. From his point of view, things had to look terrible. He knew she was the Cat Burglar; that wasn't what had him so upset. It was what had happened in the van. He'd told her he'd help her if she turned herself in but what had she proceeded to do? Run out and meet her fence.

Talia closed her eyes in remorse. She wouldn't blame him if he kicked her into next week.

Silence sat heavily in the car as they drove across town. Just when she thought she couldn't stand the tension one second more, he pulled into the driveway of a nice, middle-class, ranch-style house. He'd taken her home. She didn't know if that was a good thing or not. He reached in her direction. She shrank back but he jabbed the garage door opener. Dread loomed in her chest when he pulled into the garage and closed the door behind them.

"I'm sorry," she whispered.

He finally looked at her. "Get out," he said flatly.

Talia felt tears press at her eyes. She truly was sorry. She was sorry she'd hurt him. She was sorry things had gotten so messed up. Most of all, she was sorry she'd ever moved to this horrible town.

Miserably, she followed him into the house. He dropped Brent's box onto the coffee table in the living room and whipped off his leather jacket. It went sailing across the room. "Do you have any idea the position you've put me in?" he roared.

She flinched. His temper was finally turning loose. Shame made her want to curl into a little ball but she forced her chin to stay up. She deserved this. "I didn't mean to put you in the middle."

"Well, that's smack dab where I've landed." His glare dropped down to the briefcase she still held tightly in her hand. "Get rid of that thing!"

She quickly set it on the floor.

"Don't show me that," he said as he raked both hands through his hair. "I can't see what's in that case."

Confusion made her stand upright slowly. He hadn't taken her to the police station and he didn't want to search her briefcase. What was going on?

She watched as he began pacing heavily around the room.

"I can't believe you showed up at Winston's," he said. "I didn't know you were using him."

Uneasiness pricked at the back of her neck. "Then why were you there?"

"This wasn't about the Cat Burglar," he said, flinging one hand into the air. "We've been watching the professor for nearly six months. He was suspected of fencing stolen art but we weren't able to prove it until today when he tried to sell a painting to an undercover cop."

Talia's air seeped out of her lungs. It hadn't even been about her! She'd stumbled into something that wouldn't have touched her if she'd just stayed away. Dismay made her stomach sour.

Riley changed directions and came right at her. "What were you going to give him anyway? When could you possibly have swiped anything?"

She braced herself. Oh, God. He couldn't find out about Ramona now. It would make things even worse—if that were possible.

"I watched you all night long." He came to a dead stop and his eyebrows lifted dramatically. "Oh, that's low, baby."

"Riley," she said, her voice like sandpaper. "Please understand. None of this had anything to do with you."

"That little striptease sure as hell had something to do with me." He planted his hands on his hips. "Godammit, Talia. I should warm your bottom for this!"

The air sizzled between them.

"In fact," he said more softly. "That's not such a bad idea."

A distinct glint lit his eyes and she looked at him in shock. He wasn't kidding.

Mortification washed through her. She knew she had to pay, but not like that. Fight or flight kicked in and she bolted toward the door.

He hooked her about the waist before she'd gotten three steps. "You need a keeper, woman."

Her heart slammed against her rib cage. She didn't like the sound of that. She flailed at him but he was too strong. The room spun as he carried her to the couch. When he sat down, he plopped her on her belly over his lap. She immediately tried to leverage herself up. He put his hand flat on her backside and pushed her back down.

"I had other plans for this ass but this will have to do," he said.

She squirmed on his lap with indignation. She'd never seen this side of him. There was no tenderness in him at all, no leniency. He was incensed by her betrayal and intent on showing her how much. She batted at his hands as he pushed up her skirt.

"You got rid of the nylons but you found some panties, I see."

"Don't," she said when he began peeling them off. The degradation was too much, especially from him. Twisting around, she grabbed for her underwear. Mercilessly, he pushed her hands aside.

The struggle became a battle of wills. She kicked at him, hoping that the heels of her boots would connect, but he pushed her panties down her thighs and her legs got tangled. He shifted her hips, throwing her off balance. The position thrust her bare butt cheeks up into the air. Humiliation rushed through her and she tensed. She still wasn't ready when the first slap came ringing down hard.

"Ow!" Her body jackknifed. That was no love tap. "Let me go."

"Do you know what kind of hell you've put me through?" he said harshly.

Another smack came down crisply on her tender cheeks and Talia let out a cry. His bare hand was as biting as a paddle. Her butt clenched and her skin stung. She shimmied her hips to try to get away but suffered two more slaps on the ass.

Hot pain rolled through her and she gasped. She hadn't been spanked since she was a child but her response was all adult now. Naked as she was, the heat was coursing over her skin and collecting in the most embarrassing place. Her fingers curled into the cushion beneath her. She was horrified by her reaction.

"Rich snobs have been breathing down my neck," Riley said. "The commissioner himself has stopped by my desk more times than I can count. Even your sugar daddy, Roger Thorton, has been making a royal ass of himself."

"Uncle Roger?" she said on a high note.

"You call him *uncle*?" His hand came down in a series of sharp smacks.

Her breath hissed out her lips as she tried to cope with the stinging in her backside. Her ass felt like it was on fire. It throbbed with every beat of her heart. Worse yet, the pulse between her legs was starting to match the rhythm.

"I should throw this pretty red ass of yours in jail," he said as his flat palm connected again. "Maybe that would teach you a lesson."

Her body writhed. Oh, God. He had to stop.

"I'm not proud of what I've done," she gasped.

"Neither am I." A swift rap on the underside of her cheeks caught her by surprise and every muscle in her body clenched.

"Aiyeee!" she screeched. Her backside was a mass of raw nerve endings but the sensitivity was pouring over into her pussy and her breasts. Her heels came up into the air as she dug her knees into the sofa. She couldn't take much more.

She was either going to cry or come.

She didn't know which would be more mortifying.

Riley was breathing nearly as hard as she was. She could feel his rib cage expanding and contracting against her waist.

"Why couldn't you have trusted me just a little?" he asked, his voice strained. "Did that fuck in the van mean nothing to you?"

A whimper left her throat. He couldn't talk about fucking now. He simply couldn't.

He finally stopped spanking her but his hand lay flat on her backside. That was almost worse. Talia moaned as her nerve endings pricked and burned. She tried to roll away but he held her in place. If only he'd move that touch between her legs... A tear of frustration slipped down her cheek.

"You've got my head so screwed up, woman. Just look at what you've got me doing," he muttered. His hand stroked over her red cheeks. "Hell, you should go straight to my captain. Get me thrown off the case. Maybe that's the answer to this all."

"No!" She was the bad one, not him.

And she *really* wanted to be bad now. She had no shame left. Shifting, she tried to get his hand where she needed it the most. Instead, his fingers toyed with the crevice of her ass, driving her to near distraction.

"What am I going to do with you?" he said tiredly.

Couldn't he tell?

She groaned but she knew that wasn't what he was asking of her. He was thinking ahead to her future.

Their future.

Fear suddenly overrode her agitation. Somehow, somewhere, the two of them had become intertwined. What happened to her affected him and the implications weren't good.

She was going down, she knew — but she didn't want to pull him down with her.

Her breaths went short as the reality of the situation hit her. Letting her go wasn't an option, either. She couldn't ask that of him. She knew him too well. His conscience would crucify him — and she couldn't hurt him like that anymore. He was a good man and a good cop. He'd lose whatever respect he had for her if she didn't accept the punishment she deserved.

Somehow, the thought of losing his respect made more tears press at her eyes than all the swats he'd given her behind.

Defeated, her body went limp. She lay her cheek against the cushion beneath her, finally accepting her fate. "Arrest me," she whispered.

"What?" he asked, bending down to hear.

"Make love to me again," she heard herself saying, "but then take me in. It's the only thing you can do."

His head snapped back. "What the— No! Fuck no!"

The words were impulsive and regret immediately flooded his face. Pressure formed in Talia's chest as she watched him. He was torn between being a man and being a cop. She knew she had to push him in the right direction.

"Riley," she said gently. "It's time."

A muscle ticked in his jaw and he stared at her for what seemed like a lifetime. All the emotion that had ever been between them seemed to congregate in that space and moment. She knew. She could feel it expanding inside her chest. Finally, something clicked behind his eyes.

"I said 'no'."

The hand on her bottom slowly moved and her breath caught. Fire trailed across her skin and she groaned aloud when his hand dropped between her legs. This was what she'd wanted so badly. He caught her firmly just like she needed and she ground her forehead against the couch. Two fingers sought entrance. She was so wet, she took them easily.

"You're the most frustrating, consternating woman I've ever met. You've done some stupid things but I can't condemn you for them," he said as his fingers stroked her intimately. "Your heart was in the right place and it's the biggest heart I've ever met."

"Mmm," she murmured involuntarily. She tried to fight off the arousal crashing through her system. "Don't put your job on the line. Not for me."

"Don't worry about that. We'll work it out later," he said gruffly. His fingers wiggled inside her more aggressively. "We've got something more important to take care of right now. If I heard right, you just asked me to fuck you."

"But Riley..."

"Later."

He leaned over her and she flinched as his sweatshirt brushed over her buttocks. Even that soft touch was too much on her sensitive skin. She heard him rummaging around in something and she twisted around to see what he was doing. She froze when she saw The Box.

He came up with a plump little African man that sent her heart to racing. "No," she said, instinctively backing away.

"Relax."

She couldn't. She'd conceded enough to him already. He couldn't make her submit any more. She tried to push herself up onto her elbows and knees but he easily overpowered her. Her neck craned around. "Please, Riley. No."

"Trust me."

He was asking too much. "It's too big."

"It's just right."

She tensed hard but felt the tip press against her pussy lips.

"Oh," she sighed. Her muscles nearly melted. She'd take it there. She settled back down onto his lap and spread her legs wider. Her pussy was starving to be filled. She was embarrassed that the spanking had made her cream but it let the phallus slide in easily. He worked it in deep. She moaned when he began spinning it inside her tender cunt.

"I was so angry when I found these in Winston's office, I actually saw red," Riley said, his voice going hoarse. She felt the hand on her lower back stiffen. "I saw his lab. Did you—"

"No," she said quickly. She knew he was already jealous of Roger and Brent. "My relationship with the professor was purely collegial."

"Then he never used these?"

She blushed as her thoughts jumped to Jennifer. "Not on me."

"Good."

He began pumping the figurine in and out of her, wetting the polished wood with her sticky juices. Her hips began to rock but she groaned in despair when he inexplicably pulled the sex toy out of her.

He didn't leave her alone for long. He moved the knobby head of the carving to another secret spot and her back bowed.

"Ah!" she gasped in surprise. "Riley!"

"This is what this little guy was meant to do," he said as he pressed the African man firmly against the bud of her anus.

Shock made her slow to react and she grabbed for him clumsily. He caught her hand with his free one and held tight.

"You asked me to fuck you, Talia. Let me."

Her brain stopped functioning. All she could think about was the wicked device at her back door. Her body fought the unnatural intrusion but the pressure was inexorable and unavoidable. Her sphincter surrendered and the butt plug slipped inside.

She clutched so hard at Riley's hand, their fingers turned white.

The pressure was all-encompassing and oh-so-intimate. What hadn't seemed so big in her pussy felt huge up her ass. She was inexperienced with anal sex. All she'd ever taken back there before were Riley's fingers. The butt plug felt just as big, but much, much harder. She felt stretched to the point of discomfort.

"Easy," he crooned as he pushed the devious little man further into her. "I know you'll like this. You loved it when I touched you there."

She wasn't so sure. She swiveled her hips to try to get away from the mounting pressure. She let go of his hand and reached back to try to pull the plug out but he pressed her wrist against the small of her back.

"Just a little more. There. How does that feel, baby?"

Feel? She felt invaded, stretched, debased—and horribly aroused. The dark pleasure was too much to bear.

His hand caressed her tender backside. "That's what I thought," he said softly.

The plug was lodged deep inside her—so deep Talia was afraid to breathe. She moaned when he left it there. A similar pressure began in her pussy and she jolted.

He'd taken another piece from the set and was now inserting it in her cunt. It was one of the larger pieces of the set. She could tell the moment it passed her lips and began to seek entrance.

"No!" The denial burst from her lips even as her back bowed with pleasure.

"No?" he asked, stopping halfway.

"No... I don't know. Oh, God. It's too much!"

"Do you want me to stop?"

"Yes. No. I've never— Take the other one out."

"You'll hate me if I do."

"Riley, please..."

"Please, what, babe?" He began moving the sex toy in her pussy, giving short thrusts that sent pleasure spiraling through her.

"Oooooo."

"I'll take that as a yes." He pushed hard and her pussy opened to take the dildo to the hilt.

Talia's eyes closed tightly as her mind spun out of control. The pressure was overwhelming. She was filled to the point where she couldn't take any more. The discomfort made her toes curl but she couldn't find any relief. The only relief she would find would be a climax but that lingered laughingly just out of her reach.

She reached for her clit.

"Oh no, you don't. You asked me for that." The room spun again as Riley rolled her onto her back. He scooted out from underneath her and she watched as he savagely attacked his clothes.

Her arousal mounted impossibly higher as he stripped. She'd never seen him naked before.

But God, she wanted to.

He pulled his sweatshirt over his head. It went flying and nearly knocked over the lamp behind him. He ripped his T-shirt as he jerked it upward and she murmured in need. His body was mouthwatering. All sinew and muscle. His pecs were rock hard, and his belly was flat and rippled. The muscles in his arms bulged as he threw aside the shirt and reached for his jeans. The zipper nearly broke as he yanked it down. He kicked off his shoes and pushed down his clothes in one smooth motion. His socks followed and he rose before her in all his glory.

Talia swallowed hard. She'd seen *that* before but its size still shocked her. His cock was full and standing up like a battering ram. His balls were plump and pulled up tight. Unconsciously, she opened her legs wider as he dropped to his knees before her.

He caught her ankle and lifted her leg so it was draped across the back of the couch. He pushed the other over the side so her toes touched the floor. The wooden pieces shifted inside her and her neck arched. "Ahhhhh."

He settled over her and she clutched his shoulders so tightly her fingernails left half-moons on his skin. The weight of his body intensified the full feeling inside of her. She felt close to bursting.

"I can't turn you in, Talia," he said into her ear. "You need me too much."

He kissed her and she fought for her climax. She just couldn't quite get there.

"Do you need me, babe?"

"Yes," she cried. She needed him. Inside her. Pumping hard. "I need *you*, Riley. Not these *things*."

He heard the pleading in her voice and reached between her legs. He pulled the dildo out of her vagina so quickly, her body spasmed. He didn't make her wait. His hot, hard flesh took the African man's spot and thrust into her.

She cried out. He'd left the butt plug in and she felt him moving against it. Dark waves of pleasure crashed over her and she clung to him. She wrapped her legs around his waist and the wood shifted deep inside her. It was enough to push her over the top.

"Riley," she cried out as her fingernails bit into his back.

He rode her hard through the orgasm and past it. Sweat dripped from his forehead as he pounded into her, bringing her to another sharp peak. Talia came three times before Riley's head snapped back and his hips jerked uncontrollably. When he fell replete on top of her, she held on for all she was worth. It was a long time before he stirred.

"This is it, Talia," he finally said, his harsh breaths brushing against her hair. "You've got to stop. The New Covington Cat Burglar has to disappear."

"I know," she said.

"No, I don't think you do. We need to get some things straight right here and right now."

He propped himself up on his elbows. His chest heaved as he looked down at her. "I know why you steal and, God help me, I even admire you for it. When I figured out the risks you were putting yourself through for those kids, I had to shake my head."

He gently cupped her face. "But there's more to it than that."

She looked up at him in confusion. "No, that's why I—"

He pressed his thumb to her lips, cutting off the words.

"Just listen." He brushed her hair back. "There's a deeper reason why you keep putting yourself in harm's way and I'm not talking about revenge, although that was a driving force, too. I know you don't want to hear this, baby, but you've got a serious self-esteem problem."

"Self-esteem... I do not!" Talia had never been so surprisingly offended in her life.

His weight didn't budge from atop her. "You've told me how difficult it was growing up in New Covington the way you did. You said you didn't fit in anywhere. Brent Harrington obviously did a number on you and you're still letting him do it."

She was flabbergasted. She couldn't believe what she was hearing. "I didn't *let* him do anything."

"Maybe not, but he's an issue for later. It's your brother who pisses me off the most."

"My brother?" she said, her jaw dropping. She'd had enough of this. She shoved at his shoulders, trying to get him to move off of her. "I love my brother."

He caught her wrists and held them against the cushions. "And he loves you. He just likes to hold it over your head how your father left the family business to him."

Her mouth snapped shut. She couldn't deny it but she'd never admitted as much to anybody other than Sadie. She looked up at Riley warily. Where was he going with all this?

"I saw how he treated you at the auction," he said. A trace of leftover fire lit his eyes. "I wanted to introduce my fist to his face."

She shook her head. "That's just Adam. I don't think he means to do it."

"Then tell him to stop."

The hard look in Riley's eyes made her take pause. There was emotion a mile deep there. He didn't like how her brother treated her. She blinked hard to fight the moisture that suddenly gathered in her tear ducts.

"You haven't, because you think he's right. You think your father left the company to him because he trusted him more. Loved him more."

She flinched. The words hit her like fists.

"Damn you, Riley. That's enough." Anguish clogged her throat and tears began to trickle down her cheeks. He was digging up things she hadn't wanted to face, things that had festered deep inside her for years.

She tried to look away. He gently turned her back to him and brushed a kiss against her forehead.

"You've got it all screwed up in your head," he said softly. "I didn't know your father but it's pretty easy to figure him out."

"Why are you saying these things to me?" she choked out. She didn't want to have this discussion now. She didn't want to have it ever.

"Because you need to hear them. You're too close. You can't see the obvious."

"Maybe I don't want to see it!"

"Think about it, baby," he said persistently. "What, out of everything in this world, did your father hold dearest to his heart?"

She shook her head. Not only was he poking at her deepest insecurities, he was still embedded inside her. It made it impossible to think. Impossible to cope.

"It wasn't his company," he said with certainty.

Of course, it was. She'd adored her father. She'd worshipped him. Riley might not have known him but she had. If there was anything her father treasured, it was—

She blinked as the lightbulb went on inside her head.

"My mother," she whispered.

"Exactly." He used his thumb to wipe a tear from her cheekbone. "I studied up on you and your foundation, you know. Your mom was an art teacher in the public school system."

Talia's lips began to tremble. "My father started the after-school program in her memory after she died."

"And he entrusted it to *you*."

Shame slapped her full in the face. Oh, God, it was true. Her father had left her an incredible gift but she hadn't appreciated it for what it was worth. Much worse, she'd sullied that memory in the vilest way.

She began crying in earnest. She felt Riley's arms wrap around her. He rolled them onto their sides and tucked her up against him. He held her tightly as sorrow racked her entire body.

Talia hadn't known she stored so much water inside her. Finally, she reached for her composure. She tried to wipe the dampness from her face but he beat her to it. He grabbed a tissue from a box on the end table. He passed one to her and used another to blot her cheeks.

"Your intentions were admirable, baby, but I don't think your father would have liked what you've done in the name of his foundation."

"No," she said miserably as she blew her nose. "He'd be so disappointed in me."

"You've got to find another way to support the school programs. The money is tainted. Is that the kind of role model you want to be for Linc? For comic book Bobby?"

"No," she said on another sob. She shook her head to keep from starting a new bout of tears. "You're right. I need to find another solution."

The look on Riley's face was intense as he looked her straight in the eye. "Good, because if you don't, I'll have to arrest you whether I want to or not. Somebody's got to stop your downward spiral and I'd rather it be me."

He leaned forward and she opened her mouth for his hot kiss. Her breath caught, though, when his hand slipped into the cleavage of her ass. He carefully grasped the base of the butt plug. He watched her closely as he pulled it out of her.

Giving it up was almost as hard as taking it. Talia closed her eyes and shivered as the hard thickness left her. There was another hard thickness left, though, and it was growing bigger with every breath she took. He was fully aroused again.

"There are a lot of things I want to do to you, sweetheart," he said as his fingers brushed over the rosebud opening. "Arresting you is not one."

She knew what he was asking and her heart swelled inside her chest.

"Will you let me?" he whispered.

She looked into his deep dark eyes and felt something inside her squeeze tight. "Yes," she whispered.

He wanted to be her first.

She wanted him to be her first, her last and her only.

Chapter Sixteen

The radio alarm went off way too early the next morning. Talia winced and burrowed more solidly against the warm body behind her. She wasn't ready to wake up; she'd gotten virtually no sleep. Riley had kept her busy for what had remained of yesterday and most of the night.

Very, very busy.

Tiredly, she opened her eyes. Dawn had barely broken but she could see the shambles the room was in. Her pillow was leaning endwise against the wall and somehow the sheet had ended up in a wad underneath the dresser. The comforter was half off the bed, which was amazing since the mattress itself had gotten knocked cockeyed on the box springs. She didn't think they'd missed a flat surface in the room.

She closed her eyes more tightly. She wasn't going to be ready to get up for another ten hours, at least.

Unfortunately, the alarm was intent on kicking her out of bed. She tried to block it out but Riley wasn't into easy-listening music. Steven Tyler was wailing about being back in the saddle again. Talia groaned. No more riding. She needed sleep.

Behind her, Riley shifted. "Shit," he said tiredly.

"Turn it off," she begged.

"Can't. Gotta work."

Work. At the police station. He'd promised to help her but she wasn't ready to go back to the real world yet. "No. Stay here with me."

He grunted. "Don't tempt me."

Grumpily, she yanked on the comforter, pulling it over to her side. He might have to work but she owned her own business. She wasn't getting up until she was good and ready.

His arm wrapped around her. His hand cupped her breast in a possessive manner she was beginning to become accustomed to and his lips found a sensitive spot on the side of her neck. "Cold?"

"No." He'd kept her hot and bothered all night. "Just tired."

"Me, too. We really went at it."

She blushed. If they'd forgotten to try a position, she wasn't familiar with it. He'd taught her several new ones, in fact. She stretched and immediately felt the soreness in her body. "Oh!" she gasped.

He'd become so attuned to her, he knew without asking. His hand slid down to her buttocks and one finger slipped into the crevice. He rubbed her puckered opening lightly. "All right?"

Her breath caught. She nodded quickly but he didn't remove his hand.

"Do you need anything? I have some ointment in the bathroom."

"It's fine."

"You're just not used to feeling sensitive back there." He nipped at her ear. "I like it. It will make you think of me."

It already was. Memories of the debauched things they'd done flashed through her head as his fingers played. Her heart rate picked up as she remembered him carrying her into the room and laying her flat on her stomach on the bed. He'd slid a pillow under her hips and retrieved lubricant from the bedside stand... After that, things got a little hazy.

Talia licked her dry lips. She remembered resisting the invasion but he'd gone slowly. He'd soothed her with soft words and gentle touches. The harsh breaths, sharp cries and sounds of slapping flesh had come later.

Heat collected in her sex. She remembered pressure, pain and a dark, fierce pleasure that had consumed her. She remembered clenching the sheet until it had ripped. Maybe that was how it had ended up on the floor...

Embarrassed, she pressed her face into the pillow they shared. Yes, she'd be sore all day but she'd also be wet. With every step she took, she'd be reminded of what he'd done to her and how she'd reveled in it.

"It'll get easier," he whispered in her ear as he stroked her delicately.

There was no question they'd do it again. And again and again and again. They'd both liked it too much. It would always be their special thing. She knew her relationships with other men bothered him. This was the one gift she could give him to let him know that jealousy wasn't necessary.

Impulsively, she rolled over and kissed him. "I don't ever want it to be easy."

A wicked expression spread across his face. "I told you you'd like it."

"Yeah? Well, I did some things that you liked, too."

His lips turned upward in a smile that had her heart flipping. "Speaking of which..."

She whooped as he rolled her onto her back and climbed on top of her. The music on the radio gave way to the news and he reached over to swat at it. She knew where his mind was heading but the name "Winston" caught her attention.

"Wait," she said as she caught his hand. "They're talking about the professor."

"Anton Winston, a professor of art history at New Covington College, was taken into custody yesterday after reportedly trying to sell a portrait stolen from New Covington's Heritage Museum," the reporter said. "Mr. Brent Harrington III, President of the Council for the Arts, had this to say about the arrest."

Talia cringed when she heard Brent's cocky voice come over the airwaves. He was the last person she wanted to think of as she was lying in Riley's bed.

"I'm thrilled that the New Covington Cat Burglar has finally been caught," he said.

"What?" She pushed Riley off of her and sat straight up. "Winston's not the Cat Burglar!"

Riley gestured for her to quiet down so he could hear. Reaching over to the radio, he turned up the volume.

"This arrest is the first step in assuring the safety of the citizens of our fine town," Brent said with an authority he didn't possess. "Unfortunately, I've been extremely disappointed with the way our police department has handled this case."

Talia's head snapped so hard toward Riley, she nearly gave herself whiplash.

"You've got to be shitting me," he muttered.

"I have faith in our legal system," Brent continued, "but I see no other recourse for myself and the other victims of this serial thief than to request an outside review of the department's actions—or lack thereof. I have a meeting scheduled with the commissioner tomorrow afternoon to discuss the matter."

"Police department officials had no comment," the reporter said. "Winston is currently at the Hayward County jail awaiting bail. We'll keep you updated on this story as it progresses."

Riley's hand flashed out and killed the alarm. He threw his legs over the side of the bed. "That fucking son of a bitch," he said as he stomped to the dresser.

"Winston isn't the Cat Burglar," Talia said. *She was!* The professor had done nothing but help her...by fencing the New Covington Cat Burglar's spoils. She ran a hand over her face. Her moral compass might be off-kilter but she knew one thing for certain. The professor couldn't pay for her crimes. She pulled the comforter to her chest and sat up on her haunches. "What are we going to do?"

Riley threw her a look. "*We* aren't going to do anything. I'll handle this."

"But it's my fault."

He opened drawers and started pulling out clothes. "It's not your fault that the media didn't check their facts. We didn't even charge Winston with the Cat Burglar thefts. I don't know where they got that."

Queasiness suddenly hit her stomach. "I do."

The muscles in his back clenched and the drawer slammed shut with a bang. "Harrington. Fucking son of a bitch."

Talia scrambled out of bed, taking the comforter with her. She suddenly understood what was going on. She was responsible for this, but in more ways than Riley could understand. "I'll go talk to Brent—or maybe I should see the professor first."

He caught the tail end of the comforter and jerked her to a stop. "You're not going anywhere."

"But—"

"No 'buts' about it. You go back to your shop and act like everything's normal. I'll go down to the station and try to clear the professor before he cracks under the pressure and gives you up. He's got to have an alibi for at least one or two of the robberies."

Talia reached out and laid her hand on Riley's chest, stopping him in his tracks. There was one thing he was forgetting and it was the thing that worried her the most. "Brent's going after you, too. You've got to protect yourself."

He cupped her by the back of her neck and pulled her to him. The look he gave her was red-hot. "Bring him on."

She wasn't so confident. She knew Brent a lot better than he did. When the Turd got something in his mind, he was relentless. And in this town, he had the ways and means to do just about anything. Just look at how quickly he'd managed to schedule a meeting with the police commissioner. She dropped the comforter and wrapped both arms around Riley's waist. "He's going for your badge."

"I can handle his preppy white ass."

She shook her head. He wasn't listening. "Take me down to the station with you. I'll turn myself in and he'll back off. I know he will."

"Like hell." He lifted her so he could look her in the eye. "We already talked about this. You're not to say anything."

She wrapped herself around him like a vine and clung. "I'm not going to let him take you down."

He gently stroked her back. "He won't. I mean it, baby. Stay out of this. I've been looking forward to going a round or two with that bastard for a long time."

Tension screamed in her veins. She didn't doubt he could clean Brent's clock but that wasn't the kind of fight he was in for. "He fights dirty."

"So do I." He gave her a hard kiss but then peeled her off of him. "I've got to get going."

She stood in numbed silence as he picked up his clothes and headed to the bathroom. He stopped with his hand on the doorjamb, though, giving her a delicious view of his backside. "And get rid of whatever is in that briefcase," he said flatly. "I don't care how. Just do it today."

Talia moved weakly to the bed. She sat down with a thump and heard the shower start. There was no way she could make him understand—not without telling him more than he wanted to hear.

Because this wasn't about the New Covington Cat Burglar anymore. This was about her, Talia Sizemore.

Brent had warned her. He'd told her that he wouldn't let a common, blue-collared police detective have her. She'd just never expected him to go to these lengths.

She dropped her face into her hands. She'd underestimated him, big time. This ploy involving the Cat Burglar was about one thing and one thing only. He was going after Riley. She hadn't expected that. He'd always come after her before. She'd made the mistake of believing she could fend him off.

She nearly laughed at her stupidity. She hadn't fended off anything. She'd just delayed it.

Her body tingled. Brent had been very clear on what she was and wasn't to do and she'd just broken his cardinal rule. She looked around the disheveled room. She'd broken it more times than she could count.

Hopelessness weighed heavily on her shoulders. She'd been a fool to think she could end things so easily. Brent wasn't going to allow himself to be cast aside like an old shoe. He wasn't going to stop until she was truly his private plaything.

She reached for the pillow and hugged it to her chest. Their sick relationship had started all this. Now the professor was in trouble and Riley's job and reputation were in danger.

Panic suddenly assailed her. She couldn't leave things like this. She couldn't let Riley try to clean up after her. He didn't know the things she knew. He could walk right into Brent's trap, not even realizing it.

She wasn't the one who needed protection. He was.

Anxiety made her stomach turn. She had to do something. But what?

What could she do to divert the attention from the professor, yet at the same time throw a kink in Brent's plans?

An idea crystallized in her head but it wasn't one she liked. She looked at the bathroom door, feeling almost nauseous.

There was no way around it.

She had to go out for one last heist.

She let out a shuddering breath and raked a hand through her hair. She'd have to break her promise to Riley but she couldn't see any other solution. The only surefire way to prove the professor's innocence was to do another job while he was in custody. He'd still be facing the fencing charges but at least he wouldn't have to defend himself from unjust claims. And if she was creative enough, she might also be able to stop Brent from ruining Riley.

Riley.

Tears pressed at her eyes. This would be the last straw for him. She'd lose him if she did this. Their relationship was too new and fragile.

A sob escaped her but she stiffened her spine. Her feelings were immaterial. She was the one who'd created this mess. She had to clean it up. Protecting Riley from the fallout was more important than anything.

At least they'd had one night of happiness together.

"Just think," she said out loud. She wiped her damp cheek and forced herself to back away from her emotions. She had one shot at doing this and she needed to do it right. For his sake. Her heart rate began to slow from its frantic pace as the plan began to form in her head.

The "who" was obvious. Brent Harrington the Turd was going to pay and he was going to pay big. She could deal with the things he'd done to her but now he was going after Riley. That pushed things to another level. The man had to be stopped and she was going to be the one to do it.

The "what" was more difficult. She had to lift something that would hit Brent hard enough in the pocketbook to make him wince. But what? And how was she supposed to fence whatever she lifted? Without the professor, that was going to be difficult.

The professor...

Brent...

A memory of her fateful night in Harrington's office entered her head. She remembered seeing something—something valuable, sentimental and, if she played her cards right, sellable. The picture was so vivid, she could see things in Technicolor.

Of course!

She flopped across the bed and reached for the phone. She needed to call a cab.

She had a lot of work to do and a short time to do it. For tonight, Harrington was going to get what was coming to him.

Chapter Seventeen

The night was dark and portentous as Talia stood on Harrington property looking up at the second floor balcony. It was only poetic that she'd end up here. Things had come full circle.

It was time to put them to rest.

It had been a long day. Her plan had come together in pieces and she'd had to scramble to get things ready. As she looked upward, though, it made the hard work worthwhile. Things had come together amazingly well. The sky was overcast with clouds. The cold spell had finally snapped and the forty-degree temperature made it easier to work. Snow had melted over the course of the day, rendering her hike across the grounds virtually untraceable.

Still, she felt uneasy.

She usually spent more time planning a hit, especially one as complicated as this. The key to safety was in the details. She'd spent weeks staking out Edward Jones to learn his habits. Although she'd moved on Ramona earlier than she'd intended, she'd had at least three weeks of preparation time put in for that job, too. For this, there hadn't been the luxury of time.

The media was having a field day with Professor Winston and the story had only gotten hotter when Ramona had reported the robbery at her condo. After that, poor Riley hadn't been able to shake them, either. She hadn't been in contact with him but he'd been interviewed on the six o'clock news—if one could call a terse "no comment" response an interview.

Those two short words told her a lot. He was exhausted and losing his patience. If she'd had any reservations about what she was about to do, that put them behind her. She had to lure the media away—put the hounds off their scent. If things went according to plan, she'd soon add a new twist to the story. Neither Riley nor the professor would be bothered after that.

"But you will, Brent," she said as she pulled the ski mask over her head.

There was no turning back now.

Before she could lose her nerve, she tossed her grappling hook up to the balcony. It snagged on the first try. She gave it an experimental tug and double-checked her equipment. Her adrenaline started pumping and she took a deep, bracing breath.

Focusing on everything she'd learned, she started up the rope. An ascender and toeholds in the siding helped her make her way. She used her legs as much as she could but her arms were fatigued by the time she climbed over the balcony railing. Hastily, she dropped into a crouch. As quiet as she'd been, some people were light sleepers.

The silence was interminable but she waited until she'd caught her breath and regained her equilibrium. Recklessness would serve no purpose. Each step of her plan needed to be executed precisely.

She looked through the sliding glass door into Brent's home office. The house was dark but she watched the shadows for movement.

There was none.

"Be quick, be silent and be safe," she reminded herself.

Reaching into her bag of supplies, she pulled out her trusty glasscutter. Shelli had told her all about the new security system she and Brent had installed after the robbery. High-end or not, the sliding glass door still worked on a circuit principle. As long as it was closed, the circuit was operative. Open the door, break the loop and the alarm went off.

Simple.

As long as she didn't open the door, they'd never know she was here.

Staying low, she cut an opening in the windowpane large enough to pass through. The glass was heavy as she pulled it out and laid it out of the way. Watching the edges, she carefully slipped inside.

Her target was hanging on the wall in full display right where she remembered it. First, though, she had something else to take care of.

Opening her pouch, she pulled out Ramona's crystal paperweight. She peeled back the protective cloth as she scanned the room. Where should she put it?

"Perfect," she said when she spotted Brent's briefcase sitting open on the desk. She slipped the paperweight inside and closed the lid as if to hide it. The piece would surely be found when the police crime scene team scoured the room for clues.

That was when the real fun would begin.

Moving with purpose, she approached Brent's collection of antique riding equipment. It was what she'd come for. She scanned the bridles and spurs, looking for one particular piece.

There it was.

The riding whip.

Ignoring her zinging nerves, she evaluated it with a professional eye. A good chunk of her day had been spent doing her homework. She knew what she'd seen the night Brent had brought her here; she just needed to make sure. If the whip was authentic, it was worth a fortune.

"Nice patina on the handle," she whispered. "Cracks in the leather loop, but that's to be expected."

Her heart flipped when she saw the family crest. Tooled elaborately into the leather handle was the name Borgia.

"You idiot," she whispered. "Don't you know this is worth more than anything you have on display downstairs?"

Exhilaration made her want to yank the frame off the wall and run. Experience told her to be careful. With a vigilant touch, she slid her gloved hands around the edges. It didn't feel as if it was hooked up to an alarm. Clicking on her penlight, she peeked behind the frame. Sure enough, all she saw was a nail.

"Imbecile." She lowered the display. The frame was too bulky and heavy to carry, so she took valuable time pulling off the backing. With a feather touch, she lifted the whip. It was heavier than she'd anticipated, but in excellent shape.

It would bring a good price.

Especially if she sold it to someone in, say, the *Professor's* crowd.

Reaching back, she undid the carrying case that was strapped to her back. She carefully tucked the whip inside.

Excitement unfurled in her veins but she tamped it down ruthlessly.

She hadn't gotten away with anything yet.

Her nerves were singing as she moved back toward the sliding glass door. "Out the hole and down the rope. Out the hole and down the rope."

A soft clicking sound behind her abruptly halted her mantra.

Glancing over her shoulder, she saw the door handle turning in the moonlight.

Her heart slammed into her rib cage. *No!*

Twirling around, she looked for an escape. There was no time to run. No time to hide. She watched in unmitigated horror as the door swung open.

Brent walked in, dressed only in pajama bottoms.

Her senses screamed. The house had been dark for an hour. What was he doing awake?

He hit the light switch distractedly, but suddenly sensed her presence. His head snapped up and she froze like a deer in the headlights.

"What the hell?" Papers dropped from his hands and he took on a defensive posture. "You!"

Talia exploded into action.

She dove for the sliding glass door and ducked through the hole. Behind her, Brent recovered from his shock.

"Get back here, thief!" Footsteps pounded across the room.

She lunged for the balcony railing. She couldn't get caught. Not now. *Not by him!!!* Her hands shook as she tried to attach her harness to the rope. The sliding glass door slid open with a bang just as she swung her leg over the edge. The alarm shrieked, nearly perforating her eardrums.

"Oh, no, you don't." Brent charged at her just as she was beginning to push off. Reaching out wildly, his hands took hold of her vest.

Talia let out a screech. He had her!

She was dangling perilously over the edge. Remembering her climbing courses, she wrapped her leg around the rope even as she pushed at Brent's arms.

He was too strong. He pulled her right over the railing and dumped her on the ground. The grappling hook turned loose. The rope slithered around her leg like a fast-moving snake. She tried to stomp down on it but he knocked her off-balance. She watched as her only means of escape shot across the floor.

Just as it was about to fall over the edge, the grappling hook caught by a tip. It teetered precariously, ready to let go at any second.

She cried out in dismay and the sound made Brent come up short.

"A woman? You're a *woman*?" In typical Turd fashion, he thrust his hand between her legs and groped. "I'll be damned."

His touch repulsed her but it gave her the opening she needed. She hooked her leg around the back of his knee. He buckled like a house of cards and she pushed him to the side. He fell on all fours. Not giving him time to recover, she jumped on top of him and sprawled toward the rope.

"Hey!" he yelled. "Get back here."

Her weight hindered him for only a second but it was all she needed. When he scrambled toward her, she was ready.

Talia knew she didn't have the advantage of strength but she did have the element of surprise. That, plus adrenaline, helped her to entangle the rope around Brent's hands when he grabbed for her. Using her weight, she rolled and pulled it taut.

"What the—" He let out a roar when he realized his hands were bound.

He tried to rear upright but she looped the end around the bottom of the railing. Bracing her foot against the corner pole, she pulled tight.

"I don't care if you are a woman. I'm going to kick your ass!"

He lunged at her, trying to use his body weight to throw her off her task. Her shoulder shuddered as he crashed into her but she wasn't letting go of the rope for anything. Her hands were sweating inside her gloves and the ski mask was nearly suffocating her. Using her last bit of strength, she knotted off the rope and threw the grappling hook over the side for weight.

"You bitch!"

On hands and knees, Talia crawled away back into the house. Leaning against the side of the desk, she fought for breath.

Brent kicked at her like a donkey and her temper flared. The asshole. She dug an extra piece of rope out of her bag. Dodging his kicks, she quickly tied off his ankles.

Take that you Turd, she thought.

Standing up, she brushed off her hands and looked down at her work. He was as good as hog-tied.

It suited him.

Feeling battered and bruised, she backed away into the office. She'd have to go out through the house and she didn't have much time. The security system had already called the police. Turning on her heel, she rushed across the room.

"You can run, you cunt, but you can't hide," Brent called. "You'll never get away with doing this. Not to a Harrington."

Talia stopped cold. A Harrington. *Oh, you self-righteous pig.*

She knew she should ignore him and go but she couldn't. There was no way she was going to just walk away this time. Resolutely, she turned on her heel. His lifted ass called to her. The temptation was just too much. Heart pumping, she stomped back to the balcony. She'd show him what she could get away with.

"You deserve this," she hissed.

Bending over, she caught the tie of his pajama bottoms. He gasped in surprise and tried to shuffle away on his knees. The rope only let him get so far. Talia trailed her gloved finger along his waistband and he looked at her with wide eyes.

"No," he whispered, his smugness suddenly gone.

She smiled behind her ski mask. With a swift tug, she yanked both his pajamas and boxers down to his knees. The vision was one she'd remember for years—as was the assault on her tender ears. Brent's white ass gleamed in the moonlight and his dick hung limp between his legs. More colorful were the curses that sprang from his lips. The blue streak nearly ignited the night air.

Dropping onto her knees, she reached for him.

He'd wounded her pride. Let's see how he liked it.

"Ah!" he cried when she wrapped her gloved fingers around his cock. "Don't... You can't... Oh, God."

Detachedly, she watched his face as she jerked him off. His teeth gritted and beads of sweat rolled off his forehead. Time was short, so she used every trick she knew to work up a good, thick hard-on. When his cock was pointing toward his belly, she rocked back on her heels. He just needed the crowning touch. Digging into her pocket, she found a five-dollar bill. Her movements were sharp and precise as she rolled it up.

"What are you doing? What are you going to do with that?"

She grabbed his butt cheek and he howled with mortification. He shook his hips like madman but she stuffed the money into his crack. With a quick pat on the ass, she stood.

"You're not worth $120," she muttered as she hurried toward the door.

Talia was stunned at her own audacity but she needed to get out of the house before she could wonder over it. The alarm was screeching like a banshee.

She rushed out into the hallway and turned toward the staircase. Her entire body jerked with surprise when she found herself face-to-face with Brent's disheveled wife. Shelli screamed and lifted a tennis racket. Talia took a step back to defend herself but she needn't have bothered.

The perfect fashion doll fell into an ungainly dead faint.

Talia instinctively caught her as she dropped. Her knees nearly buckled under the added weight but she lowered Shelli until she lay on the floor.

It was too much. Bracing her hands on her knees, Talia fought her own light-headedness. Her breaths were too quick and too light. She shook her head to clear it. She couldn't falter now. "Get out," she snapped at herself. "Now!"

She ran like she'd never run in her life.

Her steps pounded down the second floor hallway. Remembering her daydream, she hopped up onto the banister. She slid down like a bullet and was running again before her feet even hit the floor.

"Back door. Use the back door."

On the winged feet of Mercury, she flew across the room. She exited through the back and disappeared into the shadows of the trees.

It wasn't until she was in her car driving away from the scene that she allowed herself to think of Brent. When she did, she started laughing uncontrollably. She couldn't believe she'd done that to him. When it came right down to it, though, vindication was sweet.

At least her humiliation had been done in private.

Some very surprised policemen were going to find Brent Harrington III wallowing in his.

Chapter Eighteen

Riley was dead tired. He'd been at the station for more hours than he could count. He was hungry and his head ached. Most of all, though, he was sick to death of having to listen to Brent and Shelli Harrington whine when he wanted to be out looking for Talia.

When he got his hands on her... He let out a grunt and rubbed his pounding temple. Hell, he didn't know what he'd do once he found her. His first inclination was to paddle her behind again. Close on its heels, though, was the desire to just pull her close. Every time he thought about her dangling over that balcony railing, he got a little nauseous.

What had she been thinking?

She'd made a promise.

Shelli started sniffling again and he fought back a curse. Leaning back in his chair, he stared across his desk at the couple. They'd been robbed and assaulted, although from what he'd been able to make out, Brent had attacked first. He understood why they were so upset. Nobody deserved to have the sanctity of their home disturbed.

But if he had to listen to one more of the blonde twit's irritating sniffles, he was going to snap.

"Mr. Harrington," he said, trying to fend off another bout of tears. "Can you give me a better description of the intruder?"

"Haven't you been listening to me? It was a woman."

If possible, Riley's attitude cooled even more. "In case you haven't noticed, women make up half of the population around here. I need more details. You've told me she was wearing a ski mask but can you give me her height? Her weight? Would you recognize her voice if you heard it again?"

"Damn it, she was robbing my house! I didn't stop to take notes."

Riley set his pencil down and counted to ten. His patience was wearing thin.

"Fine," he said through clenched teeth. "Answer another question for me. Why did she leave you in the state she did? It seemed to be rather symbolic."

Harrington slumped so far down in his chair, he practically slid out of it. "I don't want to talk about that."

Riley felt his gut fire. "We're going to talk about it until I get some answers."

Shelli could go home for all he cared; his questions were for this one. Talk about being found in a compromising position. It was the laugh of the stationhouse.

Unfortunately, he failed to see the humor. He knew Talia.

He wanted to know what had happened on that goddamned balcony.

"I was utterly humiliated in my own home," Brent snarled. "Why do you insist on harping on it? I was the victim. Do you hear me? The victim!"

"The five-dollar bill," Riley pressed. "Does that have any significance to you?"

Harrington's face went bright red and he let loose with a string of curses. Riley fought to keep his cool. He wanted to pound some answers out of the guy.

What had he done to make Talia act like that?

And just where the hell was she?

"Damn," he muttered under his breath. This was getting him nowhere. He should be out there looking for her.

Frustrated, he raked a hand through his hair. He'd been trying to track her down ever since the call had first come in from the dispatcher. Sadie hadn't known where she was. He'd even broken down and called her brother in Boston but he hadn't known either. It was as if she'd fallen off the face of the earth.

He was going crazy wondering if she was all right.

And he was beyond furious that she'd pulled this stunt. He'd warned her to stay out of things and she'd agreed. Or so he thought. That was what really stung. After everything they'd been through, he'd thought they'd finally formed an unbreakable connection but she'd lied to his face. He didn't know if he could cover for her this time.

Or if he really should.

Shelli began hiccupping with tears. "I...I think... Oh, this is so hard. She was a big woman, maybe six feet tall. When she...ac-accosted me... Oh, Brennnnnt."

She collapsed onto her husband's shoulder.

Riley hit him with a glare. "Is that right?"

Harrington looked uncomfortable. "Yeah, she was pretty good-sized. She had to be to wrestle me around like that, didn't she?"

Riley grunted. Talia, big? *Give him a break*. Her legs were impossibly long but she wasn't anywhere near six feet tall and he could circle her waist with his hands. As for wrestling, he could grapple her into any position he wanted.

Of course, she hadn't been fighting him off...

He shook his head to clear his brain. He couldn't let himself think about the other night. He was screwed up enough as it was.

He couldn't condone what she'd done. For God's sake, she'd climbed a two-story house, broken in to a man's office, left the guy hog-tied and the wife unconscious, and walked off with... What was it? He looked down at his notes. A fifteenth-century riding whip?

"What can you tell me about the stolen property?" he asked, forcing himself to finish the interview. "Why did she take that particular item? Does it have any value?"

Harrington's chin came up. "Of course, it has value. Would I put it on display if it was a piece of junk?"

Riley shrugged. "It takes one to know one."

Harrington slapped his hand against the arm of his chair. "I'll have you know that whip was owned by Rodrigo de Borgia, formally known as Pope Alexander VI."

"Borgia?" There was something about that name.

Ah, shit!

Riley's gut began to churn. He knew why she'd taken that piece.

It was the one thing he hadn't been able to figure out. He knew why she'd hit the Harringtons. Brent had put the professor in a precarious position and she felt responsible. He just hadn't understood why the whip or how she planned to move it without a fence's help.

He got it now and it worried the hell out of him.

If he remembered his history correctly, the Borgia family was infamous for many things including extortion, bribery, cruelty and, most of all, sexual excess. From what he'd found in Winston's laboratory, the man knew a thing or two about the history of sex. While he might not be available to act as a fence, Talia could still make connections in his field of research. The whip would probably sell itself.

Riley pinched the bridge of his nose tightly. He hated the idea of her running around in that crowd. He had to go get her. His chair scraped against the linoleum floor as he stood.

His attention was diverted, though, when the squad room was suddenly filled with a riot of motion and color.

"There he is! Thief! You menace! Thieeeeeeeef!"

The shrill screams echoed off the walls. Detective Carroway jumped so badly, he spilled coffee all the way down his tie.

Activity in the busy bay was disrupted as the braying woman waddled her way across the room.

"You scoundrel! How dare you take my things? You lowdown, common criminal."

Riley quickly rounded his desk as the woman bore down upon them. "Ms. Gellar. Thank you for coming down. If you'll just wait over here—"

She moved a lot faster than it seemed. She scuttled around Carroway, behind a hooker being charged with solicitation and past two uniformed cops. Yelling as she was, she attracted attention. Still, no one expected it when she let loose with her purse and walloped Brent Harrington III alongside the head.

"Ow!" he howled, his feet lifting from the floor in surprise.

"Ms. Gellar!" Riley launched himself at her. "Stop that. I can't let you— *Ramona!*"

The old lady got in two more good whacks before he was able to get the purse away from her. "Really, ma'am. I can't let you attack him like this."

Even though it was nice to see. He'd wanted to kick the shit out of the jerk for weeks.

Harrington held the back of his head as he looked up in total stupefaction. "What the fuck is wrong with you?"

The woman bristled until red streaks of fury glowed from her cheekbones. "Don't you use that kind of language with me. If you think the police are bad, wait until I get my hands on you, you overgrown hoodlum."

Riley's weight transferred to the balls of his feet when she suddenly turned on him.

"Have you arrested him yet?"

"No, ma'am." He fought not to flinch when her mouth pursed in dissatisfaction. "We're still trying to piece together all the facts. Mr. Harrington claims that the New Covington Cat Burglar planted your paperweight in his briefcase."

"And you believe that dreck?" Ramona said in a huff. "My pretties are very, very valuable. No thief worth his salt would take one and give it to somebody else."

"It wasn't a man," Shelli said self-importantly. "The Cat Burglar is a woman."

That earned Brent a pinch on the ear.

"Ow! What was that for?"

Ramona leaned over him like an avenging angel. "Don't think you can get away with lying, Mr. Snooty Pants. I've known you since you were wiping snot off your nose with your sleeve. If there's a woman involved, you're working with her."

"Ms. Gellar," Riley said firmly. He caught her by the arm and led her around to the other side of the desk. "You have to stop doing that. If you don't, I'll be forced to arrest you."

"Arrest me? He's the one who needs to be behind bars. He's partnering with that Cat Burglar person, I tell you. That's what he's doing."

"He is not!" Shelli trilled. "You wouldn't say that if you'd seen what she did to him. She left him tied to our balcony with a...*with a five-dollar bill shoved up his private parts!*"

The scandalous whisper echoed throughout the room. Silent laughter rolled in waves but Ramona Gellar wasn't amused. "Don't you get foul with me, missy. I'll tell your mother."

"Mother is already on her way here," Shelli sniffed impudently.

And so, the battle was on.

Riley lifted a hand to his aching temple and wondered what he'd done to deserve this special kind of hell. He couldn't deal with this now. He needed to get out of here and—

That was when he felt her.

He didn't see her enter the room and he certainly couldn't hear her over the din.

He just felt her presence.

Looking toward the door, he saw Talia. She was dressed to kill in a white coat and a red suit with a skirt that showed off her mouthwatering legs. His heart began to thud in his chest.

"No," he whispered under his breath. There was only one reason why she would have come here.

She was going to turn herself in.

Everything inside him rebelled at the idea. Cop or not, he didn't want her behind bars. His tired brain started whirring. He had to figure a way to get her out of the station before she did something stupid.

Or before Harrington saw her and put two and two together.

Too late. He watched helplessly as she began moving toward him. More than a few heads snapped in her direction. He glared at his coworkers, but found it hard to take his eyes off her himself. Even with dark circles of fatigue under her eyes, she was drop-dead gorgeous. His nerve endings began to zing when she stopped a foot away from him.

"Can we talk?" she said loud enough for his ears only.

He stared at her hard but she couldn't meet his gaze. Instead, she focused her attention on the ruckus in the room. Ramona and the Harringtons were still going at it full-bore. She didn't smile. She didn't think it was funny. Something about the way her shoulders relaxed intrigued him, though. She was content with the way the socialites were tearing into each other.

A lightbulb flared inside his head.

Of course, she was content. She'd planned this fiasco! She'd planted that paperweight not only to draw suspicion away from the professor, but also to shine it on Harrington.

"Carroway," he called. Oh yeah, they were going to have a talk but they were going to do it in private.

Beside him, he felt Talia's nervousness crank up a notch. She turned toward him and his own tension peaked. "Don't," he warned. "Don't say a word until we're alone."

"Wait. I came here for a reason."

Her voice wavered but it was the look in her eyes that made him uneasy. They were filled with fear and regret, yet unwavering resolve. She thought she needed to put things right.

His muscles clenched. She was bound and determined to do something. Whatever it was, he wasn't going to be able to stop her.

"Talia," he said, his throat tightening.

She surprised him by pulling her purse out from under her arm. Her hands shook as she opened it and took out what looked to be a check. Tentatively, she passed it to him.

"What's this?" he asked in confusion.

"It's a donation," she said. She licked her lips, but raised her voice so everyone could hear. "Despite recent news reports, not everyone in this town is unhappy with the police department's work. This is for the New Covington Police *Retirement* Fund."

"Hey!" Applause and whoops filled the air, sticking it to Harrington all the more. "That's all right."

Riley didn't care. Nervous tears wet Talia's eyes but he'd caught the way she'd emphasized "retirement". His gut clenched. Looking down at the check, he saw that the word was circled.

His anger returned with a rush. He didn't need to ask where she'd gotten the money. She probably thought the irony was poetic—especially with Harrington sitting not five feet away. "Damn you," he hissed.

He knew what she was trying to tell him but, once again, she'd put him in an impossible situation.

It was enough to spark him into action. Leaving Carroway to handle Ramona and the Harringtons, he took her arm and began looking for someplace private. "Come with me. Now."

The lieutenant's office was empty. He led her inside and slammed the door behind them. For good measure, he locked it and closed the blinds. Turning, he walked right up to her.

"Is this supposed to make everything all right?" he asked, thrusting the check into her face. "Retirement. I get it. You're saying that this was your last time but, know what? I've heard it before."

"Riley, please let me explain."

"I don't need an explanation." He tossed the check to the side and it fluttered to the ground. "You swore to me you were through with the New Covington Cat Burglar routine. You looked me right in the eye."

She paled. "I know—and I knew you'd be angry with me. I just had to clean up the mess I'd made."

"This is how you fix things?" Reaching out, he caught her by the shoulders. It was all he could do not to shake her. "How am I ever supposed to believe a word you say again?"

He stopped cold when she let out a gasp of pain. Not emotional pain. Physical.

"What the hell?"

She stepped back but he followed, pushing her coat off her shoulders as he went. She batted at his hands but he undid the buttons on her suit jacket. Gently, he slipped it off her shoulders. Her clothes dropped to the floor with a soft whoosh.

The sight that greeted his eyes made his knees go weak. "Oh, baby."

His anger dissolved in a flash. She wore only a bra underneath but that wasn't what grabbed his attention. The massive bruise covering her shoulder and spreading down her arm did that all by itself.

She shivered and the air shuddered out of his lungs. He didn't trust his legs to hold him. Catching her by the waist, he pulled her with him as he settled his hips back against the lieutenant's desk.

"God, Talia. You were hurt."

"It's not as bad as it looks."

"Stop lying to me." He pulled her close between his spread legs. With a groan, he leaned his head on her chest. The rainbow of colors marring her soft skin made him ache inside. "Harrington told me about the fight. I get queasy every time I think about you hanging from that rope. You could have been killed!"

She stood tense in his embrace as if she didn't know how to take his sudden change of mood. "I'm fine," she said cautiously. "Nothing happened."

"Your shoulder is purple. That's not nothing." He wrapped his arms around her waist in a bear hug and buried his face between her soft breasts. He thought he'd been worried before. Now that he'd seen proof of how violent the struggle had been, he didn't think he could handle it. The "what if"s were nearly making him sick. "You were so lucky, baby. Did you ever stop to think about what you would have done if he'd pulled a gun on you? For God's sake, he owns a factory full of them."

Almost timidly, she stroked the back of his neck.

"I told you I know Brent better than you," she said softly. "His mother never allowed guns in her house. Neither does Shelli."

Riley finally lifted his head. He could spend his whole life studying this woman and never figure her out. "But why? Why do this? Why put yourself on the line like this? Was it to clear the professor? I told you I'd handle that."

She swallowed hard, but looked him straight in the eye. "He came after you."

Riley went still. "Say that again?"

"He knew how I felt about you, so he went after you." Her shaky voice hardened. "I couldn't allow it."

Little zaps of electricity shot down Riley's spine. If there was one thing he knew for certain about her, it was that she'd throw herself in front of a freight train for the people she cared about.

The zaps grew until his entire body was buzzing with energy.

He had to hear it. He needed to know.

"Just how do you feel about me?" he asked hoarsely.

Color drained from her cheeks. She hadn't meant to let that much slip.

"I know how vicious Brent can be," she said evasively. "I couldn't let him hurt you because of me."

"Answer the question, Talia. How do you feel about me?"

* * * * *

Talia looked at Riley with something close to terror ringing in her chest. She'd been so afraid to come here. She'd thought she couldn't be more frightened than when she'd approached the researcher from the Nautington Institute with the Borgia whip. Nothing, though, came close to the fear she felt now.

She couldn't tell him.

He'd been hunting her like prey for months. One night together didn't change that. He was a cop and she was a criminal. It could never work. He'd already told her that he couldn't believe anything she said.

"I admire you, Riley," she admitted. She laid her hands on his shoulders, needing to touch him just this one last time. "You're an honest, hardworking man with morals a mile deep. I know I've been a thorn in your side. You must hate me but one day I hope you can look back on everything and realize how good you were for me."

"Hate you?"

Her lips curled in remorse. "I've done some horrible things. You made me see that."

"Damn it, woman!"

The world suddenly spun and Talia let out a yelp. When she regained her equilibrium, she found herself sitting on the desk where he'd been—only her skirt was up around her waist. His hands were already working on the tabs of her garter belt.

"Where did you get the idiotic idea that I hated you?" he asked, anger tingeing his voice. Her garter turned loose and he began tugging at her panties.

Talia gasped and reached for his shoulders when he rocked her back on the desk. What was he doing? She'd played this scenario a thousand times in her head but he'd never reacted like this. "I've caused nothing but trouble for you. I lied to you. I made your job miserable."

"You think that's all I care about? My job?"

She cried out sharply when he pushed her flat onto her back and thrust two fingers into her. She was dry and the penetration was uncomfortable. She looked up at him, confused and more than a little apprehensive. He braced his free hand beside her head as he leaned down over her.

"I don't hate you, Talia. If anything, I'm a little too much in love with you."

She jolted with shock. *He loved her?* Pleasure ran through her and, to her embarrassment, she felt herself cream. Wicked satisfaction shone in his eyes.

"Feels like you don't hate me so much, either."

He scissored his fingers inside her and her back arched. "Ah, Riley."

"Tell me," he demanded. "Tell me how you feel."

She hesitated.

"Now, damn it!"

"I love you. Completely."

His body tensed. The cop in him faded into the background and his mouth came crashing down on hers. His tongue dove deep.

Talia welcomed the rapacious kiss.

He loved her.

That changed everything.

Sudden hunger seized her and she reached for the zipper of his pants. She needed his big cock inside her. She'd thought she'd killed their chances. He'd just given her a sliver of hope but she needed more than words. She needed him.

Her hands were so shaky, he reached down to help. When her fingers wrapped around his big tool, they both sighed.

"God, yes," Riley grunted as he started loosening his tie. "Just like that, baby."

"Hurry," she said, lifting her hips. She didn't need any preliminaries. If she were any more ready, she'd be coming. "Make love to me, Riley."

She didn't have to beg. He tore off his shirt and threw it aside. She ran her hands up his strong arms as he caught her by the hips and lifted her. Automatically, her stocking-covered legs wrapped high around his waist.

Arousal made Talia a quivering mess. With the way he had her tilted upward, she could see everything. The muscles in his chest contracted as he took her weight. His abs clenched as he guided his pulsing cock to her opening.

Her eyes widened. The intimacy was more than a little shocking. She'd never watched him disappear into her before.

He penetrated her with just the head and their bodies shuddered.

Oh, God. That was incredible—watching it and feeling it at the same time.

The sight of his cock burrowing, inch by inch, into her cunt made Talia's juices run. It eased his penetration and he slid in deeply. Gripping his forearms tightly, she ground her swollen pussy lips against his tight balls. His fingers dug into her hips and her back bowed with pleasure.

"Fuck!" he groaned.

He began plunging into her and she let out a cry of pleasure.

"Shhh," he said. Leaning down, he silenced her moans with a hard kiss. "People are going to hear."

"I don't care." She had him. Her body writhed, knocking a stapler and a pencil holder off the lieutenant's desk. Riley didn't pause in his rhythm. With each thrust, she lifted her hips to meet him. Spellbound, she watched as he pumped in and out of her.

The effect was shattering and she felt her toes beginning to curl inside her red high heels.

"It's too soon," she said on a high note. Her fingernails began scoring trails down his biceps. She wanted this to last forever.

"Hold on," he said in a low voice.

His touch was almost rough as he pulled her right to the very edge of the desk where he could get at her best. The position had him bumping hard against her clit with every thrust.

"Come on, baby," he grunted. His hips began hammering at her more quickly and the bouncing free tabs on her garter belt clicked against the desk. "Come for me."

He was penetrating her as deep as he could go with every lunge. Talia's teeth clenched and fireworks sparked behind her closed eyelids. She could feel every millimeter of him as he filled her.

"Give it to me, Talia. Show me how much you love me."

Energy coursed through her body and left though her fingertips and toes.

"Yes!" she cried as her pussy clenched.

She rode the wave as it crested. From a distance, she heard him call out her name. His back arched as his cock spurted its wad.

Exhausted, she collapsed onto the desk. Sweat covered her body and she could feel the blotter beneath her sticking to her back. Breathing hard, Riley leaned over her. Bracing both hands aside her head, he let his neck hang limp as he waited for his strength to return.

"Damn," he breathed in surprise. He looked at her and shook his head. "You keep surprising me."

"You, too." Enticed, she let her fingers stroke up and down the taut muscles of his arms. When she'd decided to come here, she'd never expected this to happen. She'd never expected to be with him again.

Lifting her, he stumbled back to a chair, nearly falling when his pants tangled around his legs. He sat down hard and pulled her close. She straddled his legs and swiveled her hips to keep him inside her.

Concern knit his brow when he saw her shoulder. Carefully, he brushed a kiss across it. "Okay?"

"Better than okay," she purred as she snuggled against him. She was perfect. Her shoulder ached, fatigue weighed on her and the muscles in her neck sang from the stress she'd carried there. None of it mattered, though. Not now.

He reached between them and expertly popped the front closure of her bra. She sighed in delight when her nipples pressed against his warm, hard chest. She dipped her face into the crook of his neck and breathed deeply. Being with him felt so right.

His hand came up to cup the back of her head. "We still need to talk about what happened on that balcony," he said quietly. "Specifically Harrington's boner and the five-dollar bill."

Talia went quiet. She didn't want that to come crashing down on her now. "No," she whispered, not caring how weak it made her look.

He took a deep breath. "One day we're going to have to."

"Not today. Please."

Uneasiness nipped at her but she stubbornly ignored it. He wasn't the sort of man who could let things like that go but she wanted just this one moment in time. Was that so much to ask?

"Tell me this much," he said, kissing the top of her head. "Is he eventually going to figure out it was you?"

Her heart began to thud in her chest. "Probably."

She felt tears start to climb up her throat. She could ignore their problems all she wanted but they weren't going away. Their connection could only take them so far. There were circumstances out there they couldn't control.

"Okay," he said calmly. Hooking a finger under her chin, he made her look into his eyes. "Then when that happens, we'll deal with it together. Do you understand me?"

Her heart skipped a beat and she looked at him in amazement. Was he truly going to stand by her? Through everything?

He cupped her face. "I know you, baby. When things get risky, you put yourself on the line to save other people. There will be no more of that. No more running off on your own. We're in this together. Got it?"

"But what about your job?" she asked. It was the one glitch in her plan that she hadn't been able to figure out. "If you don't arrest someone for the crime spree, will it cause problems?"

He shrugged carelessly. "The case will just be left open indefinitely. It happens."

"But the media. I don't know how to—"

"Don't worry about them. They'll latch onto Harrington and forget about me. And if you just disappear, it will only add to your mystique."

She bit her lip. "Are you sure?"

"Everyone loves the New Covington Cat Burglar. Nobody wants to see her caught."

"But what about you? Will your conscience be able to handle it?"

He flicked her nipple and her breath caught.

"Remember all those comic books I've been buying?" His dark eyes sparked with intensity. "The Patroller married Lady Midnight."

Talia's heart began thundering.

Dipping his head, Riley gave her nipple a quick lick. "Just promise me once and for all that our kitty cat is sheathing her claws and I'll be able to deal with it."

She ran her fingernails across his shoulders as desire started rising in her again. She didn't deserve this man but she was going to do everything in her power to keep him.

"They're sheathed, Kinkade," she whispered. "For everyone but you."

About the author:

Kimberly Dean likes the freedom of imagination allowed in writing romantica. When not slaving over a keyboard, she enjoys reading, sports, movies, and loud rock-n-roll.

Kimberly welcomes mail from readers. You can write to her c/o Ellora's Cave Publishing at 1056 Home Avenue, Akron OH 44310-3502.

Why an electronic book?

We live in the Information Age—an exciting time in the history of human civilization in which technology rules supreme and continues to progress in leaps and bounds every minute of every hour of every day. For a multitude of reasons, more and more avid literary fans are opting to purchase e-books instead of paperbacks. The question to those not yet initiated to the world of electronic reading is simply: *why?*

1. *Price.* An electronic title at Ellora's Cave Publishing and Cerridwen Press runs anywhere from 40-75% less than the cover price of the <u>exact same title</u> in paperback format. Why? Cold mathematics. It is less expensive to publish an e-book than it is to publish a paperback, so the savings are passed along to the consumer.
2. *Space.* Running out of room to house your paperback books? That is one worry you will never have with electronic novels. For a low one-time cost, you can purchase a handheld computer designed specifically for e-reading purposes. Many e-readers are larger than the average handheld, giving you plenty of screen room. Better yet, hundreds of titles can be stored within your new library—a single microchip. (Please note that Ellora's Cave and Cerridwen Press does not endorse any specific brands. You can check our website at www.ellorascave.com or

www.cerridwenpress.com for customer recommendations we make available to new consumers.)
3. *Mobility.* Because your new library now consists of only a microchip, your entire cache of books can be taken with you wherever you go.
4. *Personal preferences are accounted for.* Are the words you are currently reading too small? Too **large**? Too…**ANNOYING**? Paperback books cannot be modified according to personal preferences, but e-books can.
5. *Instant gratification.* Is it the middle of the night and all the bookstores are closed? Are you tired of waiting days — sometimes weeks — for online and offline bookstores to ship the novels you bought? Ellora's Cave Publishing sells instantaneous downloads 24 hours a day, 7 days a week, 365 days a year. Our e-book delivery system is 100% automated, meaning your order is filled as soon as you pay for it.

Those are a few of the top reasons why electronic novels are displacing paperbacks for many an avid reader. As always, Ellora's Cave and Cerridwen Press welcomes your questions and comments. We invite you to email us at service@ellorascave.com, service@cerridwenpress.com or write to us directly at: 1056 Home Ave. Akron OH 44310-3502.

NEED A MORE EXCITING
WAY TO PLAN YOUR DAY?

ELLORA'S
CAVEMEN
2006 CALENDAR

COMING THIS FALL

The Ellora's Cave Library

Stay up to date with Ellora's Cave Titles in Print with our Quarterly Catalog.

To recieve a catalog,
send an email with your name
and mailing address to:

CATALOG@ELLORASCAVE.COM

or send a letter or postcard
with your mailing address to:
Catalog Request
c/o Ellora's Cave Publishing, Inc.
1337 Commerce Drive #13
Stow, OH 44224

LadyJaided

The premier magazine for today's sensual woman

Lady Jaided magazine is devoted to exploring the sexuality and sensuality of women. While there are many similarities between the sexual experiences of men and women, there are just as many if not more differences. Our focus is on the female experience and on giving voice and credence to it. Lady Jaided will include everything from trends, politics, science and history to gossip, humor and celebrity interviews, but our focus will remain on female sexuality and sensuality.

A Sneak Peek at Upcoming Stories

Clan of the Cave Woman
Women's sexuality throughout history.

The Sarandon Syndrome
What's behind the attraction between older women and younger men.

The Last Taboo
Why some women – even feminists – have bondage fantasies

Girls' Eyes for Queer Guys
An in-depth look at the attraction between straight women and gay men

Available Spring 2005

www.LadyJaided.com

Lady Jaided Regular Features

Jaid's Tirade
Jaid Black's erotic romance novels sell throughout the world, and her publishing company Ellora's Cave is one of the largest and most successful e-book publishers in the world. What is less well known about Jaid Black, a.k.a. Tina Engler is her long record as a political activist. Whether she's discussing sex or politics (or both), expect to see her get up on her soapbox and do what she does best: offend the greedy, the holier-than-thous, and the apathetic! Don't miss out on her monthly column.

Devilish Dot's G-Spot
Married to the same man for 20 years, Dorothy Araiza still basks in a sex life to be envied. What Dot loves just as much as achieving the Big O is helping other women realize their full sexual potential. Dot gives talks and advice on everything from which sex toys to buy (or not to buy) to which positions give you the best climax.

On the Road with Lady K
Publisher, author, world traveler and Lady of Barrow, Kathryn Falk shares insider information on the most romantic places in the world.

Kandidly Kay
This Lois Lane cum Dave Barry is a domestic goddess by day and a hard-hitting sexual deviancy reporter by night. Adored for her stunning wit and knack for delivering one-liners, this Rodney Dangerfield of reporting will !eave no stone unturned in her search for the bizarre truth.

A Model World
CJ Hollenbach returns to his roots. The blond heartthrob from Ohio has twice been seen in Playgirl magazine and countless other publications. He has appeared on several national TV shows including The Jerry Springer Show (God help him!) and has been interviewed for Entertainment Tonight, CNN and The Today Show. He has been involved in the romance industry for the past 12 years, appearing on dozens of romance novel covers and calendars. CJ's specialty is personal interviews, in which people have a tendency to tell him everything.

Hot Mama Cooks
Sex is her food, and food is her sex. Hot Mama gives aphrodisiac a whole new meaning. Join her every month for her latest sensual adventure -- with bonus recipe!

Empress on the Mount
Brash, outrageous, and undeniably irreverent, this advice columnist from down under will either leave you in stitches or recovering from hang-jaw as you gawk at her answers to reader questions on relationships and life.

Erotic Fiction from Ellora's Cave
The debut issue will feature part one of "Ferocious," a three-part erotic serial written especially for Lady Jaided by the popular Sherri L. King.

COMING TO A BOOKSTORE NEAR YOU!

ELLORA'S CAVE
2005

BEST SELLING AUTHORS TOUR

Discover for yourself why readers can't get enough of the multiple award-winning publisher Ellora's Cave. Whether you prefer e-books or paperbacks, be sure to visit EC on the web at www.ellorascave.com for an erotic reading experience that will leave you breathless.

www.ellorascave.com

Printed in the United States
32769LVS00002B/49-390